COURTING
DISASTER

Truly

Julie Edelson

Also by Julie Edelson

NO NEWS IS GOOD

BAD HOUSEKEEPING

COURTING DISASTER

Julie Edelson

𝒵

ZOLAND BOOKS

Cambridge, Massachusetts

First edition published in 1999 by
Zoland Books, Inc.
384 Huron Avenue
Cambridge, Massachusetts 02138

FIRST EDITION

Book design by Boskydell Studio
Printed in the United States of America

05 04 03 02 01 00 99   8 7 6 5 4 3 2 1

This book is printed on acid-free paper, and its binding
materials have been chosen for strength and durability.

Library of Congress Cataloging-in-Publication Data

Edelson, Julie.
    Courting disaster : a novel / by Julie Edelson. — 1st ed.
        p.   cm.
    ISBN 1-58195-003-9
    I. Title.
PS3555.D44C68   199
813'.54—dc21   98-54310
                                                                  CIP

For Roy,
and the ties that bear
but never bind

The author gratefully acknowledges the input, uptake, and back talk of Roy, Abbie, and Aaron Hantgan; Virginia Edelson; Susan Baum; Mike Carson; Florry Shadletsky; Hermine Stover; Sara Patton; Bill Meyers; Jay Jerome; Julie Huff-Jerome; Dave Rutter; Dana Nelson; Mattia Rocco; Francesca Tosetti; Mary Sorci-Thomas; Ginger Kahn; Rena Jones; Katie Shugart; John McAllister; Marybeth Blackwell-Chapman; Yvonne McConnico; Cathie and Court White; Leslie Poole; Bob Wykle; Lisa Childress; Luli, Jim, Dean, and Jes Sanderford; Nicasio Martinez; Elen Knott; Becky Gould Gibson; Ginny Weiler; Walter Shaw; Sol Miguel-Prendes; Judy Kem; Linda Howe; David Rosenbaum; Harold Hodes; Larry Katz; Ross Feld; Al Ferrari; Janice Goldblum; Bonnie Toeniessen; and the legal counsel of William B. Gibson and Ken Zick.

Contents

This is what I did   1

1   *Just Do It*   4

2   *What Comes Naturally*   39

3   *If It Feels Good*   75

4   *The Right Thing*   115

5   *Till You Get Enough*   151

6   *I Just Do*   182

7   *Thanks*   214

8   *In the Road*   247

What's done is done   278

COURTING DISASTER

This is what I did

It was ten years ago, two weeks before Christmas. Another dreary Christmas we'd have to spend with my in-laws, marking time between meals, and failing them, every one of us, in every way, at every moment. We'd motor north through the perilous mountains, away from our own mild winter, in the gasping, ten-year-old Dodge that couldn't die, to the very buckle of the Rust Belt — I mean there's a live bait vending machine on Main Street, next to an empty shop window offering "Rat Poison" and "Knives Sharpened" on cardboard signs, and not a man in Joe's family has held a regular job since the glass factory folded. Last February, one of them blew his brains out for his son to discover when he came home from school. Waste disposal is the growth industry. I'd already picked and lost the annual fight over going.

That night we'd been invited out for dinner. I got in the door from work and the day-care center with my five-year old, Vince, on full blast, "I'm starving!" and Marcia was on the phone to cancel. Her youngest had come down with chicken pox.

Now I'd been looking forward to this dinner. Marcia was funny, and Ron had the latest music; he'd jump up from the table — "You like that? Wait'll you hear this!" — and our kids quietly conspired in a mischief so complex it never materialized. I remembered Tess's chicken pox. She languished on the couch watching *The Price Is Right* while I dabbed her with calamine and read her nature books that all seemed to feature glossy telephoto shots of tooth lacerating flesh. In October, Vince had been home for ten days with an ear infection. I'd used up my leave, personal and sick — although you're not supposed to use your sick leave to look after somebody else — I guess you dump them on the cart for the leprosarium and rush to the office.

So I thought, Hell, he's bound to get it sometime; why not during vacation when it won't cost anything? It made sense to Marcia. Joe, too. We had a great time. It was the first time I heard "I Don't Like Mondays."

Vince broke out at his grandparents'. I felt smart. There was no snow, but a steady cold drizzle made the mud spill down the stripped gullies and the coal stink hang, so we didn't mind. We parked him in front of the TV and the artificial tree and brought him plenty of liquids and amused ourselves amusing him. The grandparents loved it. We were finally playing to their strength: confinement. Tess, farmed out to cousins in the afternoons, was jealous.

And when his fever spiked, I gave him aspirin. When he became drowsy, when he vomited, I stroked him, I held him. You don't call the doctor over every little thing; they make you feel weak and foolish — womanish. And, of course, the bill.

Then Tess was pestering him, she snatched away his stuffed stegosaurus, and he didn't respond. His lips were blue, his skin the translucent blue of breast milk, milk glass, and I couldn't rouse him. The in-laws' doctor, pulled from his table, said take him to the emergency room. In the car, his eyes rolled back, his limbs went rigid and twitched. Joe tore down the steep gravel slush, zigzagged the crowded turnpike, as though it didn't matter if any of us made it. My heart slammed around inside me as if it had ripped from its roots.

Two days later, Vince died. Reye's syndrome. The aspirin.

I have a dream where Vince is running toward me. He gets bigger and bigger as he gets closer until there's only his huge laughing face, and it breaks over me like a bottle, and I wake up soaking wet.

Chapter 1

Just Do It

Angie slides behind the wheel and sits until the noise drains out of her head. Phones. The chirp and razz still twanging her like a sensitive filling tuned to the whine of the planet. Early shift on the crisis hot line — Misery Central. Never that bad before the stores close. By the time she sinks the key, she's anticipating Mason's grip, his silky purple throb, and the hairs on her arms bristle. The radio blares on with the motor. She hurls into the curving blackness, and if that truck wants to race, she eggs it on to the one-lane bridge, where she flies in front — eat my exhaust. Although she crawls up the long rutted driveway, the crate lurches to a stop, shudders, rattles like a beggar's cup. Completely off, it ticks.

Mason's pickup, Judi's Audi, Cindi's Honda, Kristi's Escort huddle in the glare from the back-door light. She gets out. The wind saws the branches, but she catches the Indigo Girls, warbling praise to the smell of their sweat. The Lilies are in. She can't bear the idea of walking past them, their lewd sanction of what they think they understand — and, worse yet, maybe they do — about her sexual itch. Mason says they're just curious. She could make an effort. She has a lot to share. Right. She hates the way he cuts them slack. His cool. What's that about "I find thee neither hot nor cold but lukewarm. I spit thee out of my mouth'? She thinks about going home. Any place you hang yourself is home.

Mason comes out of the garage. Angie has the panicked, shuttling look of a midstreet squirrel. He latches her waist, and his tongue melts to her strong undertow. Beneath the cold enamel, she gives off the same metallic heat as her car. Dangerous, he thinks, like an ordinary wall socket; he also thinks, springing wood, Get me some. "Hello there."

He always says this. She's told him he sounds like Grover, a wheezy blue hair ball on *Sesame Street* who walks the kids through their fears as though you could get the jump on life. He watched it with his own kids until their mother surprised him at Christmas with a big gold ring to match the one she'd bought herself. He put it to his nose. She didn't laugh. He considered her pout, these two nappy toddlers, and all that sad tawdry wanna-be swank, and split. She forced him out, he says. Talk about jump, says Angie, picturing the dumbstruck kids on the couch. Mason likes aggravating Angie, knowing how. He likes knowing how.

The branches scrape. Angie plugs her lips against Mason's like an eraser. "What you doing in the garage?" she asks. "You got you another ve-hic-cle?"

"Baby, you know I's a one-vehicle man." He pulls her into his warm down vest. He smells like freshly planed pine. She smells medicinal, like a Mentho-Lyptus cough drop. They rub crotches; hers grabs, and his eyes fire. He feels everything, she thinks, and then immediately she knows he doesn't. His rugged hands appreciate her tone. "Moved out here Saturday," he tells her. "The whole shootin' match."

"You're kidding me."

Crooking her head in his elbow, he steers her inside. "You gone like it" — he contracts from her astringency — "after while."

It sits on a concrete slab. Pink insulation stuffed between the studs. There's a window in the door they came in and another to the left over his desk that reflects hanging shelves of glowing candles: romance. Or fire hazard. The flames sway and merge on the panes like Busby Berkeley chorines. He's draped the double doors with patchwork quilts and wedged his college textbooks — she recognizes Paul Samuelson's *Economics* — in the gap between them and the slab, a statement that bothers her even as she understands it. Would it bother her if he were white? The usual unaskable question. An uneasy chair — it slumps and balls its fists — faces the TV, VCR, and audio system, its back to the woodworking machinery and tools. Behind more of his clever rope-and-plank shelves, on a midnight blue Iranian rug he shipped back from his post-Nam bum around the world, sit the bed, an armoire, and a night table and, on that, a bottle of Jack Daniel's and a single glass artfully arranged in the soft radiance of a hurricane lamp. Kerosene space heater, the kind that kills old folks every winter, putting out. Quilts, candles, ceramics: gifts from women. Wooden furniture — sinuous and smooth as a horse's flank — built by Mason. Somehow he's making the garage pretty, like a sheikh's tent. It infuriates her. She spins on him. "Christ, Mason, it's fifty degrees outside and frigid in here. Where you gonna take a shit?"

"In the big house." Can't she see the hours he spent busting his butt to get it ready for her? That shoot from the lip — it's what he *likes* about her. How many women do you have to make it with before you understand one? (Before you understand yourself?) "I've put up with worse." A board over a hole. No board. Clogged hole. No hole. What would she know? Parking her creamy ass on a throne all her life. In fifteen minutes, he'll invite her to sit on his face. "Give us some privacy, dig. Thought you'd like that."

"Let me guess — this was their idea." She jigs her head toward the house.

He squares up. "Not exactly. They got they own bit, and I don't relate." Tartly, "Seem to get on 'em. You hear what I'm sayin'."

"The Great Compromiser," she scoffs.

"Meets the Great Equalizer." Let her think what she wants; he's got her number. He dips for the remote and on swirls Pharaoh Sanders. He produces a j, ashtray, matches. "Interesting matchup," he says, cracking one for her. "Not since Jake the Snake took on Brutus Beefcake —"

She drops her purse and brings her mouth to the light, her gaze as stark blue as a desert noon. He sets the ashtray within reach.

"Let me get this straight." She drags. "You found this old derelict —" The house had been a hunting lodge. It has a stone fireplace, oak floors, eat-in kitchen, four baths. "You fixed it up" — stabbing the joint like a stick of chalk — "fell in love with it" — the shimmering music feels like a summer shower — "wanted to live in it" — a supple baritone rolls in, the soft soap; she's not falling for it — "so you recruited the Lilies as house-mates" — exhaling — "and now they've moved you into the garage." Joe, Angie thinks, her husband and standard of mas-culinity, would have summarily dumped their worldly goods by the side of the road. She taps off her ashes.

Mason doesn't smoke: inebriants are the agents of genocide, chemical weapons in the race war. She's pluming like a cockatoo, a choo-choo; he's stationary, collected, seething. Where is he going with this high-handed white bitch? "Right now I got to have their rent to pay off my loans. Someday I'll soak these fools for the jack to make sole owner." He laughs shortly. "Came down here to do Soul City, dig." Found poverty and bullshit: two things he didn't need more of. He doubts she ever heard of it. "Now it's sole owner. Times do change."

She's passed the exit for Soul City on some interstate. It struck her as a joke, a bizarre theme park. Blue-collar blacks creating a new world in Klan country? She sees Mason brandishing a hammer, making vows. Bring up the soundtrack: "A Change Is Gonna Come." The baritone on the CD has started gargling. She doesn't know shit about Soul City. What she knows about is selfish, manipulative young women. "You cut all their wood?"

Mason imagines Judi with the chain saw — Olyve Oyl wielding an alligator. They can't hardly keep a fire going.

"They clean?" she pursues. "Do windows?"

"They need some education in that direction. They expect —"

Yeah, Angie's daughter Tess expects — a generation of self-righteous incompetents. All they can do is push our buttons — all we taught them. "What about the garden?"

"Wouldn't let 'em near the garden. Don't know beets from burdock. Scared of bees. Tried to mow with the plow." He's agitating for a laugh. Does he need it that bad? Not the pussy, although thinking about it — the swing of her breasts when she bucks, her grunts and cries, no holds barred — the strings in his gut tug his dick. No, it's the laugh. Another gold star from the white academy, yeah, okay, but also lightening her load. Her face looks pinched. Of course, she's toking. "And then there's the weed. You don't want 'em to have that on you."

"Ah." She salaams the joint. Has to relight.

He tosses her the matches. Leon Thomas humming Allah ain't gettin' it. Mason clicks the disc to Keith Jarrett. With the opening trill, Angie seems to unfurl, like a slo-mo rose in a Moody Bible film.

"Thanks." She allows, "This feels good. You know that guy I was telling you about — Chemo Sabe — he's in chemotherapy? Super-Christian dude all appalled at having to deal with me?" She waves alarmed mitts. Mason nods. The flicker from the candles lights the wiry tips of his beard. He looks as warm as a bear. Or — why do they say cold as dirt? — warm as the encompassing embrace of turned earth. "Your dope's given him his appetite back. He gripes he gets off on it, too, poor thing. Sometimes I think only the real pills get better —" She stops because she thinks, The good die young, and sees Vince in the hospital bed, siphoned by machines. "Anyway, he's running low."

"These folks you supply" — Mason slopes against his desk, pulling at his mustache — "how'd they react if they knew the nigger was behind it — riskin' his ass — outta the goodness?" He drops a shot of humor into the resentment: boilermaker. "Like how'd they treat me on an elevator."

"You don't get good because you're sick, I know that." In addition to the hot line, Angie volunteers eight hours a week caring for the terminally ill. That's how she met Mason, at a funeral six months ago. Or what do they call it? Memorial? Remembrance? Not wake — no stiff and no liquor. This was for a sweet old darling from his church, Miss Dealie — pancreatic cancer. Angie used to sing her "Baby Face." She was in at the same time as this white bitch with a heart problem who called you dummy and wouldn't let Erna bathe her. Then it was, "Erna's so intelligent she must have some white blood." *She* got better. Had to be sent home. When Erna takes shit from some bigot in the name of unconditional love, Angie wants to scream. "This garage bullshit makes me want to scream," she tells Mason, crushing the roach, "or scratch your eyes out. Don't you know tomorrow never comes? And meanwhile you're living in a garage."

"'Preciate you buttin' into my business. Meantime, you won't have to exercise yourself over makin' so much noise" — he snarls a grin — "out here in the Jiffy Lube."

Low blow. She sees the sulky faces of the Lilies — all right, she doesn't know them — sitting around the TV, almost audibly clucking when she and Mason come out of his room, slanting sidelongs at his groin, his hands. "The fucking handyman —"

"That's up to me." He's thinking how ugly her mouth can be — big horse teeth. Clamped to his dick — her tongue undulating like a squid. He's been wondering when she'd file a claim. Married women, in his experience, go for binding arbitration or at least no-fault insurance early on. Security, even in adventure — purchase. Angie's avoided all negotiations not sensual. So that falling back, unsprung, undone, and she's a draft stirring the candles, he has felt — used. The black stud. Does she really think he would dip his wick in those silly limp lilies?

"Ask me if I care," she retorts. And why should he tolerate her sick, ridiculous excesses, her pus-pallid cellulite, squeezing into her stingy schedule? Hey, Mason, I got an hour; drop your pants. She throws a quick look at his knotted arms, the taut line of his lips. This is supposed to be fun. "I'm outta here."

"Suit yourself."

She doesn't want to go. She wants him to eat her out until the yammer in her brain jams and the tension spasms, novas. Has she talked her way out of it yet? "I'm glad I'm not your union rep, mister." Or your pimp, she thinks.

"Wait'll I Sheetrock it." He takes her wrist and draws her to him. His eyes insist on her assent. It galls her, which also trips her switch. "Previous owner had a workshop out here, so I got all the juice I'll ever need. Have us a fine little one-room country shack."

Thunk. She recognizes the blues riff — "Tobacco Road"? but *us*? Look out!

"How 'bout your very own shithouse, seat carved to the specifications of your sweet ofay ass" — he mellows down, groping it; good gum, he thinks — "hand-rubbed till it shine like glass." His grin prods hers. "Quit your bitchin', baby. Let's get to it."

She tries to check her watch, but he forces her arm behind her back and pastes one on. The pressure of his wanting her pries her open. They shuffle to the bed, and he lifts her onto it. She clasps his neck. "I'm thinking slave quarters, Mason." It catches in her dry craw like an aspirin. What are friends for?

"And where you live, baby?" Mason's eyes shrivel to raisins. "Tell me 'bout that little room you gots all to yourself."

Angie yips a laugh. She feels penetrated, turned out. This piano player never seems to come to the point. "You got any music that's a little less — cerebral?" She brushes off the watch cap to kiss his downy bald spot. She wants to suck him steaming, she wants to snug him like the meat in a dumpling and steam.

Mason half-rises to aim the control: Eiseleys. They grin.

"You are good," Angie admits; that, or she's doing the same things every time she's here and forgetting. "But I'm never taking my shoes off."

His tongue pulses in her mouth like a sparrow. He boosts aboard and pours her glass, settles against the pillows. They sit knee to knee. The whiskey ribbons down her throat. She hitches her legs over his thighs, hunkers closer, and feels his dowser twitch. The only sentient being on the planet that's always glad to see her. "Sorry," she yields, resting her elbows on his shoulders.

He unlaces and pulls off her sneakers, one at a time. "Yeah. Well. Just don't mother me."

"Hey, man, I just spent two solid hours mothering. I'm a professional mother." She can't hear the word without *fucker* implied.

"Bad tonight?" He licks his fingertips and massages the bones in her neck.

"No, uh-uh." Her nipples are pricked up from the chill. She arches into his vest to scuff them against his waffled cotton chest, nibbles his ear, the mahogany knob of his cheek. "You heard about that kid died in the wreck? Crashed into a tree?"

He links his hands over the small of her back, slips down inside her pants to grasp the cool swell of her hips. "Drugs or alcohol?"

"He wasn't driving. Girl Tess has known since grade school — claims she abstains. She walked away without a scratch. Tess played with them both. I've kissed their boo-boos."

He tables her glass and kisses the spokes by her eye.

"Think about *her*, you know? Hard to bone up for the big test when everybody knows you just snuffed the Most Popular Boy."

"I hear you." He thinks about making a "bone up" joke, his fingers grazing the dewy corn silk of her muff. Tasteless. He never understands how they move from these heavy raps to laughing out their asses, tussling like puppies. No matter how he works at it, he can't shape their time together. Green wood. Or warped.

She licks the rim of his nostril. "So all the teens in town want to script themselves into the tragedy. I musta heard from twenty of his best friends. Spread himself kinda thin, in life as in death."

"You cold, woman," he burrs in her ear, while her body softens under his hands like wax. She pulls back and fixes a serious blink on him, like a nun on a schoolroom vandal.

She's thinking about a guy who called tonight. Moved back South from Alaska a month ago, and he can't cool off. Can't sleep — he's sweltering, dripping sweat. He keeps the windows up, runs the air conditioner. The wife is freezing. She shuts; he opens. Tonight she stormed out, took the Blazer, he doesn't know if she's coming back. The marriage is falling apart; he wants to talk global warming, El Niño, the hole in the ozone, the climatic effects of volcanic eruptions in the Philippines. Angie told him, "Hey, buster, this ain't weather watch. There's kids out there trying to ice themselves." He said, "Lucky they got you to shoot the breeze with. I feel colder already." He sounded three sheets to the wind. He ought to trade homesteads with Mason, she thinks. Something keeps her from mentioning him. It's not ethics.

Mason feels up inside her to find where she's gone. Complicated women — his weakness. This relationship is all wrong, going nowhere — nowhere to go — she's white, she's married, she's got kids, she's a head case, but she gets to him. Her hardness, her straight grain. Pisses him off. What he is and what he ought be two entirely different things. "Don't mean nothin'," he murmurs. "Drive on."

The wry floods back into her eyes, and she sees him, the dense unknown jungle of his past. "Yeah. So I tell 'em, Look, kids, don't drink and drive, that's the message. They don't wanna hear it. Wanna talk premonitions. In what ways they resemble the deceased. Born under a bad sign. They're making a shrine out of the tree — Barbie's Dream Mausoleum."

Mason snorts. She nuzzles the tender skin between his neckband and beard, teasing herself on her seam. He sheds his vest, pulls her sweater up and off, clicks open and skims off her bra. He hefts her breast against his palm. His long spatulate fingers cage its fullness, pluck out the nipple, diddle it, his tongue nipped between his teeth, and his eyes white crescents under languid lids. The rounded contours of his face sheen like eggplant. She tastes their close texture, tuned so tight she vibrates. Their lips meld, tongues flux. She cracks wide, climbing his sides, pops the snap on his jeans, reaches in, frees his pole; he bobbles her up onto it, and she grinds, arching back, moaning. His face nests in her soft acclivity, its hidden mossy scent; he probes the globes of her ass; she's scratching off his shirt — "Please! Mason! Yes! No!" — raking the black knots of hair — "Please!" — scribbling his plummy nipples — "Please! No! Please! Yes!" — clutching his flesh like hunks of bread, hungry — "Please!" — aching with hunger. They peel off their pants, slap hot mons together, gripping, he's slipping in — "No, not yet, please!" He reaches for the condom. "Mason, no. Not yet. I'll *say* when." His tongue down her throat, his dick slipping in. "Mason! Damn it!" She cuffs him. He flops on his back to get the damned rubber on. They agree on this. Her tubes are tied, but it's not birth they're worried about. As they're prepping to coast into the lifeforce, a pause — memento mori — a fool's cap on the death's-head. But now she preempts his struggle. "What you doin', woman?" She wrestles him on top of her, wedges his dick between her breasts to lick its tip, ruffing her nipples against his sealskin shaft, "Slower, man, got to make it last me. Please, go with me on this. Do what I tell you." His back tingles. Up on his knees, feeling behind him for her little starter, slick, humming — "Oh yes!" — they ride into that storm.

Right before she left the hot line, the guy from Alaska had called again. Got Pearl. Asked for Ms. Frostbite. Pearl knew who he meant. Angie finds herself replaying the conversation on the drive home.

"How you doin', Angel?"

"Alaska."

"You're quick."

"I'm all ears. And it's Angie. What's up?"

"Not a whole heckuva lot. But don' hang up on me, okay? I've tried eve'body else."

"What'd they say?"

"Same's you. Good-bye."

"It comes to that. Any sign of the wife?"

"She's prolly at her sister's. She got people all over the state — don' worry 'bout her. See, tha's part a the problem. I snatched her outta the bazoom a her family and drug her off to the ends a the earth where we knew nobody — wun' nobody. Had to hike twenny mile to the airstrip. Nearest town — place called Purgatory —"

"I love it —"

"Oh yeah. Alaska's pure poetry. She thought she'd like it, too. She din'. The dark, you know. Fog like a blindfold. Skeeters, blackflies, all that mess. Said the silence hurt her ears. Said she could hear her blood pump. And she's a tough nut. She can split a cord a hardwood in nothin' flat and skin a mink — quick as a wink." He giggled.

"Sounds like you better go get her back —"

"She'll be back. She loves me, poor bitch."

"Don't press your luck."

"Plus, she took the Blazer —"

"Look —"

"Wan' me to tell you some more about Alaska?"

"You got a problem I can help you with?"

He laughed.

"You drinking, man?"

"No-oh. Wha' makes you say that? Ain' it enough I'm sweatin' my brains buck naked at thirty degrees? I'm sittin' in the crossdraft between the air conditioner and the open window, buck naked — buck" — he popped the *b* — "naked, burnin' up. My wife's lef' me, I got no job and no prospects, no in-surance, I'm livin' off the goodwill a her kin what I ain' never had a good word for, my dog up an' died —"

Angie hooted. Pearl and Rob surveyed her like haughty waiters. They've got to retrain her.

Alaska has a loud, rushing laugh, like high-class rapids. "Now how you so sure my dog din' die? You don' mock a man over his dog, lady."

"Look, *you* got family, Alaska?"

"Have I got family? Man, have I got family. Minus Ol' Blue, a course. Hog farmers outta Smithfield. You not from around here, are you?"

"Last twenty years."

"I could tell by the way you talk. Where from?"

"Ohio."

"How old?"

"Old enough."

"Sound about twelve. You got a beautiful voice."

"Cause it's still talking to you."

He laughed. "You may be right. I was thinkin' Wynonna. You really wanna hear all this? Okay. My momma still runs the place in Smithfield with her sister Retta and a hired man. Daddy died in 'eighty-five. He was a hell-raiser, I tell you. He drank, ran around, beat me, beat my momma, maybe he was screwin' my sister —"

"Jesus!"

"Ooh, wha's it mean when you freak the hot line?"

"Should I yawn? 'Oh, not incest again.' It freaks me. My dad —"

"What?"

"Never mind."

"Come on. Get honest. Iss a two-way connection."

"You don't need to —"

"You don' know what I need. Tell me. Unload. You got to."

"It's nothing really. I was just gonna say my dad was sweet. I'm like the only person left without a cop-out."

"I'll excuse that 'cop-out' since we's gettin' hones'. When'd he pass?"

"It's been about five years."

"Pretty long — not so long."

"Yeah. I miss him. Although he could also be a bigot and a stuffed shirt."

Alaska laughed.

Angie cupped the mouthpiece. "I used to lie in bed with him until I was — I don't know — too old, eighteen? I'd cuddle up in his armpit, and he'd pat my bottom while we watched TV. I never

thought about it. You tell that around here, man, you get a thera-
pist up in your face. 'You ever wake up boot-scooting in spangles
at Cowboy's Nightlife?' "

"My sister's goin' through that right now. Rememberin' all this
shit. Man, I don' remember nothin'. Correction. I remember
some things. I seen some ugly things." His voice strained up like a
rusty swing. "And I loved him. I loved that man."

"Hey," she said.

He snuffed up a long strand of snot, heaved a sigh. "I've taken
up enough a your time."

"It's true."

He laughed.

"No, I mean we're tying up your line," Angie explained. "Your
wife might be trying to call."

"Tha's right. You right. Thanks for talkin' me through this."

"Sure."

"Can I call you again?"

"You wanna talk to somebody else next time," she told him.
"See if they got a better line on how to help you."

"Not so mean."

"Not half."

"Then they won' be able to help. You know, Angel, in Alaska,
there's the outlaws and the do-gooders, and the do-gooders ain'
good for nothin' a-tall."

Sitting at the long light near the K-mart, a place she sits so fre-
quently she expects to die there, Angie realizes she wants to hear
the end of this story. She's smiling. Bad sign.

She comes in the back door purring, buffed. "Cream Puff" might
be written on her bumper. Joe is at the kitchen table. Papers glare
up. One fist, closed on a pen, drums them; the other, his tight
mouth. The checkbook and the calculator are out. His gaze cuts

between them, not up at her. She just got laid, he thinks. She oozes well-being.

Nick perches on a chair, drinking juice, in knit pajamas. He looks like a circus performer stranded in a bus station waiting room. His eyes shine darkly, level on her. *Children of the Damned*, she thinks and snorts. Nick smiles down into his cup.

She prefers to come into an empty house; second best, a sleeping house. Slug one down, staring out the window at Mrs. Fulton's fifty-foot oak, until something tells her what she's supposed to do next. Joe's obviously got an issue. How does he get the edge so fast? She says, "Hey."

His forehead puckers. "We need to talk."

"Now?" she asks from the hall. Muffled hip-hop above, a high skitter of laughter: Tess. Angie never would have predicted there could be music that would make her want to ax an amplifier, and Tess has been through whole schools of them. She stops in the bedroom to hide her purse. Tess steals — what's yours is mine — turning Angie's last remaining hippie ideals about trust and sharing to shit. It kills Joe. He's heard himself say he doesn't care if he never sees her again. Angie can appreciate the irony, the logic, in light of Vince. But she doesn't want to shell out for it, too. The problem is she can't remember where she hides the purse. Tess is smart and relentless, so Angie has to keep thinking up and rotating the good spots. The main thing to avoid is compulsively checking, unable to tell if anything's missing. Dead certainty is one hundred percent better than nagging suspicion. But it takes pains. Or: they could let her steal from them and then punish her — like God did Eve. Angie would rather lose track of her ID in the blender for a month.

She goes to the kitchen and pours Scotch over rocks. Joe's fixed himself coffee; all his family can drink coffee night and day and still wake up looking like death warmed over. He's massaging his face in its steam when she finally braves confrontation.

Her scuttling around is driving him nuts. "What's wrong with now?" he asks.

"What are you doing up?" She instinctively dives on the little scapegoat.

Nick slurps the last of his juice and lowers the plastic tumbler to equipoise midchest. He's a robot that turns into a Camaro. "Thirsty."

Her eyes crinkle, and he smirks. "Better hit the sheets," she tells him. "It's very late. You'll be a mess tomorrow."

"More of a mess than you?" The snide comes with the smirk.

"We have this worked out," Joe puts in.

At the same time, Angie asks Nick, "You wanna be?"

Nick trots to sling the tumbler in the sink like a grenade. He makes a blasting sound with his cheeks, shakes. Another close one. He returns to fling his arms around Angie's ass and plant a kiss on her crotch, purely a matter of height and haste, as though he's stuck in overdrive, or enemy cars are harrying him through his bedtime ritual.

Joe surrounds his son, rocks him. Three years after Vince, Joe said, Let's have another one. He said it in bed. He showed Angie his hollows, gouged to accept another child. He said it would help Tess, then ten. He spoke to Angie's spine — the moving lips tickling, his face hidden — confession — thinning her on his pin. She doesn't remember saying yes, only the delicious release from her contraceptive duties, like finally being able to close her eyes. When they gave her Nick in the hospital, she thought, Mistake. If he hadn't been so beautiful, she would have eaten him. And then the pity of it won her — poor Nick. Poor Nick always knew how to milk that. He's a little older now than Vince then. He has the same obsession with cars, robots, and dinosaurs, he likes the same books, he says the same things. As he recapitulates Vince, he wrings her heart. He must see that. Joe, it charms, melts. Helpless helpless. They could have kept all those toys.

Nick plods up the stairs listening for something to snag him and drag him back down. At the landing, he guns his engine.

"Why do we resist unconsciousness?" Angie asks, taking a chair beside Joe. He looks at her glass and then into her eyes, his mouth masked by his hand. His eyes are coal chutes, heaping such enormities into hers. She drinks. "So how you doing?"

His hands fall between his knees. "I've been studying the finances, trying to figure out how we're going to afford Christmas, let alone college —"

She feels like his whole front line just collapsed on her. "So you're bored? Happy, maybe — I mean, no *Christmas!*" She salts that old wound. "Pissed off? Am I getting warmer? How cold am I?" She hears the echo. The consensus seems to be in.

"How come you're so late? Usually you have the courtesy to —" He isn't interested in this himself. He picks up the pen and starts drumming the table.

"I had to bring some shit by the Sore." The shelter where she does terminal care, answers the hot line, is called the Open Door. "Adult diapers, in fact. Everybody was just sitting down to supper. Thought I'd spell Erna and hang with Janelle, and it got involved."

"Oh, excuse me, I should have known — Mother of Theresa — on a mission from God. This Janelle die on you?"

"Almost." Angie smiles. Finishes her drink. Play this out — the upper hand. So what if it happened last week? He's so fucking wronged. "This woman — I'm not supposed to talk about her, I don't get why, but I've actually signed, like, an oath about it — anyway, a former Starlette, if you can believe that. She's got AIDS."

Joe stops drumming, starts biting the pen. Wrong again. Totally insensitive. No surprise.

"Must weigh seventy, eighty pounds. I can lift her myself. Anyway, I'm massaging her hands, and she's staring at this studio portrait of herself where she looks — stunning. Really. Like a star. I don't know what she's thinking, but it can't be good, you know, so I comment, I stew about how to say it, I tell her, 'You're beautiful.' 'Was,' she says. I can see this is a golden opportunity for uplift, but, well" — Angie shrugs — "that was it. The points I could've scored for the Lord! They've tried to baptize her twice." Joe gives up a smile. She'll take it. "So then we're comparing hands — she's got some dementia, she's not always all there, and what's my excuse? — but they do look funny together, hers clearly meant to caress the dugs of goats and mine to grub turnips, and then she says, out of the blue, 'I never thought I'd ever stop hating white people.'"

"Whoa." Joe sits back and bounces the pen off the papers. Accused and absolved in the same breath by a Starlette! It's very vivid to him, even though he's never been near the Open Door, like any sane person who didn't have to. He gives Angie the once-over for the first time since she came in. She looks good. He thought as a result of screwing. But it's that spacy serenity that descends over her when she attends the dying. Looking at her splits him open like a milkweed pod — dry white fluff in his chest. Does she want something from him? A touch? Where? How? Her body is a haunted house.

"Yeah," she says, hooding her eyes, "I was blown away."

He waits. That's it? No wider ramifications, insights to be gained, contradictions exposed? Bullshit. He almost grins. Okay, it happened, but not just now. Just now she was fucking the nigger. He stomps on the word — *nigger* — you don't judge your political correctness when you're thinking about the guy humping

COURTING DISASTER ◆ 22

your wife. He'll extend her a little credit for the story, though. Jesus. "Yeah, well, while you were toiling in the fields of the Lord, I got a call from the Spanish teacher. Blessed Tess disrupted class today — shouting match with Brian Something — totally innocent victim. Mrs. Whatever never heard such language in her life, making me wonder about her life and where she learned Spanish. Tess had to be sent to the office. Three days of in-school suspension. Feels we should know. How can she teach?"

"Have you talked to Tess?" Angie leans her elbows on the table. "Because I know this Brian. He's — He carries a baseball bat under the seat of his van. He takes our lawn ornaments for rides —"

Joe cocks his head. "What are you talking about?"

"Those concrete ducks. Two, three in the morning. He puts them back."

Joe pretends he didn't hear this. "She's grounded till hell freezes over."

"Oh, great. And what's to prevent her killing one or all four of us?"

"Hope." Joe listens to that again and likes it. "You tell me. Ange, we've got to teach her a lesson. She's got to know there are limits to what people will tolerate. Consequences. Or she'll never have a mate or hold a job." His eyes try to pin hers, but it's more like dogfighting a Zero. "You've got to take this seriously."

"When you say seriously, I think Sarajevo, Somalia, Samaritan Inn. Not Mrs. Espagnol."

"Fuck." He hunches forward, and she sits back. His disgust weights his shoulders: a yoke. "Get off it," he pushes into her, hard.

It clocks her. He's got a point. But some of Joe's reactions to Tess lately seem off the wall. She remembers her own father's bewildering bouts of hostility after she hit puberty. And Joe never pictures what they're actually going to *do.* "Okay, but I mean it. What's to make her obey? What do we do if she won't?"

Joe flashes on Tess the last time he confiscated her car keys, screaming on the landing. The noise spewing from the rupture in her rubbery face, "I hope I die! I hope you die, I hope you fucking die you fucking —" and so on. The nervous cat peeling first up, then down the stairs. The dog's hacking "What? What? What? What? What?" in the yard. He remembers feeling nauseated by his daughter, formerly a dazzling prismatic streak across his often blank existence. This hideous thing had devoured her. He wanted to tear into it and rip her out. Her braying like the Klaxon on the destroyer where he spent his nineteenth year, lobbing fire on friend and foe alike. He was pounding up the stairs, shoving her into her room, roughly, because he didn't want to touch her, slamming the door, barring it against the sharp aftershocks of teen jock adrenaline, her insane inhuman screeching. Glass breaking, windows rattling, plaster crumbling. The dog. He held himself like a tornado. Where was Angie to stop him?

He feels deflated. She's got a point. "I don't know. That's what I'm telling you. I want help, that's what I'm saying. I'm saying it, okay? Isn't that what I'm supposed to do? I'm acknowledging *need.*"

He says *need* with distaste, like *bleed.* Tess, after Angie told her about the curse: "Mama, you bleed?" The deep sweetness of her sympathy.

"We've got to work together on this," Joe's saying. "Talk about it. Not next week."

"Yeah, but not tonight." She feels like she's turning to lead, head first. "Aren't you tired?"

"Ange, you've got to get a job."

Angie tents her fingers over her nose and mouth: prayer for sedation.

"Look, Nick's in school practically all day. Tess will soon be in college — or jail — and your mother may need to be in a home. My folks aren't getting any younger, and since they sold the restaurant, I don't know what they're living on. Nobody is allowed to get sick. We've got a twenty-year mortgage on a house that might not last that long, two junk cars running on their ankles, an insurance payment that looks like my weight on Jupiter, and I have to fucking walk to work." His hand extends gracefully toward her on its back. His big brown eyes appeal. "We need the money, honey."

She wishes she had a ready reply. She sets her fist on his generous palm. "I guess the party's over," she sighs. No laugh. She wishes she'd brought the Scotch to the table. "But what am I gonna do? What can I do? What is there?"

"Why don't you go back to teaching?" He kneads the lump of her hand. He's blading the thin ice over Vince — their hearts still frozen on him — they flay when they try to pull away. He speaks gingerly. "You were a great teacher."

He knows the answer to this one. "I've got nothing to teach." The Svengali act. She taught him through law school. Okay, she owes him, but not that much. "I don't belong among youth. And I think we can assume healing is out." She lets that percolate while she gets up to refill her glass. "What about sales? 'Tellya what I'm gonna do forya —' Hey, maybe I should govern! Yeah! Or run the nuclear power plant. Now I'm into it. You got the paper? Let's get the paper." She picks it off a chair and flaps it on the table, wallowing the bank statements to the floor. "Let's not waste another second. That job is out there, and I'm gonna find it or die trying!"

What did he say? What put the bug up her ass? He watches her as if someone will interview him later, ask him to describe exactly what took place on the night of November seventeenth, 1993.

"Okay, let's see. Oh geez, did you see this story?" She forgets she's in the middle of a snit.

"I didn't have *time* —" He mashes on it.

"Two girls fighting outside the junior high, best friends, fooling around. One pushes, the other falls; the school bus runs over her head."

Joe buries his face in his arms.

"Can you imagine that kid? The one who pushed? That's what it means to be punished by God."

"But about this job." Smothered by his sweater. The still small voice.

"Oh yeah, right, where are my priorities? Out of my way, you're blocking the light of my future. 'Go to the light!'" she hams. "Fortune-teller? *Sister* Angela? 'You will die! But not before your check clears —'"

Joe rises like something from the primordial mudsuck. He sips cold coffee and bares his teeth. "Little Orphan Angie. I'm not asking you to become CEO of RJR —"

"Although" — paging through — "Up in smoke!"

"You don't have to launch a career. A job, part-time, temporary, anything. Something!"

"Well, all right, look here."

She stretches over the want ads, her ass looming next to his head. He wants to whack her.

"Jonestown needs a police chief. What they need is to rename the town. Don't they keep thinking cyanide Kool-Aid?" A few years ago, Mason got canned from his university carpenter job for nailing a protest to the door of a fraternity hosting a Jonestown party. She smiles thinking of him whamming the hammer at 7:00 A.M., the lame white boys shambling down, wondering what attitude to cop. 'Yo! Bro! 'Sup?' A story Joe would like, but not right now. "Can you feature me in law enforcement? I know there's a local opening — did you hear about this? On a tip from a sixteen-year-old in custody — 'if you know about somebody selling, we'll let you go' — cops bust this guy's door in with a seventy-

five-pound battering ram; he blasts one of them away. 'Over a little mess of marijuana,' the judge said yesterday, chiding the cops,
and sentencing the *cop killer* (black; twenty-four-year-old white
cop) to life with no possibility of parole."

"POP," says Joe. "Possibility of parole."

"Over two-tenths of an ounce."

"I know his lawyer. We commiserate at Cagney's." Joe polishes
off the coffee anyway. It has the appropriate taste of bile. "So this
job."

"What's wrong with me, Joe?" Angie flops into the chair. She
watches him scroll down the list. "Why do I give a shit? What
should I be doing?"

"What would you like to do? Isn't that how people normally approach this?" When they get off their high horse. When they have
to sell it in the street like the rest of us. And take what they can get.

She doesn't say, I like to fuck. Especially as she doesn't like to
fuck him. He could be packaging her, licking and pasting on
stamps, folding, stapling. He's always been selfish; now he's slap-
dash. The silence during the act is suffocating. "I liked singing
with the Amphetamines. I guess I'm kinda past it for showbiz."
And her wasted Starlette. Erna gloated to Angie, imposing a hug,
"At least she died saved." Merciful Erna, poised with her finger
bowl at the lip of the grave. Angie flexes her mouth ruefully. "You
know, my Minnesota Multiphasic said I was so antisocial I should
become a farmer." She must have told him this and repeated it
within earshot four hundred million times. Just like her mother.
She concedes, "I like other people to do the talking."

"Maybe you can get something along those lines." Joe tilts his
chair back, earnest, attentive, *fair*. Soon he'll poke his thumbs in
his belt. Mindless, but striking the properly folksy pose. Works on
his clients. But then look where they wound up. "It's a service
economy. Use your connections at the Sore —"

"Great name for a gang. You know? Watch out for — the Sore! The Few, the Proud — Ooh! we could start a track team —"

The legs bang down. Nothing irritates him like her smart-ass banter when he's trying. "You should consider advertising —"

"Telemarketing! That's what I do now. Phone sex!"

"By the way, your mother phoned. She had a little accident."

"How little?"

"I couldn't help overhearing." Tess appears in the doorway in rumpled grunge, pulls up a chair, sniffs Angie's glass. "Have you thought about bartending?"

"Another country heard from —" Angie appraises her daughter. Tess seems to be deliberately sabotaging her physical assets. What hair she hasn't shaved is matted in dreads. Her nose is pierced, her ears, her eyebrow, her navel; it hurts to look at her, like those medieval renderings of Saint Sebastian, patron of pincushions. Impaled on the moment. She smells like a third-world third-class compartment. Angie can see no reason to delay the inevitable — an impulse that on reflection has always played her false. "I hear you been bad."

"Anybody want to play cards?" Pulling a deck out of her overalls and thumbnailing a farting sound off the edge, Tess casts a look of loathing at Joe.

Joe shags it and shunts it off Angie — flippancy!

"And Brian!" Tess lays out a game of solitaire. "He was as much to blame as me — more! But does he get in trouble? The rich prep?"

"That's not the version I got from Mrs. Espagnol." At the same time, Joe remembers little Tess once asking him, "What's a virgin?" and when he had haltingly but conscientiously explained, she frowned. "No, I mean like the original Hollywood virgin." She's infected his brain with these tender traces. Time-released. Shit.

"Mrs. who? Oh. Mrs. Hines." Red four on black five. "Stupid old bitch."

"She speaks highly of you, too."

"Were you there? Why do you automatically take her side?"

"Which of you is doing time?"

"Which is why I shouldn't be grounded." Move up the ace. She turns with gorilla stolidity on Angie, who thinks, All that is light shall be made heavy, everything bright made dull. "This is so dumb. Okay, I disrupted class — we never do anything in that class — and believe me, he started it — but, okay, I contributed. Mr. Albert explained it to me — he's pretty cool. I have to spend the next three days in ISS —"

"In-school suspension," Angie tells Joe. In case he's thinking leg-irons, she adds, "It's in the *library.*"

"The *media center* — with Mr. Ledford. *Coach* Ledford." Tess pushes out her cheek with her tongue. "So why should I also be grounded?" Back to the indifferent tides of red and black. "I didn't do anything to *you.*"

Unfortunately, it makes sense to Angie. Joe's waiting for her to present their argument — sobriety test. "You're grounded until your father and I have a chance to discuss it," she says crisply. She has lunched with family interventionists at the Sore.

"Does that mean I can't go to Charlotte Saturday night for the Parliament Funkadelic show? The tickets cost twenty-five dollars —" This game isn't working out. She masses the cards and starts chopping them back to disorder.

Angie cringes for Tess's greed and bad timing, as if she's jumped the buzzer on a quiz show and it's a cinchy one. "Where'd you get the money?" she feints.

Joe jabs. "Are you kidding me? You just don't get it. You made a mistake, and now you have to pay. That's it. And you don't set the terms. You don't tell us —"

Angie is touched by that instinctive *us* as much as she knows he'll use it against her later.

"— we tell you. You wanna know what you did to us?" Joe twists up out of his chair as though a guyline has snapped, he's dangling over an abyss, he can't look down. The cards crackle and pop in Tess's hands like frying meat. "You disgraced us. You're not fit to leave this house. You can't be trusted. And there is no way in hell you're going to Charlotte. Let that be the end of it." Clenched, showing his back.

Tess glowers, thinking of how most directly to torture her father. Split, mix, bridge, collapse. She'll kill herself. Overdose — why should she suffer? Go out on a wave of pleasure like nothing she's felt before and let him find her in her vomit, find the note in vomit, pick the note out of her vomit. The hiss of her words etching into his brain — the riffle of the deck. She doesn't have the stuff on her or the money, but she knows where to get both. It'll just have to wait. She imagines his face at the funeral. Then a steel plate slices down in her mind. And first, she's going to Charlotte. She raps the pack true.

"This is all going too fast for me." Angie presses her head. Two minutes into an argument, it's like they've spent two weeks in a life raft. "Why don't you tell us exactly what happened in class? I mean, what are we talking about here? And has anybody noticed the time?"

"What's the point?" Tess grudges every word, but they boil out. She's not telling them how Brian comes on to her but screws her best friend and anything else that'll stay put long enough, and she's supposed to play dumb; how he bullshits her for hours on the phone every night, stoned out of his gourd, and doesn't know her the next day and rags on her to the sorry low-life dorks he hangs with; she only sees his stupid ugly face when he's lying and begging and sniveling and wants to dig her nails into it and shred it. "You're just looking for an excuse to punish me. You hate to see me have a good time. You hate me for not being dead." She has to champ her teeth to keep from telegraphing her next move. She smells Vince when she took away his stuffed dinosaur — that pond-scum smell — tastes it, like a slow drip from her nose to the back of her throat. His face is fuzzy, but that smell. They must see her tears. Why doesn't one of them hug her? She lets the cards spill. Fifty-two pickup.

"I said the end." Joe doesn't know why he has to say this any more than he knows how he can. His teeth are the bars of a cage. They must realize he's close to detonating. He never saw his old man hit a woman, but his mother never let it go this far; she would have slapped his sisters — a long time ago. Years. He bears his body to bed like a tub of scalding water. There's never an end.

Three in the morning, Angie's in the den on the phone with her friend Mimi in Pasadena — 'Dexedrine' to her 'Valvoline' in the Amphetamines back at Kent State. She's got a Scotch in her left hand and a joint in her right and no feeling in either. The house is cold — austerity measure. She can't tell if she's crying or just dribbling like a public water fountain. She can't sleep.

"— when the creep calls me, soused, wants to bitch about Lana, and my thinker goes on red alert." Mimi is talking about her ex. "It all came back to me. I'm like Nemesis: 'You get down on your knees to her or never darken her door again!' Next day, Lana calls. 'Everything you said about him was trooooo!' Oh, to be twenty-five and a moron again! They moved not far from here. He's doing great for the most part — rolling in it. And doesn't that piss you off? If I'd known then what I know now about alcohol, I'd never have tasted the filthy stuff, but fortunately it's too late."

"I wouldn't want to go a day without it."

"Off to AA pronto, sister."

"I can't, Dex — that higher power crap —"

"Since when do you have to agree with the whole agenda? You take what you can use."

"Everybody getting honest, and I'm taking what I can use? I'd feel like a fucking reporter." Hushed, "'We're here live at the bottom of the barrel —'" Straight, "And I can't handle another time commitment."

"Then you'll just have to show some starch and stop drinking. Did you know I've gone Hasidic?"

"No shit! For the outfit, I bet — big black number? Ain't it kinda hot?"

"No, seriously, I'm devout. Go to temple regular. My parents are stymied. I have to wear a wig? so I've got this humongous beehive, and I stuff it with Gummi rats and clip-on Christmas-tree birds, and everybody gets a big kick out of that, or I wear a Stetson. We belt back peppered vodka and dance and wait on the Messiah — by the way, any day now! David suspects the vodka, but it's the sweat. And the discourse." She laughs shrilly. Angie wonders what time it is there. "You pale-piscaliens don't know how to party. You know what I found out recently? There are white Baptists!"

Angie laughs. "I coulda told you."

"You might try a gospel church where you are," Mimi suggests. "Or — do you have voodoo? You dance till the spirit mounts you! Sounds right up your alley! Or go to a rave and mosh."

"My daughter moshes. I'm too volatile. Put me in a pit, I want a beak and claws. Yes to gospel music. But I have to tell you, if the Lord were to shine his countenance down upon me, I'd go straight to the devil and sign on. You know? Because where was he when I needed him? Talk about delinquent child support."

"You gotta let it go, Valve," Mimi says gently. "Ten years —"

Angie waits out the choke. "You're right. And now Joe wants me to get a job."

"Perish the thought! What a nerve!"

"'What can a bourgeoise do?'" Angie pipes.

"''Cept to sing in a rock/roll band,'" Mimi responds. They cackle. "We had potential —"

"If not mass appeal. Have you heard from the Speed Queen?"

"Not since she started working for Integra Systems. I told you about that? Computer consultant. She loves it — and it sure beats the poor-paying schemes of the past. She got most cruelly ditched by the midwife and is tentatively dating — get this — a man!"

"Diet of crow. Alas!"

"Yeah, but she's rich."

"How's the wonderful world of wallpaper?"

"You should have said, 'What's the latest wrinkle?' Absurdly lucrative. Which is lucky, because David got laid off."

"No! Shit!"

"He'll find something — architects are versatile. But we have to worry all-a-time money now, which is a stone drag. Anyway, you could do worse than wallpaper."

"Haven't I tried?"

"What are you saying? You do all that good! For nothing!"

"Hunh." Angie sees Tess, Joe, Nick, Mason, the people at the Sore, even that guy tonight — Alaska — a breadline fading into infinity. "I'm certain I'm doing harm. If history means anything. Everybody I deal with, I think how much better off they'd be talking to anybody else. But there's so many of them — and there ain't nobody else."

"So whatcha gonna do, child?"

"Get a job, shana-nada. Only I'm having a lot of trouble figuring how I'm gonna fit it all in —"

"You still fooling with that black guy?"

"De-ex!"

"Spare my blushes —"

"Not much longer. He don't need nobody fooling with him."

"Woo! Charity!" Mimi gibes.

"Besides, it's totally fucked." Angie sees her loins locked with Mason's like the layers of a Boston cream pie. And she's telling *him* to take stock. She realizes she's entering — she's already entered — another season. Fall.

"Don't they kill you for rubbing nasties with Negroes down there?" Mimi asks.

"Yes! I understand where you live they just kill you."

"The world over, darling. Gone to the dogs. The worms! I tend my own garden."

"I bet."

"I'm serious. The riots? It was bad enough when Watts was burning — again! — but when yuppies started making off with wide-screen TVs, you had to wonder. What's that eh-eh noise? The FBI! 'Up against the wall, motherfucker! Off the pig!'"

"Call waiting. Must be for Tess — one of her partners in crime. Ignore it."

"'I hear you knocking. . . .' Listen, totally off the subject, this is funny. Hannah had a friend sleep over the other night? And the next day I find this note in the trash that says, 'Be quiet! My parents are fighting, and I want to hear what they say.'"

Angie laughs. "Did you ever think you'd paw through your kid's trash? And that's another thing. Tess and Joe!"

"Tell me about it. Since David's been home? You walk in from work, it's the Golan Heights."

"So how do you deal with it?"

"Is this on a day when it's not Hannah and me?"

"Exactly. Joe thinks she's headed for hell in a handbasket, and

I'm giving the occasional push. She seems like a typical teenage mess to me. I think I've skewed my sense of urgency at the Open Sore."

Mimi's voice mollifies. "You ever think of leaving Joe? Starting fresh?"

"Only in the sense that I think of leaving life." Angie breathes. "But there's Tess — and Nick." Mimi's never seen Nick in person. "And Joe." She tells their names like beads, feeling their weight, their furrows and ridges — their relief. "I can't do any more to them."

"Oh, Valve!"

"I love them, Dex. Is that selfish?"

"Sweetie, of course not! Typical mush-for-brains. Listen, you'll love this —"

Joe can hear the faint lap of her voice out in the den. On the phone. Except for the bill, it doesn't matter. He can't sleep. He just wishes she'd talk either softer or louder so he'd stop trying to make out what she's saying. As long as it's not Pasadena — those marathons with Mimi literally eat his lunch.

The cat curled to his cock sighs and reflexively licks itself, flips over. His thrill for the night. His nerves feel raw. He's seen guys burned raw, skin flaking up like cellophane, in pain no drug could ease, so he's aware he's indulging himself. His pain isn't that bad. Doesn't compare. When Vince —

All right.

When Vince died, they were taken to another room — a quiet room, somebody's idea of a comforting room. Vince wasn't in it, like all the rooms in their future. Angie looked gray, like a blasted stump. Joe felt mangled. Although advised in dulcet tones to sit, they both banged around like amputees with cheap new prosthetic limbs. He finally grabbed her to get her to stop. In her eyes he read their sob story, which was what Vince — a sunny, a really sparkling boy — had become. Wince.

But Tess was out there alone with Joe's parents, in their olive green and gold parlor smelling of tomato sauce and lemon Pledge and death, trying to compress into a tiny dense dot and, pop! disappear — period, finished, *basta*. Or no, that was him, not Tess — not ferocious Tess, Tess the Tiger. She would disappear to reemerge, simply, somewhere else. He felt caught in her vortex. And the way to get to her had to be through the holes in Angie's eyes, now showing his stupefied reflection. He said thickly, "You must know I don't blame you."

Angie heard "blame." The shutter snapped — freeze-frame. And she smiled.

He embraced her to hide both their faces.

But Tess — she even looks like wreckage. When did he give up on her? When she stopped playing ball and started pitching fits? When her moods and mistakes began to have the same net effect as meanness and vice? When she got too hard for him?

Or was it Nick? He groans, and the cat rustles. The thought of his son expands his chest as spontaneously as the smell of spring. Mea culpa. How will he react the first time Nick lies, cheats, steals, exults in cruelty, tells him to fuck off? Which is inevitable, because there ain't no original sin. Will Joe wash his hands of him? Are his children disposable? Throw them away when they show their age?

Or only the girl?

And what about his marriage?

He's glad he didn't tell Angie about calling Elena Soto. She's a psychologist; she's testified for him in court a couple of times. He wanted to ask her professional opinion about Tess, about Angie: Why isn't she getting over it? How patient does he have to be? He needs someone to talk to. Someone objective, with answers.

But he's also interested in her — Elena. Is he playing some kind of juvenile game on himself? Angie takes lovers; he'll take a lover. The exotic ethnic aspect? Pathetic.

And then there's the little matter of what a babe like Elena might see in him. "Forty-six years of frustration coming at you, sweet cheeks!"

But after all this time, hasn't he earned some R and R? He's been faithful, he's been generous — anyway, he's been there — he doesn't want out, he just wants — a soft touch. Before he goes soft altogether. Satisfaction. Elena was telling him that the last time she went home to Brooklyn, she was on the beach, and these two guys approached her, selling jewelry. She asked them, "Did you make it? Where's it from?" and they said, "Rio." They'd come from Brazil. "What's it like? Why'd you leave?" Like, leave Rio? "It's crazy," they said. "Everybody just wants to party, morning, noon, and night." They couldn't take it. They had to get out.

Joe smiles thinking about Elena's shivery laugh. How, when she walks, every inch of her jiggles. Angie is blond, rawboned, elastic as an Ace bandage. Her jaw makes him think of Samson scything the Philistines; her eyes are like chlorinated water. Elena overflowing a bikini. Suddenly, he hears Elena's earrings tinkling beside him as he explains to his parents — for some reason they're at a table at the back of the old restaurant — crumbs, glasses of red wine, busboys clearing around them — that he's divorcing Angie, he's moving to Rio with this plump honey to do nothing but fuck. He sees their wizened faces taking in the sheer dark meat of her, crossing themselves before they enlist the Vatican army and the Knights of Columbus to defend the sacrament of marriage against the unholy blandishments of the flesh. "But she's Catholic!" he'll say.

"Meaty beaty big and bouncy." He wants to laugh out loud to release the bubbles rumbling up in his stomach like a Lava lamp.

He pulls the covers over his shoulder when he hears Angie hang up. He pretends to be fast asleep.

Tess is in bed, scrunched under a sleeping bag — on top of her sheets, blankets — in what she plans to wear to school tomorrow, with Mutt breathing wetly against her ribs. She's decided to run away rather than kill herself, for a lot of reasons. First, Brent and Megan. Megan just drove Brent into a tree and killed him, and she'll die too if Tess totally cuts out on her like that. Second, Ashley, Jen, Cath, Arlen, Suds, really, all the kids, would be destroyed. Third, everything in her life has been so shit up to now that her luck's got to change. If she can hang on through May and get into college, she's gone by September, and with father's funding. Fourth, her mother. She doesn't want to think too much about her. In her dreams sometimes, her mother is a screaming witch, but Tess sees only the silent face right before she starts in. Five, Nick. She doesn't want what happened to her with Vince to happen to him. Six, her father. In his out-of-it tight jeans and his almost-Elvis hair, making her put antifreeze in her car and change her oil. No, fuck him. Fuck him!

Because she can't go without her car. For one thing, how is she supposed to have a cigarette? Joe says if he catches her smoking, he'll dock her allowance. Which is so stupid, since it means he knows he's paying for her habit anyway. But he won't listen. He has to be the man, the father, the law. Like balls were brains. Mr. Albert, he's very manly — he played football — and she can tell him anything. Maybe too much. Her bowels churn as she remembers sitting in his office, hinting around about her mother's drinking — she almost blabbed about the pot — as an excuse for going apeshit in Spanish. Turning in her mother so as not to rat on Brian. God!

But she can't stand how her mother buys into Joe's deal. Not that they don't argue, but when it comes down to it, she always lets him win. And wants Tess to roll over, too, no matter how stupid and crazy he's being. "What are you really giving up?" she asks Tess, looking like she's being bricked into a wall. "A chance to shout?" She loses all her energy dealing with other peoples' problems, so when she comes home, she wants the Waltons. And you can't say anything, because it's like you're slamming the homeless and AIDS victims. Why can't she sell real estate or work in a bank or teach, for Christ's sake? At least then they'd live decently. Normally. They must be the only family in the world without a microwave or a VCR. But no. "I've got to look at myself in the mirror," she says. She ought to look — like she lives in a box — anyway, she's got to get her halo on straight. They're both so controlling and judgmental and full of shit.

So tomorrow Tess will go to school, okay, only she won't come home. Or only to pick up her car. If she can't find her keys, she'll make Brian hot-wire it. Cath and Jen have a place over in Lockwood Close, where she can stay for a while. She's got a little cash she took off her grandmother — the way that old lady leaves money around, you can't help it — but she'll need to pull in some markers or else get real creative if this goes on very long. Which, she has the feeling, it could.

Nick pedals his legs in his sleep. In the dream, he's speeding over the big white bridge to the beach — no side rails, it's like a long lick — and at the height of its arc, he lifts and hurtles into the night, the wind, the stars — he's flying! He's going so fast!

You have to. Or you fall.

Chapter 2

What Comes Naturally

"Did I wake you?" Mrs. Foster laughs.

It's 8:00 A.M. Tess is long gone, on foot, toting, along with her backpack, a chip on her shoulder the size of the cross; Joe took off more recently with Nick, a crankcase from lack of sleep. Angie has been scanning the want ads. She's amazed by the speed with which she plummets from professional to administrative to clerical. She's trying to picture saying, "Can I take your order?" to a table of healthy adults. The black-and-white waitress uniform turns into a nun's habit: order. She hears, "Get up and get it yourself." "Course not, Mom. What's up?"

"Well, I don't want to alarm you, but —" She laughs. Mrs. Foster laughs almost continuously, like she needs a washer replaced. Right to tight, thinks Angie. "I had a little accident yesterday in the Thruway parking lot."

"Are you okay?"

The laughter burbles. "I'm fine. Doris and I were going over to the sale at Davis and then to pick up some cake at Dewey's for the bridge club, and this girl, she came out of nowhere! Cut right in front of me. I swerved, but it was too late. The whole right side of the car is crumpled, but, thank God, no one was hurt. Doris — she bore the brunt of it, but you know Doris, she's indestructible.

COURTING DISASTER ◆ 40

The other little girl — she had children with her. I'd never forgive myself if I'd —" The laugh sputters.

Angie wonders whether her mother is stupid, tactless, or malicious, not for the first time, and not dating from Vince's death. She settles on tactless. "Have the doctor check you over anyway. Doris, too. Sometimes you get whiplash, you don't even know it. Did you phone your insurance?"

"Don't they phone me?"

"Yeah, right, your fender bender just lit up the Nationwide Big Board. Tilt! 'There goes Agnes Foster over in Emphysema, North Carolina. Fax her some cash!' Is it coming in your mail slot yet?"

"What you won't think of."

The everlasting wind chimes. Angie remembers Tess being trained in tornado preparedness in grade school. After a week of instruction, she told Angie, "If you feel a breeze, scream."

"I thought the police took care of it." Mrs. Foster laughs. "You won't believe this — it was that same little boy who helped me when I thought my car was stolen. You remember."

Mrs. Foster had parked at Doris's apartment complex. They went out for lunch, and Doris drove her home. When Mrs. Foster looked for her car the next day, it was missing. She notified the police. As the investigation entered its second week, Doris called to ask Agnes to move her car out of the visitor space — people were complaining. Agnes laughs remembering. "I've got a head like a tack."

Angie also remembers. The "little boy" is a six-foot black cop in his late twenties who suggested Angie keep a closer eye on her mother. Outside, Mutt is barking in perfect unison with the pangs in her sinus cavities. "No, Mom, you've got to call your insurance company, and they follow up."

"Well, then, I'll do that."

"Right away. Like, now. Set those wheels in motion. If you want me to help —" Angie really doesn't want to go over to her mother's, a retirement condo barricaded by chatty neighbors who can bleed hours out of you before you make it back to your car.

Mrs. Foster laughs. "Maybe so. Maybe later. I think I can still handle a phone call."

"So where *is* your car?" A laugh shakes Angie as if they're on the same train. The Toonerville Trolley. She moves to rap on the glass in the back door to shut Mutt up. The cat, Palooka, scratches his eagerness to join the fray. She lets him out. He rips through the unraked yard.

"I had the AAA drag it to the body shop. The dealer place. It's expensive, but they know me there. They said it could be a month."

"They'll let you have a loaner?"

"Oh, it drives, you see, but I was too upset."

"Mom, you've got to get an estimate. You take the car to the in-surance assessor, then they pay."

"I'm not so sure. I was the one turning. I know it wasn't my fault — this girl was going like a bat out of hell — but they have all these rules. My insurance is so high. And they've been good to us. I can afford it. Your father didn't leave me penniless."

"Good to you? Mom, you pay them vast sums of money. Call them, please."

"I want to talk to Joe first. He'll know what to do. I'll call him at work, right after I get done with you."

Won't Joe be thrilled? He calls her the Ticklish Dictator. And he objects to any interruption in his pursuit of the elusive buck — or is it truth, justice, and the American way? — since most of his clients are DWI, battering kin, or holding up Hop-Ins. He's come a long way from the ideals of southern poverty law. But it lets Angie off the hook.

"What I need from you is a ride to my hairdresser. I look a fright. I'd ask one of the girls, but I've imposed on them too much already. And I need a few things at the grocery. And I guess you'll have to take me to the doctor, but God knows when."

Maybe this is Angie's weasel out of the workforce. "Sorry, Joe, my mother." Joe won't go for it. To Joe, Angie's mother is like a crazy hat Angie insists on wearing — a tiara. She should take it off and put it in a vault. Unlike his mother, built like a vault and twice as perky — a Steeler in support hose. And maybe Angie doesn't want out. The idea of a job is beginning to appeal to her, especially as an alternative to carting her mother around. "Ma, I got bad news. Joe says I gotta get a job."

Mrs. Foster laughs. "Why, that's marvelous! Of course he's right. A bright girl like you wasting that classy education waiting on bums. If I've told him once, I've told him a thousand times, you need to get out. You'll go back to teaching —"

"Wait a minute — I've got an idea. Tess is grounded for the next week, maybe two. Joe's taken away her keys. You can drive her car."

Angela has no sense of an old lady's dignity. Theresa's car is plastered with bumper stickers — ABORTION SHOULD BE MANDATORY! What can that mean? Mrs. Foster has often felt they will get Tess killed. Shot! And for good reason. Mrs. Foster suspects that in addition to promoting the slaughter of the defenseless unborn, Theresa may be a Satanist. That, or drugs. Look at her! She's got all these doodads stuck in her, like some ghastly voodoo doll. And tattoos! Why does Joe permit it? Of course, if you think about it, devil worship is not such a far cry from the Roman Church — take *The Exorcist*. German shepherds disappearing, cows mutilated, mysterious bonfires — you read about it all the time in the papers. And Angela is just the type of liberal, indulgent, oblivious modern mother to let that grow up right under her nose. Vincent, after all. Theresa is another sad consequence. "You're too hard on that girl." She laughs.

"You'll like driving it, Mom," Angie's saying. "It's so maneuverable."

Mrs. Foster is also not sure she can drive any car but her own. She's only learned to drive since Richard's death, because everybody said she had to, even with Angela right there. "Those little cars scare me. What if I'd been in one when I got hit? Your father used to say any accident you have in a compact will be fatal. And is it a stick shift? Because I can't drive stick shift." No, ho, ho! — the laugh rumbles under her words like a mole.

It's automatic. Angie was left this car by one of her charges at the Sore. Formerly a mean drunk, when he began dying, his family, never able to please him before, turned him over to the blindness of strangers. Angie would wheel him outside so he could smoke — lung cancer. He'd get her to bend down and gutter in her ear, "Let's go to my room and have a ball." He liked her to read to him from Merle Haggard's autobiography. Care at the Sore is free, so his wife considered the bequest breaking even. Angie ran Sore errands in it until the transmission died, and they let her keep it. Dropped from above for Tess's sixteenth birthday like Sleeping Beauty's spinning wheel, the rebuilt only set them back a grand. At the time, Tess was playing soccer six days a week, and mobilizing her seemed worth the freight, even if it meant selling Angie's piano. "You don't expect me to be caught dead in this gnarly piece of shit?" she thanked them.

"It'll help you get your nerve back," Angie tells her mother. "You won't be stuck at home or dependent on others. Look, let me get my act together and hit this one office temp —"

"Angela! We didn't spend all that —"

"— and try to line something up — that shouldn't take long — and then I'll bring you over here; we'll drive around the block till you feel comfortable with it. Have supper with us."

Mrs. Foster feels let down. Can't Angela tell she's being brave, protecting her from painful exhibitions of emotion? Agnes doesn't want to hear any more about Theresa's awful car or temporary employment — she sees middle-aged Angela clerking in a snooty department store like the one where she wage-slaved, right out of eighth grade and any hope of advancement, until rescued by Richard and his ball-bearing plant — she sees her own father sitting over his coffee cup at the kitchen table when she left, when she came home, slurring, "iss onl' tempry" — and she doesn't want supper — always so tense and indigestible and late — they'd probably make her drive home in the dark by herself. She just wants her hair fixed. "Maybe so."

"Or — when's your appointment? Take a cab over here. I'll leave you the keys and registration."

"I'll call you right back after I've talked to Joe." Mrs. Foster laughs. "Don't you go anywhere."

But Joe's not there. Agnes doesn't believe it — she thinks he's ducking her call. Mr. Big Shot. If he has so much business, why don't they put in a second bathroom? Unless he's trying to bilk something out of her. Richard always said Joe had false hopes, but, to be honest, they were both glad to see Angela married, even to a wop. She'll get Doris to drive her to the beauty parlor, and the hell with it. Hasn't she been through enough?

Joe's at breakfast with Elena. He called her, and she said yes. It's the first impulsive thing he's done in years, and he feels about sixteen — twittery. They're at some dive she suggested — RESTARAUNT in gold script on the window warming his back — everyone else is black, and he's taking in his grease allotment for the duration. It tastes great. Elena's talking about the psychological costs of de facto segregation in the schools, but all he can think about is whether she'll go to bed with him and how to work it out in practical terms — her place? (does she have a boyfriend?); a motel? (near his parents, there's a motel that supplies a free six-pack with the $14.95 "short stay"); a love nest? — Jesus! — how much would that come to, and how could he hide it, and when and how should he pitch it to her? He's not letting himself think about how it will feel. Like this grease. Good. His cock practically wags. Now she's asked him a question, or that's how it looks. "Sorry," he says.

"Where are you?" She dishes up the doe eyes. The irises are sprayed with flecks of gold.

His saliva surges — the wolf. What do his eyes give away? Should he tell her he was raised in a small family restaurant, under the heading *sharing?* A walk through that woods? He's got no desire to rehash the past. "This is great."

"Yes, I come in here often. Of course, I've got to stay with the coffee mostly" — self-deprecating smile; he wants to squeeze her cushioned arm — "and your gringo idea of coffee — well. But it's relaxing. It puts the whole thing on hold. Tell me — I'm feeling a little confused. When you called — did something happen at home? Is there an emergency?"

Every time he sets down his mug, an ample waitress in stretch pants fills it. It's like a game. She saunters, but she's there. She tosses out little tubs of cream. He wishes he knew her well enough to tease her. The sunshine beats through the dusty window. He enjoys the sweat inside his collar; he hopes his ears aren't lit up. He feels like a shop cat or an aging diplomat in a Graham Greene novel and imagines becoming a regular: a hot meal, served with a newspaper, jokes, to the chink of china, the spit of the grill, the hum of muted voices. Elena's already transforming downtown Monotony into a clean, well-lighted place. He can hardly contain his elation. "Yes and no." Her lips are the color of chocolate cherries. "I do need your help" — his voice sticks — "but this —" This is his chance; "this was just —" He can't do it. He tries smiling.

COURTING DISASTER ◆ 46

"Maybe I need a friend more than a counselor — " Shyness, like a tight vest.

"A friend." She conceals her expression under a napkin. "That could present some problems for me, don't you see?"

He snarfs down the last of his fried eggs and pushes the plate away. "I don't want to make any problems for you." He slops back against the padded booth. His shirt clings like silt. She gets it. He feels like a pig.

"So what is happening?" Her eyes are canny, amused, as though this is cute.

He folds his hands and leans forward, speaking in the dead-level voice he reserves for witnesses who retract on the stand. "My daughter is a foulmouthed ingrate I would like to beat into sub-mission. My wife, Lady Bountiful to the dying and otherwise life-challenged, drinks like a fish and is fucking" — he wants to say, a monkey; Elena's brow stitches, but she doesn't look away; he won't let her; she has to see him, as is — "a monkey — the flavor of the month — but she won't fuck me, and, yes, I mind, a thou-sand times. I have a six-year-old son who in my best moments I think I should leave in a basket on St. Anthony's doorstep. I just make the money. I'm bored to death. And I want to start a torrid affair with the one person who can maybe help me resolve this mess or at least console me for the impossibility of escape."

Elena sits back. She feels waylaid. For the first time since she moved to this haven for hypocrites, she sparks — it's a man! Their eyes are tied; he's making her look through a microscope at the brute matter of his soul. She searches for her official line — no married men! — while her breasts swell and her heart gulps. She doesn't trust him; she's not sure she likes him. Good-looking, Ital-ian, married — she knows what they are. And racist to boot. She's speeding down a dimly lit one-way street in the wrong neighbor-hood. Dios mío! Does she still have any options?

"I'm sorry," he says. She looks like she's been blindsided by an eighteen-wheeler. The waitress leaves the check.

"It's not much of a deal for me," Elena says quietly.

"I know." He stands up, claps a couple of bucks on the table. "Why did I eat so much?"

She grips his sleeve and raises those soft eyes. "Can we start over? And take it much slower?" She cranes around the room, gathering her purse, her coat, then back to his face. "It's not nine-thirty in the morning."

He has to prevent himself from throwing himself on her.

"Y'all enjoy your meal?"

"Very much."

"Y'all hurry back, now, y'hea'?"

He's going to have to buy condoms! He might have to buy a car!

Angie exits the temporary agency into chrome glint and the sweet scent of exhaust and tobacco. She's wearing her funeral getup: heels. Turns out, she's marketable. They accepted her not wanting to teach; no one mentioned her age; they seemed impressed she'd been to college. She exclaimed, "I can type!" in the same last-ditch, dug-in way Typhoid Mary told Ellis Island authorities, "I can cook!" She knows the rudiments of computer use from the Open Door. She feels as though she's collecting a paycheck already. She hopes Joe will be pleased with her.

And she has time to change and go walking before she retrieves Nick, maybe for the last time. Today, she'll have to talk to someone about after-school care and break the news to Nico, unfortunately in that order. She doesn't know how he'll take it. He usually plays with his buddy Shane up the street until supper — the two of them bursting in and out of their kitchens with the bravado of hoodlum bikers, downing oceans of fruit drink, conniving in bad weather in front of the tube how to make millions off their toy designs, prank-calling the 800 number for the free video from the Hair Club for Men. Their noise reassures her like Bach.

Tess's car is not in the driveway; the keys are gone. Mrs. Foster must have borrowed it after all. Angie's only surprised she doesn't have to jump through any more hoops, that there's no package of matronly underpants or some stale cake or worthless crocheted potholders and a cheery note: "Don't thank me." Angie chalks it up to bad hair. She imagines her mother cloaked like an Arab terrorist, careening the Bratmobile to her hairdresser appointment. Unless Tess took it — And what's Angie going to do about that now? One anxiety at a time.

She plugs in her Walkman and runs down the steps. Every day she logs the same four miles in the same hour, winding up at Nick's school to bring the boys home. It's her exercise regimen; also a chance to immerse in the particularity of the day and to play with the kids. Following residential streets that join two floodplains-become-municipal-parks, her route offers the highest tree-to-human ratio in her radius and a short parallel with the train tracks, a spur between factories, where the engineer toots at her. Otherwise, she drowns sound — barking dogs, honking men — and rumination with music. Any change smarts her eye like a mote. A few days ago, she spied some blankets, like risen islands, in the dense shade of a clump of old magnolias below the high school gym. She thought picnic. She thought gnats up your nose and bees in your beer. She's seen rats eating French fries here.

But they've remained. She can't fix their contours in her memory well enough to tell if they're moving or expanding, if that Dream Team promotional cup, for example, means housekeeping or runoff. One of them is what her mother calls a com-

forter — inside, the batting would disintegrate and mold with
damp. One's a pink number, pilled and filthy. The gleam of a
garbage bag? It's supposed to get down in the thirties tonight —
that frosty fuck in Mason's bunker. Exposure.

So today, possibly her last day, she carries a sandwich and a
drink in her fanny pack. She feels conspicuous leaving the side-
walk. She has to force her feet down the slope. She knows people
watch her, set their watches by her — the engineer. She pulls out
her earphones, and the fallen leaves chatch as though she's chewing her path. The closer she gets to these cloth drifts, the clearer it
is she won't know if they're dump or domicile till the troll grabs
her foot. She stops to listen. Cars, squirrels, a plane grumbling.
Gym class — whistles, and the kids seem to bawl "Sieg Heil" —
more likely, "one, two," "left, right." Nothing else. A smell — the
mildewed blankets, rotting leaves, something carboniferous, and
a stench like the creek. She nags herself to squat, drawing out the
sandwich in tinfoil, the Mylar pouch of juice. She's down? Get
down. Go the distance.

"Hey! Is somebody here? I thought you might be hungry. It's
peanut butter and jelly, so it won't spoil for a while, and a fruit
drink with a straw you poke in the side. I'm putting them on this
root." A knuckle of the nearest tree. She feels like a complete jerk.
"You know, there's places you can stay — the stone church up the
hill? They'll see you're taken care of. You don't have to be hungry
and cold. Nobody —" She stops herself saying, nobody will hurt
you. She waits what seems like a long time, the time it takes to
measure a child's fever or to beat a birthday cake mix. Then her
crouch, the talking to blankets remind her of Tess and Vince
covering the living room furniture with blankets, playing secret
hideout. When she stands, her knees crack like gunshots.

Nick and Shane are waiting at the meeting spot by the school
entrance in war paint and construction paper feathers: Thanks-

giving Indians. They agree to clamber the willow while she talks to the principal, Mrs. Leinbach.

"What for? What'd I do?" Nick calls after her.

When Angie comes back out — luckily, admission is a question of money, not space — the boys are wading the creek. Their shoes are slung over a branch by the laces. In their giant clothes — shirts so big they look like dresses and shorts they insist they aren't cold in — their thin, tanned limbs awake a tenderness that puts her at a distinct disadvantage. Huck and Tom. "Get out of that water! Are you trying to catch pneumonia?" They scale the bank and shoe up. Soon, they're swatting each other with willow switches. "Cut that out before you get hurt," she orders.

"So what's the deal?" Nick asks, falling in step beside her.

"Is Nick in trouble for —" Shane intercepts a warning and clams up.

"You're not in any trouble. I don't think." She peers down at him. She's the wrong height. "Thing is, I'm trying to get a job."

"Hooray! Will you buy me a Sega Genesis?"

"What it'll mean to you is after-school care —"

"I can take care of myself. Or that lady at Shane's — Mizz Hairston — she will. Or make Tess."

"Not possible, kid. It's gotta be the after-school program." They could communicate better at eye-level. She should have taken this day on her knees.

"After-school is for dweebs," Nick tells her. "All they do is play dodgeball and color. What about Shane? What's he s'posed to do?"

"You'll have weekends together."

"Except for all the dumb stuff you make us do."

They trudge along. Nick kicks Angie's shoe several times, bumps her with his lunch box. She's not asking how his day was.

Into this oppressive silence, Shane suggests, "Maybe my mom will put me in after-school, too."

"Yeah!" Nick ignites. "We'll take over! We'll make them" — Gentlemen, start your engines! — "do what we want!" He capers ahead, banging the lunch box on his butt. He looks like a mummer.

Shane dances toward him. "Billy Lucas is in after-school," he chants. "We'll whup his ass! Wahoo!"

"Billy Lucas is a after-school fool. He thinks he's so cool. He's covered in drool. He pees in the pool. He's a big fat fool —"

"Hey, you two! Lighten up on this Billy Lucas! I'm sure he's got a point of view."

"Like a dumb old mule —"

At the bridge over the creek, Nick stops and pushes back his thick, wet curls. Both boys are panting; their paint is smeared; they smell like cheese. "What kind of job?" Nick asks.

Lord of the Flies, she thinks, wanting to smooth his hair and smooch him. "Dunno yet. What they give me, till I see what I can get."

"I thought you had a job. With those sick people and all. They gave you Tess's hunk a junk."

"I'm a volunteer. It doesn't pay."

"I wouldn't do a job that doesn't pay. If you get one that pays good —"

" — pays well —"

" — weh-hell, will you give me a Camaro?"

"Ferrari Testarossa," Shane whispers. "Red."

"Can we make a little detour?" Angie surprises herself by asking. "I wanna see something over by the gym."

"What?"

How to explain? She certainly doesn't want them nosing around those blankets. "Never mind. Skip it."

"Can we stay here and play Pooh sticks?"

"Too far. We can play Pooh sticks for a minute, and then you can jump on the mats near the track. But you gotta stay where I can see you every single second."

"Deal."

The food is gone. So are the blankets. Silvery trash disposed on the root like sloughed skin. Angie tries to interpret whether it says thank you or fuck you, kneeling before it like an anthropologist or a supplicant until she balls it up to throw away. She's tingling. The boys are on her heels: "Your mom sure hates a litterbug!"

What has she done? Hounded the poor creature to better or worse? How can she follow up — if this is her last jaunt through the park? Don't start what you can't finish. Don't make promises you can't keep.

By suppertime they know something's up with Tess. However generally slovenly, she's always punctual, ever since her first wristwatch. If she's held up, she calls, collect. Things of hers are missing — her sleeping bag. Mrs. Foster hasn't got her car. She says Angela talked her into retrieving her own from the body shop. She laughs and says Tess must be halfway to — Timbuktu. Angie hangs up, rhyming. Tess's friends are clueless.

So the conversation centers on not the job the agency has lined up for Angie — in the business office of a furniture showroom — but Tess. Angie has made celebratory, consolatory crepes she and Joe can't eat. They guzzle wine. They ask each other questions only Tess can answer. Joe comes close to asking how Angie can be so stupid. Nick asks if he can have Tess's room. What can they do? Wait and see.

Joe closets himself with Nick. Angie does the dishes, kills the wine, tries to watch TV, asks for the car, decamps for the Sore. First, she thinks to deliver that ounce to Chemo Sabe before Joe comes across it. She ransacks the trunk, the glove box, delves under the seats. She was pretty out of it last night. Has she already hidden it in the house? She did take it with her from Mason's? She remembers the Seal-a-Meal in her hand, but when? Mason doesn't have a phone in the garage. She's screwed. Her heart is a fist.

"It's him again. Asking for you. By name."

Angie picks up the receiver like a fat girl picking up an éclair in company.

"You might need to ask yourself," Heather adds with a worried smile before transferring, "if this is entirely healthy."

What *is?* Angie doesn't ask. Heather knows. And only twenty-two! She has reams of printed matter saying so. She has it on disk. She makes it widely available on the Internet. And she's too sweet to kid about it. "Alaska?"

"Hey, Angel! I thought they wun' let me through. Fuckin' female five-o. Who are these people?"

"Good people. You oughta give them a try."

"Gimme a break. How you doin'?"

"Better than you."

"Tha's for damn sure."

"Is your wife back?"

"She ain' comin'. She says. Man? As if I care. Listen, I don' wanna talk about her. Can we have a conversation? You like sports?"

"Hoop. What's your wife's name?"

"How 'bout Barkley? You like Barkley?"

"Of course — a bad boy. And he's got grit. If Jordan hadn't quit — Jordan, he can fly. He's from here, and he can fly." But Angie is seeing Tess as Amelia Earhart one Halloween, gamely saluting the camera before takeoff. Tess refusing to stop flapping her angel wings during the church Christmas play, refusing to take them off afterwards, refusing to give them back. Tess has wings tattooed on her ankles. Center forward, flying down the soccer field, mud and curls flying. Tess, flown. Angie cannot lose another child. What to do, what to do?

"Wha's wrong?"

"Wow! You're on the wrong side of the phone."

"Seriously."

"Seriously. What's happening with you? What can we do to help?"

"Don' gimme that we shit. You are helpin'. Tell me wha's wrong. You show me yours, I'll show you mine."

"Strictly verboten."

"Think Barkley."

"You first."

"Now you got me cornered. I'm dangerous when I'm cornered."

"Don't dramatize. I can always hang up."

"Don' you ever hang up on me. I might drop dead. Then how'd you feel? You carry a burden like that forever. I know what I'm talkin' about."

"Extortion."

"Damn! You're right. Ha! Sorry. Damn!" He swallows. "Okay. My wife's named Louise — Weezie. She's my second. First — Margie's an accountant. Smart as a whip. Put on a few too many pounds, maybe, but good lookin' all the same. She still calls. My second — Weezie, that is — reg'lar Playboy cennerfold, and tough as nails, or so I thought. Married her right before Alaska cause I knew I'd need the help and the, uh, companionship —"

"What were you doing in Alaska?"

"Fishin'." He guffaws. "Seriously. Trappin'. Livin'. Tryin'a make it real."

"Yes."

"Like the way you say that. When my momma and Aunt Retta get to talkin', momma calls her 'sosta,' and they say, 'yes,' like that, soft, like they had all the time in the world. Or testifyin'. 'Yes, Jesus.' Like a stone ploppin' in still water, ripplin' out. 'Yes.' Say it."

"You put me uptight."

"Yeah, I know. I fuck with people. Famous for it. So, Weezie. She got herself pregnant."

"Neat trick. No thanks to you."

"Yeah, I hear you. But wha's the big deal? A billion women've done it, even in Alaska. I've birthed all kinds a animals. So's she. I don' get wha's the big deal."

"It's a big deal. Precious cargo. Treacherous waters."

"You got kids?" he asks.

"So that's why she wanted to come home?"

"Jus' when we were gettin' the hang of it. We'd lasted the winter, this summer was wonnerful for fish, I'd brought down a moose, and we were tradin' off it, puttin' some up. I said I'd take her to Fairbanks. She said it was a whore's town. Said there wun' a clean pair a hands. Stuck-up bitch. So, okay, Anchorage. She was callin' the shots by then. She ain' even due to drop for another three month. I shoulda let her find her own way back."

"She wanted to feel safe. Is it her first? A lot can go wrong, you know that. How old is she?"

"Twenny-five. But don' let that fool you — she's been around. Listen, she knew wha' she was gettin' into. One a these women wants eve'thin' you want till she gets her hooks into you and come to find she's all mouth. Remember you said you's all ears?"

"Have you cooled off any yet?"

"Say wha'?"

"Last time we spoke, you couldn't cool off —"

"Oh yeah. Tha's still true. I'm sittin' here naked as the day I was born, cold air pourin' over me, pourin' sweat. Weezie use to call me her furnace; she'd put her hands up inside my collar to warm 'em. Out huntin' at thirty below, I can sweat. But tha's not what you're askin'. I guess when you been raised like I have, you have a hard time seein' the woman's side. I'm tryin'. My sister says that when my pa was messin' with her, I was the only one she could turn to for protection. And I don' remember a goddamn thing about it."

"I don't know what's going on with your wife, Alaska, but when you're pregnant you're really scared you'll screw it up."

"I know that feelin' well enough."

Actually, after the nausea passed, she'd never felt more confident. She'd deliberately puff out her belly when she walked past reflective surfaces — swagger. Right from conception and before any notion of gender, she thought of Tess as backup. She tells him this — in complete disregard of the hot line rules about personal exchange. She just hopes she's not betraying Weezie. "It hits every woman differently, but it hits hard. My friend Mimi says it's because we're thinking for two. No, look, I screwed it up later on. My daughter? She's run away. Like today, tonight." She sees Tess alone in the dark on some lost highway in her truculent clunker, running on empty, all those bumper stickers just asking for it, and wishes she could enclose her again. Here come the waterworks.

"Damn! How old?"

"Seventeen."

"Aw, she be back soon's she runs outta money. You musta married out the cradle."

"I'm forty-three." She should say fifty. Eighty! Too vain. And it's hardly comforting to contemplate what Tess will trade on when she runs out of money.

"I'm thirty-eight. Kinda old to be foundin' my dynasty, I hear you. Tha's part of it. Day late, dolla' short. Why'd she run?"

"Who knows? Some bullshit at school. I knew we had problems, but I didn't know how bad. My husband's been telling me, I guess Tess has been telling me" — she sees their lips moving underwater —"but —"

"You been all ears to the wrong people. You need to quit wastin' your time on trash like me and go home right now to your husband."

"Maybe. I feel so useless and restless there." Picturing herself watching TV with Joe, Angie's skin shrinks. She clicks her mind back to Alaska, to Weezie: soul-surfing with a remote. "But don't get me wrong. Kids are great. Everything good about me I owe to my kids. I'm not just saying that. Get straight with your wife and start looking forward to your baby. The baby will change things." She only lets herself see the little ones she held in snapshots. Long ago and far away. "They give you all the real you can handle."

There's a silence in which she can hear his breathing, Heather's patter on another line, the buzz of the fluorescent lights, Rob and Ben clowning in the hall.

"Angel, you been so hones' with me, I gotta get hones' with you. You were right about my drinkin'."

Everything goes dark — Weezie and the baby in free fall, down a well. "How long you been at it?"

"Days. Weeks. I don' know. There's all these bottles. I don' know where they comin' from."

"You gotta stop sometime, pal. The sooner the better. Let me put you in touch with AA."

"You don' unnerstand. I been in the program on and off for years. Mos'ly off. I got a sponsor. I'm jus' ashamed to call him."

"Hey! He's heard it all before. You got a disease. Don't let that shame crap get in the way. Call him."

"Tha's right, you right. How you make eve'thin' seem so positive? I think I can beat this. I got enough here I think I can taper off. If I can jus' get some sleep. But I start shakin', I get scared. I've had seizures."

"Call a cab, get to the hospital. Where are you? I'll take you. They'll bring you down safely there."

"You know how many times I been in the hospital? In jail? I don' wanna be incarcerated."

"What are you now?"

He snorts. "You got that right. I mean, here I sit, shitfaced, hopeless, helpless as an infant, puttin' it all on the woman — you wouldn't believe the things I put that woman through, and her pregnant. But, God knows, that was her doin'. I mean, I know I'm the problem, but I'm not all a the problem. See if you can figure this. I'm away a lot, okay? Followin' the fish, the game — spent a little time on the coast this summer" — he lilts — "Melancholy Bay."

"'Come to me, my —'"

"Yeah. You got a beautiful voice, you know it? So part a her deal is she wants me to be with her more, right? So I bring her back here, I'm with her every fuckin' minute, and she leaves me. Does that make sense to you? She's always applyin' the needle, and she knows exactly what that does to me." In a high, wheedling voice, "'I got my needs, too-oo.'"

"She does," Angie enunciates.

"Yeah, but — I don' wanna make excuses, but the whole time in Alaska, I never touched a drop till she started fussin' about home. And I was sorely tempted. You know what i's like up there — eve'body drinks or drugs. But I was almos' happy. I thought Alaska was the answer to my prayers. And she took it away from me."

"It's still there. Look, you've got one problem. Stop drinking."

"I's not that simple."

"Sure it is. Why you wanna make it harder?"

He laughs. "Tha's funny. You know, my sponsor, black guy, beautiful guy, must be in his sixties — he's lived it, man, he's done it all, and now he's got ten years of sobriety behind him. He says, 'If it ain' simple, it ain' spiritual.'"

"Wow! Say that again?" Angie writes it down on her wrist. "Certainly call him."

"Yeah. In the program they teach you eve'thin' happens for a reason. I have a lotta trouble with that, but right now I'm thinkin', how'd I hook up with you? You know? I feel truly blessed. You go on home, sweet Angel, find your daughter. You done your good deed for the day."

"Alaska? Call your sponsor. Or go to the hospital. You gotta stop drinking —"

"I'm tryin', I swear, I'm tryin'. Husband, huh? Too bad. I was gonna seduce you."

"Right. Look —"

"Hey, Angel, I'm good. I can open you in ways you can' even imagine. Wha's he like? He do you right?"

"Stop drinking. Whatever it takes —"

"I bet you never been done by a man before —"

The line crackles into a strident dial tone. "Alaska?" He seems to have dropped the phone. Angie hangs up and looks at her empty hands. She feels the lines slipped through them. Squiggly blue lines on her wrist, incomprehensible as her veins.

Joe's just let Mutt in. The poor guy totters to his water dish, chomps a few desultory smacks of "Cycle 9 — for the dead dog," Joe thinks, in the unctuous tones of the dog food commercial. Mutt tags Joe to the living room and lies down on his feet. Works the sad look. They got Mutt for Tess's second birthday, two months before Vince was born, trying to pull off the old bait and switch. Much more successful, actually, than the anatomically correct male doll from Mimi, the head of which Tess smashed during nursery renovation. After Tess fell asleep, Mutt would wriggle out of her stranglehold and trot out to sit on Angie's lap, so that she used to claim he hatched Vince. Now, every night, he teeters up the stairs to Tess's room. If she's not there, he limps down again to wait for her — the worried father, Nana in *Peter Pan*. It makes Joe want to kick him. He leans down to scruff the dog's neck. When he stops, Mutt rolls up the sad eyes to let him know it's too soon. Palooka attaches to Joe's thigh. He's the fucking peaceable kingdom.

L.A. Law is on. Joe loathes lawyer shows, but he watches. What he'd like to see is "Local Law": the arsenic poisoner's prosecutor, who, during the trial, was negotiating the broadcast rights to her exclusive story while her underpublicized lover was taking a hammer to her husband, who had made too many assumptions about *his* cut. The prosecutors in the Little Rascals day-care litigation, who, if they didn't actually plant memories of playing doctor on pirate ships and flying saucers in the heads of the nippers, certainly let the accused who pled guilty walk and those who pled innocent rot. The defense attorney, now serving in the state legislature but with national aspirations, who secured the survivalist's sweetie custody of her two sons over the protests of his client's parents, whom she murdered before they could testify against her — what does L.A. know about la-la land?

He had a plea bargain today. He wishes he'd told Angie about it. She's been following the case; she'll love it. Thirty-eight-year-old black, sporting dreadlocks, busted selling pot out of an ice-cream truck. His defense? Freedom of religion — he's Rastafarian. The twenty bags were for his "own spiritual use." Strangely enough, Joe couldn't put it over. D.A. offers five years' probation on a seven-year suspended sentence with a promise Rast won't ever again inhale. Without so much as a glance at Joe, Rasta asks for the hard time. You'd have thought it was *Name That Tune*. In fact, Angie wanted Joe to defend him on the grounds that the ditzy little jingle drove him to it: the Ding Dong Defense. "Play it all through the trial. Talk about courtroom theatrics! You could write law here. Think of the wider ramifications — get Muzak banned." As it is, he could be paroled in two months. Joe had been saving the story for dinner, but Tess.

Tess! She can turn sleeping over at a friend's to defy parental authority into Anne Frank hiding from the Nazis. Since she took almost none of her stuff (their stuff), she hasn't totally bagged her future. She's too shrewd and too lazy to blow a sure thing, no matter how it cramps her style. The hard part comes next, when she wants back: how will they handle her? And Nick, because he's studying every move. In Tess's room — a bomb crater — evaluating the situation, he thought about stabbing a butcher knife into her teddy bear's chest. He'd like to leave it at that. Just once, the last word. He needs Angie to restore his perspective, to clarify why they need this shit. But he was so annoyed, he managed to chase her off, too.

Trouble is, he can't stop feeling happy. He's in love. Dull roots, spring rain, all that. Or — call it that. Angie's got a job. She's excited about it — wait'll she sees what hours of mindless drudgery at minimum wage buy — but it's a step. Soon she'll be teaching again, engaged, yes, that's what he wants for her, bright and bubbly and bringing in enough dough to support herself, so he can take some time off, preferably touring Brazil in an ice-cream truck with Elena. Angie can have summers with whoever; Joe will be generous — he'll take Nick. He sees them romping a sugar beach beside a turquoise sea under a mango sun.

Why not call Elena? She'll have a strategy on Tess, and Joe can win some points showing her his vulnerable side, listening to her advice. Why is his heart skidding? The phone goes off in his hand. Mutt woofs. He hears, "Shit!" Loud music. It's Tess.

"Is Mom there?"

"Tess! Where are you? What the hell's going on?" Joe jolts, sending Palooka diving for cover. Mutt, the sentinel, stands up wearily. The blaring music has Joe imagining Tess in some combat zone bar, surrounded by predators filing their teeth. What if he's all wrong about her staying with a friend, and she's on the streets? He's believing whatever lets him keep mooning over Elena while Tess slips into darkness. Selfish slime.

"I wanna talk to Mom."

"She's at the Door —"

"I shoulda known. Glad I didn't interfere with her *commitments*. I'll call her there."

"Wait a minute!" But he can hear her waiting; he can almost feel her bated breath in his ear. "What's going on, Tess? You've got us worried sick." He does feel sick.

"Yeah, I can tell. I wanted her to know I'm all right. I'm staying with friends — you don't know them — and I'll keep going to school. But don't hassle me, or I'll quit."

"Don't you threaten me." He swallows the bees swarming in his throat. "Can you explain this to me? You screwed up, so you're punishing us? The people who love you most in the world."

"You're confusing me!" Tess hangs up.

"What are you doing for money?" Joe asks the dead line. He's trembling. He should be relieved. It's exactly as inane as he thought. Tomorrow, Angie — no, her job. Shit. Okay, *he*'ll go to school — he'll *make* time — get the whole thing straightened out. Drag the little brat home by the ear if he has to, lock her in, sell her car. Confiscate her car.

Then what?

Or do nothing. See how she likes life on her own.

The local news comes on. The majority white aldermen have voted to disband the civilian police review board created last year when two black suspects died in custody. Led by a twenty-four-year-old Bob Jones graduate who says he "knows in his heart what's good for the community," the margin was five to four, over vociferous protests by the black aldermen, ministers, civic and business leaders of both races, and members of the police force, including the chief.

Earlier today, the all-white school board unveiled its redistricting plan to curtail busing, which it acknowledges will increase racial imbalance but will also bring back the neighborhood schools and family values it knows the community wants.

Tragedy struck in broad daylight when an eighteen-year-old white skinhead shot to death two sixteen-year-olds, one black, one white, for walking down his street together.

A drug-related drive-by shooting on the east side has left one man dead and one critically wounded.

Asleep in the backseat en route from Texas to a Thanksgiving reunion in Norfolk, a little girl is in critical condition tonight after her mother's car was riddled with bullets by two youths taking pot-shots from an embankment.

A handicapped woman, who arrived in court towing an oxygen tank, was convicted on four felony drug charges for possession with intent to sell five bottles of moonshine and the two bags of marijuana found in her bra. She said she needed the money to pay for chemotherapy.

Coming up: the shelling of Sarajevo, but first —

Is it too late to call Elena?

Mutt shoves his skull under Joe's hand. Joe pets it, numbly watching the weather. It's going to be beautiful.

She's just missed her mother at the Open Door. Tess puts down the phone. Cath and Jen, Brian, Brad, and Kevin are in the next room chugging brews, smoking the number she gave up as thanks for taking her in, and talking about tripping for the show Saturday night. It's lucky she finished her homework in ISS. Nobody else seems to be starving; they seem to live on Cap'n Crunch. She chipped in some fruit and cheese, microwave pasta, to help out because, glad as they are to have her, it's a bitch meeting the rent, even in this shithole, shuddering with their Nirvana and Snoop Doggy Dogg from downstairs.

She'll definitely have to find a job. Jen cashiers at the Revco, but Cath works at this cool boutique where she gets not only discounts on clothes and accessories but whatever she can snake. It's a hoot. She was telling about how Monday on her lunch break she lifted the assistant manager's credit card and bought herself a really fly leather jacket that Jen is going to paint for her and then snuck the plastic back, and nobody the wiser. Tess has a lot to learn.

Tomorrow she'll go to the mall and see if anyplace needs afternoon or evening help. She knows it won't be easy — her only experience is as a counselor-in-training at Y camp. That's why she's holding back on the dope; she might have to sell it or trade it. Anything but flipping burgers. She's already taken out her studs, the nose ring, her dreads, brushed and washed and styled her hair into this cornball cutesy look. Her father would love it. Joe won't let her work during school — he's constantly on her case about grades and college and career — his subtle way of reminding her she owes him. But this shit-eating zoid in the dresser mirror is exactly the person he wants her to be. It'll be great to see his face when she walks in like little Miss Wonderbread and shows him her pay stubs and her report card. If it goes that far.

She wishes she'd reached her mother. She wants to hear what she'd say. Tess feels hollow. Is this freedom? Huh. She's just hungry. She should make herself something.

But she doesn't feel very social. The couch where they're discussing how to score and when to drop the acid is where she's supposed to sleep. There's only the two rooms. The door cracks, and Brian comes in. He's so gorked he almost falls over his own big feet. "Why don't you turn on a light?"

"Why don't you sit on it and rotate?" She can see fine in the streetlight. She likes it black and white.

He parks on the mattress beside her. His backwards ball cap crimps into his eyebrows, and he takes it off, tries to put it on her. "What'd you do to yourself?" He combs his fingers into her hair.

"Ouch! Keep your hands to yourself. I'm not one of your sluts." Swamped by his aftershave, like whiffing a bottle of fabric softener. Combined with the smoke and beer, it sets her teeth. "Let me remind you about Ashley, your girlfriend? My best friend?"

"Looks nice," he says.

His befuddled eyes look like oil slicks. "Yeah, in the dark we all look nice. It's just to get a job."

He sags back. "You look like you used to." He prods her arm. "Lie down so we can talk."

"In your dreams."

"Aw, c'mon. I won't try anything. You still mad about yesterday?"

"No." There's nothing she wants so much as to lie down in someone's arms. "I love sitting in ISS with that wuss Ledford telling us what a rebel he was before he got Christ."

"Sor-ree. I mean, I said I was sorry. Little joke! How's I s'posed to know you'd go off? You so crazy. You goin' out for varsity soccer this spring?" He keeps reaching for her hair.

"Don't you listen? It depends." She hasn't thought that far. She only just realized it's Thanksgiving next week. Her mother makes this dynamite pumpkin pie with ginger. Food again. He's making her so tense.

He runs the flat of his hand up and down her spine. "'Member that time we scrimmaged with you all? I couldn't believe how fast you were. I bet you could get a scholarship."

Yeah, and where would that get her? Bust her ass for two bum knees? What could be more stupid and pointless than a great girl soccer player? "This bullshit work on Ashley?"

"Don't be so tough. Lie down."

Tess descends like a drawbridge. Brian adjusts the pillows so that she's niched into his shoulder. His mouth and eyes are smiling. One hand sits on her hip; the other fiddles with her hair. His shirt is soft. In the next room, they're laughing. They've put on the TV. She's dozing off. The thumping bass from downstairs is like the tide. She's warm. His lips are in her hair, his hand has wandered to her tit. "You don't know how much I like you," he murmurs.

She doesn't have the energy to resist. Besides, it feels good. A twinkling through her body, her nipples thumbs-up, and between her legs a kind of lip smacking that ticks her off, but it's strong. He starts poking her there. He pops her jeans and slides his hand into her panties. Maybe it's time to get this over with. The Great Mystery of Sex — she hates mysteries, stuff people act all superior for knowing. She wishes she could tell him how to move that finger. It's in the wrong place, he's up inside the spongy part of her, and she feels a hangnail or something; anyway, it's Brian, the lying creep, who's supposed to be in love with her best friend and who thinks he's God's gift, and he can have any girl. She socks his arm. "Cut it out."

He pretends he's still snoozy. "C'mon. You like it. Touch me." He nudges this — like a zucchini — against her. "You know you want to."

Now he's telling her what she wants? "Get fucked." She tries to sit up.

He holds her. It makes her wild. She wrenches up.

"Ow! What?"

"Leave me alone, okay?"

"I won't — I mean — I'll —"

"Just get outta here!"

His voice moves closer. "I've got protection. If you —"

"No. I mean it."

"What'd I do?"

"You know?" She wants him to get how pissed she is and that he's nothing to her. That stupid stubborn look — she could be Ledford lecturing him, or his mom. "Tomorrow it'll be all over school, 'I laid Tess DiPietro.' Well, fuck that shit."

"Is that what you think?"

What's she supposed to say? No. Psych! She stalks out to join the others. The light slits her eyes. She gets an apple and jounces onto the arm of the couch beside Cath, eating noisily. "Anybody wanna play cards?"

Brian comes out and falls in a chair near his boots. He hackles his hair back with the plastic adjustment of his ball cap again and again.

"Hey, girlfriend," says Cath, "wha's shakin'? I think I'm 'bout to crash. Hope the sheets ain't wet."

"That's a new look for you, isn't it, Tess?" Kevin observes. "Like you're wearing someone else's head."

"Whose? Brian's?" cackles Brad. Jen slaps his arm.

"Will you give me some?" Kevin simpers.

"You wanna play spit?" Tess asks through the apple.

Brian walks out without a word. Brad and Kevin hustle into their boots, their jackets. From out front they hear thunder, splintering.

"There's my ride," says Kevin.

He and Brad hurry out. Jen runs to the window. "Tess!"

Tess lets herself be dragged down to the parking lot. Her windshield is smashed. Glass glitters everywhere. The driver's side door is bent so it grazes the tire, and there's a deep dent in the hood. Brian's van is gone. The others are grabbing her, carrying on. If she opens her mouth, the blast will reduce the whole world to dust. Somebody's going to pay for this.

It looks like the filming of a demonstration rather than the real thing because of the dominance of the television crews. The microphones in pools of white light are lures, snagging the big fish. Various Lois Lanes trawl for an angle. As Angie remembers it, once the TV arrived, it was all over but the whimpering. She remembers the night Dr. King was murdered; Chicago, 1968; Dupont Circle, '69 — night made it worse. She remembers floundering in grandiose emotions like terror and rage, once in a while an admiration for heroics and humor verging on awe. That all seemed real but wasn't. City Hall and downtown, frozen since 1929, might be part of a train set layout. Where's King Kong? The thought shames her. She edges through the crowd searching for Mason.

She spots him in a group of black men, his arms folded in the thoughtful, shall-not-be-moved stance that first attracted her. There's no way she can extract him, and not because she's married — because she's blond. She'll wait for the crowd to disperse.

But he's coming toward her. His directness moves her. She's watching the approach of Brutus, Marc Antony? Who was the noblest Roman? She thinks of waving him off. If she's his destination, he's going seriously astray. Out now. How?

"Hey, Ange, what's up? Ain't this some deal." He keeps his arms tied over his chest. She looks weedy and wan, less like forbidden fruit than a desiccated discard. Strange fruit — he sees a body swinging from a tree. He's a damn fool. He'll tell the brothers she's well-connected.

"I heard about it from Judi. Trying to track you down."

He cants his brow — why?

"She seemed to think you sniffed a cross burning and rode out into the night to right wrongs or wrong rights, whatever. She'll look after your sound system until you're paroled. I got the more mundane details from the radio. This town is sick."

Chirp chirp — he listens to about half of what she says. "They need a two-thirds majority. Second vote next week. Got to pressure the woman from the northwest district to change her vote. This won't stand."

"Kenniston, man, he's some piece a work. He needs to die."

Stroking his beard, Mason regards the alderman's spotlighted mouth, pale and hairless as a fish belly. "Well, you ain't gone change his mind," he says under his hand.

She laughs. "No, really, I'm volunteering. The mess I'm in, shooting a public figure is as good a way out as any."

She could be announcing a K-mart special. He will never get used to the frivolity of white people. "So what's up? You were huntin' me?"

"You did give me that ounce last night?" Although no one is anywhere near them and she mutters, he looks like he's been goosed. His paranoia gives her some inkling of his ego. "Tess ran away, and I can't find it."

"Shit." Nobody anywhere near them, but no telling how far her fluty voice carries. He should shut her up, but he's suddenly sure he wants to shut her off. No more hassle, no more complications. He's tired of this. "Typical. You didn't just forget where you put it?"

She draws up from her confidential slouch. He seems to forget where he puts it. "That's why I'm talkin' to you, buddy. That's why I went through twenty questions with that idiot Judi —" Marblemouthing, mastered during silent lunch in junior high. His antsy attitude takes her back to telling fibs, hiding under boys' beds, swallowing gum. Idle fears.

"What'd you tell her?" he asks sharply.

"The phone number of your ex-wife's collection agent."

"Hey, all I wanna know is where the next one's comin' from —"

He'll pull up the weed; he was only growing it for her sick folks — playing root doctor — and because it's a nice plant to grow, okay, and to fuck with the man a little, okay. Will he have to evict the Lilies? He *ain't* moving.

"Yeah, I understand that. I'm not stupid." She can't catch his eye. What's with him? Why isn't he on her side? A few hours ago he was behind her all the way, backed her to the hilt, et cetera. The woman is always the butt of the joke. "But you're not the one with the problem. Of course, maybe I'm not thinking too clearly, since my daughter — that's the flesh of my flesh? — just ran away. I don't know where she is or how she is. I only know she's carrying."

"She be back soon as she runs dry. Question is, she gone brag about scorin' off her mama. You answer me that one."

His clasped arms look like fortifications; his swiveling head is the guard tower light. "What do you know about it?" she snaps. "You ran away from your kids."

He should never have told her about his kids. "Don't criticize what you can't understand."

"Jesus — Bob Dylan! The times they ain't a-changin' fast enough."

"What you talkin' about?" Why is he embarrassed to know? The Panthers quoted Bob Dylan. He sees himself in college, trying to relate to Bob Dylan, but it sound like chicken squawk, mean about as much as fingernails scraping a blackboard. All the humiliation of his education — and him, asking for it, saying, 'Please, sir, may I, sir, I want some more, sir.' So much shit in his head. If he's quoting anybody, it'll be Malcolm. Curtis Mayfield! He's not quoting anybody. "All I'm sayin' is, don't compare. Don't think you know what it means for a black man to lose his children."

She looks in his obsidian eyes, and her mouth goes dry. She's never told him about Vince. He's trusted her; she never trusted him — she used him. She fucked him, she fucked with him, she fucked him over. She's the fuckup. She's trashing him, and she's the fuckup. She's always the fuckup.

He can't stand that punched look. They start up with you, and then they act hurt, suddenly childish. What's she got to be hurt about? "You know your daughter. You mean to tell me at this late date you can't hide your shit from her any better? You didn't care enough. You couldn't be bothered. You people just don't get it. Here you come, mouthin' off, 'We should kill him.' That kind of trifling bullshit gets folks killed, you hear me? and I don't mean you and Kenniston. The shit goes so deep — you don't know the half. This ain't nothin'. Tip of the shitberg." His mouth feels dirty. "You know, folks tell me, you try to be friends with them, but in the end they sell you out. Every time."

His voice so low and pulsating it seems to come from inside her. He deserves a reply. "Mason, I'm sorry. You're right. Look — Tess doesn't know about you. Not your name, nothing. I'll keep away from you. You don't have to worry. There's nothing to connect us." She won't stain his face with her gaze.

He ponders her flush, her slippery eyes. Some of them won't quit; they say it's over, then they turn up on the phone like it's yesterday. Not her. This is it. The end. He feels winded. He's not sure how they got here. He knows he's right, but he don't feel right.

Later, he'll go over it slowly. Or maybe get blind drunk and forget he ever knew her. Take up with some little fluff, dumb as a post. "How you know your daughter ran away? How you know she ain't somewhere too stoned to drive?"

Angie shrugs. "Malice aforethought. She took her sleeping bag. And she always calls."

"Up to now." Maybe there's no real issue here. That would be funny.

"Although it is nice to think of her out there somewhere too stoned to drive." She looks up hopelessly.

He has to restrain himself from tracing the forlorn line of her cheek. "Gone miss you, lady."

He don't know the hoof of it. Her libido is screaming, Who's in charge? "You were always too good for me, kid."

Mason opens his arms, and Angie leans against his chest. To him, she feels like something missing. To her, he feels like a clean bed in a quiet boardinghouse at the end of a long and winding road.

On the City Hall steps, Reverend McFadden, his Old Testament vehemence cutting a wide swath, has just called Alderman Kenniston a racist. Kenniston drawls with the complacency of someone recently interred that he doesn't have to ask his plenty-of-black-friends to speak for him. The microphones mob toward him. "This is not a color issue," Kenniston is sad to inform the misguided from his lofty height; he's got the mike. The dissent remains inarticulate — the ostinato. It all seems orchestrated. "How many people does the poor cop have to answer to?"

"All of the people!" roars McFadden.

The cameras wheel to record the people's response.

"The poor cop?" Angie wonders aloud. "Why doesn't that compute? Is it the gun, the Mace, the pepper spray, the billyclub, the power structure —?"

"Did you get that?" a young woman, glazed like a doughnut with ambition, asks her camera assistant. She pushes her microphone at Angie. Mason dissolves into the background. "Who do you represent?"

The cheese stands alone, Angie thinks. She was never meant to sing lead.

"We're returning you live to City Hall for a wrap-up of tonight's top story —"

Angie's still not home, and she must have left the Sore an hour ago. Joe wants to go to bed, but he ought to tell her he spoke to Tess. And then he realizes he's looking at her, behind a hectoring crowd, a nattering newsbabe, locked up with the nigger. This certainly gives him carte blanche. He should be on the horn to Elena, making reservations — shit, in her arms.

Oh, and now he can hear her. Give them your name, why don't you? Be sure they get the spelling.

But her delivery — pure Betty Boop — tickles him. When my baby steps in it, he thinks with something indistinguishable from pride, she sinks waist deep.

Jen sits Tess on the couch, waiting impatiently for her to freak. Which she won't. She's got too much to figure. She lights up a cigarette. Kevin says if she doesn't call the cops, she can't recover on the insurance, but she obviously can't call the cops. Cath might have some advice, but she's passed out in the bedroom. The TV's still on, yak yak yak, so she can't think. Some black-white bullshit downtown. Behind the shouting, she catches a familiar sweater, a gleam of hair.

"There's my mom," she tells Jen, but she's telling herself. "The blond bag with the black stud."

"You're shittin' me!" Jen's new take on the scope of Tess's problems. Her *mother!* She can see Tess making Oprah one of these days.

Tess wants to knock her ashes off on Jen's sympathetic hand. She bites down, and the cinders cascade her chest. The black guy has an incredible body. Her mother looks like a complete stranger. Tess can't take her in — is she old? ugly? beautiful? sane? Now she's saying something. She's on the screen for maybe two seconds; they seem to have torn Tess's brain in two. "I guess she doesn't miss me very much," she says.

Chapter 3

If It Feels Good

It's a ten-minute drive on the senile interstate — exes rather than cloverleafs and potholes like missing molars — to the rambling old brick school building that houses the showroom and mail-order sales for an upscale furniture factory. Maybe, between auto maintenance and child care, Angie will lose money by working. After coordinating with Shane's mother and a very weird Joe — buoyant, like the *Hindenburg* — Angie reports promptly at eight to a rangy young woman named Valjean, who says, "Hot dog!" and presents her with the clerical analogue of Cinderella's chore list. Angie sorts it out in two hours and asks what next. Valjean slews her a look.

Since then, Angie's photocopied every piece of paper extant, including the boss's will. She's been inside the machine, force-fed it toner, coaxed it through hallucinated jams and overheated breakdowns. It works best when you make no demands on it; i.e., unplugged. Hence, tedious manual collating, requiring acres of table, in a former classroom; Angie might be handing out some fateful standardized test to anxious little ghosts. Her fingers and face, especially her nostrils, are smudged, as though she's been down the mine forty years. It's a good thing the funeral getup is navy. Everyone drops by to meet her and entertain her with the scoop on whoever just left. Everyone tells her what a lunatic asylum this is. Constant wailing radio: The Lover's Complaint. One of the sales reps makes a pass so fatuous she has to avoid the break room and skip lunch. The boss wants to find a way to use her voice, but not to hear anything she has to say. Valjean starts to wobble when she sees her coming.

Toward four o'clock, Valjean drags Angie into her cubicle and confides her ambitions, her conflicts with the boss, her family problems. Angie is privately calling her La Misérable. Valjean says Angie is lucky her husband encourages her to work. "You have it all," she marvels. She lets Angie go early because she skipped breaks and lunch. Valjean wants her to be happy here.

Angie hasn't had to think all day. This is great.

Joe calls the school to learn that Tess isn't there. So much for her credibility. He speaks to the vice principal, Mr. Albert, who assures him Tess is deep-down, underneath it all, a nice girl. Joe interprets this to mean she's white and middle-class. Under the botulism is a nice tomato, but so what? Albert will arrange a three-way conference as soon as Tess returns. His concern makes Joe hostile and competitive. If she's not back by Thanksgiving —

Jesus, Thanksgiving! What's Joe going to tell his parents when they call and want to talk to Tess? They'll treat this like the hostage crisis, and he's the Ayatollah. He hopes that over the weekend he and Angie can cook up a scheme — a tiger trap or at least a cover story. (He hopes that Elena will meet him later for coffee, for beer, for anything at all. He hopes he can keep his skin on till then.)

Tess can't face school. Or Brian. She can't get over this sick feeling she made him trash her car. She hasn't slept a wink. It's stupid, but on top of everything else, she missed Mutt. She has only one recorded absence, and as long as she remembers to forge an excuse, she can do her three days of ISS — they have to be consecutive — next week, before Thanksgiving, which should be a slide since everybody goes brain-dead around holidays. If she times it right, she shouldn't have to see anybody.

She's also really not sure how she's going to get to school; she couldn't face her car, either. Maybe if she ignores it, it'll go away. Meanwhile, she'll have to find a ride. Maybe Megan — whoops! Maybe Megan needs a driver. Maybe Tess can boost her grandmother's wheels — the old lady will think she left them someplace again, she'll be too embarrassed to mention it for a month, and by then Tess won't need them — no way she's losing out on Christmas.

She borrows an outfit off Cath and *takes the bus* to the mall and fills out a million applications. Then at the CD Superstore they need a cashier immediately because they just booted this girl who was stealing them blind, and the stock boy was in Legal and Political Systems with Tess last year and vouches for her when he recognizes it *is* her — duh. She tells them she has lots of experience behind a register, only not this kind, not a computer. How hard can it be?

Can she start right now? Can she work this weekend?

She gets off at five. She bums a lift back to the apartment with Chad (the stock boy), who also springs for a slice and a Coke. Her pockets are crammed with frilly undies she filched asking about work at Victoria's Secret. She lights a cig and dials the Crimestoppers number. She tells them Brian will be carrying tomorrow, when and where to find him. She drops the butt almost unsmoked in a cereal bowl. Her mouth feels as dank and foul as the tunnel under the train tracks where the boys piss and tag and beat up on each other.

She leans back on the couch and drifts into an interesting

nightmare. She'd like to see how it ends, but Cath and Jen come in, freaked because Cath got canned — the manager finally caught on — but not to the leather jacket, and, hey, it was a shit job anyway. Way cool about Tess's job. CDs! Cath says, "Don't forget your friends." They're taking Tess to the Rockola and much later to Ziggy's to hear Jehovah's Waitresses because it's Friday night, baby — party party weekend.

The panties go down real well. And maybe somebody at Ziggy's will buy her ticket to P-Funk.

Angie has time to walk her four miles before she's due to pick Nick up at after-school. But she motors past the high school gym, where the blankets sprawl under the magnolias again. Yes! Who's hooked? She races home to change, to make a sandwich — two! a selection! — and with a can of juice and an apple, rushes back. She leaves them on the protruding root, like a giant crow's foot, hunkering down to say that the cheese will go off and awkwardly adding, although she's cutting it close, how glad she is to see — what? A crash pad for weevils? Another dependent? *Nothing at all?*

She bops to the school. She hasn't talked to anybody who's actively dying today or who resents the hell out of her or who is just a means to her dirty ends or who needs a lot more than she's got. Hot dog! She *is* lucky. Buy Nick a frozen yogurt. Spoil his appetite.

The kids are coloring in turkey work sheets. Nick's not there. Billy Lucas was acting ugly to him, and he ran off. Nobody answered at the numbers she gave them — Joe, her mother, Shane's mother. She listens long enough to decide they're assessing blame, then explodes for Shane's house — they're out. To her car? Canvas the neighborhood? First call the police? Her heart engorges her throat like a goiter.

She remembers asking Nick what he would do if a stranger told him his mother was hurt and wanted him to come: "You can take care of yourself."

What if he said he was a Power Ranger?

"He'd have to show me."

What if the stranger had candy?

"What kind?"

The only thing that's holding her together is her absolute faith that she's a cipher in a statistical universe.

The front door is unlocked, his key in it. She gags calling his name. A noise out back. She threads her way — noting in the den the blithering TV, the lunch box and coat on the floor, Palooka sitting on them, still and portentous as a figurehead, a sphinx — what goes on four feet in the morning, two at noon, and three in the evening? — as though she's rising through masses of water, to the surface, to the light, to — the kitchen. And the bends.

Outside, in the yard, Nick is standing over something. He fits perfectly in her stooped embrace, like Africa against South America. Except her chest is heaving. He twists her a bluntly needy look.

Mutt lies stiff on the slates. His eyes are periods and his teeth show: pearly gates.

"Oh, man —" Nick burrows his head in her gut.

After a while, she summons the strength to detach Nico and carry Mutt into the house, setting him out of sight on the washing machine in the cold pantry. His woodenness repels her. A flea hops onto her upper lip, and it takes the grim restraint of a surgeon not to slap at it and roll Mutt even closer to her face. They'll bury him in the yard, but Nick wants a box. It's dark; also past time for her to start supper. Nick asks how she can think of food at a time like this. She's staring at the stove, listening to the furnace bluster and Nick's beautiful footfalls, like a waterfall, when he hauls in the big cardboard dress-up box. They dump it, and she puts Mutt in the pillowcase that served all three of her children as a ghost costume — finally giving up the ghost, she thinks — and then into the box, which is tricky because he's rigid. She hears a line from some movie: "We'll have to break his legs." Uh-uh.

But in a preposterous position for final rest — hanging by his toenails — he fits. She tapes the flaps closed to U.S. postal specifications and washes and washes her hands. Where's Joe? She sneaks a shot. Nick's there, in snow boots, with the shovel.

"I dunno, kid. Let's eat something and wait for your old man."

"Don't be such a wimp. All you have to do is —" His eyes don't move off hers. "I'll dig."

He can barely support the weight of the shovel. Angie props it against the wall and beckons him to the glass of apple juice she's put on the table. She opens a can of soup. She threw together some soda bread yesterday, mainly as blanket bait; now, she feels, it speaks well for her. "Don't you think your dad will want to be here?"

Nick pictures them standing over a grave at night, a full moon with a brown ring around it and wispy, pink-silver clouds or, no, a storm — black clouds, big wind, and howling, only Mutt's the dead one. He sits down to the juice with a look of defeat and rakes back his hair. "Tess," he says. The picture doesn't work without her. He kicks off the boots.

Angie sits. "Tess." Tess the tidal wave, out there somewhere, building. The fluid incarnations of Tess dash her memory, chased by a dopey, adoring dog. Tears pop into her eyes. She really has to hold up her head with her hands. "I don't know how long we can wait, and I don't know how to reach her."

"She's gonna be —" Nick checks his mother and quickly looks away.

"Yeah." They sit. Palooka glides in and, eventually perceiving that his dinner will be delayed, nests in the pile of dress-up. Angie spots her wedding gown, cut down first into the angel costume, then into a clown tunic with big black buttons. She wishes she'd wadded it — all of it, all the pretend — into Mutt's coffin, to muffle any thudding during burial. Nick drains his juice. "You wanna tell me what happened at after-school?" she asks him.

Burning glance. "Billy Lucas was bein' his same old stupid self, and I got tired of it."

"Yeah, but, hon, you can't just take off like that. I was really scared."

"Why do I have to go to dumb old after-school?"

"You know why."

"Well, next time, I'm gonna flatten Billy Lucas."

"What is it with this kid?"

"He said you kissed a nigger on TV."

Angie rocks back in her chair.

"He said he saw you. On the *news*." Nick ladles on the contempt. "He said his mother let him stay up to see Arrested Development on Arsenio. Not!"

Angie tracks this idea through a maze of dead ends. Yes, there were TV cameras. She remembers blinding lights. Maybe it looked like she was kissing Mason. Maybe she was. Yes, any kid in Nick's class would recognize her; she picks him up every day. But are there really mothers who let their six-year-olds watch late-night talk shows? "It's possible," she admits.

"On the *news*?"

"There was this —" How's she going to explain?

He shrugs his indifference. "I mean, it's not news. You kiss a lotta people." He expertly impersonates Joe: "All you babes do."

"What's a nigger?" she asks. She almost can't say it.

What game is she playing? He frowns at her. "Billy Lucas is a nigger."

"Wow." The soup is bubbling. She splits it between them and sets the bowls on the table with slabs of buttered bread, grated cheese, more juice for Nick, and more Scotch for her. While she doles out cat food to placate Palooka, she tries to convey why she hates the word *nigger* without making Nick feel bad about himself or Billy Lucas. Nick looks skeptical and spent. Another time. Yeah, when she's less inadequate.

Her thoughts toll. Okay, if Billy Lucas saw her on TV, did Joe? Is that why he's not here and hasn't phoned? Maybe he's left her. Whoa! Maybe Tess saw, too. She's already gone. Maybe she'll make Dallas by nightfall. *Do* Dallas. Maybe Mrs. Foster saw. Still crawling toward the telephone for help. Maybe Mason's mother saw, his wife, his wife's collection agent, every narc in town, J. Edgar Fucking Hoover. Maybe the Open — saw. Maybe Mutt saw and collapsed. Angie covers her mouth and starts laughing.

Nick comes around the table and gently strokes her hair. "Don't cry, Mom."

Angie surges with an emotion she thought she'd never feel again. It floods her like an injection of light. He's Nick! He's new! He's *here*! Vince — Vince didn't get this far. She has to wait before she takes him in her lap so that she won't crush him, bruise him with it. Finally, she folds him against her, kisses his head, and falters into "Mockingbird": "Hush, little baby —"

"I *hate* that song." Nick swats her face. "The kid is so piggy! Sing 'You Got What It Takes.'"

Joe and Elena are having a beer at the bar of the Rockola. It's noisy, but she likes the frosted glasses, the shiny, plastic, metallic look she associates with things gringo: cool. Antiseptic. You could have a baby on this bar. He's talking about his daughter, trying to be cool, but he's sweating. Even his eyes sweat, big stains under them. His white shirt — cuffs rolled so she can trace the hairs running to his wrists like swashed grass — must be permanent press. An intimate funk, salty, clings to him. She imagines him laboring under a fresh sheet, light switching with the wind, or on the sheet, under her, working, sweating. Cool. That's definitely what's wanted.

Joe knows he's due home, that he should call. Time keeps on slipping, slipping, and here he is, divulging his personal problems, using his daughter, for Christ's sake, to worm his way into the soft, tight, sensitive acceptance of Elena. He loves this squirmy wrongness. He sees himself gripping the bars of a brass bed, her, naked, slowly pumping him, tick tock. Talk about your pendulum. Pendejo, that's what she's thinking. How can he turn her around? How much time will it take? How much time does he have? Does he remember how? Did he ever know? "So what's your advice?" he asks her. "Whatever you tell me, I'm doing it."

Elena smiles into her beer. Too much smiling. He's got the intense bounce of a fighter. "You're making me too important."

"No."

In front of her, only mirrors. All around her, big bland comical cool loud laid-back white guys, like milk-swollen infants. And Joe. She chances a look. Hot. How long has it been? A year? Two? Since she was really gone on someone, since she really gave it up. "I can't talk about your daughter right now."

He flutters her crinkly hair. He imagines nosing into a muff like mink. Luxuriant. Moist. Ooh, that smell. Every hair on his body is standing. He remembers where he is. He juts up. His cock is egging him on like an obnoxious buddy. God, it's hot. "Then tell me about yourself." Jesus! His tongue is hanging out so far he's tripping over it. One step forward, twenty years back.

She plays with the water beading on the bar. "You know? I'm thinking — I guess to my family it seemed like I ran away. When I went to college. They couldn't understand it. I'm the youngest of four daughters. My sisters, they all got married right out of high school. And I had a boyfriend — they really liked him. He was the best of the bunch — respectable, good job, light skin, everything." She dimples quizzically.

Joe's listening, but he has trouble getting past the beauty of her skin. Her fingertips, like red grapes, her copper eyes.

"Papi — he was calling Eduardo 'my son.'" Her lips purse. "So when I said, no, I'm sorry, I'm going to college, they were, like, why? what for? what's wrong with you?" She wants him to see how sweet this is: the crowded household; her tough, perplexed little father, wrinkled as a walnut; her exasperated mother, "If you were ugly!" striving to prepare the meal that would change Elena's mind, enlisting the sarcastic sisters over the dishes, "Talk sense to her!"

"Aren't they the ones supposed to say —?" but he can't feature any of his own sisters passing up marriage for her intellectual ambitions. He shoves Tess's mutinous scowl out of his mind. The image of Elena, even as a teen, primed with filial love and loyalty, laughingly rejecting everything men held out to her, thrills him. He's staring at her mouth. She must be a fantastic lay. Going after what she wants. Very experienced.

She laughs. "They already knew I was trouble." How does she look to him? Fat? Attractive — for a fat woman? Too dark? He's been handsome a long time. His wife is probably thin, flatchested, anemic — blond. How many others has he been through? She corrects her posture: voluptuous. "Did you know I was a park ranger?" She wants to impress him.

"I love it." He grins. "You wear one of those hats?"

"Mmm. Like a juicer." She pulps an imaginary lemon.

He laughs delightedly. He unconsciously rounds his palms over the smooth, tight pants.

"And a gun." She slicks her finger up her wet glass and raises a sculpted eyebrow. "The best part was the gun."

She's coming on to him! The sly curve of her mouth, the unbelievable lift of her breast. He'll kill himself if he fucks this up.

He looks so flustered — it's hilarious. "And seeing people's reaction when I tell them about the gun." She laughs. "Men, especially." She wobbles her shoulders. "Ain't you gonna ask me if I ever used it?"

God, she's a psychologist. His reactions must be transparent to her. Not to say the rocket in his pocket. "Did you?"

"Not once! Unless you count target practice. I'm a crack shot." She brings her red-lacquered fingernail to her lips and blows on it.

Sweet Jesus, those lips! Her sparkling eyes. The freckles like exclamation points. The only thing in their sights is the dumb hulk of him. "This was in Brooklyn?" He's losing track.

"Puerto Rico. Near Arecibo — the big antenna? — there's a park. I spent a lot of summers there, even after we moved to Brooklyn." Her life suddenly seems so rich, so gorgeous. She wonders if he knows any Spanish. "You been to la isla?"

"Elena." What's he got that will work on her? What's the shortest distance between two points? "Do you know how beautiful you are?"

His voice is as soft as the sea in a shell, as urgent as drowning. When he says *beautiful*, she believes it. The match in her box lights. She glows.

"Do you know how much I want you?"

A woman with hair like something you find in your drain laughs shrilly. Someone tunes the TV over the bar to ESPN: beach volleyball.

"Now? Tonight?" she asks.

He's reduced to nodding.

She puts her hand to his cheek, partly instinct — he looks like he could unravel — partly testing how far he'll go in public. He stays fixed as a bull's-eye. "What about your family?" She has to say it. "Joe, you're married!"

"You're telling me?" His eyes twinge. "I'm scared to death."

Those must be the magic words. "Let's go." She might be talking to the moon. For broke. She claps twice. "Vámonos, guapo."

He hops to the balls of his feet, takes care of the check, while she scrabbles up her bag and anchors her shoe to her heel. They head for her car, his hand steering lightly at her waist, her hips swinging like the Liberty Bell, as though behind them crowds are cheering, and he's raising his gloves.

As soon as he's gone, Tess sits up. Jesus! You're not going to tell her that was a client. Both her parents! Heard of a white sale? Somewhere in this town, there must be a black sale. Buy one, get one free.

Jen's mouth is open. "Her father!" she tells Cath. "And on TV last night —"

Cath's eyes get that greedy shine.

Well, well, well. Tess's leaving home seems to have revived the love-in. Has she wrecked their marriage? Was she the dead bolt, the pin in the grenade? Her abdomen convulses. Or has this been going on all along? While they were telling her, "You're not going out on a school night!" At least Joe didn't see *her*. She imagines him dragging her out of the booth by the hair, shouting, smashing things, then hugging her — that's TV. Real would be he recognizes her and looks away, goes right on dogging that black bimbo with the big butt.

Anyhow, now she's got some bargaining chips; not one, but two, three secret weapons. An arsenal.

Why does she feel so bummed?

Maybe they're glad to have her out of the way. Maybe she's finally done exactly what they wanted.

Elena lives on the top floor of a converted 1920s YMCA. Above the street entrance the word BOYS is carved into the concrete. She leads Joe up the stairs, twaddling. Her apartment reminds him of his aunt Bambina's. Every surface is littered with brittle little things, some religious, the walls checkered with photos and prints in assorted frames. Plants fill the tall windows and dangle off tables, the TV, the stereo. She has a squawking parrot named Ponce, a cat named Cacique. He can't identify the smell — too many smells. She motions him to an armchair that receives his ass like a sling.

"Rum okay? It's Palo Viejo. Or beer?"

Old stick? — auspicious. Joe realizes he's famished. One good snort, and he'll pass out. And the beer will make him piss.

"Look around," she invites brightly, retiring to the kitchen.

Joe keeps his hands in his lap. He's afraid he'll destroy something if he moves, and if he doesn't, he may sprout. The parrot makes noises reminiscent of family violence. Cacique sheds long silver hairs against Joe's trouser legs.

Elena reappears with drinks and a plate of thinly sliced cheese, meat, a gummy amber substance that looks like it seeped out of a tree, bread, and olives. She remonstrates with the parrot and puts on some hincky Latin music. They sit together at a round table that nods every time he sets his elbow on it. She urges him to eat, but he's worried about farting. He can't remember how to make conversation. So, you wanna fuck, or what?

Elena is trying to describe the view from her window when she was a child, the innumerable gradations of green, the flowers, the climb of the sun, what it was like being warm all the time, strutting along the dusty street shoeless and shirtless and trailing a duck that had imprinted on her, and everyone knowing their names, hers and the duck's. What a treat she is! Fresh, fascinating! Joe listens, spellbound, too absorbed to eat. "Of course, if we'd stayed there, I might still be barefoot, trailing the little ducks." She thinks about showing him her photo albums. "Actually, Don Pato found his way into a cruel neighbor. Oh, how I cried!"

But she's laughing. There's a smear of the gummy stuff on her tooth. Her silver earrings tinkle and shimmer. Joe feels time pressing on him. He puts his hand on her collarbone. She feels like velvet. She leans in, lustrous, and their mouths meet. She tastes fruity. The table teeters. Maybe he can make a big mess on the carpet.

His kiss feels more like promotion than passion. She softens her mouth, but he shunts the tongue in again like a jimmy. He's pale when he draws back, a nakedness in his eyes that persuades her to be patient. He moves his hand down to her breast, and she bulges into it, licks the corner of his lip, sucks his earlobe. His stubble burns.

He's wondering, do they discuss the condom: who, how, when, where? But she rises and leads him into the next room, the bedroom, which is primarily pink, encrusted with patterns and textures, gilt, like pirate treasure on a coral reef. Giant crucifix. An ornate mirrored vanity with little bottles, the Virgin trampling — he hopes that's a snake. Under a pink spread, an old wooden fourposter staked out like a protective relative: stop! The bedside lamp is shaded in pink. Speakers transmit the scratchy music that makes him think of manic mice, he's sorry, dancing donkeys. She lights some sickly sweet candles. She probably likes the man to undress her, wears a bra that requires a manual.

She slides her hands up inside his jacket and has it off him before he knows it. She puts her finger through his belt and it's open, too. She's Houdini! He grins at her, grazing her straining sides. She throws her hem over her head. Her lacy red bra presents her breasts like a caterer. He's nipping them, licking — although her perfume uncomfortably calls to mind talcuming his babies — pincing the deep cleft of her buns, shaped by a tiny thong of red silk. She detaches the bra, and when she sashays into the bathroom a minute, he undoes his buttons, drops shirt, pants, undershirt, briefs, shoes, socks. Nowhere short of a dream has he felt so encumbered by layers of clothing.

She's pulled back the bedspread and reclines against the pillows. His cock tells her everything about how she looks. The condom is somewhere in his clothes. He gets it and turns away to ram it on. What a view! He must be the clumsiest man on earth. He doesn't have the gall to extinguish all these subtle lights. Hell, he'd walk a mile over broken glass to come in her shadow. He approaches her from the other side of the bed.

"Thanks." She smiles at his rubbered member. His chest, his shoulders, hairy hairy. "I put on my diaphragm, too. Raincoats and hats! Let's put on boots!"

The parrot shrieks. Hysterical drums crest. He wants to wipe that smile off her face. He falls on her like the pie-eating contest, like five-minute supermarket giveaway. The old mattress wheezes, clumps between them like knuckles grasping for a share of the sheet. She thrusts him to his side, facing her. He's nothing but thatch and bone — elbows, knees, even his nose bungs, and his cock is prodding. She sucks his finger and puts it to her labia, glues his cock to her clitoris and rocks. Her internal organs start sloshing around, colliding. He clamps her wrists high over her head so she can only move her hips, pinned under his thigh, and she picks up the rhythm of the claves, clinching him in on the downbeat, while he tongues her nipples to groping fingers. Once sunk in her clutching wetness, he goes off like the fireworks finale. She's imploding, rising, coming —

Joe glumps out with a sclop. He falls back and feels sleep tow him down with the droop of his eyelids. Wow! He pries them up and steals a look at the clock under the lamp. Jesus. He never called home.

Elena is clicking. She feels the air stirring around her scoured skin. Glop slogs out of her. She throws her sticky leg over his groin, questions his nipple with her long red fingernail: come again?

He cups the ball of her shoulder. Plush. He's limp as a sigh. His kiss scuds.

All right, then; she's hungry. She cranks on one elbow to look at him. He's bleary. Maybe they'll order a pizza, eat it naked in front of the TV. Then she'll take him, right there. She wants to show him what she can do — floor him. Show him what he can do. She curls like a grub.

He brushes her electric hair with the back of his hand. "Your face is the only sky I want to see right now."

He means "only." She hears "now."

"But I gotta go." He's actually reaching for his clothes when Cacique leaps on his balls. He screams, curses.

Good, thinks Elena. What's she supposed to do? *Read?* Watch TV? Eat the whole fucking pizza herself? She hopes he doesn't expect her to give him a lift! She tries to pull the damp rope of sheet over her. If he thinks this is it, that he can work her up and kiss her off, he's got another thing coming.

"I'll call you," he says.

He doesn't seem to notice she's pissed, even smacking a kiss on her. It's automatic, no doubt: kiss the woman, turn out the lights, shut the door.

Big finish. Ray Barretto brings down the house.

Angie and Nick are snuggled on the couch watching *King Kong vs. Godzilla,* a big bowl of buttered popcorn on the coffee table.

Nick lifts his eyes to Joe. "I'm rooting for Zilla. Mom says we have to root for the mammal."

Joe smiles without focusing at Angie. He's probably prevented her relieving untold suffering at the Sore. Or fucking her brains. "I'll be right back." He goes to the bedroom and gets rid of his briefcase, doffs his suit. It's dirty, disheveled, whiskered with silver fur. Do they own a clothes brush? Ha. Daring daylight raid on the dry cleaner's in his future. He goes into the bathroom, removes the condom. Now what? Not that she goes through the garbage, but sometimes Mutt — He flushes it. He prays it won't clog the sixty-four-year-old sclerotic pipes. He feels saturated with Elena's perfume. He showers. If anybody asks, he'll say —

"Hey!" He's interrupted some serious discussion. He sits at the far end of the couch in jeans and turtleneck, toweling off his head.

Nick centers himself, expecting Joe to paw and kiss him. Joe tousles his son's hair. Nick looks back and forth between his parents.

"Hey, yourself." Angie smiles at Joe.

She shifts her weight, and her hair slants forward like a sun-shot scrim in a summer breeze. Something quiet, strange, about her. Can she tell already?

"Long day, huh?" she asks. Joe looks exhausted. The news about Mutt will keep. "Can I fix you something? A drink? Some soup?"

He's about to launch into his alibi — last-minute meeting, a quick bite at the Hardee's — he stops himself. "That'd be nice," he says.

"Soup'll have to be canned, but there's soda bread —"

"You know what I'd like? A grilled cheese sandwich —" He can't believe he's doing this. Like *he*'s the injured party, the one in need of comfort. Then again, remembering her performance last night, he is.

"Coming right up."

And she's doing it. Is this normal? He can't remember normal. "Heavy on the mustard. Downtown they treat mustard like a controlled substance. And a big glass of milk."

"You got it."

On her way out, she holds up her hand like a catcher's mitt, and he tosses her the towel. He notices her narrow waist, her high ass. How does she always get the drop on him? "Hey, how was your day?" he calls after her. He forgot this was her first day at some job.

"Insane. I'll tell you later." Angie imagines he's been drinking for hours, and not beer, hard stuff, since he's coating his stomach with milk and didn't call for a lift and had to shower. Because of Tess or her? She wonders about him walking home. He seems to have drunk himself sober.

"But when Mothra comes on later?" Nick edges his butt against his father. "Mom said I could stay up. It's Mothra versus Zilla. I mean, then what?"

Joe kisses Nick's head. "Didn't you go to after-school today? How was it?"

Nick whicks up his thick lashes and frowns. "I mean, who do you back?"

"Lizard over bug. All the way."

Nick punches the air triumphantly. The commercials end, and the film comes back on. "Zilla's really pissed," Nick whispers. "They been messin' with her baby."

"You know these fire-breathing females. After-school?"

Nick makes a puke-face and puts his finger to his lips.

Angie returns for the showdown between ape and reptile. She sets the plate and glass on the coffee table and sits where she was. She's made enough sandwiches for a party. Nick and Joe dive on them.

"You remember Tess sided with Godzilla," she says, clacking the ice in her cup.

"Ma-ahm!" The mouth full.

"Nee-co! It's not like there's dialogue. Tess was so distraught when Godzilla —"

"Don't! You're spoiling it!"

His parents touch eyes. Joe remembers. Tess was so distraught when Godzilla tumbled into the fiery pit, she wept bitterly and had to spend the night between them. Neither of them could believe it. She was fairly big — nine? ten? Before or after Nick? They kept trying to kid her about it, and her lips would quiver — Joe thought she was fighting laughter, but she was inconsolable. "Don't you get it, Tess?" he'd argued, two in the morning. "There's a sequel. Godzilla's still in one piece. She *likes* it hot." Years after Vince, but, yeah, definitely, before Nick. A reason for Nick. "Never thought we'd raise a bunch a dang lizard lovers!" Joe's cowpoke.

Nick wriggles, suppressing laughter. Angie laughs.

"Any word from the wayward daughter?" Joe asks.

Angie shakes no and lifts an interrogative eyebrow. He shakes no and shows his palm to say, there's more.

In the long break before the Mothra movie, Angie gets up and lowers the sound, nods at Nick, returns to the couch.

"Joe?" Nick paints Joe's thigh with his greasy fingers. "I hate to tell you, but — Mutt's dead. I found him."

Joe sweeps Angie's face. It's muzzled by her cup.

"I came home from after-school" — Nick pauses, eyes steady on the screen, but his mom doesn't interrupt to tell Joe how he ran away (he's afraid Joe will yell at him) — "and when I went to get a snack, Palooka wanted in, and Mutt was dead outside. He was — like —" Nick demonstrates rigor mortis. It's pretty graphic. Joe bunches his son to him. "Mutt was dead. We couldn't close his eyes. We put him in the dress-up box. And now we gotta bury him. We waited for you, but — what are we gonna do about Tess?"

Joe sees his son finding the dead dog. Angie, comforting him: her evening. He thinks about what he was up to while all this was happening, and he's suffused with perfume and the sulfurous smell of sex, the beautiful, soft envelopment of Elena, the happiness, even now, of his muscles. He feels as though he's packed with hot oatmeal.

And then he lets himself think about Tess. Baby Tess and Mutt cheek by jowl in her crib. He's blinking away tears, and he sees tears on Angie, tears on Nico, like they're all wearing contacts.

"Tess wasn't at school today," he tells them, "so I didn't talk to her. I left a message for her to come home for Thanksgiving."

"Do you think she'll come?" Angie asks. She doesn't let herself explore the reasons why Tess was not at school or the range of places she might be instead. Joe saying *Tess* in the same sentence with *Thanksgiving* makes her think they'll be together soon. "Can we wait that long on Mutt?"

"I don't know." She knows he doesn't know. She knows more about death than he does, from the Sore. But he likes her asking, casting him as the father. He kisses Nick's head. "We'll think of something," he says recklessly.

"Mutt was a great dog." Nick is asking.

Joe thinks that by the time Nick came along, Mutt was basically an embarrassment, like a hawking, spitting, shuffling old smoker. Gramps.

"He hatched Vince," Angie says.

"We'll think of something," Joe assures them.

Nick goes to turn up the volume. The tiny Japanese girls who travel with Mothra are singing over the credits in their glass-breaking voices. Nick returns to Angie's arms and treads Joe's thigh with his toes.

Angie never understands what's going on in this movie. When Nick drowses out, she and Joe bed him down on the couch, silently fetching his pillow and blanket, the crucial stuffed animals.

In their own bed, Angie cuddles Joe spoon fashion. There's no way he can get it up. He feels her flannel nightgown like it's the circumference of a circle of hell. Should he say he has a headache?

Angie sighs contentedly. He's letting her hold him without trying to fuck her. He feels and smells so good — so familiar — his body as firm and flossy as ever. He hasn't changed a bit.

Angie's up at six and decides to go walking. She loves the empty streets, the noisy birds, the blossoming light. First, she feeds Palooka, makes coffee and, while she's at it, a couple of sandwiches she puts in the fanny pack with an orange and a Capri Sun. When she gets back she'll fix pancakes or popovers or French toast for the boys, and they'll plan their next move.

The blankets are gone, but there's a note. Blobby ballpoint on grimy looseleaf paper, a failed algebra test, creased soft as a lawn handkerchief, secured by the juice can. "Spare Me," it says.

Spare me what? Change? The food? Why eat it? Why come back for more? The tinfoil? She can't just leave unwrapped sandwiches; it's not sanitary. She wonders about Blank's vocabulary. She writes, "What?" under "Spare Me" and puts the next round on top of it.

When she gets home, Nick's up watching cartoons, vigorously petting the cat. She goes to work on the popovers, and Joe appears when the stove bell rings. They sit at the kitchen table; although the cartoons entice Nick, he wants to be in on any decision about Mutt. He also likes dribbling jelly and margarine into the hollow of his popover, which would not be allowed in the den. He wants his own cup of coffee and gets it.

"So, Mutt." He grits his spoon in the sugar bowl.

Joe sets down his mug to say, "We buy an ice chest and seal it with duct tape. If he starts to stink, we plant him. Otherwise, we wait for Tess."

Nick and Angie look at him. At each other. "I wanna help make the cross," Nick says.

Angie asks, "What next? How about we settle this bullshit in Bosnia?"

"What are you doing today?" Joe's on a roll. "Wanna rent a canoe?"

Nick sees himself in an orange life vest, paddling deep and pushing the water back, so they're flying. "Can Shane come?"

Angie sees them skimming the silver surface of the lake, startling a kingfisher, the resident blue heron. She has other commitments: Chemo Sabe must be wondering where she is; she's signed up for terminal care at the Sore. "Shouldn't we hang around in case Tess calls?"

"What's the chance of her calling on a Saturday? Doesn't she have a concert tonight?"

"Yeah. In Charlotte. You think we should go? Grab her as she's going in —" Because the show's at the coliseum, Angie sees herself and Tess in fright wigs and sequined bathing suits wrestling before a rabid crowd. Jake the Snake and who?

"And then what?" Joe thinks of something Elena said last night — her mother, trying to win her over with a meal. "She's got to want to come back. Something in it for her and something in it for us. I say Thanksgiving. Soften her up with stuffing and then sock it to her — the ten commandments of love."

"Bong bong." Angie rings her juice glass. Sonorous: "One —"

"One: No running away. Stand and fight. Let's really write them up. We'll all sign." He can't go into it in front of Nick, but

Angie follows. Thou shalt not steal or thou wilt not drive, and so forth. "Tomorrow, when we make the cross."

"Sunnnnn-dayyyyy," Nick bellows, like the ad for Raceway Park Joe's always quoting.

"And of course we'll have to listen to her gripes and make concessions," Joe adds.

"You sure are smart all of a sudden," Angie admires. "Who you been talking to? Gandhi? Jimmy Hoffa?"

Joe looks away. Is she kidding? Is she hinting at something? He feels so dense. He's got to remember to tell Elena what a good thing she is, how much he's already learned from her. In retrospect, he didn't handle last night very well. He meant to call her, but he crashed, and now it's probably too early, and the canoe trip is in motion. Nick's got Shane on the phone. Angie's organizing a picnic. She's singing. Nick's laughing. The coffee is strong and hot, the kitchen drenched in sunlight — a golden autumn day. The only thing that seems normal to him is putting the dead dog in the cooler. He feels like the rock in a hard place. Go with the flow, he tells himself. Get back, Jojo.

On the way home from the lake, they buy not only a cooler but an answering machine in case Tess calls. Nick's sleeping over at Shane's; Joe takes the car to meet a friend from work and drops Angie off at the Sore. She's slightly sunburned, achy, and she hasn't had a drink all day, although she's thought of it, if only to congratulate herself for not having thought of it more often. She's sitting with a sixty-year-old former textile worker, known as Pepper when he pitched for the Gastonia Smoke, eroded by disease to a bronze skeleton. He's feeling lively, having just put away half a sausage biscuit Laurie went out on a special mission to procure, since there's never anything as sinful as sausage in the Sore fridge.

Laurie's dolled up for a date, and Pepper teases her about forsaking him; she leaves in a flurry of giggles, blushes, and kisses. Angie's a definite letdown. But she atones by unearthing a Mighty Clouds of Joy tape to replace the New Age pap in the boom box.

Erna's next door in the office, catching up on her notes, keeping company with Henry and tabs on Carol. Carol's been in a coma for weeks. Her labored breathing indicates she's going out soon. Everybody hopes she'll hold on till tomorrow; her family's visiting right after church.

Henry's new, young: AIDS. He designs cross-stitch. On the office couch, under a merciless light, he fills in tiny boxes on graph paper with colored pencils — his square in the national AIDS quilt. It has to be the ultimate, and, start to finish, he wants to do it himself. He can't get it just right. He keeps adding figures that totally change the composition.

Pepper's telling Angie about somebody singing at a big game, or he's not talking about baseball at all. He has no teeth, and Angie is really bad at interpreting, asking questions that lead nowhere in a language he doesn't speak, but it sure beats reading the Bible. Sometimes she wonders about the inspiring exchanges her cohorts report. Now he wants to use the john. Every time he farts he says, "'Scuse me," and she's about to reply, Bless you. In spite of how thin he is, she can't move him by herself. He hates the bedpan. She goes for Erna.

"Bet you can belt 'em out —" Pepper flirts as she enters.

"You'd lose that bet!" Erna laughs. She's tall, full-chested, also black, so people are always asssuming she can sing, or else he *is* talking about baseball. "That's one thing I can't do. Choir director said he'd teach me to sing or quit. Honey, he quit!"

The two women clear the covers, and Angie presses the button that raises the bed's head. Pepper can swivel his legs but needs help standing. It's important not to yank him so that the skin won't shear away from the tissue. Erna knows how to do everything. She's a nurse. Despite sole responsibility for two teenage daughters, she works her shift, comes here, and works with the dying. She once told Angie that what she likes about her regular job is that some of the people get well. "I'm tellin' you darlin', I went to a new church last Sunday, I was really cuttin' loose, and didn't these huffy people get up directly and change their seats?"

Once he's on the pot, they give him some privacy. "He's about due to be turned," Erna says, looking at the wall chart. "Let's give him his meds and get him settled for the night."

Angie piles the pillows on a chair, while Erna tautens the sheets — wrinkles raise sores. Pepper calls out. Angie puts on gloves and wipes his ass, first with paper, then a washcloth. He's a mess and impatient, he's got a monster hemorrhoid that must sting like crazy, and a qualified mercy stops her before she's satisfied with her efforts. He pulls up around Erna's neck, and when they tango back to the bed — she's cooing pleasantries like a pigeon — Angie deposits the washcloth in a plastic container, chucks the gloves, washes her hands, puts on a fresh pair of gloves, sprays and mops down the bathroom with disinfectant, chucks the gloves, and washes her hands.

Erna's got him lying a little too low. Leveling the bed, on the count of three, they heft him up and onto his left side, then raise the bed head to a thirty-degree angle. Angie props pillows behind his back, between his knees, and under his head. She voices doubt about her swabbing, and, donning gloves again, they clean him thoroughly and dab medicated cream on his inflamed butt. Angie disposes of the washcloth and their gloves, washes, puts on new gloves, sponges the table and anything they may have touched, as Erna Vaselines his big bat, asking him what church he belongs to, and he looks completely disoriented. She washes and comes back with pain pills and a stool softener. She suggests that Angie massage more Vaseline into his legs, knees, hands, his rough elbows. "Angie's got the healing touch," Erna tells Pepper. When she leaves the room, it gets bigger and darker. Angie is happy to lubricate Pepper's gnarled appendages, humming "Amen" behind the Mighty Clouds of Joy while the night hardens behind the drapes.

Pepper falls asleep. Angie gloves, double-bags the trash, and takes it to the Dumpster in the alley. The cold air refreshes her like a swim. She stops in the office to ask if she should run a wash, which provokes a diatribe from Henry on the blotching of his duds by dim-bulb staff dousing them with bleach, part of the universal protocol before which they are all helpless. Dan from the crisis line is there. This one caller insists he must talk to Angie-only and has somehow talked them into letting him talk to Angie-only. Erna guesses she can spare her, unless Henry plans to blow a gasket. "Just keep her out of my drawers," sniffs Henry, and they all laugh.

Angie and Dan tramp past cutthroat card games and the AA meeting, quiet reconciliations and noisy arbitration, through mighty clouds of incense, cooked cabbage, coffee, and tobacco smoke, to the top floor, where the hot line operates. Dan calmly reviews the rules. She feels like Mary, Queen of Scots, going to the block; like Mary, Queen of Scots, she knows it's her own doing. "Rules were made to be broken!" she'll cry before the ax falls.

He's left his number. It's busy on the first try, but after a cup of coffee, she connects.

"Angel! At last! I can' believe you callin' me. Where you been?"

She hears his parched throat. She can almost smell his breath. She wants him to pass the glass over. "My dog died!" She laughs.

"You shittin' me."

"He was real old. How are you?"

"Not so good. I been makin' kind of a pain in the ass a myself ove' there, I guess you heard."

"Yeah, what is this shit? Where's your curiosity? Your sense of adventure? Thought you'd like — sampling."

"Don' joke. I's special between us, you know that. I can tell you anythin'. I han' had that since — Hey, din' your daughter run away? Have I got that right? She home yet?"

"My husband spoke to her. She's not far." Angie likes his concern; she'd like to describe what's been happening to someone at a remove, who might be able to take in the whole picture. "So set 'em up Joe —" Now she can taste the alcohol. (Call Mimi, first thing.) "Look, buddy —"

"You sound differ'nt. Lighter. Or — brighter —"

She's struck. She knows she should say, Just tell me about yourself, but she lays it on the line: "This is fucked."

"Course i's fucked. You fucked, I'm fucked, our girls're gone, our dogs died. Tha's what i's all about, Angel. Tha's why God sent you to me."

He's as seductive as a sheer drop. "Bullshit. Don't jerk me around. You still drinking?"

"I'm tryin'a stop. Believe me. I'm doin' my best. Do I sound that whacked?"

"You sound — coherent."

"Thanks," he says dryly. "I swear I'm tryin', I'm doin' what I tol' you — taperin' off. Drink enough to sleep tonight, and tomorrow take what comes."

"I don't get that — drinking not to drink. Why's it gonna be better tomorrow?"

"Maybe i's not." He coughs a laugh.

"Yeah, okay," she concedes, "but you have to put some effort —"

"Listen, Angel, I have to tell you somethin' — and I have to be drunk to do it. Okay? Will you take my word for it? Reason I got started this time — Weezie leavin', tha' was a forgone conclusion — but this month, seven years ago, my wife and my boy were killed —" His voice breaks.

"She's an accountant, still calls." Angie's lips are numb.

"You think I'm lyin'? I'd never lie to you. If I'm lyin' to you, I'm lyin' to myself. Tha' was Margie. I fell in love with Rosemarie while I was still married to Margie — never very proud a that. We were both workin' in this environmental coalition —" He laughs. "Took me for a ignorant redneck, din' you? Promised myself a long time ago tha' no amount a education was gone distance me from what I am and where I'm from. You unnerstand."

"Yes."

"But I'm a certified en-vironmental engineer; even worked for the EPA awhile till I got tired a doin' nothin'. Rosemarie — well, she was a wild thing, free, angry, and smart? Like you. She din' care about no ceremony — hell, she was married to a good friend a mine — so we never bothered. But she was my wife" — he chokes — "and my son" — again — "he was my *life.*"

Maybe it's the caffeine, but she's shaking.

"Car accident. Drunk driver. Not me. I swear. They were goin' to some Kudzu Alliance meetin'; I had to work. I only started drinkin' after that. Din' rightly see why not. You know what I'm sayin'. But I sure as hell don' drive."

Angie's never told anybody about Vince. She can't. He's the poisoned appled lodged in her throat as she lies inert in her glass coffin. So why does she feel like she's holding out on this total stranger?

Alaska blows his nose. "Some drunks, tha's the first thing they do — get behind the wheel. Guess I'm lucky in that regard, or I'd surely be dead and God knows who with me. There's this country singer? His wife hid the keys on him one time, an he took off to the liquor store on the lawn tractor." When he laughs, he seems to be scraping out metal shavings. "I was drinkin' straight gin — still workin', mind you, goin' through the motions, goin' home at night an drinkin' to feel somethin'. Then it got outta hand. Woke up in jail. Woke up in restraints in the psycho ward. Blackouts? Angel, if you tol' me I committed murder, I'd have to say, maybe so. Can you imagine that?"

Angie can't speak.

"Wha's wrong, Angel? Me? M'I bringin' you down? I'm sorry. I jus' wanted you to know I don' always fall to pieces like this. Here's to los' love and squandered dreams."

Angie still can't speak.

"Can I call y'again sometime?"

"My son Vince died," she croaks. "He was five." There's a long silence in which she hears his raspy breathing. She's trying to determine if she feels better, like when she's lifting her head out of the toilet bowl.

"I knew that. How'd I know that? How'd it happen?"

"But you gotta think about the baby Weezie's carrying. You're getting a second chance —"

"It's a mistake —"

"No, no!" Now she knows what this is all about: her words are coming back to haunt her. Echoes off the sheer drop between lost souls. She can spare him — spare him! — her mistakes. She's ringing the changes. Sanctuary! A laugh ripples her voice. "It just looks that way because you're drinking —"

"I'm fadin', Angel. I'll be in touch —"

"Alaska, wait —"

"Thanks for callin'." He's gone. Never mind. She pockets his number. There's always next time. She falls back from the phone like she's run — won — the first heat.

*

Elena insists on dinner at her place. If she thinks he's interested in her domestic skills or staging some kind of Bake-Off with Angie, she's wasting her time. Has he told her he grew up in a restaurant? He'd as soon tie on a feed bag as sit down to a banquet. And he wanted to blow some big bucks on her to show he's not using her, take her out someplace fancy and public to show he's cool. He hopes she doesn't think that calling her two nights in a row means they're shacking up. Should he spell this out? She says, "Let's just kick back." Fine. He's zapped from sun and wind and paddling and the constant jabber of six-year-olds. He promises himself not to jump her bones but checks to see the Trojans are in his wallet. Like the Greeks in the horse.

She greets him in purple spandex leggings and a sloppy white T-shirt that keeps falling off her bare shoulders and surprises him with a long kiss he tries to get in on, but she plumbs and sluices and sops as though next she puts in a crown. "You want to eat, fine," she murmurs; "we don't have to."

He grips the neck of his polite wine bottle. It might as well be his tongue. His cock. A vacuum cleaner — "Just plug the little wonder in!" He wants to wipe off his mouth. "What do *you* want?" he asks.

Good question. She draws back. Brooding last night about how to approach their next meeting, horny as hell, riding her finger in and out of turbulent consciousness, moving through the day's tasks obsessing over what he did, what he didn't do, what she did, what she should have done, what it meant, his phone call simply merged with her fantasies. Looking at this stranger — she's never seen him in jeans — he could be a delivery man or Al Pacino or Al Bundy or Ted Bundy — and what does she look like? Oprah on oysters, Clown Cleopatra — she wants to eat.

He studies her murky eyes and smells food. "Let's eat."

She takes the wine and hands him a rum drink. He sits at the rickety table, wondering if he's supposed to get in her way in the kitchen. The music is a little more subdued, but when the horns shriek, so does the parrot. Cacique — the fucking feminist avenger — picks his claws on the cluttered windowsill.

He must be used to the royal treatment at home. She opens the wine, lugs out the arroz con pollo, the beans, the plátanos fritos, the salad. Stuff me, she thinks. She doesn't bother lighting the candles.

They both eat a lot and quickly.

"You got some sun," she observes over her fork.

Big red honker, very sexy. Does she want to hear about Saturday at the lake with the wife and kids? He asks what she's been doing.

I couldn't concentrate on anything but you. I cooked all day for you. I worked my fingers to the bone for you! Fucking sufrida. She was up for this last night. "Nothing."

The table rocks between them. "I could maybe fix this," looking under its skirts. He's thinking a shim of folded cardboard.

"When?" she demands. Put up or shut up.

He feels pinched. His aunt Bambina used to pinch. His mother walloped you across the back of the head. People saw, heard, remarked. Aunt Bambina minced around deadpan so that even the welt seemed like a false accusation. "Gee, I don't know. What with Thanksgiving —" Twenty things pending at the office, the conference with Albert, and then he'll be playing paterfamilias — he sees himself sharpening the carving knife — conning Tess back into the fold, Angie off the sauce, and his mother-in-law, the Laughing Hyena, into *Father Knows Best.* Better keep everybody's mouth full at all times. And, of course, Mutt's last rites. Then he realizes Elena, from the big, warm, happy family, may be alone

on Thanksgiving. He thinks of inviting her over. Why did he bring
it up? "You got any cardboard?"

"I thought you meant carpentry. Cardboard I can do myself."
Cardboard is what he gave her last night. She wishes she'd bought
Chinese takeout and rented a movie and told him to fuck himself.
"There's dessert. You want coffee?"

"Coffee, please. Dessert — maybe later. That was great." His
stomach distended like a bagpipe. "So, what do you think about —"
He flails for a neutral topic. Hastily rejecting the civilian police review board — did you see my wife on TV the other night? — he
recalls the front page. "— the Haitian refuge situation?" Jesus! Is
he the biggest racist on earth? Hunh. Not even in the building.
This reflection only sours his mood.

"Haiti!" she exclaims. Why not the police review board? Rodney King! Michael Jackson!

Her breasts mound up like two huge scoops of vanilla ice
cream, cherries in the whipped cream on top, and he thinks of an
obscene banana split.

"Haiti!" She clears her eyes. He wants Haiti? She'll give him
Haiti up the wazoo. "Haiti is the future."

There's a shine on her, like caramel. She makes no move to
start the coffee. He refills their wineglasses.

"Haiti has hardly any trees left, entiendes? They make char-
coal, sí? they burn their *trees*, see, that hold on to their *soil*? see, for
fuel, see, because there's nothing else. So, okay — no trees, no
soil, no fuel. People bathe in sewer water because drinking water
is so scarce. Disease, infant mortality, life expectancy? The worst.
Unemployment over fifty percent. Eighty percent illiteracy. Shall
we address the current regime? Go back to Papa Doc, the Ton-
tons Macoute? Do I have to tell you the role played by the U.S.?
Bueno: a few weeks before the most recent elections, the Haitian
army received one point five million dollars from the U.S. Con-

gress. The soldiers massacred people as they stood in line to vote. You can read about these things. Nonetheless, proud heritage, amazing culture, crazy with talent — Do you know their history? Have you seen their art?"

"No." She's nailing the nearest representative of yanqui imperialism: Go home! Her hairdo suddenly looks like a beret. "Okay, hard times. I'm with you. So now they all want to leave."

She hikes her chin. "You used it up — The rats have taken over. Don't think it won't happen here."

"Yeah, I see. Meantime, we take them all in. I'm with you. Open door policy" — and there's Angie, angel of the soup kitchen, lifting her spoon — her skirt — beside the golden door — she *is* the golden door — "Welcome Wagon. So how we gonna pay for the massive social services they'll need? The health care?" He grins at her. Has he offended her on every level yet? "By the way, you look sensational without your bra."

He takes her sugar, right, and then she goes quietly back to Puerto Pobre where she belongs? The rights of the master. And don't interrupt his sacred family Thanksgiving. Thanksgiving! Thanks for what? Fucking Anglos invite the Indians to their own house for dinner: we'll pray, and you bring the food, okay? Deal? "Oh, now you throw me flowers, huh? You win many arguments like that, hombre?"

His lips twitch. "I don't know that I've ever won an argument with a woman." Well, in court. And Angie going to work. Which strangely seems to have coincided with the ground opening up under them. "Or let's say — when I have, I've had cause to wonder what exactly it is I've won."

"This is old news, amigo" — Elena is aloof, like she's posing nude for a classroom of amateur painters — "the sly woman getting her way by letting the man win." His wife, probably some country club ice queen. "Even winning isn't enough for you guys.

By the way, I like the color of your balls." She rounds her mouth and lifts her tongue.

Bitchiness — yes! "Wanna step inside and settle this?" He inclines his head toward the bedroom with his thumbs in his belt and legs indolently stretched to her chair. What the hell?

He looks younger tonight. She wants to make him hard, make him moan, make him lose it. She finishes off her wine. "Joe, excuse me for asking, but who've you had sex with besides your wife in the last ten years?" He hurls her a look of rank disbelief, and she hurries on, "I only ask because — maybe — the condom — I mean, there are other ways we could —" Her throat is closing.

His head lowers and his back lifts as though something's stabbing it. "And you can be so sure everybody you've ever fucked was — what? Pure?" He imagines her gang-banging. Guys in do-rags with beepers and diamonds in their teeth. "I guess it's pretty obvious I'm no Don Juan" — he thinks about throwing Vince at her. His pretext for fidelity? he really is vile scum — "but my wife —" He pictures Angie's staring martyrdom in his bed. "You wanna talk Haitians? You know when you give blood, they ask you, 'Have you ever had sex with anyone who's had sex with a Haitian?' Well, *I don't know.*"

She tries to absorb this. She hasn't been listening; his wife is a slut! His pain pulls her to him. She splays her hands over his ribs and plays big chords. She kisses him so lightly his eyelids shiver, and a little salt brims.

He loves the flow of her breasts under the T-shirt, the sleek slopes of her ass.

She loves his tears. She tunnels into his hair. "I just want to explore with you," she whispers, defining his cheekbones, his long nose, his jaw with her lips. "The condom — it was stupid, but I thought —"

He chews her mouth, cleaving her thighs. "Show me." He's so excited he's afraid he'll bite her.

She bites back. She's lathering. "Let's see what comes up."

Pepper's asleep. Erna's reading Scripture to Henry with her glasses slipped down her nose, the broad bittersweet planes of her concentration, his blanched concentration gleaming in separate pools of lamplight. Angie goes to check on Carol. Her eyes are open, like the water in a fish tank without any fish. She smells like milk and shit. Her breathing catches and rasps. The feeding tube ticks. Angie caresses her curd white forehead, her baby-fine curls, before changing the diaper. Sometime into the long procedure, Carol's breathing catches and stops. Catches and racks. Catches and stops.

When Angie finishes the change, Carol's dead. Angie kisses her good-bye. She stands petting her hair, looking at the smiling photos, cards, and colorful drawings on the walls. Carol taught girls in detention, who seem to have loved her. Carol's people are always gusting in, laughing, helping. Any other time, her husband, Sam, would be here. He's her second — editor of the city's black newspaper — they only had four years together. He's at home with their child.

Angie goes for Erna. They return to the room and snap the overhead light on. Erna assures herself Carol's dead and disconnects the feeding tube.

"I thought she'd hang on till her sister got here," Erna says. "Lives in Arizona." She looks over her misted glasses. "How *you* doin', child?"

"I'm fine," Angie says. "You know."

They rest their foreheads together, which is a dip for Erna.

"Did you feel her spirit rise?" Erna's breath smells like wintergreen.

"It's all around us." Angie's thinking about the pictures on the walls.

"Praise the Lord!"

"Praise Carol and Sam and all their friends and relations," Angie argues.

"Whatever. Amen. And now I got to make some phone calls." Erna pauses. "You know? It's so late. Maybe I'll wait till tomorrow. What they don't know won't hurt them. Specially if they're asleep."

Cath and Jen bomb in. Tess pretends she's sleeping, but they turn on all the lights and jump on the couch and start gaggling at her like prison bed check.

"Brian —!"

"— got busted! They met him when he came out of his house and found the stuff on him and took him down. Kev saw almost the whole thing!"

"Five minutes later and —"

"Jesus!" Tess welters up, sniffling and rubbing her eyes. "What time is it?" She squinches at them in their thrift-shop flash, one on each side, like some kid movie where the next thing you know they're blasting back through time with talking animals. "Didja go to the show?"

"Yeah, it was kickin'!" says Jen. "They did this thing where —"

"Yeah, too bad you had to miss it. What about Brian?" Cath asks cagily.

Tess shrugs and yawns. "I bet he's already out."

"No, man, acid ain't like pot." Cath's head shakes like the needle on a scale. "It's a big deal. Kev said. Like *years*. Brian's *screwed*. Roll us a number."

"I'm going back to sleep. I had to work all day, remember?"

"Yeah, so you said. Kinda interestin', you gettin' this job all of a sudden so you couldn't go —"

"Good thing, too, what with you losing yours —"

"And Brian trashin' your car the night before —" Cath wheedles.

"Did I ask him?"

"All I wanna know is, you gonna finger us when we do somethin' you don't like?"

"Ca-ath!" Jen's eyes flit to the ceiling like flies.

"Finger you for what? When'd you ever buy your own?" Tess retorts, pulling her sleeping bag around her.

"Yeah, back atcha, bitch! Snitch-bitch! Who's moochin' off who here?"

"If that's what you think, fine, I'm history."

"Tess!" Jen pleads. "Cath doesn't —"

Cath, in fact, looks like she just tripped Miss America.

"But think about it, genius. I'm the one holding, and Brian knows all about it. He could just as easily turn me in." Tess's eyes fill. "And I don't have rich parents to bail me out." At the moment, she's got nobody. What was she thinking? She must be crazy. She sincerely wonders if she's crazy. Maybe the next stop is the loony bin.

"Yeah, Cath," says Jen. Tess's tears convince her, absolutely.

"Do I have to leave now?" Tess asks. "Can it wait till morning?" Or she can sleep in her car and get shot like that little girl from Texas or Michael Jordan's father.

"It can wait as long as you want, far as I'm concerned." Jen hugs Tess's shoulder.

Cath gets tired of always being the heavy. She thought it, and of course she had to say it. Jen even said it, before, on the drive back, although she always goes along with Brad and Kevin or whatever asshole guy she's with. Cath doesn't want to wake up some morning with cops in her cornflakes. And what about Brian? He's their friend, too. "If I'm wrong —" sizing up Tess —"I'm sorry."

"Let's do that number," Jen suggests. It's how her mom and stepfather patch things up after a fight.

Tess goes to roll one on the coffee table, while Cath and Jen see what's to eat and whisper about her. Tomorrow — today — Tess will either have to find another place to stay or go home. If she still has a home. Her parents may have already split up. Probably thanks to her. And she hasn't figured out what to tell Joe about her car. There's nobody she can ask. This was never going to work out anyway — that Cath is poison. Tess just wanted some space and to go to the show, which she missed anyway, and to show Joe something — what? Maybe she can stay over at Megan's. Drive her to school, cheer her up, help her cope. Or Ashley's. Ashley's mom is cool. Except Ashley's Brian's girl.

"Anybody in the mood for cards?" Tess lights the j, tokes, passes off, picks up the deck. Long night ahead.

Angie won't call Chemo Sabe from an Open Door phone, but she knows he's an insomniac. Charged up, a little afraid to go home to the Scotch, she mouses the dark, spooky blocks to his apartment in the rehabbed old Y to tell him she doesn't have the pot but will keep looking. He's bundled in a woolen cap, ironed pajamas, a bathrobe, socks, and slippers, like Beaver Cleaver, and offers her milk and cookies he can't stomach, like she's Santa. He takes it on the chin, like someone who has to believe you get what you deserve.

Leaving the building, she spots the family car at the curb. Great. Joe must be out drinking again; there's nothing else he'd be doing around here at this hour. Should she track him down? Make like she was feeling sociable, cruising the more single-minded saloons. Drive him home. Explain how everything's changed. Coming from her — he'll be sure to listen. Talk is cheap between them — maybe because he earns his living questioning people's word, concocting arguments to get the guilty off; maybe because she's heard it all more than once at the Sore. She'll have to show him. Be there, sober, when he gets in. Night after night. Right.

She picks up the pace. The temperature's dropped below freezing, and she's wearing a sweater, no hat, no gloves. Loud clack of skateboards, the technopop throb of a rave, raucous laughter from Recreation Billiards. Three men hunch in a doorwell across the street. Her hair feels neon. She tries to contract to a line, a trajectory. "Hey, good lookin'" — from the left, fifty feet down the alley —"where you goin' in such an all-fired hurry?" Is it always like this, or just Saturdays, or something about the cold? "Look at the legs on that!" She wonders where Tess is, if she's got a coat. Blank, on the cold cold ground. A car slows to shadow her. She ducks into a McDonald's, gets her breath, then, on an impulse, buys a Happy Meal — easy to carry, warm her hands — for Blank. It's the most direct way home, the way she always goes. The bad guys are prowling the streets, not the trees. Shortcut through a parking lot where two months ago a woman was raped and killed coming out of choir practice. Yesterday she'd have quoted the odds on lightning striking twice. Tonight, she runs.

Telling herself that nobody else is crazy enough to be in the park on a night like this, but remembering the Central Park jogger, she tears down to the magnolias through the dry leaves. She sounds like Godzilla scourging Tokyo; her breath smokes. The blankets hump and straggle, but they don't move or snore. The trash, under a rock — she finds it by feel and substitutes the burger box. "It's hot," she quavers. Not a sound. She sits a minute, feeling her heart knock, freezing her butt. Should she shake Blank, wake Blank, take Blank's pulse? She thinks of Dian Fossey with the gorillas in the mist. Yeah, and what happened to her? She thinks primal; she thinks tribal. She thinks nuts. She highballs down the crackling hill. Somewhere behind her, did somebody blow a raspberry?

Back home, she finds the note with the trash. In the same blobby ballpoint, it reads: 'Song and dance.' She fans it over her laughter like a Victorian deb in a costume drama.

Tomorrow, it's ham. And then turkey.

Chapter 4

The Right Thing

Nick and Shane barrel up the front steps about 10:00 A.M. to find the newspaper just sitting there and the house locked and the porch light on and Palooka clawing and crying to be let in. Nick is slammed by a million G's — they're all dead! — they've all run away! — although the car's parked in the drive as usual. Palooka must have been out the whole night, and there's tough cats and big mean dogs and no Mutt, and Palooka's ear was half torn off when they got him. Nick's angry, also desperate to pee, and he doesn't have his key. While Shane beats on the door, Nick whips out his thing and takes a whiz on Angie's flower bush, right through the railing and in the face of the old lady across the street who's always saying their house looks like nobody lives in it. Shane cracks up. He has to go to church soon, and Nick wants him to see them making the cross and writing the ten commandments that Tess has to obey. Shane hates Tess. "Make her kiss your butt," he advises.

Joe finally answers in his underwear, all burly like he's crawling with spiders and sort of blue and smelling pissy. His dingy sack of balls is right at their eye level. The boys stalk past him without responding to his touch or his jokes, except for Palooka, who lets

COURTING DISASTER ◆ 116

loose a mad meow. Joe trails them into the kitchen, pausing only to turn up the thermostat.

"What stinks?" Shane whispers.

It could be the litter box. "We gonna make the cross?" Nick scowls at Joe.

Joe hasn't sealed Mutt in the cooler yet. Jesus! First things first: "Have you guys eaten?" He yawns so they can see inside his yellow and metal maw. His eyes are muggy. Lint in his hair. He scratches it up in tufts.

The coffee's brewed, and Joe's feeding Palooka when in pads Angie in her raggy old nightgown. Her hair looks green. The house is freezing, and they're barefoot and in rags and underpants and greasy-looking and smelling putrid, like bums. Shane's parents never look or smell like this. Nick remembers one time the teacher told the class to wear their Sunday clothes to an assembly, and he asked, "What is that? Like my pajamas?" and everybody laughed. Precious, who has long silky red hair, is still talking about it.

"Have you guys eaten?" Angie asks, flumping down at the table. She runs her tongue over her gunky teeth.

"Shane's mom made pancakes that spelled out our names. Hours ago."

Shane's birthday comes one month before Nick's, and each year his mother pulls off some confectionery coup in addition to Putt-Putt and roller skating. Last year, it was a spherical cake, iced blue and green and white to look like the globe, with flags on toothpicks, and sparklers at the poles. Angie's cakes, mixed from a box, fissure. Frosting drools in. She takes the kids to the park and runs them around the track and hands out tinfoil medals for such dubious achievements as style, attitude, best bruise, most sweat, until they've all got a chestful, and then they come home and eat her disaster cakes. Where are those popovers she made yesterday? The cooler idea isn't working.

"Then you'll be thirsty," Joe brogues like the Lucky Charms leprechaun, setting glasses on the table. "Belly up to the bar, boys."

Nick reluctantly takes his chair, and Shane copies him. "He gots to go to church, and he wants to see me make Mutt's cross." Nick knows this won't happen for a long time, if ever. They'll want coffee, showers. His nails pit his palms. He wishes he were going to church with people who always smell like candy and don't sleep in their Sunday clothes.

There's banging out front. "Hell-lo-ho?" The door opens and shuts. Clicks across the wooden floor. "Hell-lo-ho! Are you decent?"

Not her! It's Grandma Foster. Joe, approaching the table with steaming coffee mugs, plunks them down, looks around wildly, finally ties on an apron, and sits, smoothing it over his lap. Angie stifles laughter behind her hand with her eyes winkling on Nick's, exactly like Precious Jewel Crutchfield. Shane is eating this up. How's he gonna tell it at school?

"Hello, darlings! Am I too early?" Mrs. Foster laughs, peering at her watch.

She smells like those killer poppies in *The Wizard of Oz*, and she's wearing a dark suit and a bottle-cap hat and gloves like a meter maid and carrying a hard purse that swacks you in the face when she walks with you, and her features are outlined and colored in, which makes Nick imagine her waking up with a blank face, and her heels chip-chip-chip like the dentist's pick, and she laughs all the time, but you can tell she doesn't think anything is funny.

"You slept late for once, and here I am! I just wanted to hear if anything's happened with," she mouthes, "Theresa."

She makes to kiss him, but Nick repels her with his force field. He wants to yell, Tess! Like he's blind or retarded or something. Tess, Tess, Teeeeessss!

Angie gets up to give Mrs. Foster her seat. "Well, Tess called Thursday night, so we know she's in town." Her voice sounds hiccupy. She pours a cup of coffee for Mrs. Foster.

"Well, that's marvelous! I knew Joe wouldn't just be sitting here if you hadn't heard. Honey, you know I take cream." Pulling off her gloves.

Angie returns with the canned milk and sits on the step stool and puts her hand behind Joe, biting her lips. Joe looks like he's listening to a speech, with his legs and hands crossed, but now and then he starts and cants an eyebrow at Angie.

"I really shouldn't — I'm on my way to church. Maybe Nicholas would like to come with me? There's a special children's service." Mrs. Foster sips. "But I see he's got a little friend."

Nick revs quietly as a signal to split.

"I gotta go," Shane says, jumping up.

"I'll walk you."

Joe stays Nick's arm.

Shane's out the back door already: zero to sixty in nothing flat. "That's okay! See ya! Thanks, Mrs. D, Mr. D!"

"Angela, darling, I don't like to say it, but something in this kitchen smells ripe. You don't want to cook bad meat. Look what happened to those children at the fast-food place in Seattle! They actually died!"

Nick can hear Shane screeching "Nick-oh-las!" down the street. "Can I please go?" he mutters to Joe. Where? Anywhere!

"You don't want to come to church with me, darling? We'll sing, and there'll be good things to eat! Cookies!" She tastes her purply upper lip with her pointy tongue. "I've got time for you to change." She moves her watch away to look at it, brings it to her ear.

Into what? "Mutt died," he says, "and I'm making the cross."

"Oh, I'm so sorry." Mrs. Foster bugs her eyes at Angela and Joe.

Why didn't somebody tell her? She goggles at Nick. "But you have to understand, he was a very, very old man in dog-years. He's happier now. He's in heaven, with Vincent" — she laughs — "and your grandfather Foster."

"And Elvis," Joe says between his teeth, taking Angie's hand, "and Rin Tin Tin."

Nick checks Joe's expression. Heaven is a dumb joke only chumps fall for. He wishes it weren't. He's always wanted to meet this Vince.

"You know? I was thinking. Instead of a cross —" Angie reaches for her coffee, takes a sip, makes a face. Her knee judders like she's idling. "What if we planted a tree for Mutt?"

"You said a cross! You promised!" Nick is off his chair. It crashes to the floor. Palooka turboboosts to the top of the refrigerator.

"Yeah, but Nick, look, trees grow. We could drive out to the nursery, maybe stop at the Dairy Queen on the way? Then, come home, dig a hole —"

"You said a cross!" Nick bellows, kicking the chair legs. They kick back. It inflames him. He kicks and kicks, waiting for someone to stop him. It hurts! Palooka knocks the napkins and magnets and pictures off the refrigerator.

"Nich-o-las." Mrs. Foster chuckles, dragging down the syllables.

Nico-loss. Nick-alas. Nicol-ass!

"Nick, get hold of yourself," Joe commands.

Nick picks up the chair and dashes it on the linoleum and keeps kicking. Palooka falls behind the refrigerator with a bloodcurdling scream. Angie to the rescue. This has happened before. She tackles the fridge like a sumo wrestler and totters it away from the wall as she's saying, "Just listen a minute —" Palooka jangles out, dazed.

"No! A cross! Now!" Nick howls. "Noooooooooooow!" Palooka scrams.

Before his son destroys the chair, Joe spurts up — like he's wearing a skirt! — captures Nick's arms, and takes a sneaker smack in the groin. Sucking in his breath and stiff as a forklift, he carries the little dervish from the room.

Mrs. Foster gets a load of Joe's retreat and holds Angela responsible — did she have to breed with such a hairy son of a bitch?

"Well," Angie says, "I guess we'll be nailing the cross this afternoon. Care to join us?"

Shouting and stamping. Angie tries to convince herself Joe and Nick are cavorting around Nick's room, throwing things, slapping five. She returns to the step stool.

"Have you done your grocery shopping yet?" her mother asks.

Angie wipes down her mouth. "Can't say I've given it a moment's thought."

"Well, you must! You don't mean to tell me you haven't bought your turkey yet? There may not be any turkeys left after today!"

"Nation's largest turkey-producing state —" Angie goes to hotten her cup. "Although I heard that all the good ones are taken." She wafts the pot at her mother, who frowns at her watch again and elbows up her purse.

"That's not that smell? Your turkey?"

Angie replaces the pot and spritzes some cleanser from under the sink hither and yon. She thinks about spraying it under her arms, into her mouth. "No, Mom."

"Because you know every Thanksgiving, people kill themselves by improperly thawing their turkeys."

Angie sits.

"You really don't have your turkey! I swear! You're worse than I am!" Mrs. Foster laughs. "I'll have lunch with the girls, and then we'll go shopping."

"Mom, I can't. I've got laundry, and — you saw Nick."

"Isn't he a little old for that sort of tantrum?"

Angie considers how to answer. If only he were less old? "What's your advice?"

"Well, I don't know." Mrs. Foster can't remember when anyone last asked her advice. It's a trick! "I've read about these hyper children. I think it's Maureen's nephew has to take some kind of drugs. Talk to them at the school — they'll know."

"Hey, thanks, I'll do that. Drug him. Okay!"

"Well, then" — Mrs. Foster laughs; there's always something cruel lurking in Angela's mouth — "when *do* you want to go?"

"Where?"

"Shopping!"

"Are the stores open Thursday?"

"Thursday *is* Thanksgiving," Mrs. Foster honks. What planet does her daughter live on? She probably damaged her brain back in college like so many of them. Come to think of it, that would explain a lot. "What's wrong with tomorrow?"

"Work," Angie says.

"Work!" That stupid temporary job. "What possessed you — right before Thanksgiving?"

"I think it was Christmas. Sugarplum funding. Mom, look, I'll just play it by ear. *You* don't have to go —"

"Of course I do! You won't remember half the things we need. You'll come home with three colors of wine and no cranberry sauce. And you better get some Lysol. How are you going to —?" She breaks off, seeing Angela wandering the aisles of the Kroger barefoot, in her nightgown, pushing an empty cart, without a list. It's open twenty-four hours. "We could go tonight," she suggests warily. Robert Stack in the Stygian parking lot, narrating the circumstances of her abduction.

"How about Wednesday night?"

"We'll have raw turkey, I'm telling you. What's wrong with Tuesday?"

"I've got a funeral."

Mrs. Foster half-rises, sits again. "You don't mean this foolish business with the dog?"

"No, it's that place I volunteer — the Open Door."

A haven for drug addicts and welfare mooches. "So you don't *have* to go. Tuesday night, then!" She's up.

"Mom, I wanna go. I'm going. Wednesday night or nothing."

"What about the turkey?" Mrs. Foster fidgets. She must be so late. Where will she park? "How will it thaw?"

"If it's a problem, we'll eat something else."

"What?" Mrs. Foster bites her gloves. "Ham?"

Angie laughs. "Pumpkin! Rice! Ice cream!" The *dog*!

"Rice!" Mrs. Foster pivots and hurtles toward her car. She can just picture it! Rice! Shoveling it in with chopsticks! "Pick me up directly after five. Have your list! Be ready!"

"Mom, I — Be careful on the steps!"

The front door slams. Something in another room falls.

Why the fuck is Angie on the wagon when the humor of all this would certainly be enhanced by a shot? There's beer, wine — it's mother's milk to Joe. And what about Joe? — wean. Well, for now, she's testing herself, and it's a simple yes-or-no question.

She sniffs down her nightgown — maybe the cat box is contributing — maybe they have to come to a decision about Mutt sooner than later. Remembering she brought home some incense from the Sore, she fetches it and lights it in a saucer. Joe returns showered and dressed and sits at the table with another cup of coffee. He looks haggard.

"You got in late last night," Angie remarks, stroking back his forelock.

He shies her hand off. "Yeah, okay, I'm sorry, I didn't get around to putting Mutt in the cooler. What's *that* smell?"

Angie explains the incense. How's she going to broach the subject of his drinking with him already so defensive?

Joe slugs into the pantry, opens the cooler, crushes the foul-smelling box inside it — thank Christ it fits! — and whacks the lid down. He'll tape it later. He'd upchuck in the sink if Angie weren't there washing Palooka's bowl. He staggers back to the table. The sweet smoke reminds him of Elena's place. Also of lying around some girl's apartment with a lot of stoned people younger than himself who'd never been anywhere and knew everything, excruciating Indian music boring through his skull. The things he's done to get laid. If it's all about pleasure, boy, has he been living wrong! "Maybe put in some ice?" he calls. Angie's moved to the pantry, changing the litter and scrubbing the floor around it. He pictures the soggy cardboard; he's not opening that cooler again. "Or — what'd we do with my old footlocker?"

"You mean my night table. Maybe we gotta put Mutt in the ground. We can still hold a ceremony when Tess comes."

He sees himself and Nick spading the yard, the breeze drying their sweat. Presenting Tess with the mute earth. "Let's hold out another day. I'll see her tomorrow, unless —" He claps his mouth. Elena's expecting him to take her to breakfast, and he's got the conference with Albert where, hopefully, Tess will resurface. How could it have slipped his mind? He remembers last night, and waves of fetid softness engulf him. What mind? "You couldn't blow off the job?"

Angie resumes her place at the table with more coffee. "Not if I want to work through this agency again — Why? You have a conflict?"

Yeah, last night, I forgot all about Tess and invited my tootsie to breakfast. "How much you actually making?"

She doesn't want to calculate her value right now, right after

COURTING DISASTER ♦ 124

her mother. "The thing is, I like it. You don't bring it home with you. You meet new people you really don't care about. It's like going to the movies."

"It's like a robot," Joe comments.

"Is you is or RUR my baby?" Angie croons. "I like the way you blew off my mom. You missed an opportunity to talk turkey. I hope you set Nick straight on the cross."

"It's not funny," Joe bridles.

"Is too!"

Joe battens down his hatches. It's *not* funny. "What'd you think you were doing, goosing me in front of them?" Fucking tease; fucking fraud. "You been drinking?"

"No." Angie holds up the Girl Scouts' Honor fingers. Joe looks at her coldly and looks away. She can't tell if he believes her. Why is he being so nasty? Maybe he's hung over. "How about you?" she asks quietly.

He really hates that look — that incredulous, stood-up-in-the-pouring-rain look. Okay, maybe he's off base. This time. Makes a change. She managed to miss the ugly scuffle with Nick. "I had to give Nick a pop on the bottom."

Had to? Joe knows how she feels about spanking. Not allowed. He thinks it shows seriousness and teaches absolutes. They've never fought this out. It must be D day.

"He was hysterical. He's confined to his room for the next hour, and then we'll discuss it. The mouth on him! Just like his sister." Joe looks away. "I'm not saying this is your fault, but these kids are out of control. We've raised two undisciplined, uncouth, un-caring —"

"Oh, Joe, no" — Angie leans in — "that's not what's wrong with them." Who's out of control? Who hit who? Who blames who?

She's telling him he's wrong about his own kids? Just because she's the mother, she's got a lock on the truth? He sees her pleading this in a custody hearing. He sees Elena waiting to testify. He sees the Queen of Hearts behind the bench. "Sociopaths," he says. Angie's shaking her head — the teacher — with her eyes shut. "Monsters!"

"No, Joe, look. The other day — whatever day Mutt died — Nick — he was so sweet to me. He'd run away from after-school —"

"He what?"

"Oh, man, this is one convoluted —"

"You weren't going to tell me?"

"Course I was, but —"

"So he's in the care of total incompetents —" While she's out generating paper — destroying the trees! depleting the ozone! — at $4.60 an hour.

"No, it's just that he's new —"

"What are you saying? They mislaid him?"

"I mean, it was his first day, and — oh, there's this whole horrible racial component." She tells him about Billy Lucas, neatly excising the part that touches on her TV appearance. "I don't think it's *because* Billy Lucas is black — this shit between them — but Nick doesn't have any black friends that I know of and —"

Joe listens, tracing his hairline. "Why don't we look into St. Anthony's? Okay, I know what you're going to say, but you could put your religious compunctions aside until he's learned some discipline and long division. Or take him out of school altogether. This friend of mine, a black psychologist, was saying that the public schools —" He sees Elena's earnest face across the table in that restaurant, between his legs last night —

"Ooh, your friend have kids?" Angie interrupts. "Ask them to dinner. Thanksgiving!"

He shivers. "You could teach him here at home —"

"Are you out of your mind?" She and Nick reading Greek

myths — And then she serves him his own children! — field trips to the Nature Science Center — So how long *does* it take for a twenty-pound dog to decompose at a fairly constant sixty-five degrees Fahrenheit? — or the Open Sore — This nice man is dying of plague because he butt-fucked without a scumbag. And he's worried about Nick at school! "Nick doesn't need any more time alone with me. He needs the other kids. How else will he work through this Billy Lucas?"

Is *he* out of *his* mind? "You're just proving my point. Both kids running away? If you'd been here — both times —"

"Whoa! Wait a minute." Angie's gonged by the steel striker he's malleted — Test Your Strength, indeed. "I thought you wanted me to work. Me going to work was your idea. This is about when to bury the dog, right?"

Joe feels like a complete failure. He envisions himself on the talk-show circuit, like the father of that baby-faced serial killer who ate his victims. "Ange, I'm really afraid they're in serious trouble. Maybe they need psychiatric help. Maybe we all do."

At the same time, she's saying, "Maybe we could put on everything we own and drop the thermostat to zero." Nick's hour is almost up, and she's got to do the laundry. Won't the dryer warm the room? She also remembers Alaska. She's never getting to the hot line today, and her mother thinks they're going grocery shopping tonight. She'll try to call him later, make sure he's — alive, like the Uruguayan soccer team stranded in the frozen Andes.

Joe double-takes. She's lost it. He gets up to get a couple of brews. It's close enough to noon.

The phone rings. Mrs. Foster's had a little accident. The EMS are taking her to the county hospital.

Tess packs stealthily, although you'd need a drill team to wake Cath and Jen. She thinks about snaking something, something

really obvious, like the leather jacket — what could they say? On
the other hand, why let on how much they cost her? She doesn't
even take Cath's blouse she's been wearing to work as if she just
forgot. She doesn't leave a note, either. It's a write-off. A learning
experience. There's no trust in this world.

But when she shuts the door, she wishes she'd kept a key.

Somebody's hosed the pavement around her car. There's still
broken glass on the seat and the dash. She swipes at it and dinks
her hand. The engine starts. Spectacular crunch when she inches
forward. She kills it. Joe will not understand if she slashes the tires
driving home. She'll have to leave it here. Tell him Brian did it,
on account of Spanish. This should make her look more plausi-
ble, more innocent, which of course, when you think about it for
five minutes, she is. This is good. Okay, she *had* to come home,
even though she didn't want to, even though she could have held
out forever otherwise, so she can get to school, to work. Then he'll
drive her to the Superstore — Hardee's first! grilled chicken
combo and a vanilla shake! — and while she's putting in her
hours, maybe he'll have the car towed. Do the insurance. Deal
with the cops. Be the daddy.

She must look so cool, lounging in this broken-glass, junked-
out car, having a smoke, especially to the Bible-beaters charging
uphill to church, especially to their slicked-down, dressed-up
brats. She lights another. Then she doesn't know what else to do,
so, brushing the chips off her ass, shouldering her possessions, she
trudges the three miles home.

The house seems deserted. No car. She doesn't hear the same
six sexist songs on classic rock radio that always accompany Joe's
Sunday chores. Her mom could be at the Sore and Nick at
Shane's; Joe jogging? At the office? But where's Mutt? He should
be barking gleefully.

She goes around back and lets herself in. There's really nobody here. From the smell in the kitchen, nobody's been here for some time. Mutt's dishes are gone. Palooka's litter is clean; his dishes, empty. Almost nothing in the refrigerator. No Thanksgiving.

Tess goes to the front porch for some air. She hasn't even taken off her pack. She'd imagined them all being here: her mom's hug, Mutt's slobber, Nick glad to see her, although not showing it, Joe finally coming across with a hug. She doesn't want them walking in one at a time, from — where? Their lovers? Ready to go off, looking for a reason to leave again, finding *her*. Making her explain over and over.

She's not going upstairs to see if they threw out her stuff. They wouldn't throw out Mutt? That's insane!

Maybe they went on vacation. Disney World! Without her!

She sobs over cigarettes and solitaire for maybe half an hour, hoping they'll pull up. Everybody in the West End gets an eyeful. Then thirsty, cold, starving, her feet killing her, her heart choking, she hobbles to Megan's. At least Tess won't have to put on a happy face for *her*.

"So she can have our room, and we can move upstairs, into the front room, unless Tess —"

"That'd work," says Joe, "except for the bathroom. How much does one of those full-service places run? I mean, would it be comparable financially to —"

Mrs. Foster is sitting bolt upright in the backseat of their dreadful old Chevy with the greasy snack bags and leaky drink containers and the felt ceiling cloth swagging on her hair — where's her hat? — and her broken wrist in a cast. She's being brave and chipper, and this is the thanks she gets: they're arguing about where she's going to sleep and how they're going to look after her. Permanent arrangements. Doesn't she get a say? They'll put her in that Open Sore place, with all those gays and coloreds, and everybody dies!

You'd think she ran her car into that post on purpose. Didn't she refuse the drugs the doctors offered her? The *Reader's Digest* has so many stories about the dangers, especially for people her age. And she refused to allow them to keep her overnight, although she's pretty sure *she's* covered. She even tried to prevent them taking her in the ambulance — Angela would have come eventually. She knows that if they had left her alone a minute, she would have been able to — well, what? The wrist *is* broken.

It's funny, though; the car accident had nothing to do with that. She broke it tripping over the curb, scurrying to church. And the next thing she knew, a hundred helpful hecklers. "I just want to see you stand up." Like a trained seal! I just want to see you buzz off! she should have shouted. She just wanted to sit still. And yet she tried to stand, she actually tried to smile and reassure the idiots she was all right, leaning on that wrist and seeing stars!

But it's got nothing to do with her driving or her competency. The more she asserts herself, the more tolerant they become, as if she *were* addled by drugs or age. What about bridge club? What's to become of her beautiful apartment? Her lovely things? Mrs. Foster's eyes fill. Will somebody please notice how brave she's being!

Nicholas pats her leg. He scoots beside her, his two fingers in his mouth, just like Vincent? — no, Theresa — no, maybe it was always Nicholas with the two fingers, although you'd think he'd have outgrown it — he'll have buck teeth. It's too bad he's on her broken wrist side. (It's too bad she broke her right wrist.) She tries to pat back, but it hurts. He squints his eyes sympathetically.

As long as it's not his room, he thinks.

"Anybody up for lunch?" Joe asks the rearview mirror. "How about a pizza?"

Nick isn't speaking to him ever again.

Mrs. Foster loathes tomato sauce. This is going to be hell.

After a long day of hurry-up-and-wait at the drugstore and the hardware store and a comfort supper that's riding pretty low, they finally badger Mrs. Foster into taking her pain pills and going to bed. Joe much admires Angie's economy of motion and gentle co-ercion; he was thinking whips and chains. The cooler — duct-taped and double-garbage-bagged — has been displaced to the dirt basement, where possums have sometimes been discovered, not to mention mutant forms of insect life. The laundry is done. The cross is made; Joe and Nick dado the joint with hand tools and chisel Mutt's name on the lateral in block letters. They're proud of themselves and display it in the pantry window. Tomor-row — when? — they'll sand, stain, and varnish it and paint the letters gold. Nick wants to write, "A Great Dog!" on the other side. Tess may have some ideas. They're exhausted. The ten com-mandments are on hold. Joe and Nick have settled down to watch *The Terminator.*

Angie seizes the time to phone Alaska. She can think of several good reasons for no answer while it rings. The cross canceling the view out the pantry window reminds her of the Klan; she's been wondering how Mason would have made it. Lashed it, she'd bet; he does all these nifty things with rope. She'd like to call him and ask.

Clatter. "H'lo?"

Alaska sounds like he's coming out of the depths of something: the deep freeze. Too much Mutt! Why is she doing this? The compulsion to tie up loose ends. Umbilical cord. The rope to hang you — not worth. "Alaska. It's Angie, from the crisis line? Did I wake you?"

"Angel! No! I was jus' thinkin' 'bout you. I can' b'lieve you called."

"How's it going, sport?"

"Not ver' well, to be hones' with you."

"Is there anything I can do?"

"How'd you get my number?"

"You left it at the hot line, remember?"

"Tha's right. I remember now. Truth is, I was half asleep. You not at home?"

"I am." She can hear him kneading his face.

"I can' b'lieve you callin' me from your home. Your family — your husband — Hey, how's your daughter?"

"Still not home." Tess's image through a sudden haze of tears as though behind a rain-grimed Greyhound window. Wait!

"And you thought about me? Wha' can I say?" He's liquefying. "God mus' be watchin' out for me."

Angie pictures God's cold monocle, glittering down at a tiny speck in an ocean of snow. It fills her with an ache that could be longing. The same God that watched her kill Vince?

"'Member you offered — take me to the hospital?"

"What's your address?" This is sheer madness. But it doesn't seem like a moment for analysis — not at his expense. She tells Joe she has to go to the Sore. She shouldn't be long. Does he mind if she takes the car?

Joe's glad, because when Nick sacks out he'll get a chance to call Elena and explain about the conference with Tess and Albert tomorrow and schmooze a little. He feels the warm grotto of her neck, her pillowy lips. But something about the way Angie asks — since when does she tell him how long she'll be? — it smells like a quickie with whosis. Why does he care?

What if her fucking mother wakes up?

He'll tell her Angie had to see a man about a horse. The one she rode in on.

Alaska lives on the second story of a ticky-tack development. It vibrates with TV and bass, and when she knocks, the whole structure seems ready to cave in. People in other apartments put out their heads. Ripple at the Venetian blinds. Finally, chains chitter, the lock chocks. The door opens inward.

He's lean, tallish, stringy blond hair pulled back in a ponytail, and a scraggly ginger beard. Light blue eyes in a leather-tanned face. She'd imagined him dark. Why? He could be her brother. He's also stark naked. Buck naked, she thinks. He's standing behind the door, half-smiling down at the baseboard. He's got no pockets to put his hands in. It's freezing. The place smells like the Welch's grape fields in late fall — where are the bees? Except he's slapped on some pinewoods cologne.

"Angel," he says in the caressive tone of a huckster for cold relief medication, "thought you might be the police." He leads her in; diffident touch. "They was jus' here askin' 'bout some junked car in the parkin' lot. Maybe i's mine!" He giggles.

"You don't look ready," she observes. His bare butt reminds her not of Joe's hairy chimp but of Nick's poufy white Parker House rolls. Maybe because his belly bows slightly. Otherwise, he looks very powerful, his musculature a treatise on manual labor. He has scars, bruises. "I'm on kind of a tight schedule."

"I'm tryin'. Is it too col' for you?" He's dithering at the air conditioner. "Wha' am I talkin' about? Freeze a slab a beef in here."

"Don't worry about it. Let's just get going."

"Truth is, I'm kinda embarrassed." He smiles sheepishly and flares his hands over his genitals like a fan dancer.

She shakes no. His nakedness seems perfectly ordinary. What's not right here is her. "Please get dressed so we can go. It could take them a while to admit you."

"An' you're beautiful!" He shines at her. "I knew you would be."

"What kinda health coverage you got?"

"You lookin' at it." He postures like Mr. Universe. "She's kind, she's beautiful, and she's interested in my health coverage. Why we goin' anywhere? You wan' a drink?"

Yes. "Could you cut the crap and get a move on?"

The choppy laugh. "Yes, ma'am! You wanna spank me? Please!"

In fact. "I'm outta here in one second."

"I'm sorry, but you so beautiful. Seriously. Okay if I take a shower?"

"You tell me."

"I think it'd help. I'd feel better. I'm so dirty."

"Okay. But please hurry."

"I'm tryin'." He staggers into the other room. She hears drawers slide, water running. There are bottles everywhere. Bottles in paper sacks, plastic sacks, bottles burgeoning out of the trash can, mushrooming at its feet. Sticky spills. Shitty-sweet smell. She avoids the kitchen. Wonderful things on the walls and shelves: figures, masks, totems; clear reds, black. Photographs of smiling people with blowing hair backed by mountains. Bottles. The squeegee noise of skin against ceramic and a hard thump.

"You all right?"

"Think so —"

She finds him on the floor with his paws in the air like a shooting-gallery bear, openmouthed. The shower spraying the room. "Can you get up?"

"Think so —"

Angie turns off the water, then bends to put her hand behind his head so he won't slip and bunk it on the sink. He folds to sit. "Ooh, tits!" he says into her chest. He cups the air around them. "Nice ones." She stiffens. His eyes harden. "And you got a real nice ass on you."

"You gonna be able to do this, buddy?"

"I'm tryin' —"

"Yeah, everything you know." She straightens up.

He grins. "I like you."

"Look, pal —"

"But that ain' eve'thin' I know. Not even close." He gets up to the commode. The bedroom air conditioner chugs. She goes to snuff it. He catches her around the waist from behind and rests his drippy head on her back.

"Angel" — he sighs — "sorry I'm such a fuckup. I need a hug."

She faces around. "Alaska. I'm here to take you to the hospital. That's it."

"Too bad." He stands and moves his hands up into her hair and holds her head like he's about to shoot a free throw. "How much you know 'bout alcoholics?"

She feels like he's holding her over something.

"An alcoholic has to have tha' las' drink. He's got to feel he can put his hand on it" — his hand grazes her breast; his eyes smile sadly — "i's the only thing makes him feel safe." He kisses her with an inquiring delicacy that takes her off guard. "Angel, I ain' got enough in me to make it to the hospital." His lips as light as husks. "You gone have to take me to the store and lemme buy a bottle." He touches her cheek as if turning a fragile page in an old Bible. "God, you're beautiful." His bright eyes. "I don' wanna drive — *you* unnerstand." And there are their dead sons, floating in that bright blue water. He kisses her again, lightly circling his palm over her nipple, sheathing her tongue in winy silk. "You know we have to," he whispers.

"No," she says. She looks at him, amazed. His eyes, with their almost white lashes, seem so defenseless. She imagines the stinging snowlight bleaching them. "No we don't," she says, almost laughing. It's a first. She's always said yes to hunger and curiosity. Or, "why not?" She's taking so long to figure this out that he's not getting it; he thinks she wants coaxing; he's rolling her breasts, her ass — his warm lips trickling over her features, as provocative as mosquitoes.

"We could come back here firs'," he murmurs. "Deal with this thing. You know we have to. This don' happen ever' day — i's a miracle —"

Her skin peaks. She's moist. She's disgusted. Not a minute ago, he was looking up at her from the tiles of Heartbreak Hotel. "Alaska, no."

Stropping his dick and balls and against her thigh. "You can lie to yourself, but you can' lie to me."

"Look, man, no." She pushes back. It's the end of an era. It's the day after the last day of her life.

Blades glint in his eyes and teeth; he yanks her hair. "I could be rough with you —" He rubs up her breasts with his chest.

"No." Registering, appalled, the chills. "Look, man, you're a drunk." She doesn't know why she's not afraid of him. He just seems naked in the wilderness. "I'm here to take you to the hospital. You get that next bottle, you're not gonna wanna go, and so on until you drop dead. There aren't enough bottles —"

He slacks back onto his disheveled sheets and bobs up and down. "Then I'm not goin'. You been wastin' your time."

"Is that what this is all about? Another bottle? Shit." She feels like an empty herself. He pushes her buttons like she's a fucking vending machine. "You just want me to buy you a bottle."

"I swear to you, Angel, tha' was the furthes' thing from my mind. But when I thought about the 'mergency room — I tol' you I've had seizures — I got so scared —"

"Man, *this* is what's scary." The exasperated thrust of her fingers sums it up: the four icy walls, the stink, the wily captive, working the main chance.

"You don' unnerstand. Lemme tell you a story 'bout Lymon, my sponsor? He's once in Memphis, on the street, drunk, broke. I's snowin'. He goes to the hospital. He explains his situation bes' he can to the doctor, tells him he's gone commit suicide they don' let him in. 'Fine,' says the doctor. Fuckin' Indian son of a bitch. 'Jus' do it someplace else.'"

Alaska's laugh rattles her. "Yeah, okay. Look, I'll buy you one. One, that's it. On the way to the hospital. Can you please put your clothes on?"

Slow smile. "An' I sure as hell din' slap a move on you for a bottle. Honey, tha' was pure —" His penis looks pink, newborn; he tugs it, sliding an oily eye down her hips, "'Bout the hardes' I been in — le's jus' say some time."

She's rifling his bureau and tosses Jockeys at him. "I'm humbled."

He starts struggling into them. "Tha's what I like about you. Mean. Tha's what I'm use to. We coulda had us some big time."

She bonks him with his socks. "Buddy, you know? Get real! You got a pregnant wife out there —" She's reminding herself.

"Oh, that. Jesus, I'm sorry. Angel, you right. I'm so far gone. I'm such a prick. You gotta help me. You gotta stick with me. I'm such a fuckup."

"You're in love with yourself as a fuckup. Put on your pants."

"Oh, wow! Say that again —"

He brings a thermos. She doesn't argue, but when she tries to bypass the grocery, he opens the car door and makes to eject. The seat belt confounds him. She lurches left, without looking, and the door swings to. She can't bludgeon him into the hospital.

When she comes out of the Kroger, he's pissing against the wall. He takes the bag. "This it?"

"The object of the game is to get you to the hospital."

"This ain' gone get it." His face closes. "Ain' goin'."

"Then good-bye."

"Lemme tell you somethin', Angel — never threaten an alcoholic —"

"Right." She's had it.

"So fuckin' judgmental — you need to look to you own self —"

She peels out, circles the block, pulse pounding, teeth grinding. At the five-pronged intersection, she has to wait forever, beating the wheel. Why didn't she just go back in the store and buy whatever he wanted? Get him to the hospital and swill the surplus at fucking Thanksgiving. Who took whom for a ride? Who copped out? Who's the fuckup? When the light finally changes, she makes an abrupt U-turn and goes back to the lot. He's not there. Not in the store. Hopeless. She whacks her fist against — what is this? a mosaic embedded in the exterior brick of the supermarket — a dwarf blond in a bustle and a crown pushing a shopping cart. Queen Shit.

"Whatever it is, lady" — a natty black man rumbling a line of carts — "Jesus loves you."

"I seriously doubt that."

"It's a fact."

"He's got a funny way of showing it."

"I hear that." He laughs. "I guess you got that right."

Without making a conscious decision, she drives through the Krispy Kreme for two dozen doughnuts — the second is half price. She skims the box of plain-glazed down the hill at Blank. Take that, wise ass!

Monday morning, Mrs. Foster is up and about before anyone. If she knew where they hide their skillets or how to work the coffeepot, she'd surprise them with a big breakfast. Instead, she makes a list of everything they need to buy and do between now and Thanksgiving. Fortunately, she keeps a notepad and pen in her purse. Unfortunately, she can hardly read what she writes with her left hand. It all hurts, but she'll heal faster if she doesn't baby herself. That mangy cat wants something — quite possibly her life, since on one of its frenzied passes, she's going to fall flat on her face. What is the point of keeping such an unsightly, useless animal? She's told Angela about ticks.

Angie is the first to appear. She feeds the cat, makes coffee, and tries to find out if her mother will be okay on her own till five, while Mrs. Foster tells her about ticks and how much better she'd look with a little lipstick and reads her the list and asks if she has any corn bread mix or if she's going to fix oyster stuffing and studies how she makes coffee. The filter is perplexing. Also where the water goes. Angela seems tense. Probably Joe. Mrs. Foster wonders what Doris would think about moving in with her temporarily. She doesn't want to become a mother-in-law joke.

Angie feels the dainty chuff of her mother's slippers like pecking. The old lady's gown and negligee sling around her calves like in some Ginger Rogers number. Palooka has to be evicted for trying to climb them.

She'll be fine on her own — Mrs. Foster laughs — but she won't take her medicine without Angela there; she's afraid of what she might do.

Angie imagines her mother inviting the mail carrier in to rumba.

"Don't mind about me." Mrs. Foster laughs.

That's not an option. Angie scolds her for being too brave, doing too much. "Get back into bed. Catch up on your reading. Watch TV."

Mrs. Foster agrees to the painkiller. She thinks when they leave she'll dust. Somebody has to.

Joe comes in with the newspaper and dispatches several cups of black coffee and sugary doughnuts. Mrs. Foster teases him about gaining weight, recommending her own bran flakes, which she's reminded to add to the list, and reads him his horoscope and something cute from Ann Landers and what he's got to get done before Thanksgiving. He's as sullen as ever. Nicholas, who will certainly catch pneumonia dressed like that, toddles his milk and doughnuts into the den and watches violent cartoons (!) until Joe takes him to school. What is it about Catholics? She still remembers fleeing the Holy Innocents (that was the name of their school) in her neighborhood: micks and wops. Holy Terrors, even the girls. Absolutely immoral. And *smelly!*

Before leaving, Angela shows her where things are and asks what she needs.

Where to begin? "I'll manage" — Mrs. Foster lofts her cast and grimaces — "but shouldn't you be here for Theresa?"

"I will be." Angie really wants to throttle her mother. Put *her* in a cooler in the basement. But Mrs. Foster looks shrunken and old inside her glamorous nightclothes, her cast like an evening glove, her elaborate silver bouffant listing to one side. She probably carried books on her head in stilettos, not once or twice at sleep-over parties but diligently, into her twenties — to make what she could of herself. Too sad. "If you wanna help me, you'll take it easy! Call your pals." Angie hopes this unnatural charity will last at least until she herself stops being such a fuckup. "And watch your step in those damned skirts!"

*

Tess is in Mr. Albert's office, afraid she may shit her pants. Spending the night with Megan: bummer. Megan's a total wipeout, and her mom is Looking for Answers. She really pushed Tess — like racing for the goal shoulder to shoulder with a defender — Tess kept fading off. But she couldn't very well say, "Hey, lighten up!" when everything is still about Brent's death. After a supper of microwave nachos and Camels, Mrs. Stoll wanted to take Tess home; Tess agreed to call home, but the line was busy — good sign, and good luck, since Tess would have found it hard to put over her action with Mother Superior listening in. She went to bed about eight to get away from them; awake till two.

The only good thing is she left that ounce rolled up in her sleeping bag back at their place. Her locker's been searched, her pack; they made her peel off her socks and open her peanut-butter-and-jelly sandwich and take out this braid she'd twisted in her hair, and they wanted her to tell them where she's been staying. Now Albert is sitting behind his desk, very formal. It's like he doesn't remember who he is. (The school stud muffin.) She could be suspended for skipping on Friday — okay, forging the excuse was stupid, but how was she supposed to know Albert would talk to Joe and tell Ledhead she ran away? He tries to make her feel really cheap about it — honor-code violation, big whoop — he knows everybody does it, and what about him betraying her? The suspension — five days out of school and no extracurricular activities for the rest of the year — no soccer! — would go on her record for college. That's the least of it.

The kicker is Brian turned her in. His mom called the principal *at home on Sunday* and ranked on Tess. "He couldn't have! I know my son! It's that girl in the Spanish class! She planted it on him!" This is how Tess imagines it, although Mrs. Clark has always been very smooth with her. "I want her brought in!"

Tess wants to tell Albert about Brian's tenth birthday party.

Or — if he could just know. It was at this unbelievable mansion with, like, grounds — Brian's dad's. No white grown-ups. A huge cake, ice cream, hot dogs, soda, served on the poolside patio by black people in uniforms. Balloons, horseplay in the water, but no organized games, no real supervision. A lot of the kids — the whole class was invited — ate themselves sick. Tess, bored and confused, went exploring and stumbled across Brian lying under a stone bench in some ivy — wet, buggy, cicadas cheeching, mockingbirds — and they got to talking, and he asked her if she'd ever thought about before she was born. Which she had, wondering what if her mom had aborted her. And it was so amazing somebody else — a *boy* — had thought about it and would talk about it. Later, Brian's mom showed up — she looks like Krystle on *Dynasty*; Tess always wonders why she's divorced — and went off on the black people about where Brian's father and stepmother were, but not about where Brian was. Angie came for Tess a little early. She didn't make Tess go find Brian to say good-bye or make her talk about what kind of time she'd had. Tess wishes that same big strong straight Angie would walk in the door right now and get her the hell out of here. And Joe would do fine. Although he'd catch on a lot slower and ask a lot more dumb questions and be completely annoying.

But Albert — she doesn't think he'd get it even if she told it right. She doesn't know where to look or how to look. She doesn't know what she's supposed to know. So she certainly doesn't know what to say. She's thinking of whatever's sizzling up and down her intestinal tract as brimstone. "When's my dad coming?"

"Tess, you've got to get honest. If you're doing drugs and you seek assistance from us, you won't be disciplined. We'll get you help."

Help. Something you get nailed to. He talks like he's pre-recorded. What's he want out of her?

"— into a treatment program with your parents —"

Oh right. Joe's short fuse in some touchy-feely group? She can see that: "Where'd you get the pot?" they ask Tess. "From my mom. She also drinks and sleeps around and so does my dad —" The group turns into a gang. They forget all about Tess. Put her in the Children's Home. Give Nick to foster parents who beat him and make him eat shit.

"— too late for Brian. He was carrying enough that the police have to assume he intended to sell or distribute —"

"That's ridiculous." And she's been wagging this ounce all over town. Wonderful. She feels like she's digesting a jellyfish. Is it conceivable that Albert is leveling with her? Treating her like an equal? Which would mean that just when she's lost all confidence in her judgment and her ability to take care of herself, she'd better start taking care of herself. "Brian wouldn't sell drugs —"

"— they can try him as a juvenile or an adult. He'll probably be suspended for the rest of —"

"But he's rich. He doesn't have to sell anything. He wouldn't — it's part of his —" Tess searches for a word besides bullshit, "image." Albert wants honest? Tess can't remember the last time she said what she was really thinking — and in school, of all places. "Rich and white and connected? He'll get off. In this town?"

"You've got it wrong, little lady."

She's fascinated by the champ of his spiky teeth.

"This town can't afford to let rich white kids off and only put away the disadvantaged. How would Chief Stark justify that to his officers? More a reason to prosecute the wealthy white boy to the full extent of the law, as an example, to prove the integrity of his department and the system at large. You think Brian makes a good example? He could get ten years."

Albert looks like Peter Jennings on *World News Tonight*. What is she doing here? How did she get sucked down into Brian and Megan and Brent and Cath and drugs and death and dirt? Her stomach is spewing fire. Where did she get the pot?

" — whereas if you get honest and cooperate with us —"

Who so little gave a shit when her daughter ran away she snuck out to screw Brother X, pretending she's gone to hear confession on the hot line. Tess would like to try confession. She'd like to tell Albert the truth. But as soon as she's about to say, "my mother," a boulder with a human face rolls out of her heart and blocks her mouth. She's homeless, friendless, clueless, sick as a dog, trucking around the better part of an ounce from one crash pad to the next, and they're frisking her lunch. Well, she has a good idea where to put that ounce. Right back where she found it. The source. Square one.

"Cooperate in what?"

It's Joe. The handsomest man on earth until she remembers him following the fat can on that slut in the fucking Rockola the other night when he was supposed to be missing her —

" — we've done everything but strip-search her, Mr. DiPietro," Albert is saying, on his feet, shaking Joe's hand. "If she were my daughter, I'd have her drug-tested today —"

The two of them, all buddy-buddy like they're discussing their golf swings. She gets up and — it's so completely humiliating — "I have to go to the bathroom." She's just in time.

Cheeks kissing cool porcelain, magma pouring out of her writhing gut, the tears come. She's going home! After ISS, after CD Superstore, after Megan's to pick up her stuff — home. Where she can lay her burdens down.

As soon as he's back at the office, Joe calls Elena. He ought to take her to lunch, but he doesn't have the time; he's ponderously apologetic about it. She hardly has time for the phone call. She sounds crisp, maybe not pleased he's calling her at work, maybe pissed off about breakfast, maybe he's becoming a pest. Who the fuck knows? He blurts out the situation with Tess anyway. He can't help it. He went into the meeting ready to defend *grounding* her; then Albert hits him with this Brian-felony-drug-bust — "we don't know that Tess is involved, but —"

And what's Tess's angle? First Brian smashes up her car, now he's lying about her to the law? Does that make sense? Is this how the boys pull the girls' braids nowadays? She looked so young and frail. Will Joe have to spend the rest of his life checking the size of her pupils? Bankrolling treatment? He's spinning. He falls back into his desk chair and careens into the windowsill.

Elena detaches herself from the notes she's been logging on the computer. She's touched by his urgency, his coming to her for emotional and intellectual support. Maybe he's not just using her to beat off. She gives it to him: "Look, Joe, you and your wife have to face the fact that there are too many things in your lives you're not being honest about. You can't lie to children. They —"

Joe closes his eyes. Listening to her peroration on the best policy — there is no word in the language for which he has more contempt than *honesty* — he feels as old as Adam. He's called the wrong woman — the woman he could reach. The right woman — she's photocopying.

Elena hears the ocean heaving between them. "For example" — now she's letting him have it — "what are you going to tell your family about me?"

He sees those sharp red fingernails.

Angie and Nick come home to find Mrs. Foster swathed in a blanket, asleep before a roaring TV. The house is cold and dark. Angie boosts the thermostat until she sees charred wisps of five-dollar bills flitting out the chimney. No Tess.

Mrs. Foster revives when Nick changes the channel. It takes a minute before she realizes where she is. She smells him and his snack with disapproval, then groggily gropes her way to the kitchen, where Angela, in jeans, is staring into the refrigerator.

"Hey, Mom! How you doing?" Angie's determined Tess will be home tonight, and she's got to produce a lot of something her daughter likes out of a bare cupboard. Mrs. Foster looks a little wobbly. "Have a seat. What can I get you?"

"Oh, I'm fine." Mrs. Foster sits at the table and blinks her bird's eyes. "I didn't make much progress." She laughs. She wants Angela to notice that she's still in her gown. Stuck in her gown — the wrist. She even tried using her teeth. She was helpless. She feels seedy. "How was your day?"

"Good. Look, you're doing the right thing, doing nothing. You take your medication?"

"I'll take it now."

Angie pours her a glass of milk and hands her the tablet. "You know, you can turn up the heat. And put some lights on. We want you to be comfortable."

Impossible. Agnes grew up in an old house like this without a capable male or any capital. Walls like a colander; the furnace sounds like stampeding elephants. She recalls her magnificent home back in Ohio, Richard whistling over a task in his neat workshop. He'd die if he could see them in this chicken coop. "What news of Theresa?"

The front door opens, and they hear the swish of her nylon pack. Angie runs. Mrs. Foster runs too, but her body is leashed by infirmity and her skirts. She arrives in an agony of frustration to find Theresa on the couch, sobbing in Angela's embrace;

COURTING DISASTER ◆ 146

Nicholas on the floor, riveted on the cartoons, tormenting the cat.

"I told her about Mutt," he says.

Mrs. Foster stands there. She wants to tell Nicholas to turn off the TV; she wants them to join hands and say the things people say at such moments, with their heads bowed. She wishes she could quote Scripture — the return of the prodigal. But she can't quote Scripture, and she doesn't know what to say in this bright, messy den with Bugs Bunny and Elmer Fudd at her back and the dog rotting below. She's spent the day calling friends who all had to be somewhere and watching transsexuals who are suing over silicone breast implants. She feels not like a wise matriarch but like the skinny girl who stood in the doorframe while her parents paced their separate tracks, their lips sealed over unspeakable disappointments, one of them, quite likely, her. She laughs and says, "Could you give her a minute?"

Nick glares at the screen. "She asked!" Tess looks up with her open mouth and blighted face and starts bawling again. Angie stays buried in Tess's matted curls, at some expense to her hearing.

Joe comes in loosening his tie and drops his briefcase. "So where *is* your car?"

About an hour later, they gather at the dining table. Joe hasn't had a chance to tell Angie about the meeting with Albert — Mrs. Foster followed him around relating her feelings about transsexuals and pointing out chores he needs to do until he shut the bedroom door in her face. Somehow Angie comes up with minestrone and corn muffins. "Garbage soup," she calls it.

"Yuck!" says Nick.

Tess has showered and changed into clean clothes. Puffy eyes, tense, sallow. Her movements — pulling out her chair, buttering, spooning — are constricted, as though she's just off the sickbed or the rack. She's very hungry. Wherever she was, the food was lousy. Mrs. Foster holds forth on children who don't eat their vegetables, starving Africans, and beta-carotene, while everyone else digs in.

"You took out your dreads" — Angie smiles at Tess — "the studs, your nose ring."

"You look so much cuter," Mrs. Foster puts in, paying no attention to the rude faces Nicholas is making with his spoon in his mouth. There's some kind of rancid cheese in this soup. And she's leaving the kidney beans.

Tess clears her throat. "I got a job." She braces to see if Joe wants to pounce on her.

Joe doesn't know where to start. He takes a long draft of wine. Angie's drinking either water or pure alcohol. Everybody seems to be undergoing some unfathomable change of life. Okay, he's cool — they'll all go to hell on Rollerblades. He signs Nick to stop mocking.

"After school and on weekends," Tess continues. "I had to make some money." Chin into chest. "I had to take care of myself." Down a notch. "I didn't know how long."

Why? Angie can't figure her daughter. She's running away from the circus to join the rat race. Fine — no questions. Joe will fill Angie in later — for now he's going along with her: one night of welcome. "I've been working, too," she says, the gaga way she used to say, Let's tell our times tables! "It's crazy! You alphabetize, and they act like you're performing acupuncture. They wanna hire you for life." Valjean is begging her to sign on. And when Angie spent the day sweating out Alaska. She phoned all morning. She imagined him smeared across pavement, picked clean by buzzards, set on fire by itinerant sadists. A tag on his toe: Inspected by Angie. Pickled by Angie. Then, just before she left the old school for after-school, he answered. He'd been asleep. "Jus' keep callin'." He slushed back into oblivion. But Valjean noted Angie's absence only when doling out her low-fat black-bottom pie, and then as an occasion for praise — "You don't see Angie — where is she? — sittin' on her butt or hasslin' me over ever' little thing. She goes ahead and gets it done."

"Your mother was meant for better things and so were you!" Mrs. Foster laughs.

Both Angie and Tess attribute this endorsement to the shabby way they stack up against the award-winning offspring of the bridge gals rather than some fit of feminism. They lower their eyes with the doughy look of tongue-holding nuns, Joe thinks, annunciation virgins. Witches. "This is great, by the way," he says, nodding at his soup.

"Yeah, Mom," Tess says. She's about to add, I really missed your cooking, but she doesn't even want to think about the last few days, let alone open the topic for discussion.

"Don't you want to know what happened to *me*, Theresa?" Mrs. Foster cheeps, exhibiting her cast.

Show-and-tell. Nick changes the subject. "When you wanna do Mutt's funeral?"

"Nicholas! At the supper table!" Mrs. Foster's eyelashes beat to and fro, reminding Nick of the brushes at the car wash.

Tess frowns. "What do you mean? I thought — Didn't you —"

"We waited for you," Angie says.

"He's downstairs —" Mrs. Foster laughs, wrinkling her nose, "in an ice chest!"

Tess looks around vaguely, as if for servants who will remove her with the plates. "What now?"

"Me and Dad made a cross. It's in the pantry. You wanna put anything — we gotta finish it tonight. Then all we gots to do is dig a hole and say some words." Nick bays, "Ah-oooooooooooooo!"

"Nicholas!"

"Where would you like Mutt to go?" Angie asks.

Tess pauses to think, while Mrs. Foster reminds them that she has always thought they should call the humane society: more sanitary. "You don't want his remains —"

"*I* don't wanna bury him at all," Tess says. "The ground is gross. I want him cremated."

"Oh, honey!"

"And scatter his ashes —"

"No! In the yard! Under the cross! You haven't even *seen* the cross."

"He was my dog."

"He was everybody's dog!" Nick shouts. "I found him. And I want him close. Where Shane can see. And Mom can put flowers. Mutt loved the yard!" Nick is crying. "'Member he use to —"

Mrs. Foster thinks Joe should wallop Nicholas before he gets started. She's afraid of the hot soup and the glassware.

"We might have a little trouble pulling that off, Tess," Joe, thumbing away Nick's tears. "If we can't burn *leaves* —"

"Do you want to take him to —?" Angie doesn't know the name for such a place, but the expense: Hollywood extravaganza!

"No." Tess stands, rummages in her pocket, lights and lofts her disposable lighter. "I saw it in a movie. Down the creek. Covered in flowers. Floating candles." The moving flame is hypnotic. Nick looks up, muzzy.

The creek sometimes turns blue from the dye factory up the hill. Angie imagines flames bowling down the channel, consuming Nick's school. She wonders what kind of environmental catastrophe we're talking here — Exxon *Valdez*. Ask Alaska, if he regains consciousness.

"Or on a platform in a bonfire. Don't you know somebody has a farm, Mom? A field somewhere."

Mrs. Foster knows Theresa is a Satanist. Look at her! Look at the effect she's having on the others! She's been burning animals, dead and alive, for years. That's where she's been — a black mass in a field somewhere. God! Is it in the water? That doctor in — where was it? Fayetteville — crazed on LSD or something, slaughtered his wife and children, and painted devil signs in their own blood. And right around here, that Susie Something — she and her cousin, wasn't it? killed her *grandparents* before they put cyanide in the children. And that Dungeons & Dragons boy who had his parents hacked to bits by —

Nick's laughing. "Look at Grandma!"

"She's seen a ghost," says Joe.

Tess starts laughing maniacally.

Mrs. Foster's staying out of her way.

Chapter 5

Till You Get Enough

Seeing the cross finally persuaded Tess they should bury Mutt. She came up with a goofy photo of him, full face, tongue lopping. Joe showed her how to incise a shallow oval in the vertical, just below the crux, and they clipped the picture to fit and varnished over it. Stepping back from the finished product, their eyes welled with tears. They're so talented. It's such a waste.

Typical morbid wop gaud. They kept Mrs. Foster awake till God knows, drinking cocoa, festive, as if they were trimming a Christmas tree or carving pumpkins. Next they'll be sticking it on the front lawn with those tacky concrete ducks and plastic posies and wooden cutouts of bloomered rear ends and whatnot till the place looks like Rock City. Mrs. Foster is glad she has a space reserved beside Richard, or they'd do the same with her! She hopes none of her friends visits her here.

Now the kitchen reeks of shellac. She's had a headache all day. "Grandparents of Satanists" on TV, or did she dream that? Although Angela helped her dress, she has to admit that it's an ordeal to use the bathroom and very uncomfortable when she naps. She just doesn't want people to think she's a rummy, larking about in her nightclothes in the middle of the afternoon, breaking things. Unable to wash a dish, she was forced to contemplate her bleak future.

Sometimes she almost hates Richard for abandoning her. The truth is, he was scarcely there to begin with. He married her in the same way he bought a decorative barometer for the living room wall. She tried so hard, but his heart belonged — in small doses — to "his baby girl" (an immaculate conception if there ever was one; sex with Richard was mortifying, and childbirth, fully anesthetized, an ugly rumor). He never allowed himself to see the real Angela, who was hell on wheels growing up, a slovenly, immoral bitch, she hates to say it, who treated her mother, well, like shit, and who will soon be *in charge*. My God, look what happened to poor little Vincent under her care, those unsuspecting souls at the shelter. Richard, for all his sweet talk, would never lift a finger to help "his baby girl" — "Let her stew in her own juice," he'd gloat when she was failing this or needed money for that, and Mrs. Foster thought he meant "Make a man out of her," and *he* got all her love.

Not to mention that shifty, no-account ambulance chaser she married.

Mrs. Foster is becoming depressed; doubtless a side effect of the drugs. She needs to get out. She'll make Angela skip this silly funeral (always bucking for sainthood — her duty is to her family) and go grocery shopping. Mrs. Foster has refined the list so it practically strips the shelves by itself. She's very anxious about the turkey.

Theresa's arrival hardly lifts her spirits. Mrs. Foster declines her offer of a drink or a snack; she's eating nothing that girl touches unless somebody else tastes it first. Go ahead, laugh — the arsenic woman, who poisoned not only her husband and illicit lovers but her father *and her mother-in-law*, worked at *their* Kroger.

Why did all the children have to favor Joe? Theresa squats at the coffee table with a glass and a deck of cards and asks where's Nicholas, her eyes ferreting from Andy Griffith to various unsuccessful games of solitaire — such a squalid-looking girl — move the two! — and when the cat attacks, scattering the cards, she jumps a mile and curses a blue streak — gutter language. Telltale signs of something.

Third degree again today. Tess lay low in ISS, making up a missed exam, her homework; you can't even leave for lunch, so she was out of the media center only for a half hour of blinding light from Principal Teague — lucky he loves to hear himself talk — and another pressure session with Mr. Albert, who's become a real nuisance. "If you just tell us where he got it and who else is doing it and —" And, man? To get him off her case — What would it be like to spill her guts and be done with it?

She won't be done with it.

Anyway, that dork Chad still feels privileged to drive her to and from the Superstore — if he thinks this means she'll screw him, he's tripping. Everybody else is either freezing her out or swearing they're not. She can't wait for the phone to go off tonight. She'll tell them she's grounded from everything, phone included. She can't believe she's not. Her parents are acting so weird. Is it Mutt? Grandma? They wait till the old lady's back in the condo to land on Tess? That'd be a switch — beg her to stay. Move in, Grandma, please! I *want* you to tell me what to do four hundred thousand times a day!

Or maybe they don't care anymore. Preoccupied with their lovers, waiting to make their break, too guilty to pick at her. Weekends at, like, Carowinds, you see the divorced fathers ladling on the fun. The young stepmoms like they're at cheerleader tryouts. How do the divorced moms look? Beat. How do the kids look?

Crazy.

She has to keep the noise up. Brian crosses her mind like scissors, almost constantly. If only she could undo what she's done, take it back. She's really not sure she can live with this. Or Grandma constantly staring at her. Get a life, lady!

Angie and Nick stomp up the porch with groceries. Nick is whining, "Why do I have to?"

Angie's had a shitty day. She spent it "getting familiar with the files," while Valjean bared her soul in fifteen-minute increments over her eggless lemon custard pie; also, now, the receptionist. The office is turning into the Open Sore, except Angie has to face these people — they don't hang up or conk out or kick off. They're all there.

At lunch, she reached Alaska. "You want me to take you to the hospital?"

"You'd take me? After what I did?"

"I feel partly responsible —"

"God, I love you. You mus'n' never feel responsible for nothin' but good. I swear to you, Angel, if I come outta this, I'm gone do ever'thin' differ'nt. I'm gone do jus' what you tell me —"

"Whoa! Slow down, big fella!" Rustling, clunking. "Alaska?"

"Who is this?" A raw-voiced woman.

"Angie. Who's this?"

The voice turns away from the phone to tweedle, "Angie, Julie, Libby, Sally, Susie, Stacie, Julie, Mary, Terry, Sherry —"

"Gimme tha' phone, you fuckin' bitch —"

Now Angie's got an hour, max, to put supper on the table. She wants to clout her son. "Shut up!" she snipes.

She can just die, Nick hates her so much. He cannot take this many hours in school. He hates the teachers, the other kids; they won't leave him alone; he can't even read if he wants to or bounce a ball or run around, and today Billy Lucas spat on his drawing paper — big nauseating glob of spit — and when he hauled off to belt him, *he* got time-out. He comes home in the dark, starving, and it'll be bath right after supper and then read and bed, and he hasn't seen Shane or watched TV today. This sucks! All because *she* has to have more money. Selfish pig!

The bag is ripping as Angie fumbles with the doorknob.

"An-gel-la!" La-sol-fa. "You know you shouldn't speak like that to darling Ni-co-las!" Mrs. Foster laughs, extending her uninjured but useless left hand to assist. Nick, behind a grocery sack, comes close to running her over. Varrroom!

Angie jostles up her load and waits for her mother to figure out how to get out of the way. Palooka twines their legs. Tess casts up a miserable look. What do those cards tell her? Angie should be finding out, but, hey, Carol's funeral's tonight, and Sam, the be-reaved husband, must see that the white folks care. She'll explain this to Tess — sometime. Mrs. Foster follows her around while she shucks her junk, even leaning against and talking through the bathroom door. She's lonely, Angie chides herself; you left her in pain, helpless, so you could — prove something to Joe the Schmo. The hair shirt scratches and so do the violins.

In the kitchen, Nick is spitefully scarfing down peanut butter. Palooka plies her ankles. Mrs. Foster traipses after her as she puts on apron, pulls out pots and pans. There is nothing she wants so much as to pull out a tall, cold one — roll it over her forehead, her neck — and no one would even notice, it's right there, she can feel it, taste it, and what's wrong with one, anyway? And how's about a reefer five miles long? Tess drawls in and lays her cards on the table: bedraggled gypsy refugee. Angie finally perceives that her mother is haranguing her about going grocery shopping — again — tonight, for Thanksgiving.

"I'm sorry, Mom, I told you. I've got a funeral."

"Mutt's funeral!" Nick sputters out bread. "Tonight's Mutt's funeral?"

"No, it's this friend of mine from the Open Door —"

Nick bawls into coughing. Angie is afraid he's choking. Before she gets to him, Joe comes in, sets down his briefcase, picks Nick up, and carries him off.

Tess shoots Angie a frantic look. "Mom! Stop him! Don't let him hit Nick!"

Angie hates Tess's melodramatics, and Mrs. Foster's delighted distress wants damping. But, yes, she has to stop him. She tails them to the upstairs front bedroom, where she and Joe are currently camped in bags on the floor.

Joe and Nick are talking quietly, knee to knee, under the bare bulb. Joe in his incongruous suit with wing tips splayed: jackleg lawyer talking Mad Dog DiPietro into giving himself up. Joe's glance ripples over the possibility of her intrusion as though she's crouched behind a black-and-white with a bullhorn. She finds their colloquy — their dark heads bowed under the light — ineffably beautiful, like a painting by Raphael — a Consolation.

Joe considers Nick's dejection as Angie retreats. The problem isn't Mutt's funeral. He resents being jerked around — first afterschool, then Mrs. Foster moving in, the inscrutable come-and-go of Tess, whatever else he senses — the rut in the air — summarized by Mutt's permanent desertion and imputed to Angie's working. The upshot is he'd like to plant Angie as much as Mutt.

And what can Joe say? Things change; we don't have to like it; all part of growing up. He remembers promising himself he wouldn't mouth that kind of pat crap to his kids — the pat crap that slid him into joining the Navy when he might have been deferred out of the whole meaningless mess; into the plodding career that would pay his debts, support a wife, a family, a little house, the kids' education, retirement, blah blah blah. How did that blah blah blah take the shine off falling ass over ears for an Amphetamine — what a slingshot the woman is! — throwing three wholly original kids into her, and defending the rights of outrageous minorities to the pursuit of impossible happiness? "He has to get it sometime" — that's what they said about Vince's chicken pox. Then they said, "This too shall pass." Sic fucking transit. Amor vincit omnia. Fucking bullshit — he'll be buried in it. "In the name of the Father, the Son —" Buried to the ears now.

And today — Elena prating over the phone on honesty, maturity, responsibility — the Red Guards marching from her vaginal apocalypse — he wonders what pat crap he was listening to when he slid into a wanton affair with a fucking psychologist — the fount of pat crap, never mind her fantastic tits, oh, yeah, and the fact that he finds her completely adorable. Tit for tat — that must have been it. Looking at his befuddled son, Joe imagines telling him — or Tess, right? — he imagines Tess in the room, sporting her new, whipped-dog look — "Hey, kids, guess what? I'm having it off with this nice lady — oops! powerful Latina — and it's okay! because Mom is letting this African-American carpenter — a worker! — do it to her! So okay! Are you okay with that?"

It's not okay for him. He feels like a closet cross-dresser. Later tonight he's getting out of it. He can't keep standing in it and sliding.

He caresses Nick's chin, shoulders. He defends Angie to the extent that he was the one who asked her to get a job and puts it to Nick: what choice does she have about Grandma? Jerking loose the knot in his tie.

But he didn't ask her to keep licking the lepers at the Open Sore or the cock of the carpenter. He thought she'd go to work and come home and stay home. He'd like to plant her, too. Joe imagines his wife as a tree, Mrs. Fulton's fifty-foot oak, with a swing hanging from her elbow like a purse. He pulls up the ends of the tie like a noose and sticks out his tongue. Nick laughs.

Nick loves Joe so much. Watching the thoughts clump his dad's wonderful, tough, *man's* face, Nick is reassured: Joe takes things seriously. He'll fix this. Nick burrows into his father's jacket. Joe's arms close around his back like a seat belt.

Angie calls them to dinner. She's wearing her coat; she doesn't have time to eat. The food's steaming; she's leaving for the funeral.

"What is this?" Joe frowns. "You have to eat. Sit down."

"I tasted a lot, cooking."

"You're still wearing your apron," Tess points out.

"Don't you have more than one dress?" Mrs. Foster chuckles.

Angie looks down at herself. It's a comical apron — a birthday gift from Joe's mother: "I'm not Aging, I'm Marinating." She puts her hand to her mouth and sits. Joe has poured her a glass of red wine. The color is beautiful. Tess passes her a full plate. "Thanks, guys. Maybe I'm pushing it." She shrugs off her coat.

"So you're not going?" Mrs. Foster smiles slyly, tucking into her potatoes.

"I could use the car tonight," says Joe, utensils poised.

"What's happening with my car?" Tess asks.

"I really have to go to this funeral" — Angie spears a brussels sprout — "but I don't have to help set up the chairs. I won't be all that late."

"How late?" Joe asks, held like a needle over a turntable.

What's up with him? Angie wonders. This drinking with the boys is getting old. She adjusts her meaning to his. "Ten, ten-thirty."

"It's just that I need the car. I have work at the office. You couldn't walk?"

"In these shoes?" He knows a woman was murdered in the parking lot behind the church. He usually demands she take the car. Why didn't he bring his work home? Maybe he's planning a heist.

"If I'd known you were going out," he continues.

"I told you —"

"What's happening with my car? Did you have it towed?"

Tess's car! He forgot all about it. He forgot all about this funeral, too. "You think I've got nothing better to do than clean up after you, Miss? I was working. Earning our living." He prisses at Angie, "I have to work tonight."

"You forgot all about it," smugs Tess. "So much on your mind —"

She crooks an eyebrow at him as if she knows exactly what's been on his mind — thighs. "Yeah, you, for instance," he snaps. "Any bench warrants out on you I should know about?"

Mrs. Foster looks around with an experimental laugh.

"No" — Tess winches her spine — "how 'bout you? Anything we should know about you?" Fanning her eyelashes so even Angie should feel the breeze. "Or Mom?"

If you feel a breeze, scream. "All I know," Angie says, washing down the bubble and squeak with a gulp of Nick's milk — he growls his angry engine at her — untying the apron, and registering how glad she is she doesn't have to look at that stud in Tess's eyebrow anymore, "is that I really have to go to this funeral. The dead woman — she taught girls in detention. A fine person. She got out of a rotten marriage, and her new husband, also a fine person — they've only had four, five years together. Now he's got to look after their little girl and an older daughter — about Tess's age — by the first jerk —"

"That sounds like Casey Alston's mom," Tess remarks, but Angie hasn't said the second husband's black.

"You know her?" Angie loves Casey. She's sometimes wished Tess were more like her — responsible, honest.

"Yeah. Wow, poor Casey. Don't you remember? She was our goalie on Twin City."

"Oh yeah! Great goalie. I must've seen Carol then, too." She must've had her head up her ass. All she remembers is Tess, running. The yes of Tess outrunning the field to drill the ball in the net.

"I always thought you and her mom would like each other." Especially seeing the tastes they had in common. Tess pictures the two old bags double-dating 2 Live Crew. God, she's heartless. Poor Casey. "What'd she die of?"

"Cancer." Angie lowers her eyes. "A quick one."

Those dodgy peepers. Funeral, huh? Would she stoop this low to go fuck whosis? Joe knows she needs the car to see him. She's never made an issue of walking to the Sore before; comes on like he's a fear-mongering bigot when he suggests she's not rapeproof. Of course, she's not usually dressed like this. "Why don't I drop you off," he volunteers cagily, "and maybe you can bum a lift home?" He doubts *he* would go to see Elena over a friend's dead body.

At the same time, Mrs. Foster sighs. "It's such a shame when someone young and vital, with everything to live for, dies. The good Lord must have wanted —"

"You wanna come?" Angie asks abruptly.

"Who?" Mrs. Foster startles.

"You. Everybody. You were saying you wanted to get out. I know Casey would like to see Tess. Joe can drop us off and take the car, if you don't mind picking us up later —" So he can't say she's stranding him at home with her mother. They'll never take her up on this.

"Oh, I couldn't!" Mrs. Foster laughs. She thinks of the Open Door as the Open Hatch. She'd have to be inoculated!

"I'll go." Tess finished her homework in ISS. She doesn't want to answer the phone tonight — she's deathly afraid Brian will call — this fear is out of *Friday the 13th* — a razor coming up behind you in the mirror. And she'd like to talk to Casey — someone who hopefully never heard of Brian. Talk about — soccer. Soccer or death, one.

"Can I?" Nick asks Joe. If Tess gets to go. He's also curious about funerals. Do you have to look at the body? What about the smell? Is it creepy? When do you do what?

"Sure," says Angie.

"What are you talking about?" Joe sees himself tearing from Elena's embrace — or, no, he's calling it off — tears, threats, recriminations; she might even throw things — to chauffeur his nutty family home from bringing in the sheaves. "He can't go out on a school night, and neither can she —"

They arrive as the Swinging Doors — two acoustic guitars and sundry voices — are selling the Sore Song. It sounds like the alma matter of Holi High, with lots of dos and don'ts and thees and thous and inverted syntax. A tape of it plays at every meal. Angie has been known to hide the cassette. It means things are about to start. Trish hasn't gone for the high one yet.

The large room is crowded. Headlights rinse the storefront windows, and the music competes with the grumble of sporadic traffic, the odd shout. The tables have been pushed to the perimeter and folding chairs arranged in an oval, five or six deep. Heather and Tim pack in more. Angie greets them, then passes chairs along to Tess, who tries to pass one to Mrs. Foster until the old lady stops doddering and clucking and holds up her plaster wrist, and Tess finally gets the message and, flushed and flustered, opens the chair for her. Nick wedges them in the thick of it, under a light.

"These are your kids." Heather smiles condolence at them. "Oh, and say, listen" — dropping low and inside — "you-know-who has called, asking for you, by name, at least fifty times. I tried to help him, but —" She inspects Angie's eyes. "We need to have a meeting and process this —"

Joe's picking them up at ten. They settle just as Trish nails the high one. A man Angie thinks of as the Sorehead — missionary physician gone New Age — welcomes everyone, briefly describes the work of the Open Door, and calls on Reverend Elliot, Carol and Sam's pastor, to speak.

Mrs. Foster doesn't know what she's doing here. She's never been in a room with more colored than white. Of course, Angela never bothered to say a *colored* funeral. In a storefront, no less. She hopes that no one speaks in tongues or runs amok near her. It smells funny. Everyone seems very dressed up, and look at her hair! And no hat! She barely had time to put on lipstick. She waggles the cast so people will not take offense and want to riot on her. She's *not* using the bathroom, no matter what. She's just got to tough it out.

Reverend Elliot is wearing a black suit rather than clerical garb. Religious services for Carol will be held Thursday at 11:00 A.M. at Galilee Baptist; inhumation to follow at Evergreen Cemetery. Tonight, however —

He digresses in praise of the special atmosphere of unconditional love and fellowship he's encountered here at the Open Door; it may be his first visit, but it won't be his last, et cetera. Angie's heard it before. How great we art! Lizard smiles from the (white) Sore Board; Angie thinks they look like Salem witch trial judges or hungry aliens, and, come to think of it, they do have strange dietary prohibitions: not merely no animal products or red food coloring, but serve the strawberries separately. Some of them won't eat bread on account of the yeast.

Tonight, however, Reverend Elliot understands, it's customary for the staff to gather with friends and family of the recently departed to share their memories and bid a fond farewell.

"Closure," someone murmurs.

"Healing."

"Amen," pronounces Reverend Elliot, and a dust of voices stirs.

Sam is seated beside him, in a silver suit, little Nicole in his lap, very frilly, trying to play with her daddy's big handkerchief, which she knows he can turn into a rabbit and a cradle with babies. Casey's next to Sam. Tess thinks she looks terrific, so old and thin, even though her eyes and nose are red. Tess remembers Vince's funeral, first at the church, then the graveyard, as though her head were in a thick black sack and the rest of her strapped to a handcart. She feels she has something to tell Casey, but the words sound dumb. Megan is also here, with her mom, and another girl Tess remembers from the Twin City team, and Adrian Charles, a black guy she's noticed at school because he wears nice sweaters. Other kids she doesn't know, some cool-looking. She feels weird about talking to them, what they might have heard about her, what Megan or her mom might say, how to pitch herself. She doesn't know how to act. She feels herself to be maximum gross: a pile of shit. Really. *Full of shit.*

There's no body. Nick is partly relieved, although then it occurs to him it might be in the basement, maybe even in a cooler — well, something like a cooler — and looking at it comes later, lined up, one at a time, like in the haunted house on Halloween. He knows he doesn't want to go any lower in this crummy building; he's thinking of the Ninja Turtles living in the sewers with a rat. And his mom, hanging out here, like April, the reporter. He wishes Joe had come. The fussy girl in pink on her father's lap is much younger than he is — a baby. She keeps showing her underpants. It's hard to think what it means, her mother being dead, because all these other ladies are huddling around and also her sister, who's as old as Tess, but he plays with the idea — if his mom were dead. He thought there'd be crying. Some of these people are enjoying themselves.

When Reverend Elliot sits, there's a lull. Then a bespectacled, twentyish brunette — Jewish, Mrs. Foster thinks, pushy — stands to thank Sam, Casey, and all Carol's friends and family for sharing Carol. She's sure that everyone who worked with Carol would vouch for the fact that she knew and felt a lot more than you'd expect from someone in a coma.

Cheery riffle of assent. Angie hopes she's not polled. She sees Mason standing against the wall with his arms over his chest, and she instinctively sits up.

Carol's chi, Christine goes on, shone through and brought serenity. Her aura was purely — green.

Angie has heard this said about sheep. Mason snorts and says something to the guy next to him, who snorts. Boy, Angie likes him. She can't believe she's going to introduce him to her mother. What was she thinking? Show Tess and Nick racial harmony or some such conceit. That's what drew people to Jonestown. She shields her laugh in her hand.

A few others — hippies and old cranks, it seems to Mrs. Foster, in need of a haircut or bald, even the women — ramble on. One codger raises her hackles intoning about death's dignity when heroic measures are refused. Dignity! She remembers the skid-row flophouse where her father died, the garbage smell, and the noise! screaming, smashing, the terrible barking sound of dead-end men. She shouldn't have been there, he shouldn't have brought her there — she shouldn't be *here*. And she *wants* heroic measures, thank you! A colored girl with a withered leg takes the floor — these people need help themselves. Mrs. Foster realizes, *This is a cult!* Next they'll be laying on hands, producing raw liver out of their chests, passing out snakes! As hard as she tried to climb above this class of people —

A stout white woman in her thirties — a dyke, Mrs. Foster assumes — rises. "I met Carol my first day on the job as a high school math teacher. Fresh out of college. I don't have to tell you all that I was scared to death." She addresses the group like a teacher, with animation and humor, including everyone. Tess can imagine a class making short work of her. She must give a lot of tests. "I'd come in to fix up my classroom, and I had nothing — no paper, no posters, I mean, nothing." She nods around the oval for consensus. "I came crying to the teacher next door — that was Carol — and she said, 'Let's us go crawl in the Dumpster.'"

Appreciative laugh.

"And that's what we did. I had my whole room out of the discards. That's the kind of teacher Carol was, and the kind of person. I feel blessed to have known her." She beams at Sam, Nicole aggressively mopping his face with the handkerchief. Casey takes her little sister onto her lap; Tess feels criticized by how gracefully. She wonders what it's like for Casey, having a black stepdad. A drag — at best.

"I've got one." A graying colored woman — in a dress much too young for her, Mrs. Foster observes; she starts to think about the sex angle. "I've been teaching in the trenches with Carol for about ten years. The story I want to tell tonight is actually hers. Her class was studying, I don't know what now, but they got to talking about saints. One of the girls asked, 'What's a saint?' which just about floored Carol. She tried to explain, 'a really good person' — she wasn't so sure what the Supreme Court would say about her going into the technicalities —"

General chuckle.

"But they looked so blank. Carol started to blank, too. How's she going to explain, oh, say, Mother Teresa?"

Tess will not respond to Mrs. Foster's tap.

"These girls don't know where Indiana is, let alone India. And who else? You know, think about it. With what they hear on TV. So she said, 'What about in your own lives? A really good person.' Blank. 'What about the people who look after you?' They go, 'But she's a prostitute,' 'She's doing crack,' 'He hits me.' Carol didn't want to touch that, so she said, 'Okay, but you know? Last week Star got punished for fighting, right; and when she came back into the room today, you all didn't tease her or cut her down, you weren't glad something bad happened to her — see, now, *that* was good.' They were stunned she could find anything good about them."

The detention teacher lets this resonate. "What I like about this story, what I'm thinking about as we sit here paying our last respects, is that Carol wouldn't stop until she showed those girls something good." Her eyes cup with tears. "And it was in themselves."

The crowd flurries like a garden in the rain. Now the downpour: students, colleagues, neighbors, friends. Carol arches in the air — a rainbow, a grin without a cat. Erna thanks Jesus. Sam, in a clotted voice, thanks them all for their kindness. Angie feels frothy.

Mason spots her. Last time he saw her lit up like this her legs were hooked over his shoulders. He attributes her radiance to the presence of her runaway daughter, her son, whom he identifies, although they look nothing like her, by their tranquillity at her side. About fifty people stand between him and the exit. Well, he doubts she'll want to introduce him to her children.

Reverend Elliot claps Sam's shoulder as he reclaims his seat. Faye, Carol's sister, rises as though someone is trying to stop her and talks about how happy Sam made Carol as though someone is arguing with her. How it makes her less angry about Carol's death and the years stolen from her by Casey's lousy father, that no-good — Casey focuses on Nicole, who wants to suck the starch in her ruffles. "You hear all this shit about black men —"

The Sorehead flags the Swinging Doors into "Amazing Grace." Everybody seems to know this one except Tess and Nick, and he's coming out of a doze, and she fakes it. Angie, eyes closed, embellishes the tune like a felt-tip pen. She doesn't feel the stares. Tess hopes nobody thinks they're together.

There are some beautiful voices — you have to give them that. Mrs. Foster doesn't know where Angela gets it. Not from her side. The idea of any member of her family — or Richard's! — singing almost convulses her. Laughing at a funeral! Although it's not like any funeral she's ever been to. She's fighting the need to pee; she's going cross-eyed. When will this end? She wonders if they sing themselves into a frenzy? Will *she* succumb? And do what? Sign over her social security?

After soliciting volunteers — and of course cash cheerfully accepted — the Sorehead asks Reverend Elliot to say a benediction. They all stand. Tess notices Angie is the only one who keeps her head up — no, Angie and Nick — he's checking the scene like it's a ball game, and she looks blind.

The service is concluded. Everyone stretches. Sam is swamped. Casey consigns Nicole to a short, efficient woman who nips her off to scope out the refreshments. Faye cumbers Casey's shoulders like a wet sweatshirt on a wire hanger. Tess thinks this might be a good time to say hey.

"Wait a minute, babe. I'd like you to meet somebody." Angie's thinking of Mason, but Erna's hugging her. If he leaves before Angie gets a chance to — what? normalize relations? — well, chances grow slimmer. And in case her family did catch them together on TV, there's something about their friendship she wants them to witness — its legitimacy.

"This must be Tess and Nick!" Erna exclaims.

Tess and Nick wear identical vexed expressions, as if called up onstage by a hypnotist. Angie introduces Mrs. Foster, who tries to stand again, joggling her injured right hand, primping her hair, and laughing.

Erna quells these fretful motions by taking Tess's empty chair. "Don't agitate yourself, dear. What in the world happened to you?"

Mrs. Foster is gratified to be able to tell what's the matter with her, even to somebody's maid — this Erna looks a lot like Beulah. Mrs. Foster loved that show. Things were so much better then. She loved her own maid, Phyllis; how they laughed over Richard's finicking little foibles when Mrs. Foster laid out Phyllis's lunch. Someday, she'll have to explain to Angela that you don't get palsy-walsy with them; they themselves don't want that. It makes them ridicule you behind your back and steal the silver.

Angie asks Nick if he'd like to fetch Erna and Grandma some punch and cookies, and when he peels out — varoom! — she accompanies Tess to Sam and Casey, standing apart, a planet and its pale moon. Faye has been borne off like James Brown winding up the show with "Please, Please, Please" by three women — purplish, reddish, and gold — whom Angie sees as the Graces. Mason irritates the corner of her eye. She kisses Casey and shakes Sam's hand. "How you doing?" she asks him. The girls squeak each other's names and embrace. The other teens hesitantly converge on them.

"Well, you know." Sam studies his shoes. "You think you're ready, but it's tough."

"Yeah. They tell you I was with her when she died?"

"I don't know." Sam knocks his noggin. "I'm not taking too much in right now."

"She went out real peaceful," Angie assures him.

"Yeah, she made peace with it; now I got to do the same. We had time before she went into the coma, you know, so the practical matters are all taken care of." Sam's shorter than Angie and lofts yellowed eyes drizzled with red. "I can't say I don't know what to do, but I don't know where I'm going to find the strength to do it."

"Yeah," says Angie.

"I got to keep it together for my girls."

"So far so good." She smiles. She senses someone behind her and glimpses Mason putting on his down vest. She could do without her heart clopping back and forth like a tacked horse in a stall. "I'll miss seeing you —" Not only because as a newspaper editor Sam knows a lot of interesting dirt. She remembers one afternoon when, after "understanding some of Al's issues," he laid into Carol's first husband with a very appealing venom.

"Oh, I'll be back," Sam pledges. "This place is — well, I thought I might like to work with the youth program — after a while."

"Take your time." She kisses him. "This place is either the Tar Baby or the Briar Patch. Sticky." Sam really looks at her for the first time. She makes way for the next couple, tracking Mason.

"Excuse me — you're Tess's mother?" A disheveled blond, scarved in tobacco fumes, snares Angie's sleeve. "I'm Megan's mom."

A smile crimps Angie's instant response: oh yeah, the one who killed Brent in the auto accident. She can't hide her eyes. "Angie DiPietro." She feels blocked by a panhandler, scrabbling for change, as her train pulls out of the station.

"Valerie Stoll." She's rummaging in a big cloth purse. "Is it okay to smoke?"

"Sentiment is divided," Angie tells her. The Lost Souls can't help themselves or don't give a shit. The Healthies rail against it for everyone's sake. And then there are the tobacco employees, present and past, who owe their soul to the company store. Angie hates the smell of cigarettes. Mason's nabbed by a woman in blue satin — looks like he's running his number — they're both gushing. Good. (Good?)

"Better not — if nobody else is. Tess probably told you she stayed with us the other night. We should get together and talk." Megan's mother's eyes are grease spots. Mason kisses the satin doll's cheek, makes her turn around for him. "Our daughters have a lot in common." Valerie plucks Angie's sleeve again and laughs. "Neither one could tell the truth if her life depended on it."

Angie views that hand on her sleeve as the skeleton grip of the downhill double she's trying to ditch. "I'm sorry, I've got to see about my —"

"How about lunch sometime?"

"Sorry, I — Mason! Hey! Mason! Wait!"

He's almost out the door, but he meets her halfway. The satin doll and Megan's mother follow all this. Others, possibly, as well.

"Mason. It's good to see you," breathes Angie.

They both keep their arms wound around their chests.

"I see your daughter's back." She'll have to crawl a little before he wastes any more time thinking about her.

"Yes! I'd like you to meet her. Both my kids. My mother!"

He throws her an eyebrow, and she laughs. She reminds him of Saturday morning in East Potomac Park, watching a little Sunfish run into the blistering silver light. She reminds him of morning and childhood and children and other lost illusions. "Look like a cop in that getup," he gruffs. Her legs look great in heels.

She takes in her navy blue and brass. "Yeah, I've joined the forces of order. Actually, these are my funeral duds. Also, work costume — I'm temporarily employed. It's a trip — being normal. None of it makes sense!" Valjean's incorporeal pies. Tomorrow, it'll be Styrofoam meringue.

Each time she laughs her features fly apart as if she's plowing into spray. He brings his mouth to her ear. "What happened with — you know, Chemo Sabe?"

Her stupid breasts pant their little pink tongues like Pekingese. He's talking about the missing ounce. "It's still out there, but no repercussions." She sees the lights and noise that night at City Hall as though Mason were being clubbed and dragged through them — the Rodney King video. "I'm really sorry about that."

"Listen" — his lips against her ear conjure her lipping and laving his head, slip-slicking his up-straining clay with her quick fingertips — "since nothin' came down — I couldn't bring myself. Harvested, but — Hate waste, you understand. Come out tomorrow. Take it off my hands."

"Maybe —" Angie thinks Valjean will let her go as early as she wants if she promises to come back — talk about diminishing returns — like Beauty's promise to the Beast: 'Let me go, and I'll stay' — although tomorrow is Angie's last day, and, after that, she's never going back. However bad she might feel about misleading Valjean, she feels a lot worse continuing to jeopardize Mason with the pot he grew as a favor to her. And then Chemo Sabe can't eat. "Tomorrow afternoon?" She searches Mason's floating expression. He's got to know she's not playing him, if he does turn her on like a tap. "I can't stay —"

"'Round four. If it don't rain, be out in the meadow leads to the pond —" Take her in the tall grass, take her in the rain — take her in, take her out, take her any way she want it — "Think you can find me?"

"Never spent much time surveying the estate." Never spent more than half an hour out of each other. Her fault.

"Don't put myself in situations where I got to wait on no-body, dig." He rocks back on his heels, panning the crowd. "Got goin' on."

She nods. He just wants to get rid of the pot. "I'll find you. If I can't, I'll scream." She looks for her brood. "Listen, I wasn't kid-ding, I really do want you to meet —" Tess is in a circle around Casey, the two girls shaping their exchange with vivid hand jive. Nick is engaged with Erna, her arm around his waist, while Mrs. Foster nibbles a cookie, erect, clicking her gaze on and off like a chicken. And here's Joe, coming through the door, fast, purpose-ful. "Geez, there's my husband." He looks like he's double-parked. What time is it? Were they supposed to meet him? Wrong-footed again.

Mason had imagined her husband bovine. He feels a gratified twinge. It's not a case of compared to what. He's good, and Angie likes him. It occurs to him she's told him almost nothing about her husband, her family, herself. He looks at her fine-boned pro-file and thinks of those Mexican sugar skulls and realizes he's in deep trouble — he may be in love.

Joe's coming from Elena's. He showed up at her door, rehears-ing his exit lines, and she was ticked off because he hadn't called first, even though he thought they set this up at lunch. Maybe be-cause she's on the rag, smelling rusty. He loves that smell. Must be part dog. He should have licked her face, but he didn't want to give out mixed signals: he was there to break it off. He ended up bending toward her — with what half-assed expression? — and not kissing her, like her fucking priest. Like a bullshit artist.

Letting him follow her in, she started dumping on him. She re-sents being taken for granted. To him, waving his hands like a typ-ical guinea — and of course this was the wrong tack altogether — that's intimacy. The parrot squawked. She turned off the TV and sat back down on her littered sofa, surly. He took the armchair. He sat staring up the cannon of her, her eyes straying to the vacant TV screen. What's on Tuesday nights? Must be pretty compelling. He refused a drink. He apologized for interrupting her work. The parrot rawked something like "Don't say you're leaving." "Maybe I better go," he said.

"Since you're already here —" She rearranged her posture so that he felt he'd been looking at something of hers he shouldn't. "Why don't we talk about where this is headed?"

He moved to the couch — "if mine eye offend thee" — and leaned over the pile of papers and books and an empty container of Rocky Road toward her, almost on one knee. Was *she* dumping him? He wanted to say, "Let me go first," give her the big eye, kiss her hand, and walk. So it would take her a couple of minutes to realize what had happened. Cacique jumped from the windowsill to the pile of papers between them and stuck his head in the ice-cream carton. The loud licking inside this polka-dot helmet made Joe want to laugh. Very inappropriate.

"I don't want to be your dirty little secret, Joe. I can't take this so casually. I thought — well, I didn't think." Her lower lip trembled. "But one of us has to. People are going to get hurt. Your *kids*."

Joe took her hand, and Cacique looked out long enough to playfully claw Joe's wrist. Elena booted the cat off with her bare foot. Joe clasped her arch. Her foot really seemed strange to him, small, puffy like a bun, the browns and taupes seeping up fine cracks and gullies like some western landscape. He studied it, brought it to his mouth, kissed it, kneading her ankle, her calf, her thigh. He was kissing her — the papers whiffled to the floor — so soft — sucking her tongue, blearing her lips, feeling for her fat nipples until she hissed, "Shit! Let's get naked," and he cleared his eyes and looked at the time, and it was time to go.

She was really thrilled about that. She threw a book or something at him and told him to go fuck himself and a lot of other things he could almost understand, in Spanish, reminding him of the operatic nights he spent with his hands over his ears as a kid. How'd she think *he* felt about it?

He can see why some guys just want to pay for it.

And now this is good. This is great. He's got a hard-on like a hockey stick, and here's Angie — Nick's around somewhere for Christ's sake! Tess! her fucking mother! — kissing on her lover, her tits lifted like pansies. He should turn and walk. Yeah, where? He pictures that book or whatever coming at him. It's a dark, hostile, empty night out there.

And he's got to get these kids home. And her fucking mother! Shit, leave her fucking mother. She's finally in the right place — the Open Grave.

"Hey, Joe" — Angie's around his waist, kissing his stubble, and she quotes the Jimi Hendrix song. Old bedroom joke. He looks hot, tense, and smells musky. Work, huh? She imagines chiffon belly dancers disporting about the office with perfume atomizers. He's having an affair. Of course he's having an affair. What does she expect, cold-shouldering him for years? What does the other woman look like? Different, Angie hopes. She certainly smells different. Better? Is he different with her? Better? What does she do? Is she married? Children? Is she young? Better? It's heart-catching, like toiling up a roller coaster to the big drop.

He returns her kiss perfunctorily. She reminds him of an ivory paper knife.

"Are you in a hurry?" She checks his eyes. Not anymore. She feels like a mission gone haywire. "I'd like you to meet some people."

She's not giving him time to answer; she propels him straight for her boyfriend. Rage bloats his throat. This has got to be the limit. All right, he can pull it off. Sophisticated? Sure. Afterwards, he'll go home and beat himself to death.

Nick tackles his leg as Angie is saying, "Mason Saunders, this is my husband, Joe DiPietro. Joe — Mason."

The two men pump hands. Nick scrutinizes Mason without letting go of his father.

"This is my son, Nick." Angie smiles, relying on her social programming like a kamikaze. "Nick, my friend Mason."

Mason ties his arms again. "Hey!" he says. Shut my mouth, he thinks.

"Hey." Nick smiles. This must be the guy she was kissing on TV. His skin is very dark, like the school piano, and he has a big beard Nick would like to touch. Nick watches Erna sneak up behind Mason. They fall together. People around here are really mushy. And the cookies taste like dog biscuits. He looks up at Joe. "Can we go now?"

"Sure," Angie says, smiling at everybody's discomfort like a nurse giving flu shots. "Would you get Tess, please? And your coat. I'll collect Grandma."

Joe bends down. He won't be surprised by anything he finds in his son's face. "How you doing, my man?"

"Great, Dad." He doesn't want Joe to know how tired he is, or he'll never be allowed to stay up late again. He runs to get Tess.

"Ange, I got to be —" Mason zips his vest. Feets don't fail me now. White folks — crazier than shit, every last one of them. His friend John flags him. Catch up with him. Laugh this off over some wings.

"Ooh Mason, one more minute? I want you to meet my —" Angie wants to prove that Tess doesn't know him from Adam; "Joe, Erna — *the* Erna. Erna, Joe —"

This fudgy, smiling Amazon seizes Joe's arms. Is he supposed to know her?

"I feel like I know you already!" she enthuses.

What in the fuck does Angie say about him? He feels like something at the end of a tweezers — the incredible shrinking man. Mason sure isn't shy about sizing him up. Why don't they both just whip out their cocks and compare?

"You've got one wonderful wife," Erna tells him. "We're so lucky to have her around here."

Joe is at a total loss how to respond. He's afraid he may start crying.

"Hey, I'm Tess. Mom said to introduce myself."

She even looks like a question mark. Her hands work in her jacket pockets as if she's playing a concertina. Nick is behind her, oaring into his coat. Joe draws her into him like a deep breath. He hasn't touched her in years, and she's not flinching, although her legs fidget. None of that filthy tobacco smell on her. Her waist is small and firm. He kisses her beautiful hair. Nick crowds his other side. Joe feels closer to tears than ever.

"Mason." Mason lifts his beard and catches his mustache in his lower teeth. "Pleased to meet you." Daddy's girl. This child has an at-ti-tude. Spiny with it. She *knows*, but how much? He hopes she don't think he's crossed her. Looking at Angie's husband shorn up by their wary cubs, he's shocked by stabs of jealousy.

None of them has a clue what to say. Tess hopes nobody expects *her* to keep the ball rolling. Ask Malcolm if he has a smoke — a joint. Her mother has really lost it. And what's with Joe? Luckily, Mason and Erna's other friends keep tapping them — and half the Western world wants to say some dumb shit to "Angie's girl!" Jesus! She's got Casey's phone number; now let's get the hell out of here before Megan's mother can sink her teeth in.

"There wasn't a body," Nick chatters to Joe. "It wasn't the real funeral — that's at a church. Some people stood up and talked about the dead lady." He looks at Erna to make sure he isn't saying anything stupid. She's half-listening to some skinny old redhead in, like, a cape. "We sang. Nobody much cried."

The skinny dame horns in, "You see, darrrling, some of us don't think it's sad when —"

She looks like she's dead herself with her staring eyes and white skin — she's probably a vampire. Nick explains to Mason, "See, we have to have a funeral for our dog Mutt. He died. I found him."

"How —?" The boy's directness is Angie's. Mason feels warm, expanding, like kneaded dough.

"He was real old. We're gonna bury him in the yard. We made a cross — mostly me —"

"What?"

"Wood. It has a picture of Mutt." Nick does an impression, hands for ears, tongue slagging. "Tess put that in. I wrote 'A Great Dog!' in gold. It's great!" Nick's thinking now daytime and a big crowd: Shane, Molly from around the corner, kids from school (Prec-ious Jew-well Crutch-field, show her, Billy Lucas, nanny-nanny boo-boo), Erna, all the Door-people — singing. But it's gotta be something he knows. "Bingo"? What are some dog songs? "You gotta see it. We're gonna bury him Thanksgiving." He frowns at Joe: logistics. "Before dinner or after?"

Did Nick just invite Angie's lover to Thanksgiving dinner? Joe sees Mason and Elena at either side of the table with napkins around their necks, gumming drumsticks. Jesus Christ!

"Hi!" Angie tillers Mrs. Foster by the elbow.

Tess thinks her mother must be stoned out of her mind. Did she find that grass and smoke it? Maybe she found out about Joe's bimbo and got trashed and decided to pay him back. Joe's fingers are leaving dents in her ribs. Tess will die if he starts a fight. She's heard about fights, when he was in the Navy or when Angie sang in clubs, under the heading, "I was young and stupid once, too." This goosy part of her wants to see it happen. But it wouldn't be like in the movies. It wouldn't be funny later.

"Mason, this is my mother, Mrs. Agnes —"

"Mrs. Richard Foster," Mrs. Foster corrects, laughing. She knows she taught Angie better than that. She puts her cast out and then laughs again. "I've got a head like a sieve. I keep forgetting about this wrist, which I broke — you won't believe it — going to church."

Only Mason is learning this for the first time. He says, "Sorry to hear it, ma'am," holstering his own proffered handshake. Angie's mother looks like Nancy Reagan as a bag lady. He can see Angie going exactly the same way. He shoots her a smirk before he says to Nick, "I'm a carpenter. How'd you make that cross?"

Joe knew they'd be comparing their sticks. And what a surprise! Mason's is better. As Nick's fingers explore his callused palm, Mason describes lashing the two sticks together with rope so there's a place to put flowers. Why didn't Joe think of that? So easy, so obvious.

"Ours is more real," Nick tells Mason. "You gotta see it." Somewhere above, Joe snorts. "There's always a ton of food. Mom makes the best turkey. And stuffing!"

"Yeah," Joe says, hugging Tess to him and laughing. He feels the lining of his chest cracking and tumbling and fizzing in his stomach acid. "Please join us. I'm inviting a friend of mine — you remember, *honey*, the psychologist? — I forgot to tell you."

"The more the merrier," Angie lilts. Is that his lover? What did he say about the psychologist? Black! He said black. Did he mention gender? What if it's a guy? Whoa! Well, if so, she can't take it personally, right? Will he or she analyze everybody? It could be a long meal. "You coming, Erna?" She winks. "Corn pudding —"

"Yes!" Nick jumps. He bets Erna sings great — loud!

"Not unless we do some shopping." Mrs. Foster laughs.

Erna turns from another conversation. "I can't, honey, I got my own —"

"Yeah," says Mason. Thanksgiving with the fucking Pilgrims? With no decent sweet-potato pie or greens? He thinks he'd rather drive back to Lamont Street for the first time in five years and deal with his daddy's bitterness and his mama's fantasy life and his sorry-ass little brother's excuses and his stuck-up sister's plug-ugly girlfriends and a surprise cameo appearance by that woman he *failed so badly* and their kids. Have the stereo ripped out his truck.

Mrs. Foster laughs. "I don't know about you young people —" Where does Angela think the food is coming from? They don't even have a turkey. And the way the house looks! They'll think she was raised in a barn! Using the Foster family silver, the heirloom china! They should be serving, not sitting down. "But we senior citizens —" But please don't let them cook. Those cookies were made out of God knows — sawdust. Or pills! Prozac! — and she couldn't drink anything because — well, she doesn't want to dwell on it — And what was that place where they all died of Kool-Aid? That was some kind of phony church just like this. The jungle bunny mesmerizing little Nicholas — he must be one of the leaders — look at the women fawning over him, even Beulah, and Angela introducing him to Theresa! She must be crazy! Brainwashed. It's a terrible Satanic cult temple. No wonder they never have any money — Angela's giving it away! Now they'll be draining Mrs. Foster's bank account — or worse. Her will! And the children. Do they sell them or force them to perform vile acts and then take pictures of them or beat them or — sacrifice them? Did Vincent really die of Reye's syndrome? Did Richard go naturally? Did she fall, or was she pushed? The coffee! Mrs. Foster laughs. "We need our rest."

"Mom?"

Angie is turning Nick in. A faint light filters through the curtains from the street. "What is it, baby?"

"What songs about dogs do we know?" He makes room for her at the edge of the bed.

"Gee, quite a few, actually." She seals the blankets around his little body like a turnover. "That you know, too?"

"That most people know. The best one —"

"'Hound Dog,'" she answers.

"How's it go?"

Angie sings a few bars.

"It's too mean."

"Oh, I don't know. You can tell they have a close relationship. It's an Elvis song."

"Elvis!" he says scornfully. "He's some kinda alien."

"Oh, no, honey. Elvis is the best. The King. Listen, I'll tell you a story." She leans over him, propped on her elbow. "In nineteen fifty-seven —"

"Back in the day —" Nick yawns, grinning, nesting.

"Yes. Your mama would have been the same age as *you*." She tickles his tummy, and he wiggles. She slinks her hand in his oily hair and strokes his temple with her thumb. "Elvis was playing Seattle. He wasn't very old, either. Maybe Tess's age. Performing in a ballpark, fifteen thousand people. Sunset over the mountains. Big lights. Elvis came out, and there was pandemonium!" Angie mimes pandemonium. Nick smiles indulgently. "Finally, the crowd quieted down. Elvis took the mike and said" — she mellows into Elvis — "'I always like to begin my concerts with the national anthem.' That's that 'Oh say can you see' number," she explains.

Nick whaps his chest and makes a solemn face. He's been to minor league games.

"'Will you all please rise?' Elvis asked," Angie continues. "Everybody stood up. And then Elvis twanged his guitar and sang" — Angie wails in her stage voice — "'You ain't nothin' but a hound dog —'"

Nick laughs delightedly.

"The crowd went wiiiiiild!"

Nick puts his hands on his mother's face to calm her down. He says, "One we can sing at Mutt's funeral."

"Ah. I know some icky folk songs. 'Had a dog and his name was Blue —'"

"Blue?"

"Then there's 'Something something and a dog named Blue —'"

"'Scooby-Dooby-doo.'" Nick pulls up her hair and lets the strands fall. "What's up with this *blue*? I guess it's gotta be 'Hound Dog,' huh? That's the one everybody knows."

Angie pictures them singing "Hound Dog" over the grave. Doing that stiff-legged, twitchy dance Elvis did with the mike or when he belted "Jailhouse Rock." The black-and-white stripes call up skeletons. It strikes her as just right. "I could try to think of some others," she offers halfheartedly.

"Make me a tape," Nick says, heavy-lidded. "Before Thanksgiving."

"If I have to stay up all night —"

Chapter 6

I Just Do

"I tell you, darling, when I see a good-looking man nowadays, all I think is" — Mimi's voice darkens — "*disease vector.*"

It's about one in the morning. By candlelight, on the den floor, cocooned in a crocheted afghan, with phone, trying not to wake her mother across the hall, Angie's dubbing a Neil Young dog song. Cold sober. Can dentures and incontinence be far off? She might also be fifteen. Palooka is ramming her face, purring. The women have been lamenting the spiraling costs of fleshly pleasure and the plight of a mutual friend with genital warts. Angie tries to steer. "My marriage has never been threatened by looks."

"Oh, we're not talking marriage-threatening," Mimi snips, "just undie-bunching."

Angie guffaws, shoves the cat away.

"No, Valve, fess up," Mimi pursues, "we made out like bandits in the men's department. We shopped just in time and with an eye on eternity."

"Yeah, right. As I remember it, you had your eyes opened by the Wrong Brothers — a tribe more numerous than the Wongs."

Mimi shrieks her appreciation.

"But I fell for that wolfish look," Angie goes on. "You counseled me against, Dex." Palooka is back, butting her mouth, noisy as gravel.

"Against marriage, not Joe. Mercy — Joe! He always looked like he wanted to drag you off and *feed* on you. Then he turns out to be a sweetie. *Too* nice, in fact. Go figure. I'll tell you one thing, nobody ever asked me what you saw in him."

"I think he's seeing somebody," Angie says softly, shunting Palooka aside.

"Yikes! And?"

"I married him for his hunger. What can I say?"

"'Soup's on!'" Mimi shouts into the mouthpiece. "'Come and get it.'"

Angie sees her spread legs, bent at the knees from clapped feet, clanged like the iron triangle in the intro to *The Real McCoys*, and Joe hustling from chores in overalls with his pecker stuck out and "gawrsh!" expression under the titles and the theme song. She can't remember Hamlet's soliloquy or the Gettysburg Address, but she knows the words to the theme song. "What I mean is, what can *I* say?" Palooka, like an idling semi.

"The black guy?"

"All the guys." Angie would like to talk about Alaska, but she doesn't know how to explain why she's mixed up with him if it's *not* about sex. She's afraid of Mimi's disapproval. Mimi was a philosophy major. She can go categorical. She can go without Angie.

"You've always had trouble with boundaries, Valve," Mimi says. "That's why Joe married *you*. It's classic — the Sprats. You have such particular power to please each other. But you can't fake yourself out about sex, the obstinate beast, or it isn't sex; it's love or compliance or some shit. The Lord's sense of irony — no faulting it. Proof!" she adds brightly.

"I don't know, Dex, you talk about boundaries." Neil Young finishes off King, and Angie interrupts the taping to chuck Palooka across the room. Her chin and palms are furred. "I'm going through some kind of withdrawal, from sex, intoxicants —"

"Way to go, girlfriend!"

"Yeah, for hours, Dex, maybe even *day*."

"One at a time, kid. Start notching your belt."

"I'd rather be running a tab —" A huge stifled sneeze almost detaches her retinas, folds her to sitting, and blows Palooka under the couch.

"I hope you bit your tongue."

Angie wipes her nose on her sleeve. "This feels like a crisis."

"Have you thought menopause?" Mimi asks.

"Is that happening to you?"

"Intimations — scatty periods. I haven't gone delusional or croaked anybody yet. I don't think. I'm not looking in the hamper."

Angie chorts. "Of course I wish I could tell you — that's it, I'm past it, saved, no more sin for me!" She seems to be rubbing the fur into her eyes. "Okay, maybe the highs aren't as high, the lows aren't as, well, interesting, and it takes forever to recover, I still want a joint, a drink, a new sensation."

"The part that's *not* all in your mind," Mimi says, "that's the killer. The tree nobody can see falling in the forest? — it's falling on *you*."

"Part of it is my kids."

"Sure — Tess running away —"

"Like she took a breast with her — still attached." Angie imagines her breast slammed in the trunk of a car. The heat whooshes on, flickering the candlelight, crickling some papers. Palooka emerges with one of Mutt's old, lost toys, a red rubber bone with a jingle bell in it, and is rolling and tossing it noisily. Angie reclines, absently scanning her tapes and records for canine hits. "And now I'm afraid of her. You know? How'm I supposed to get her to clean up her act? When I see myself through her eyes —" She closes her eyes and shudders. "And how's she gonna come back at me? You know?"

"Darling, you're talking to a stepmother."

"I haven't really talked to her since she got home. I don't know what to say. Geez, I may have already fucked it up, huh? Aren't you supposed to deal with kids right away?"

"The good-swift-kick school. That's for little kids, hot stoves. Your almost-eighteen has probably guessed you sometimes need to think. Maybe tell her that — you're still thinking. See what she says. Nowhere near the cutlery."

"Yeah. But, see, Joe —"

"Joe! Incidentally, what makes you suspect a rival?"

Angie has been trying not to think about the rival. "He's maybe invited her? him? to Thanksgiving."

Mimi laughs. "Ooh, she-he sounds dangerous. Pluck her! Stuff her!"

Angie spouts. "And I think I invited Mason — the black guy!"

"With your mother there?"

"And we still don't have a turkey!" Angie imitates her mother's querulous laugh.

"You have at least two," Mimi suggests. "I want a full report on this meal, soup to — ahem — nuts. Thanks be, chez nous, we've reached a level of bohemianism where no one expects us to observe Thanksgiving."

Angie pulls out the Everly Brothers and puts the cold plastic box against her cheek. "So how are you guys?"

"Oh, we're fine. And we better stay that way, because we have no health insurance. Say, you couldn't loan us seventy-five thousand simoleons? Or give it to us — that would be even better."

"Geez, Meems!" Palooka bats her with the obscene bone. Angie bips him with Don and Phil.

"No, I'm kidding. We're all right. Although pretty soon I'm going to start printing and hanging a different kind of paper. If I get caught, will Joe work for food?"

"I thought he was doing that now, but maybe he's keeping up payments on a time-share in Myrtle Beach. And I just sold myself into slavery. Office temp. I seem to be paying to work."

"David would pay to work. That's what I get for marrying up in class."

"Yeah, but he builds things. I don't see why I should be paid. All I did was stand around talking. All anybody did. Phoning, Xeroxing, faxing — same thing. Same as teaching, the Sore. If I could just stop talking —"

The door flings open on a billowing silhouette and extinguishes the candle. Palooka crashes down towers of tapes — they bing Angie's head — and sprints for parts unknown.

"What's all this racket?" Mrs. Foster demands. The light flares on. She's armed with a brass duck bookend and wincing from opening the door with her bad hand. "Angela!" She laughs. "I thought it was thieves!"

She doesn't have her teeth in. Her chest sags like a river delta. Her eyes are blood-rimmed, her hair is a smokestack. Angie feels like a straw in a gale. Scream!

"You get to bed this instant! What are you doing up at this hour?" Mrs. Foster is breathless, as if she's fallen into icy water. She was prepared to discover Theresa, muttering over black candles, torturing the cat, but it's Angela. This must be how the brainwashing is done. They call, keep her awake all night reciting God knows what — spells, catechism, credit card numbers — with the candles and the incense and so on until —

"I gotta go, Dex. It's my mom."

What can Mrs. Foster do? In whom can she confide? Joe? Hardly. She sets the brass duck on top of the TV and staggers on to the bathroom, mumbling and chuckling.

Angie wonders how much her mother heard, what she makes of it, what she'll say about it, and to whom.

Mimi is beating her bare feet on her linoleum. "You're in trouble now! Oh boy!"

"Listen," Angie whispers — her mother pauses at the bathroom door to hear if she hangs up — "do you remember who did 'Please Stop Kicking My Dog Around'?"

"Richard Milhous Nixon. On the Checkers label. Follow-up to 'Leader of the Pack.'" Mimi squeals her tires.

"'I felt so helpless,'" Angie sob-sings.

The dog mix is completed, Joe and the kids are fed and out the door, her mother ensconced on the couch in the den with the phone and the newspaper, and Angie is on time for her last day at Ye Olde Schoole Fine Furniture. She doesn't hear any applause. She wears sneakers and jeans. The receptionist fiddles with accordion-pleated turkey decorations. Several sales reps don't show. Those who do stand in the halls or in the break room over Valjean's pumpkin parfait pie telling jokes. The boss tells Angie if he doesn't see her — she looks down at herself — he wants to thank her for her invaluable contribution and leaves at ten. Valjean makes one last pitch for her to stay on permanently, then releases her at lunch with half the pie in foil. It tastes like bubble bath. "You need to set your sights a good deal higher," Valjean says on the doorstep. Angie feels as if she's shaking hands with her priest after the sermon. She compliments Valjean on her dynamite handshake. Must be from rolling all that crust. She hopes they bump into each other. She does!

It's too early to go to Mason's. The sun brisks her like a dry towel. Maybe she has time to do the grocery shopping with her mother. Ugh! Drop in at the Sore, see who's died, touch base with the hot line? Maybe she should stop by Blank at the park with — what? A bucket of chicken and some cheap champagne. An ice-cream soda and two straws. Pick fleas off each other! Or why not surprise Joe at the office? This conjures Joe in his rolling desk chair, naked legs and arms spraddled like a spider, plugged into some perfect hourglass of a woman. Tears spring into her eyes. This is crazy. On to the Kroger!

She's parked next to a phone booth near the road. First, she has to make a call — loose end. She dumps Valjean's pie in the trash can and dials Alaska's number — now *this* is crazy — hoping for, and afraid of, no answer. He picks up on the third ring. He sounds — out there. Small and distant. Her heart contracts, the same way your uterus flags you down to unload an importunate child. She shuts the extraneous ear with her thumb and shouts, "I can take you to the hospital."

"How many times you gone come to my rescue, dumb bitch?"

Angie thinks about it. "I don't know." If he's too drunk to walk, she can't carry him. She sees them plummeting down the steep iron steps on their necks. "Is anybody else there?"

"No. Who?"

"Weezie?"

"Nah, she split. She jus' come over to fuck with me. You know wha' she tol' me?" His voice stretches thin. "She said I ruint her life." He breaks down. "She says I'm murder on women. Why'd she have to come over here to tell me that?" He gulps. "You ever feel suicidal, Angel?"

"Never." Not lately, anyway. This strikes her.

"A course." He clears sludge from his mouth. "You ever hear a more mis'able life than mine? An' you don' know the half. But I ain' never felt suicidal. Not even when Rosemarie — I always felt, you know, I ain' drunk enough, drugged enough, fucked enough —"

Recognition. "Maybe this time you've drunk enough."

His big laugh. "God, I love you! I'n' it amazin'? I really love you. Le's get to the hospital. What the fuck? Firs' le's get married. You know, I did that once —"

"I'll be there in fifteen minutes."

"Woke up in a motel with a case a Canadian Club and a woman I swear I'd never seen before in my life —"

"Please be dressed."

"Doin' my bes'. Listen, you not gone like this, but you gone have to bring me a bottle. Can' make it unless —"

"I'm heading out —"

"Gin. Not a lot—a fifth. Good stuff. Pay you back."

"Just get dressed."

"Seriously. I owe you so much — I'm gone give you all my money. If I jus' knew — where is my money? Ever' goddamn penny I have. Why you so kind to me?" The spanking laugh. "Wha's wrong with *you?*"

Good question. And where's her money? She's about two dollars shy of the fifth she thinks she'll need to enlist his cooperation. She obviously can't write a check. She may have enough quarters in her glove box, for parking downtown at the Sore. She opens the passenger-side door, the glove compartment, and a Seal-a-Meal of marijuana falls out. She hunches over it, staring at it, much too long. The whole time she's been agonizing about Tess, about Mason, it was here? Where she left it? How could she have missed it? Is she crazy? Or did Tess put it back? She can't tell if any of it's missing — does Mason weigh it? She can't make sense of it at all, but she's relieved it's back in her possession. The quarters are there, too.

The sun is warm, the sky's a clear, uplifting blue as she pounds

Alaska's door. She hears shuffling and pounds again. He's wearing socks. The apartment is glacial. He tries to take her in his arms; he smiles extra when he feels the paper sack. He gives off dry heat like a woodstove. His lower lip is bloody, his eyes as pink and blind as his balls. "You mus' love me," he says. "God, you're beautiful. Why don' you gimme a blow job?"

She's got him in socks and Jockeys when the front door opens, and hard heels tromp toward them. Angie wildly imagines it's her mother. Alaska looks at her as though he thinks the same thing.

A whippet of a woman in jeans and cowboy boots and a Harvard sweatshirt. "Oh great! Now idn't this special? Who in the fuck are you?"

Alaska flops down on the bed and puts his head between his hands.

"I'm Angie. I'm trying to get him to the hospital."

"'I'm Angie, and I'm a fucking asshole.'" Weezie turns eyes like frayed buttonholes on Alaska. "You fuckin' son of a bitch. Got you another facilitator. You motherfuckin' lyin' son of a bitch. You bring him a bottle?"

How can she be six months pregnant? Angie could span her pelvis with one hand. Unless she's carrying awfully high. Angie wonders if anything Alaska has told her is true. He's a drunk. He told her that. He told her he was fucked. In the traditional poet's position, Job on the dung heap, his cheek rests on his palm. His eyes are closed.

"Can you help me get him to the hospital?" Angie picks up a T-shirt from a heap on the floor and jams it over his head.

"You so fucked," Alaska says, putting his arms into the sleeves. He reaches for her hand. She lets him take it, stroke it, bring it to his cracked lips. "Now, I don' wan' you two girls fightin' over me. There's plenny to go roun' —"

"Can't you see what he is? He's the biggest —"

"Hey, I'm goin'," Alaska says and coughs, "long's I can bring my drink."

Angie looks at Weezie's exasperation. "You got another idea?"

"You know how you can tell he's lyin'?" Weezie asks. "His lips're movin'." She stalks out.

Angie passes Alaska his jeans. "Please hurry," she says.

"Doin' my bes'."

Metallic noises from the direction of the kitchen. Angie wonders if Weezie is cooking; rustling up some grub, she thinks, as if this is a cattle drive. Coffee — a great idea! She also wants to tell her, for what it's worth, that she's not screwing Alaska. He holds up his feet to receive the jeans. Angie feeds them in the legs.

"Jus' can' keep your hands off me. Go on up there and see what the fuck she's doin'." His screen wipes. "Oh, God! Don' let her empty tha' bottle!" He's blundering off the bed with his feet in the calves of the pants.

Angie's happy to flee the aftermath of the fall. As she goes to investigate, Weezie is coming back behind a fire extinguisher. Angie leaps to one side. She hears the loud whush, white noise, the whump and jang of the dropped can. Weezie strides out. "Asshole," she spits at Angie.

Angie returns to the bedroom to find it white scud. Alaska, holding his arms away from his body, a pillar of suds, the head on a beer.

"What you laughin' at?" He wipes off the soft mask. "You b'lieve this?" Foam flies from his hair, his hands. He laughs tentatively, and foam drips from his nose into his mouth.

"What a woman!" marvels Angie. "What a mess!"

He falls backward onto the creamed bed. Baked Alaska, Angie thinks, and she's off again. She wonders if she should hose him. Shave him.

But he manages to shower, and she finds a sweatsuit in the

closet. His wallet and keys turn up in a jacket near the front door. He won't leave until she pours the gin into a thermos, but then he doesn't drink it, just holds it. On the way to the emergency room, he tells her how Weezie took over the family farm at fourteen when her father died. The things she can drive, build, mend, breed, tend, grow. "I'n't she beautiful?" he asks repeatedly. "Why do such amazin' women love me so much?" Walking in, he trips over a concrete parking block, tears up his hands, and alienates the admitting nurse when she asks him if his cuts need immediate attention by boasting that he's one tough motherfucker.

"I don't mind for myself," she sneers at Angie, "but there are children present."

A one-year-old slung over its mother's forearm and a toddler standing up in a stroller are saying "pow pow" into each other's faces. Angie extracts Alaska's wallet and learns his name.

Gaping wounds and heart attacks are taken first. But after a while — he's describing setting traps in the frozen hush, smelling bear, hearing the first loud report of the ice breaking in spring, and asking if she doesn't want to kiss him — he's moved upstairs to the ward. "What a bitch you turned out to be," he calls after her, searching for her hand.

Angie blasts into the sunshine. She shoots the thermos into the trash basket from three-point land — dead ringer. It's going on four. She has to nag herself to drive carefully. She turns up the radio and sings along with Marvin Gaye, ". . . wouldn't be dog gone . . ." Hey!

Everybody thinks they know what happened to Brian. It seeps into ISS from the halls between classes like that green gas in *The Ten Commandments;* Tess is surprised she doesn't keel over. Soon she'll be the only one who doesn't know, because in the empty time when Ledford is babbling about some stupid pro football team coming to Charlotte, she's telling herself it didn't happen and, since the runaway is now a total blank, convincing herself it couldn't have. Albert calls her in and grills her "one more time" — like it's such a drag for *him* to keep going over and over it and like it'll just be once. If she gets honest, if she admits she's doing drugs, if she tells him where she scores and where Brian scored, if she gives him the names — then!

They'll leave her alone?

No. Of course not. That's just for openers. Then she can go to the ball. If the shoe fits, you've got to dance in it.

Well, fuck that shit. She always goes to the ball, man; every muscle burning, she drives that ball around all obstacles to the net. She wears cleats and digs in. The crowd is far away, screaming as incomprehensibly as the wind.

She only slips up once. "What's going to happen to Brian?" She doesn't even hear herself say it.

Albert looks down at his desk, and then his eyes hook into hers, glittering. He says the D.A. and the school are discussing Brian's case. Since he has no previous record, comes from a good home, since he's always been a model student, clean-cut, active in sports, his church youth group —

Tess's lips wrinkle. She could tell them a lot about Brian. She still holds his fate on the tip of her tongue, but now she's protecting him. She adjusts her expression accordingly. Then she remembers her car. Joe's probably already told the cops it was Brian.

"They take all these things into consideration." Albert shows his little rat teeth. "Maybe he fell in with bad company. And if he cooperates"— he barbs her eyes again — "if he gets honest and names names and tells us —"

Well, nice try, but bye, bye, Brian. Even if Joe hasn't talked to the cops or the insurance company yet, there's no way she can stop him without blowing her cover. Anyway, why should she care about Brian? It's not like she asked him to practically rape her or destroy her car; it's not like she planted the acid on him. Why does she feel like a cigarette butt's being ground out in her navel?

"And if we learn from him or another reliable source that you —"

Somewhere — in a police interrogation room or a lawyer's office or his mother's white-on-white living room — all kinds of awful people are pressuring Brian to flush Tess. She doesn't know how much damage he can do her. She can't think straight. She needs to talk it through with someone she can trust. The last one who comes to mind is her mother. She pictures Angie sitting in the armchair, listening to the dirty little story, and getting smaller and smaller or further and further away. Wouldn't everybody, even Joe, leave Tess alone if Tess put it on her mom — her bad influence? Tess has only been trying to shield her. That's natural. It's almost true. Maybe it'd be a good thing for Angie — she really does need help. She might even think of it herself. She might suggest it.

Chad doesn't show to drive Tess to the Superstore. It's too bad; she liked the busyness and the music and rapping with the customers and this one other clerk, and, although she hasn't actually seen it yet, the money. And if a total reject like Chad won't be caught dead with her, she can forget about a social life. But, anyway, it's Thanksgiving. No school till next Monday. Sometime in the next four days, she should have a chance to talk with her mom.

Elena bounces the receiver down on Joe's calls.

He says, "I'm sorry —"

No doubt! She's not letting the macho pig interfere with her work anymore. She is well out of this.

"I've been thinking about what you —"

Ha! She wears knockout red lipstick, dangling red crystal heart earrings, a tube skirt, and four-inch spikes and assaults her morning appointments with rather less than third-world patience. She's got one message today: get over it; get your shit together; ha!

"Would you listen —?"

You listen.

She's thinking about lunch. The vindictive shoes she wore to parade her backside past his building — the idea must have been to create a little plash of excitement that would draw him to the window, but the men downtown, well, strictly rape-and-kill — anyway, the shoes hurt, so she's combing the phone book for the number of the Chinese that delivers. She plans to order a quart of hot and sour soup and all the appetizers on the menu — not just the pu-pu platter — to satisfy the anaconda coiled in her stomach.

Then he crashes into her office, distraught, like some coked-up white comedian — Robin Williams as Mork. He stops, opens his jacket, exposing his whole body and soul to her firing squad. He says, "Let's do Thanksgiving."

This is the scene she's dressed for. "What are you doing here?" she says coolly, swiveling toward him and crossing her legs. Cat-woman! Her heart is pumping merengue to the words of some hackneyed old bolero. She feels fantastic.

He plonks into the clients' chair. "God, you look good."

She lets him read her infinite disdain.

"I was going to ask you to lunch." He's sweating like butter. He feels like a Sterno drunk hitting on Jessye Norman. Those thighs — they raise static. His face contorts. He harrows his hair.

"Joe." She's suddenly deeply embarrassed by the fact that she's compulsively crossing her legs. She pegs her feet behind the desk, leans forward, and actually closes her hands as if she's going to try to sell him an aspirin. "Let's face it —"

"Will you listen to me?" Joe dives so that he's holding on to her desk like a rubber raft in the ocean, those baby-seal eyes sucking hers. "I've never had an affair before. I don't know what the fuck I'm doing — you know that. I love my wife, and I don't want to hurt her or leave her, and my kids, Jesus! I'm worried sick about them"— his eyes shut — "I could *never* leave them"— now his eyes open —"but I want you. I want you! I can't see how that's bad. If you want me, too."

Whenever Elena thinks she's getting the upper hand with this guy, his underhand gets her right where it counts.

"I also really do want to invite you to Thanksgiving dinner." His head reels back, and he laughs dizzily. "I feel I should warn you" — propped on his elbows, so now he's a beach boy, working on his tan — "it's likely to be a very weird affair. You'll meet my god-awful mother-in-law, my wife's lover may show — he's also black — and we're burying the dog." Joe's head lags forward. "Who's dead, in case you're wondering." He's overwhelmed with laughter.

Elena stares at his bobbing shoulders. She pushes her chair back, kicks off these torturous shoes, walks around her desk, and sinks beside him, popping a run in her last pair of sheer panty hose. She leans her forehead against his rigid hair and puts her arms around him and mews.

He lifts his head, amazed. "Can I kiss you here?" he whispers.

"And here — and —"

Wow, he thinks.

She thinks, Whoa.

Mrs. Foster has endured a day of torment. She didn't dare take her painkillers: "Eighty-Year-Old Widow Murdered by Nephew for Insurance Money," "Rash of Dognappings Points to Satan Worship" in the state-and-local section; on the talk shows: elder abuse, conmen target older women, David Koresh's mother with an exclusive, up-close look inside Waco. She decided to call Doris and, although she hates people who air their dirty laundry, told her everything.

Doris scoffed. In the first place, she accused Mrs. Foster of an overactive imagination. She brought up the missing-car incident. She said Agnes was just moping because Angela left her alone with a broken wrist to go to work. "You never had to work," Doris said, and Mrs. Foster retorted, "I beg your pardon! If looking after Angela and Richard wasn't work, I don't know what is!"

"You don't!" Doris replied, in that smarty way she has. Doris was divorced in her forties and had to support five children by waiting tables.

There was a silence. Back in Ohio, Mrs. Foster would never have associated with her type — coarse — but she's capable and spry, and since she's also not from the South, she doesn't act sweet to your face and then blab your business to all and sundry. Mrs. Foster invited her to Thanksgiving.

"Just see what you think," she wheedled. "Don't take my word for it. See if you don't — sense something."

Doris laughed, picturing herself as America's answer to Miss Marple. She loves those British mysteries, except that she can't make out what they're saying. Agnes strikes her as something straight out of one of them — a loony old crock with stolen jewels, make that lost marbles. A cult, yet!

"I'm not worried about myself" — Mrs. Foster sniffed —"but the children! Darling little Nicholas!"

Finally, Doris agreed. After almost fifty consecutive Thanksgiving dinners, pulled off some years by the skin of her teeth, this year her youngest son's wife insists on having it — "it's too much work *at your age*" — and, not only that, insists on having it at seven o'clock in the evening instead of the traditional two in the afternoon — "such an *uncomfortable* time to eat" — so the men can get drunk watching football. Doris wouldn't mind showing up full. Stuffed!

No sooner is Mrs. Foster off the phone than she hears the front door open. Her heart stops. She feels for the Louisville Slugger she hid under the couch. Something weighing at least a hundred pounds hits the floor, and Theresa slinks past the den. Isn't she supposed to be at her job? The toilet runs, and then there's noise in the kitchen. Theresa returns to the den with a glass of something that looks like milk and a plate of cookies and almost drops them when she sees Mrs. Foster.

"Grandma! I forgot you were here!" Tess takes a deep breath and puts her snack on the coffee table. The old lady looks like *What Ever Happened to Baby Jane?* Norman Bates's mother in *Psycho.* "Boy, you sure gave me a scare! Whoo! Can I get you something?" Her grandmother's hair has the texture of Easter grass. Her eyes are staring. God, what if she's having a stroke? "Some water? Have a cookie!"

Mrs. Foster compresses her lips. She finds a chipper voice. "No, darling, that's all right. I'm fine. Maybe a sip of water?" She indicates the glass she filled herself earlier.

She sounds like a crow. The glass is empty. Tess remembers a fable where the crow fills an almost empty pitcher with rocks. What's the moral of that? "I'll get you some more."

"No, darling, never mind. I have to get up anyway." Mrs. Foster struggles to sit as if the couch is a snowbank.

"No, really, I don't mind. Please. You don't look so hot."

Mrs. Foster braces her feet in her mules and her bad arm on the arm of the couch and rises, seared with pain. Theresa pothers around her, trying to give her a hand or the glass with as much success as an organ-grinder's monkey. Mrs. Foster hurries to the bathroom, shuts the door. The doorknob falls off into the hallway; the spindle is worn smooth. She's turned on the faucet, so she doesn't hear it fall, but while she's using the commode, she hears Theresa jigging it, sees it turn. She sits, clenched. Terrible images flood her, with her skirts rucked up and her drawers around her knees. "Please, Lord," she prays, "don't let me die on the crapper!"

Theresa knocks and asks how she's doing. Mrs. Foster rights herself. What she looks like! No one will believe her side. She's afraid the door may be somehow booby-trapped. When she takes hold of the knob, something clunks in the hall. The doorknob and the post pull out. She's trapped! She thinks about breaking the window, but then what? She shoves the shaft back in and finally something grabs, and the door opens on the wide-eyed Theresa. Mrs. Foster springs back.

"Happens all the time," Tess assures her, "specially when we have company. Joe can fix it."

"You should call your father Dad or Daddy." Mrs. Foster returns to the den, where a full glass is waiting.

Tess sits on the floor at the coffee table where she's laid out a game of solitaire. "This is for you," she tells her grandmother. "It's orange juice. You need something healthy. And there's cookies. Help yourself."

The cookies have colored blobs that could be anything. Theresa passes her the glass, never taking her eyes off the cards. Mrs. Foster pretends to drink. It looks funny, but then it's in a blue plastic tumbler. Should she be gathering samples to slip Doris? How? Is there time? She's very thirsty. "I thought you had a job." She laughs.

"My ride didn't come through. I told them I took sick."

Mrs. Foster reclines, exhausted. "'O what a tangled web we weave,'" she drones, "'when first we practice to deceive.'"

"What?" Tess startles. Her gaze creeps over the walls to Mrs. Foster's face. "*What* did you just say?"

"Oh, nothing." Mrs. Foster sighs. "A poem. Don't they teach you anything in those schools?"

Great. Here they are, telling Tess "get honest," when anybody, even her batty old grandmother, can see right through her. They just want her to give *herself* away — spares them the trouble. And she's been buying into it. Jesus! No, of course, the trick is to fool them. Never let your guard down for one second. Play the game. Jack on queen. This is going to work out.

"And while we're on the subject" — Mrs. Foster sounds mad, although she sort of laughs — "hasn't anybody ever taught you a decent two-handed game of cards?"

Spit. Go Fish. Rummy. Baby games. And Indian poker, where you stick your card to your forehead so everybody can see it but you and then bet.

"Theresa. If you'll help me do something with my hair tomorrow, I'll teach you to play gin."

"What about poker?"

Angie treks through a stand of pine and white oak, past the vegetable garden, studded with rotting pumpkins, pale gourds, fresh greens, out to a close-cropped meadow and halloos Mason on the slope opposite, into which a ripe persimmon sun is oozing juice. They both trail shadows like black ribbons. Angie suddenly plumps her hand on the path, whirling over in cartwheels. Her momentum carries her to the seam where the path rises and becomes more overgrown. She regains her feet, poses like a balance, and calls, "Ta da!" Her vision is swimming. She grins giddily.

"Lucky you din't bust you butt, baby." When she reaches him, Mason frowns his amusement and offers her a hug. She pulls up short and juts her thumbs in her pockets, and he knots his arms over his chest. She's waxed with sweat, smiling.

"Whatcha doin'?" she asks.

"Propagatin'."

"Ooh!"

His eyes crease. "Cardinal flowers." He shows her the bright red, feathery blooms he's collecting in a white paper sack. "Plant 'em out in spring."

"Beautiful color!" Something she's thinking about his skin.

Something he's thinking about her hair. "They're native, but, you know, makin' themselves scarce." He slices her a sidelong. "You in a hurry?"

She imagines lounging naked on the pink-lined cushions of his lips. The tweedy texture and deft touch of his hands. How does it hurt anybody? She can't measure. "Kinda. I gotta pick up Nick."

"Get back to it tomorrow, then." He folds over the top of the sack. Apparently, no thrash in the pine needles, either. A scene he's staged in his mind once too often since last night. "I got the stuff up here in the shed."

They fall in step. "Thanks for doing this, Mason. It's really good you're getting out of it, but it's gonna help Chemo Sabe — a lot of people — so much. And listen, I'm really sorry I fucked up about that ounce." She speeds up her patter. "Today it fell out of my glove box, so maybe it was there all along, and somehow I missed it —"

"That'd be a laugh." He looks at her hard. She's focused on her feet. Probably thinking about her daughter. She has no idea what he feels about her. He'll make her a lavish going-away present, something she'll use every day, something that will get in her way and fuck with her. A full-length mirror?

"Anyway, it was a wake-up call" — her eyes skit between the dark shoals of his profile and the uneven path — "that ounce." What's that about an ounce of prevention? "I'm trying to straighten up — no booze, no smoke — caving in to family val-

ues." Her lips tweak. "But if it says something positive to Tess —"
She still wants him to pump her straight up like a bottle rocket.

He wants to remind her that splitting up was his idea, he wants
to ridicule the prospect of her becoming a staid Republican ma-
tron, and he wants to feel all that determination yield against the
ball of his index finger.

"Beautiful place," she says. "I haven't been on a farm since my
hippie days." Rolling — and sneezing — in the hay.

"Only difference between here and heaven is a screen door,"
he says, "and it's open."

Angie gawks at him. "Heaven! Here?"

"Say hell in the summer," he adds. Her hair flutters as if he
were blowing on her face.

"Wish my kids could come out here. Let 'em run and holler.
My Tess, she can run. You should see her."

They stop near the house. A few remaining dried leaves crackle
above them. "Bring 'em on out," he says. He sees running children silhouetted on the horizon. Black children.

She lifts her face as if she's going to sing. "I guess I'm saying I'd
like them to know you. I'd like to fit you into some normal, honest context in my life. Are you really coming for Thanksgiving?"

He traces her jaw, like a bow — ash, birch. What *is* she saying?
He doesn't like the sound of "fit you in." They fit just fine as is.
"You want me to?"

"Abso-fucking-lutely." She sees herself biting his beard, feels
the tough hairs between her teeth, the triangle of nubbly wool ta-
pering to his waist, curling her tongue around his root. Good-bye
to all that! Hello to handshakes and twaddle!

"What about your husband?"

She hikes her shoulders. "I dunno. He's maybe also invited —
a friend. A psychologist. I think — she's — black."

Mason drops his hand. What's she playin' on him? "Have to

think about it. Shit's in here." Parceled in plastic Ziplocs hidden in a twenty-five-pound bag of compost he totes easily to her car.

"You got a definite gift for crime," she tells him, opening the trunk.

Not her most racially sensitive remark. "'S' a nice plant. I'll miss growin' it." But dumping it in, he's glad to be done with it. He's had visions of waking up to spinning blue lights, a speedy end to recent economic and political machinations. And for what? Some pretty dated notions. "You use that compost now, you hear. I'm serious. Don't know 'bout the dope, but *this* shit is primo."

"I know just where. We gotta bury the dog — they tell you?" She gets in her car. "Come around two if you're coming."

She sails off on big white plumes — burning oil. He might drop by, although he has a date he means to keep with a sweet-potato pie. He's curious, for one thing. And maybe it's a way to tell her he's willing to go a little distance for her. The idea of starting a new relationship right now just wears him out. As he turns back to the garage where another midstream project is waiting, emptiness racks him like a yawn. He finds it hard to admit that what he's living is his life. Maybe he needs a dog.

Angie comes home rosy, with Nick in the backseat, singing "Bird Dog," and two pounds of pot concealed in a bag of muck in her trunk. Nick is wearing her Walkman — "Mizz E says don't bring it in again" — and carrying his DARE certificate — that's Drug Abuse Resistance Education, an "age-appropriate, alcohol and drug-specific curriculum to equip the students, K–12, with accurate information and life skills that empower them to avoid problems related to the use/abuse of chemical substances prior to their onset," as the accompanying flyer tells her. Today was the last day of the program.

"So whatcha know about drugs, Nico?"

"Everything."

"That's a lot!"

"Don't ask me," Nick huffs. "They went over and over it. Bleh!"

"So what if somebody —?"

"No no no no no no no! Sheesh! You know what's weird? When she gave us our things" — he flaps the diploma — "Officer Susie was in *tears!*" First, Nick felt sorry for her, and then he felt mean. "He's a bird dog," he growls. "Hey, Mom, what's a quail?"

The house is hushed. No TV, no music. Tess is up on her knees, facing Mrs. Foster over the coffee table, both veiled in cards, fingering piles of toothpicks. Their eyes are bright. Nick shows them his certificate. He likes the way his name looks, written in gold like Mutt's on the cross, although he can't read cursive yet. They can hardly be bothered to look.

"That's nice, dear." Mrs. Foster laughs. "I'll see that five and raise you two."

"Narco!" says Tess. "Congrats!"

Nick shakes her hand off his hair and pops the tape out of the Walkman and into the stereo. Rufus Thomas, "Walkin' the Dog," booms on.

"Turn that down," Mrs. Foster shouts.

"Hit me!" Tess shouts.

"No, no!" Mrs. Foster laughs. "Theresa, darling, think! What does that tell me?"

"Can I play?" Nick reduces the volume and kneels over to the table. He wants in any game that lets you hit Tess.

"Get lost, Narco."

"You're the narco. I bet you sniff crack!" Nick shows her his crack — "Nicholas!" — making a farting noise with his tongue, and goes to the kitchen to get a snack and attach the certificate to the refrigerator with magnets before they spill something on it.

Angie's period has descended like the last act of *Titus Androni-cus*. The bathroom doorknob comes off in her hand as she rushes to the toilet, and she had to jab it on and turn it with a delicacy of a safecracker when she feels herself funneling. She corks and sets about scrubbing out the stains, skulks into her bedroom in a towel to put on clean panties and a pad and a kneeless, pocketless pair of jeans. She never knows what's happening with her body any-more. Revenge of the cartwheels.

She stops in the den to say hey and to see how her mother and Tess are doing. "Dog My Cats" rocks feebly on the box, and a cut-throat game of what looks like stud poker is in progress. Nick stud-ies the cards like mug shots, while his stealthy digits creep up on Tess's cache of toothpicks. Palooka is watching over Mrs. Foster's shoulder. Angie imagines six-shooters in their laps. She takes ad-vantage of her mother's absorption to cry in mock horror, "Mom! Why aren't you dressed? What about Thanksgiving?"

"Angela!" Mrs. Foster tips her hand, and Tess devours the in-formation, grimaces at her own hand. "You did give me a turn. We're not leaving now?"

"No, I was just kidding. After supper."

"I thought so." Mrs. Foster breasts her cards and narrows her gaze on Theresa, who's contemplatively rolling her toothpicks. "Even you wouldn't go out dressed like *that*." She laughs at An-gela's exposed knees.

"Guess again," says Angie. It's what she's got.

"But you're in rags!" Nick exclaims. He feels protective and also angry and ashamed, the way he did when Officer Susie's mas-cara was streaking. In tears, in rags! Women!

"Glad rags, baby," Angie smiles: on-the-rags.

"Anyway, what's new?" Tess says. "My mom is a punk. Hey, lis-ten, I couldn't get to work today."

"My job just ended. We can celebrate."

"No, I'm ticked. My ride didn't come through. Is Dad ever gonna see about my car?"

"Of course."

"Before hell freezes over, I hope. Okay, Grandma, could you hit me again?"

Mrs. Foster sweeps up the deck. "It's no fun when you cheat. How would you like to learn to play bridge?"

Angie decamps for the kitchen before they see her as a fourth. The silence defeats her imagination. She dials Chemo Sabe. He's not in, but she leaves a perfectly transparent cryptic message on his answering machine. She's excited that he'll be able to eat Thanksgiving dinner; she hopes he hasn't already left town. She goes so far as to invite him to theirs; he can toke up — where? in the basement! obviously, no smells make it up from there. She's singing, doing laundry, stirring a curry, planning tomorrow's menu, when Joe comes in.

He drops a kiss on her head. "Hey, babe, what's up? They're awfully quiet out there."

"Learning bridge. Or planning to bomb one."

Before he can get a beer and go, Angie's arm slides inside his jacket. She brings her mouth to his and glosses his lips and again and pecks and pries, and then her tongue flows in like molten metal, he can see it, hot and bright — school trip to a steel mill — and he tightens around her slender resilience and sucks and licks and plays with her oral apparatus like a sleepy baby.

They peel apart and blink.

Wow, thinks Angie.

Whew, thinks Joe.

They retire to their corners to cool off. Joe takes a beer. He rolls it over his neck. Angie starts the rice.

Where'd he learn to kiss like that? This was not the usual one-sided smackeroo that makes her think of skulls clacking their bony chops. She wants to search the cave of his mouth with a flashlight and roust the musky bitch, conk her, clear her out, clamber in. Her breasts are crowning, her cunt is clawing. And damn her period!

How'd she get such a rise out of him when he thought, after *lunch*, he'd never get it up again. Mother of God! Where the hell is she coming from? Or should he say who? She's red as a rose. And he's turning into a fucking hydrant. What's next? His cock is nosing up like a prairie dog. What's he going to tell her about Elena coming to Thanksgiving? And when? Now? Bedtime? Jesus! Women!

"By the way" — she has to clear her throat —"the bathroom doorknob is falling off again. And Tess wants to know what you're doing about her car."

Angie and her mother are in the all-night Kroger. Mrs. Foster is very agitated. It's almost nine o'clock — pitch dark. Several unsavory-looking characters are picking up wine, cases of beer — one unshaven duo is pushing at least ten five-pound sacks of corn-meal and sugar — and a bag boy, in his thirties at least, looks mental. Mrs. Foster is not at all sure how convincing she and Angela would look swearing out a complaint. This is the Kroger where the arsenic poisoner worked.

Fortunately, there are plenty of fresh turkeys. Angie hefts a twenty-pounder into the cart and feels a sudden hot gush. The cotton between her legs should be enough to stanch the Mississippi, but she can feel it's not working. The lights are buzzing, turning blue; her womb is seizing. She bangs the bell over the butcher counter, and a female voice responds, "Can I help you?"

"Is there a bathroom I can use?" Angie shouts.

Mrs. Foster wants to sink into the earth. Everyone is staring. Why didn't Angela take care of that before she left the house? A grown woman! She never could control herself.

"No, ma'am, I'm sorry, it's just for employees."

"Where is it?"

"Ma'am? I'm sorry, I *said* —"

Blood is flooding her jeans, running down her legs. Her tubes seem to be squeezing out huge gouts like a pastry bag. "Please —" Suddenly, everything goes dark. Angie finds herself sitting on the floor, pouring blood. Rubber wheels, heels, dodge around her. Above, her mother is chattering and laughing. She prods Angie's hip sharply with the toe of her shoe. A black man in a snap-brim cap and a white coat puts his hand out. The mercy in his eyes makes Angie's water. She slips to a stand. How is she going to clean her sneakers? He leads her through some swinging doors to the toilet. Once inside, she's afraid to unzip in case only the jeans are holding her together. She grabs paper towels, buys as many pads from the vending machine as she has change, dredges the tampons out of her purse, pulls down her pants, and parks on the seat. Blood rushes the tampon she was wearing straight out of her. Massive clots plop. Her pad is soaked through, her panties sopped to tissue, her jeans heavy as if she's been wading in sewage. Eventually, she mops herself and stops herself up. She cleans the best she can. Now, she's actively crying. "State law — employees must —" She scrubs her hands and face raw.

Her mother is waiting outside the swinging doors. "There you are! I was worried! I thought you fell in. Look, I went ahead and got almost everything, except I couldn't find —"

"Ma, I gotta get outta here."

"Honey, the damage is done. It won't take me two minutes."

"Ma, look at me!" Angie is shaking. "I'm leaving."

"Well, look at me!" Mrs. Foster flourishes the cast. "You don't

see me babying myself. Look what I've accomplished! I thought
you'd be pleased. Tie your sweater around your waist."

Angie slumps over the cart. "Mom, I'm outta here."

"Well, all right, I guess I don't really need you — I've got my
checkbook. You can reimburse me when we get home. Just push
the cart up to the checkout for me. You go sit in the car, and I'll
be along directly. I'll get one of the boys to help me carry it out."

"Ma, I'm going home now." But Angie pushes the cart forward.
She's interested to see that no one questions a woman who seems
to have been disemboweled.

Mrs. Foster clicks alongside her, laughing, browsing the
shelves. "Angela! Don't be silly. The worst is over, and as soon as
I find the cranberry sauce — Hold on a second, honey —"

Some twenty minutes later, Mrs. Foster comes out into the
parking lot with the groceries. Of course, Angela hasn't moved the
car. Feeling like a target but determined to execute her appointed
task, Mrs. Foster plunges into the darkness and directs the boy to
their trunk. She knocks on the window for the key, and then Angela starts ranting that the trunk is full; they have to stow the sacks
in the backseat. What does the girl use for brains? She knew
they'd be bringing home all this food. Mrs. Foster even has to pay
the tip.

On the return trip, Mrs. Foster puts aside her aggravation. An-
gela must make an appointment with her doctor immediately.
Until they schedule the surgery, she can wear a paper diaper —
Mrs. Foster thought to pick up a couple of boxes of Serenity.

Angie's sitting on the road atlas, wearing a product called Always, but she feels as though the bleeding has tapered off. "Mom,
I think you're jumping the gun. This is the first time anything like
this has happened to me. Won't it just stop?"

"No!" Mrs. Foster laughs. "Believe you me!" Mrs. Foster goes
on to relate the horrific details of her own hysterectomy and the

bad experiences of her friends and their daughters. Angela says nothing. She smells vile. Mrs. Foster cracks the window, although of course she's already freezing in this rattletrap. She can't help thinking that Angela is rather young to be starting menopause. Could she have miscarried? My God! *Whose child was it?* And then she wonders what exactly is filling the trunk.

Strange, but Tess is feeling pretty up. Joe is so apologetic for having forgotten her car again, he doesn't say word one about Brian or school. Or maybe he's got the guilts over the bimbo. Either way, he's right where she wants him. Nick's heavy into memorizing all these wack dog tunes — there's an amazing number of sickening songs about dogs out there. No point trying to watch TV; they're playing cards. Joe is great at poker from the Navy. He's telling stories about this dog on the base they used to deal into the game, and once they stuck him in a plane in the navigator's seat with a headset to freak the landing-signal guys. Even with Nick being a total pain in the butt, she's having fun. At least she's not thinking about — anything else.

When the phone rings, she jumps.

"Answer it," Joe says. "You know it's for you."

It must be the bimbo. She talks funny — barrio accent? How'd he hook up with her? Maybe a client. On the rebound from some battering husband. Or one of those Cuban jailbirds on her way to doing major time! Tess sees her whole family with picnic baskets singing dog songs on the bus to the state correctional facility. "It's for you." Tess lays it on thick, passing him the receiver. "A woman." Boy, does he look uptight.

"Hello?"

"Joe? Elena. I'm sorry to —"

"Can you hold a second?" He covers the mouthpiece. "Hang this up for me when I get into the kitchen?"

"Pleeeease?" Tess drags it out.

The kitchen is cold. He picks up the phone and shouts, "Okay," and doesn't start talking until he hears the den phone clatter into its cradle. She's not going to back out on Thanksgiving, not after he's already bollixed up telling Angie she's coming? "Elena?"

"Hola, Joe. Can you talk?"

"Yeah, but not long. Angie and her mother went for groceries, and I've got the kids. What's up?"

"I'm sorry to bug you at home, man, but you never told me what time —?"

"In all the commotion" — he smiles, recalling that slow, low commotion, Elena, all snug and silky and slippery and smelling sweet as burnt sugar. Nick is roaring "Hound Dog" again, and Tess barks, "Will you shut up?" and that kiss of Angie's, right here where he's standing, lights up his head. Tilt!

"*Loco*motion," she says. Way loco. She has the reputation among her sisters, her friends, as the cool head, the sensible one, the decision maker. What if somebody had walked in? Perched on the desk — the blotter — with her legs wrapped around his suit coat and his pants around his ankles. That sure would have been the last of her. Blow her back to Brooklyn before you can say Little Latin Lupe-Lu. Acting out the fucking spitfire stereotype in that white-bread office, God knows the sick fantasies she'd be giving life to — the bloodless undertaker who runs the place will be trying his luck next. If he just got a load of the bites on her neck — walking around with her shoulders up to her ears like some hulking football player the rest of the day.

And this Thanksgiving business. She's realized with gut-certainty that she was just twisting Joe, seeing how much she could get away with, if he really cares about her, if he'd let her sit beside his lawfully wedded blondie, under the pretense of being *civilized.* And she's supposed to be the professional, see through these selfish little mind games. Loco! Now maybe she's got him crazy for her; he wants to be humiliated, wants to lose everything — she'll be saddled with a doting, disbarred, hundred-seventy-pound sheepdog. She called to give him the chance to back out of it.

"Come at two," he says, and, picturing her delectable cinnamon face beside the fine china plate of his wife, he feels his insides roll over. "It'll be nice to have you."

"Okay. Hasta mañana, chico." Oh brother! She sits for a long time, biting a hangnail. Maybe she just won't show up.

Joe returns to the den. Tess and Nick smolder at the TV out of striking distance from each other and don't look up. Cards and toothpicks all over the room. "Who wants popcorn?" he yawps, when the phone rings. It's his mother. He blushes to the ears. They just called to say happy Thanksgiving. She's not feeling too good, her legs as usual, and Papa's gallbladder has been acting up, but the whole family — except their only begotten son and his wife and kids, that is — is coming, even the Chicago cousins, they're flying in — of course, they got the money — but so she guesses she'll have to hold up long enough to put the food on the table. Joe is pointing at the phone and mouthing, "my mother," and waving the kids over, and they tick-tock "no way" as firmly as time bombs.

"So how about you? What you doing for the holiday?"

"We've got a full house, too," Joe says and wishes he'd said they'd be fasting, eating slivered glass. Mrs. DiPietro sees Mrs. Foster slyly taking over, especially when she hears she's actually moved in on account of her ha-ha broken wrist — God knows, Celestina don't get no break, and every part of her body crippled with arthritis. "That's nice for Angie. So who are these friends?" Putting strangers above blood. "So where are the kids?" since

Theresa's the one always picks up the phone, and she wonders if Angie and her mother have finally come up with some scheme, beyond undermining Holy Mother Church, to turn the children against them. At the grocery? At this time of night? Are they buying prepared, from the deli? That's gonna be *some* Thanksgiving.

"And Mutt died," Joe offers in place of his heartless spawn. When he gets off this phone, they're going straight to bed, both of them, and they'll be lucky if he doesn't slap them silly. "We're gonna bury him tomorrow."

"Oh, that's a shame, but we all gotta go sometime. Put it this way, he's outta his misery. Well, okay, I'll let you go. Don't worry about us. We wish you was gonna be here, we all gonna miss you, you papa especially, but we understand. See you Christmas. Have a list what you want next week."

Chapter 7

Thanks

Angie's up at five. Under cover of darkness and the big old locust tree that punctuates the drive, she transfers the Ziplocs from the bag of compost to a plastic garbage sack, which she twist-ties and returns to the trunk. You can still whiff the pot's nasty resin in the car, even over the cleanser she sprayed on the bloodstains, but nobody's going anyplace on Thanksgiving — noplace to go. The other ounce stays in the glove compartment in case Chemo Sabe wants to help himself before dinner. He left a message last night — he's coming. She kicks in her last rolling papers, her disposable lighter, and the bobby pin she used as a roach clip as if she's retiring from active duty. Alas, she cooks so much better mellow! Well, unless you actually want to *eat*. Now she's got to go make pumpkin pie and figure out how to bake all these vegetables with a twenty-pound gobbler hogging the oven. She humps the compost to the back porch. Her bleeding has slowed to heavy. Another golden day.

Everyone rises early except Tess. Joe fixes eggs, hash browns, toast, imitating his father's Etnean irascibility: "Who the hell wants this lousy egg? You gonna eat it, I hafta shove it down you troat!" Angie, trailing long silvery streamers of melody, bumps into him, kisses his stubble, absently runs a free hand up his neck, his waist, his buttocks, while she whips and melts and pours, and he gets so tense he starts to squeak. Nick watches them as if they're on TV.

Mrs. Foster thinks Angela is on drugs. She wonders if Joe knows what really happened at the Kroger or what's in the trunk. She's pretty sure he's not part of the cult, yet, but look at Angela working on him! — it's disgraceful! — and although she feels she has to remind him fatty breakfasts like this will kill you, she gorges — who knows when she'll see food she can trust again? The turkey stands headless in a pot, its wings lifted in surrender. "I'll do the dusting as soon as I finish these dishes," she laughs when Joe sits down to eat. He should have thought about what the rest of the house looks like before he created more chaos in here. He knows perfectly well she can't clean and do dishes. What's wrong with cold cereal? "We'll all be so full we won't be able to eat one bite of turkey!"

"Turkey's not for hours," Angie says. "How's the wrist this morning, Ma?"

"Fine! Isn't it amazing? These doctors today are miracle workers!" It feels like a thorny bracelet. "And anything I can't do, Nicholas will help me, won't you, darling?"

"I gotta dig Mutt's grave." Nick's not getting suckered into women's work. Let Tess.

"When'd you take your last pain pill?" Angie asks, looking for a toothpick to test the pie. It smells done.

"When I woke up." Mrs. Foster glances at the clock. "Seven-thirty."

"See, that's it." Angie pulls out the pie. Perfect, if you like a lot of cleavage. The brownies are taking longer — must be the lumps. She wonders if Joe's little honey can cook or if he just eats her. "The pills make you think you're ready to scrub floors, but you've got to heal. Maybe later you can help me set the table —"

"Smells good, Ange," Joe says. She bomps her ass against him, switching to the refrigerator.

"I know! I'll iron the tablecloth —"

"Right." Before Angie gives her disabled mother a hot iron, they'll arm-wrestle. "You go make yourself comfortable. Let us handle it. We've got lots of time before anybody's coming, and, besides, these people are our friends, Mom. They'll forgive us a little dust, a few wrinkles." Like Miss Havisham. And she threw away the ghost costume only last week.

"I'll take care of it, Agnes, don't you worry." Joe gulps the last of his coffee. He pictures his mother-in-law with an iron as something out of the Spanish Inquisition. Do they have an iron? Do they have a tablecloth? "Nico — go put on your digging clothes. Your oldest, grubbiest shoes."

"I got boots!" Nick burns rubber. Finally! Mutt's going in the ground! He's gotta call Shane.

"Well, then, I'll supervise." Mrs. Foster laughs. A little dust! Like Oklahoma! "Are you sure you shouldn't take care of the housework first, Joe? This burying the dog —"

Angie tells Joe about the compost on the back porch as she chops ingredients for the stuffing. "So if you could make the hole extra big and mix in —"

This Mason must be the last of the true romantics, Joe thinks; he bags his shit for his women.

"— I mean, is it really healthy for Nicholas to —"

Joe clears the table. He can't get past Angie without her petting him. Her mother pecking at the thin shell of him.

"— and won't your guests think it's a bit, well, strange —"

He turns the water on full and belts out "Vesti la giubba," making up most of the lyrics. He and Nick burst out the door with equal zeal. They may dig to China. The Great Escape — *into* prison — where there's nothing but men.

"Maybe we better wake up Theresa." Mrs. Foster laughs.

Angie lets her mother go wake Tess, although it means her climbing the stairs in the long nightgown and those floppy glamour-girl mules — at least the underfoot cat is out — and risks her stumbling over some new dread secret — a boy in the bed, empties rolling over the floor, reefer madness. She braces herself for the screaming tumble of retribution, but soon she's singing "Old Blue" again. "Old Blue died and he died so hard, shook the ground in my backyard —" What a cesspool of lyrics her brain is!

"Up you snakes and shake your rattles," Mrs. Foster calls, swooping off Theresa's covers. My God! The girl's slept in her clothes! Where has she been? What's she's been up to? The old woman yanks up the blinds. "It's daylight in the swamps!"

Tess creaks open an eye. Dracula turning to a corpse in the shrill sunlight, now singing "Lazy Bones." Snooping into her stuff, her shoes? Looking in the closet. If Tess weren't so tired, she'd do them both a favor: lock the old bat in.

Brian called last night, or more like two in the morning. It was weird. She picked up almost before it rang — she knew it was him. Her heart was pounding. But he was so nice!

"Don't hang up on me, Tess, please? Listen, I don't know how to say this, but I'm really sorry — about your car and everything. Right now I don't know what's gonna happen to me, and I just wanna get straight with you before —"

"What's happening with you?" Her voice was clogged like the glass pipe in the Drāno commercial.

"You wouldn't believe it. You know I got busted —"

"It's all over school," she said cautiously.

"Well, so everybody's on my case now full-time. Cops, lawyers, shrinks — I gotta listen to more bullshit than you knew existed. My mom —"

"She got me in trouble with Albert. I thought you —"

"No! I would never do that, Tess, I swear. I knew you'd think that. No, I been denying it every which way. It's on account of the fight in Spanish. Albert said something about it, and she jumped on it. I didn't tell her about your car — she was already threatening to call your parents — I had to make up this whole — No, see, that's why I'm calling. I never wanted to hurt you. You've got to know that."

Tess felt like shit, but she was trembling, too. This was like a dream conversation, the kind of daydream you have to pop before you get sloppy and can't function.

"You're like the only thing that's — I know you won't believe this, and if you do, like, so what? — but I love you. I think I've always loved you, but you're so — honest. Intense. I mean, it's hard to be with you. I can't con you like everybody else, and now I'm so tangled up in all the lies I've told, and all the lies everybody else is telling — I just want to talk to the one person who's always been straight with me and say that I am really and truly sorry."

Tess's saliva had turned to Elmer's glue. "What's gonna happen?"

"I don't know and I don't care."

"Oh, Brian, no —"

"No, no, this is good, see. That's what I'm trying to tell you — this is gonna work out. I'm gonna turn myself around. All the things you been telling me. I'm paying attention now, I'm gonna do something about it. It'd be nice if I could see you when I get my shit together, but that doesn't really matter. At least I'll have some self-respect. Thanks to you. That's all I wanted to say. I'm gonna make it, thanks to you."

Yeah, hooray for her. What now? Lower the boom? Uh, Brian? No thanks to me. Her heart had shriveled like a prune, but a smile was twitching, a cheap score.

"Well, look, I'm sorry I bothered you," he said. "I didn't want you to worry about me."

"Listen, Bri — are you allowed out?"

"Shit, Tess, now?"

"Yeah, right." She mimicked the rednecks who yell down from their monster trucks into her car window, "'Meet you at the Texaco.'" It made him laugh. In her normal tone, "No, I mean like ever. I mean like can you come over — hey, can you come to our Thanksgiving?"

"Maybe. For a little while. I think so. Yeah. Wow!"

"So come over." She couldn't help it, she was laughing. "Whenever. We'll be here all day — we gotta bury the dog — but dinner will be like about two."

"What about your parents?"

"Just tell them — tell them your name is Tony!"

"Let's go, Theresa!" Mrs. Foster whacks Tess's bottom. "Up and at 'em! Get a move on! It's Thanksgiving!"

Granny's really going to flog her until she's out of bed. How come grown-ups think it's okay to hit you, when if you ever even thought about hitting them, even in fun, they'd go completely ballistic? Like you're their dog — obedience training. Today they're burying the dog. And Brian's coming. Tess sits up. "What time is it?"

"Time to get going! Remember? You've got to do my hair!"

Give me a match, thinks Tess.

"And since when do we sleep in our clothes, young lady?"

Angie's studying her wardrobe. She seems to have nothing to wear. She's showered. The turkey's dressed, basted, browning; the other dishes are prepared and waiting in the wings for the doorbell. She's satisfied there's plenty, and it's going to be tasty. The table's set; the cloth, it turns out, a Christmas gift from Joe's parents, is permanent press. Joe, Nick, and Shane have dug a vast grave in hard clay webbed with ancient roots they cleared with the ax. It looks like the foundation of Fort Knox. They unearthed boulders, marbles, beetles, bricks, pieces of tile and asphalt shingles, a garter snake that got Palooka going, a tennis ball, and "two black worms with yellow stripes and legs" that almost came to dinner. Soaked with sweat, Joe worked with the boys on their Elvis impersonations, whirling their shirts over their heads, although he had them singing "Chain Gang," the rock 'n' roll ignoramus. Angie's thinking of her backyard rather tenderly as Graceland. Now Nick and Shane are leaping in and scrambling out of the trench, enacting some fantasy — GI Joe? postnuclear mole-mutants? born-again giant reptiles? — that ought to please Shane's mom no end when Angie shoos the little dirtball off in about half an hour. Joe is bullying the vacuum through the house. Mrs. Foster won't be satisfied, but what else is new? She and Tess spent some quality time in the bathroom, then the bedroom, and, at present, she's watching the last of the Macy's parade in her church suit and those god-awful high heels with her hair stiff and symmetrical and her face on. She laughs and oohs and ahs and cries out, "Theresa! I want you to see this! Nicholas! Angela! You have to see this! Joe! Jo-oh! Oh, Joe —"

Angie is not going to meet Joe's mistress in the funeral getup. She has a couple of dowdy numbers she wore to deflect attention at PTA functions and a spangled purple shimmy dress that made her reputation as Valvoline in the Amphetamines, but pity is not the reaction she's shooting for. She associates her jeans too closely with the recent red tides. She's taking a hard look at the curtains when Tess comes in.

"Oops!" Tess quickly averts her eyes. Her mother's pale skin and her tatty, "sexy" underwear — for some reason, Tess feels icky-sad in addition to embarrassed. Maybe from dealing with Grandma — God, the way the old lady's skin pleats over her bones. She spirals from the door. "Sorry."

"Tess! Just the person I need! Help me figure out something to wear."

Tess can't pretend she didn't hear. She slouches back. "I had to set and blow-dry Grandma" — she tugs her own mop straight up and shows her teeth — "and then I helped her get dressed. She sent me in here to fetch a hankie. Like what's wrong with her *legs?*" While she's thinking about it, Tess takes the handkerchief out of Grandma's overnight bag, which sits open on the dresser. More sad underwear — Grandma wears little girls' cotton pants with elastic legs.

From the smooth way she roots through Mrs. Foster's things, Angie wonders if the hankie isn't merely a pretext to steal and not necessarily from Mrs. Foster. What?

Tess catches herself in the mirror over the dresser. "And suddenly you guys want my help with your look — you know? A couple days ago — Tess the Mess, right?" She thinks about Brian, that night at Cath and Jen's, saying he liked how she looked, and she feels fizzy. She's putting the nose ring back in regardless.

Angie wants to say something about the runaway, but it runs away with her: I missed you when you were gone, I was nearly out of my mind, don't ever do that to me again, why did you do that, what were you thinking of, how *could* you? Avalanche! Flash flood!

Tess checks her mother's gooey eyes glomming on her in the glass. "You made me feel ugly —"

"I'm sorry," Angie says. "It's just —"

"Joe especially." Tess chokes. It's so crazy to be talking to her half-naked mother in the mirror, like talking to Barbie. Tess used to whip her Barbie around naked, by the hair.

"It's just that we think you're beautiful as you are. When you bore holes in your face and —"

"Yeah, yeah. I'm beautiful *the way you made me*, am I right?"

"Honey, I don't think we had a thing to do with it." Angie smiles ruefully. "You've always been you. I mean, day one. Doctor told me you shot out like a line drive to left field; wished he was Willie Mays. They gave you to me, wrapped in blankets and diapers and a shirt and whatnot, and I wanted a better look, so when we got alone, I stripped you, and you were, you know, gorgeous, perfect, but so then I worried you'd get cold, and I tried to dress you again? And, geez, the pins? — cloth diapers with these giant safety pins — I was afraid I was gonna lance you. And you looked up at me, like, What'd I do to deserve this?" Tess scrimps a smile in the mirror. Angie imagines herself as a siren wooing wax-stopped ears. "I don't think you have an inkling how precious you are to us." She guards her mouth with her hand.

Tess knows her mother is thinking about Vince. She feels a little bitter and a little sympathetic at the same time, like gulping hot chocolate that burns sweet in the hollow of her chest. She turns. "So what's wrong with jeans?"

Angie looks in the closet. "I'm sick of jeans." She looks back and sees herself over Tess's shoulder in the mirror. "These people coming."

Oh, sure — Joe's bimbo. And her boyfriend, what's his name? Malcolm. Ex-. Tess doesn't want any exes scarring her future. Anyhow, she's not supposed to know all this. She doesn't *want* to know all this. She wants to worry about her own sex life! But she notices the brownish bruises under her mother's eyes. Her skin seems — thin. Tess walks over to stand beside her and survey the closet. "All your stuff is old."

"You said it," Angie agrees.

"One of these days, you've got to go shopping." Tess strums the hangers. She pulls out an old dark green corduroy suit of Joe's. "Wear this. With a black T-shirt."

"You're a genius." Angie opens the buttons of the jacket and skims the cool green satin lining. She grips the pants. "I don't have a black T-shirt."

Tess laughs at the desperate way she says it. "Borrow mine. Can I try on the purple?" The shimmy dress. Angie has an issue about borrowing. She doesn't trust Tess to give things back. She's got her watch wound too tight.

"You can have it." Angie's pulling on Joe's pants. "Just be good to it. We've been through a lot."

Whoosh! Tess returns with the T-shirt. Angie is maneuvering to get a look at her legs in the dresser mirror. "You know," Tess remarks, "this house needs a full-length mirror."

"Yeah, well, meanwhile, how do my feet look?"

"What kind of shoes you got?"

Assembled, Angie looks great to herself, combination Beatle, Merry Man. She puts on mascara, blush, lip gloss, and Tess French-braids her hair. Tess also looks great in the purple shimmy dress. It's too long on her, too big. With Angie's matching satin pumps — killer. Tess is really going to wear it — Grandma will have a *purple* cow — if she can ever get into the shower. Right now, Joe is repairing the doorknob.

Angie and Tess stand far back so they can both see as much of themselves as possible in the dresser mirror. Angie puts her arm around Tess's waist, and they smile as though for a photo, and their insides cream like hot mashed potatoes.

Doris arrives while Nick and Joe are in the shower, rocking the rafters with their "wall-of-sound" car medley. She takes the steps in installments — thanking her stars she lives in a modern condo with an elevator and a professional maintenance staff — and knocks.

Mrs. Foster has been so wrapped up in the TV — actually, she doesn't have a clue what's on. She's been asleep. She never sleeps in the daytime. They must have drugged her at breakfast, which means Joe is in this up to his neck. She has no ally. She's alone.

She's next!

Nick and Joe crescendo, "Go Granny, go Granny, go Granny, go!"

Doris knocks again. Angela toddles from the kitchen. Mrs. Foster tries to collect her thoughts. What time is it? Where is the baseball bat?

"Hey, Doris!" Angie opens the door on her mother's friend. She's dressed up in a black pantsuit, a bright red blouse, and a lot of gold chain and carrying a cake box. She must be invited! Clean cups, clean cups! "Come on in."

"Ooh-whooh ooh!" from the bathroom.

"Ooh, I hope I'm not too early. Don't you look good, Angie!" Doris busses her cheek, passing her the cake and coming inside. "Work must agree with you. Your mom said you was working."

"Yeah — well, actually, I'm not sure — it was the least work I've ever done. Let me put this cake down before I drop it. Mom's in here. I'll be back with nibblies. What can I get you to drink?"

"Round round get around. . . ."

"A Bloody Mary, if you've got it. Don't bother with the celery —"

Mrs. Foster is sitting as straight as she can on the soggy sofa, smiling through tears like Loretta Young. Doris bends to embrace her, and she hangs on, which surprises the hell out of Doris — she never thought Agnes liked her all that much, especially when they've been partnered at bridge. She does seem very frail. Some of them don't come back from an episode like the wrist. Agnes gestures for Doris to sit close. "Be careful what you eat!" she hisses.

Angela comes in with a tray of drinks and some green muck and a runny tomato thing and those salty Mexican chips, also cheese and crackers, napkins. Of course, she doesn't serve them with the slightest flair, although she certainly has seen how it's done: an assortment of cute-shaped crackers topped with cheese spread and perked up with pimento or an olive or a seedless grape, displayed on a chilled glass plate. Here it's dip in the trough or saw your own and slap it on a cracker everybody else has handled, if not chewed, but there's at least a slim hope she hasn't doctored the cheese. Mrs. Foster flashes her eyes at Doris to warn her. That drink could contain real blood!

"Be careful what you eat," Angie warns them. "The guacamole and the salsa are hot."

"Oh, I love the hot food, the salsa!" Doris laughs. "With this black hair, I always thought I had a little Spanish blood in me — a touch of the tarbrush."

Elena knocks. Joe and Nick are coming out of the shower in towels. Nick beats Angie to the door, dripping, towel slipping.

"Hola!" says the woman behind it, holding a shopping bag.

Angie thinks this is the most beautiful woman she has ever seen. And in shrimp-pink mohair! She literally falls breathless against the ropes. Nick doesn't know her, and the way she's smiling at him, he feels like a total dork in the towel. He runs into the den, squealing his tires, runs out and upstairs to his room. "A streaker!" shouts Doris, swatting at his pinkened buns.

"Hey! I'm Angie. You're Joe's friend." Angie sees herself as gallant. She puts out her hand.

Elena takes it. She loves the spare, stunned look of this woman — the bone structure. Naturally, she's thin. Almost transparent. And what is she wearing? It really is a man's suit. Sweet Jesus, is she gay? Wouldn't that be a load off? "Elena Soto." Elena pronounces it with the Spanish inflection. She offers Angie the shopping bag. "Pasteles. Meat in banana leaves. My mother sent them. And I made some mushrooms, for before the meal. I hope you like them. And some wine." Why is she talking like she's fresh off the boat? In a moment, la Señora is gonna tie an apron on her.

"Great, thanks! Please, come in. We're in here."

"But you're right," Doris is saying at the same time as her face breaks in greeting, "the Latin food is very fattening. You have to be so careful."

"Hey, guys, this is Elena Soto." Angie says it carefully. "Elena, this is my mother, Agnes —"

"Mrs. Richard Foster." Mrs. Foster laughs. What now? Voodoo? What do the neighbors think when they see this procession of colored in and out? Maid service? That's a laugh.

Angie's eyes flicker at Elena. "— and her friend Doris —"

"Hi! Nice to meet you!"

Angie sets a casserole from the shopping bag down on the coffee table and lifts the lid on some good-looking, good-smelling mushrooms. Maybe they're poisonous. She pops one. "Delicious." She sighs. She's so glad she decided to mock up Mex for her whore-derves, since the woman probably is Mexican — are there black Mexicans? She motions Elena to sit. "What can I get you to drink?"

Elena ramrods at the edge of the recliner. She'll be damned if she's losing contact with the floor. "Some wine would be nice."

"Coming right up." Angie lumbers to the kitchen. She imagines heading straight out the back door with the wine, pitching into the hole.

Mrs. Foster tries to draw Doris's attention to the foul black fungus in that dish. If they don't kill you, they probably give you hallucinations.

"So!" says Doris, clapping her knees, radiating good will at the chubby little wetback, "where are you from?"

There's another knock. Angie's screwing the cork out of the bottle. She's ready to bite through its neck. Joe comes out of the bedroom, tosses the towel over the shower curtain, combs his hair, and goes to the door. It's Angie's lover. He's carrying a bottle of wine and a burlap-balled tree. He's dressed exactly like Joe, in chinos and a sweater. His sweater is nicer. "Hey, man, how you doing?" they say, almost together, pumping hands as though there's been a dry spell. "Come on in! Welcome!" Joe takes the wine from Mason, looks at the tree.

"It's a dogwood," Mason says. "It's for —"

"Yeah, I know, I think that's the next order of business. Hey, thanks" — Joe shakes the tree — "that's really nice." It's so fucking nice he could shit. The wine bottle, like a club. What if he brains Mason with it? What jury would blame him? "You wanna take it back to the yard?" Oh, that sounded good. Should have said, "boy," and directed him to the colored entrance. Very evolved. He quickly adds, "Angie's back in the kitchen," to try to explain himself.

"Yeah, sure." Yassuh, boss. What in the fuck is he doing here? Will Angie have the faintest notion what he's trying to say to her? Any way you want it, babe. A loser's proposition. Lose the tree and jet.

But Joe's got the wine; he leads the way. Turning his head toward the den, he sees Elena — she seems to be wearing peach frosting — being interrogated by his mother-in-law and some other old hag. "Hey, Elena! How'd you sneak in here?"

Elena smiles grimly. Joe looks like such an asshole, shooting her the secret smooch in front of the duennas. Lucky she didn't scoot back so he could shoot straight up her dress. And who's the stud behind him? Brings his own shade. Or is it camouflage? He better not be her date. Mother of God, it's a Mod Squad reunion! Joe's the ugly white guy, Angie's the bleeding-heart female, and this is the strong, silent type the show's producers called Linc, as in the Great Emancipator, and they called Link, as in Missing.

Angie slopes in with a glass and kisses his hairy cheek, which registers seismically on the two biddies. She draws back and admires the tree. "A dogwood" — clasping his bicep. "You *are* good." Oh wow! This is her boyfriend! She's nuts about him! Is that why Joe —?

"Who's your tailor?" Joe asks Angie, and she shows him every tooth in her head.

Mason can't believe Angie's touching him and talking to him like this with her husband, her mother, right there. Is she stoned? He feels as though not only his fly is open but his dick is sticking out of it, dribbling. And who's the sister? Tell him this ain't some kind of fool fix-up. He can pick his own women, thanks, anytime he wants — yesterday. "Birnam wood come to Dunsinane," he jokes, just to tip everybody to what they're dealing with; yeah, right, fucking house nigger. Joe snickers. Angie wonders if she needs to change her tampon.

That was a line from *Macbeth* — a play about murdering anyone who gets in the way — a benevolent old king, two tiny children, and witches. What are they going to do with that tree? Build a bonfire? Is it — a stake? Mrs. Foster tries to think of some way to communicate with Doris in code: That's him, the ringleader. The Devil Incarnate! Doris will never get it on her own. Plus, she's getting soused. Oh, they're clever!

Angie performs the introductions, handing Elena a glass of wine. She crouches at the stereo to find some mutually agreeable music to cover the awkwardness and, in the meantime, presses the play button — "How Come My Dog Don't Bark When You Come Around?" Mason and Joe travel on through the kitchen to the yard, where Mason sets the tree near the grave. "Some hole," he comments and then wants to tear out his tongue.

"Nick and his friend were heavy into it — that kid energy is awesome. Nice for me to get the old body moving, but I'll pay for it later —" Christ! He doesn't have to keep digging the hole. All he has to do is fall in it.

"Desk job, huh?" Mason doesn't know how much he's supposed to know about Joe. And for pure cussedness, it's hard to follow up that first remark. He contemplates the trench. "Feel like I'm supposed to jump in it. Cept I miss the mosquitoes, the red ants —"

"You were in country." Joe meets Mason's eyes.

In country — right. Mason expects Joe was deferred. Must've seen the movie. "You?"

"'Sixty-five," says Joe.

"'Sixty-nine, seventy."

"Shit!" A grunt, Joe figures. Either a stone killer or one of the walking wounded. He wants to be clear about his own candy-ass tour. "I enlisted, straight out of high school — Navy. Idea was, do my patriotic duty, get it on the résumé in case I ever wanted to go into politics — ambitious son of a bitch back then — stay out of it as much as possible." His eyes narrow. "Not near enough."

"I hear you. Hey, I was Navy, too. My daddy, he served on the *Mason*, dig?" He thumbs his clavicle. "Atlantic destroyer escort — all-black crew. These guys — braver than you can believe — naturally, they got the shaft. Convoy commander recommended every man onboard receive a commendation — never happened. I watched a proud man's resentment grow — you know? And it was my *name*, you hear what I'm sayin'."

"Wow," says Joe, imagining life as a walking reminder of your father's disappointment. "Heavy name."

"After while" — Mason smiles — "came to call me Junior." Joe nods. "So I'd done two years of college — I had ambitions, too — but the contradictions — you know what I'm talkin' about — so I dropped out to do some work in the community, and, bang! got my notice. Well, hell, man, I booked to that Navy recruiter be-

COURTING DISASTER ♦ 230

cause I did not want to spend no time in no jungle. Wound up a river rat."

"Jesus."

"Yeah. Want to hear something funny? I volunteered. I was bored."

Both men see the flat, cleared, and defoliated riverbanks and canals of South Vietnam as though their eyelids had been burned away. Burned bodies. Stench. Swarms of starving children, some wired to explode. Flak jackets in the heat. Remembering to brush off the mosquitoes because the sound of a slap could get some-body killed. And then the rain. Joe knows Mason would have spent weeks in the mud, in continual rain.

"Won't all that bad." Mason laughs shortly. "I pulled some duty at Cam Ranh Bay, man. That was paradise." Under the circum-stances, he stops himself saying anything about the women. He remembers some of the brothers used the boats to smuggle these five village girls into the barracks, collected payment off the white boys, who stood in line, Monday, Wednesday, Friday. Only seri-ous fighting then was with the white boys. One time they burned a cross. Outnumbered, twelve to one. Had to form a gang, for pro-tection. Paradise.

"Man, I was nineteen, I was a virgin," Joe says, thinking of Elena, "and every female over the age of ten and all her friends and relations knew my name. It was hell. Let's go in." When he and Mason are parallel, stepping up on the porch, Joe puts his hand on Mason's shoulder. Mason slaps his back. Each sees the other's eyes jellied.

Angie puts on Patsy Cline — everybody loves Patsy Cline — before she actively starts to bay. Elena has been justifying where she's from and what she does for a living, which would seem to Mrs. Foster mutually exclusive until she thinks of those women who read your palm and plunder your savings. And weren't psychologists mixed up in that disgusting Little Rascals day care scandal? And the ones who have sex with their patients and the ones who are always letting dangerous criminals walk our streets. Doris admires Elena's spunk, pulling herself up by her bootstraps, not like most of them who only want a free ride. Of course, Elena's got no kids to support like Doris did. Nick zips into the room, takes a handful of chips, sits on his mother's lap as if she's his throne, and contemplates Elena, munching.

"Don't you spoil your appetite, Master Nicholas!" Mrs. Foster laughs. God, she hates that hillbilly whining! How anybody who grew up with the sophisticated sounds of Lawrence Welk and Guy Lombardo —

"But, so, how'd you wind up here?" Angie asks Elena. Out of all the gin joints —

"Oh, it was a job, you know. I mean, a lot of the people I went to grad school with are driving taxis, working in restaurants, going back to school. It was a career move, with potential, perks." And she scored it over all the statistics working against her. How could she *not* take it? What would *that* say? "I really enjoy my work." The peevish, pimply faces of her clients appear before her, saying things like, What do *you* know about it? You can't make me. God, she hates this plodding, maudlin country music. They play it at her dentist's. If she sits back, maybe somebody gives her novocaine.

Enter Tess. The shimmy dress is roomy on her; she looks like a Vegas child bride. Her dark hair bubbles up, her skin gleams like bond paper; her nose ring and a number of earrings are back. The tattooed wings on her ankles spire above the purple satin high heels. She sits on the floor at the coffee table to form the last corner of a conversational box. When she sits, the chest of her dress shifts after her, like a double exposure.

Mrs. Foster is aghast. She looks like a harem girl! A harlot! An offering!

Angie is misty, gazing at her beautiful daughter in the beloved shimmy dress. Maybe playing "I Fall to Pieces" wasn't such a good idea. She turns it off. Nick instantly restores the dog tape and contorts to smile egregiously at her. "Bad, Bad Leroy Brown —" Was Poe like this as a child? She rocks him into a hug. "Elena, this is my daughter, Tess. Tess, Dr. Soto."

"Please call me Elena." Elena thinks Tess looks exactly like Joe: trouble.

"How do you do?" Her perfume — gag! How obvious can you get? Tess almost can't stand to look at her. And the way *she's* staring: "Ha ha! a specimen!"

"And you know Mrs. McIlleny?"

Tess scrinches at Angie. Adults are so totally bogus. "Hey, Doris. What's up?"

"Where did you get that dress?" Mrs. Foster gasps.

"It's mine," Angie intercedes. "Mom, have you had anything to eat or drink yet? Can I get you something?"

"Excuse me" — Tess interrupts Angie — "but it's mine. You gave it to me, remember? She didn't tell me to wear it, either, Grandma. I thought of that all by myself."

"I've never seen anything like it! And at Thanksgiving!"

"It looks real cute," Doris insists. She doesn't want to be confused with an old prude like Agnes. "You got a nice set of gams on you, honey."

"I think it's pretty tacky for a funeral." Nick luxuriates against Angie like a towel on a chaise lounge. He and Tess roll thick, creamy eyes over Elena.

"How do we know you?" Tess asks intently.

Mrs. Foster tunes in. Doris holds a chip shaped like an ear at her mouth.

Elena thinks, This one has lived before.

"Elena is a psychologist, sweetie. But wouldn't you enjoy your work anywhere?" Angie pursues. She feels suave and merciful. "I can't imagine anyone who doesn't have a family or a limited income wanting to live here. After New York and Puerto Rico, it must be so dull."

Elena interprets this to mean get out of town by sundown. And get your own family. Before she has to come up with something she likes about her empty womb or living single, black, and Latina in the tobacco capital of the Confederacy, Joe and Mason charge in from the back of the house, laughing heartily. At once, she recalls big family parties, the men adding that solid bass of laughter and ebullience to the finicking treble of the women, and the trampling kids, like castanets, claves, or the little frogs — coquis. She should be home right now, making that scene, but when she got caught up with Joe, she only remembered the fighting, the crying, the come-ons, the endless dirty dishes, and the endless questions about when she's going to settle down.

Nick is on his feet as soon as he hears his father's voice, watching the doorframe. Angie hears one of the men say, "You got that right!" and imagines they've been talking about her. Tess thinks about tripping Joe so that the wine he's carrying splashes all over the bimbo and he breaks his nose on the coffee table.

"Ladies, ladies, let me fill your glasses!" Joe pours wine into Elena's glass. Every time he looks at her he thinks, People *do* this! They *do!* "Agnes? No? Uh —" Who the hell is this other woman? "You're still working on that —" What is it, a transfusion? "Angie — where's your drink, woman? And, by the way, your turkey smells done, and the yams are sticking. Mason, let me get you a chair — or — Hey, is the gang all here? Maybe we should do the deed? What do you say? Put Mutt to rest, daughter? son?" His eyes roulette the walls to avoid meeting Elena's grump, Tess's glare, Angie's glitter, Mrs. Foster's grit. What is Tess wearing?

She's the ghost of Valvoline! And Angie in his old cord Beatle suit — *Help!* He seduced her in that suit — well, more or less. His women have gone retro. He needs to watch his drinking.

"I got a friend coming," Tess says, "but I don't think he'll be majorly bummed if he misses Mutt's funeral."

"Yeah, same here," says Angie, and Tess, Joe, Mason, and Mrs. Foster all think, Another one? "Guy I know from the Sore, I mean the Open Door — Justis. Give me a minute to the take the turkey out, and —" Does she have to put another leaf in the table? Where will she find more chairs? Sharp knives?

Mrs. Foster is sure Justice will be swift. She's sorry she dragged poor Doris into this. She takes a swig of whatever Joe was dispensing. She might as well take one of her pain pills, too — why not two? Make it easier.

"You work at the Open Door?" Elena asks Angie.

"Yeah. You know it?"

"Yeah. They contacted me about working with the Hispanic community, and then they also want me to do a training session for the hot-line volunteers. There's been some problems with —"

"I gotta get the cross!" Nick's wheels are spinning. "Wait'll you see it, Mason, it's awesome! Hey, look! Somebody's coming up the stairs! Tess's *boy*-friend!" he nasalizes and wags his ass.

It's Brian. Tess is already on the porch greeting him, while Angie and Nick race to the kitchen to take up their respective crosses, and Joe and Mason troop to the basement to bring up the deceased. Tess looks wild, she looks beautiful — she shifts inside her shimmering dress like a fish through reeds. Brian holds her cool, slender arms in his hands and stokes on this vision: her face floating over a place he belongs.

Tess doesn't know what she's thinking, except that he makes her feel — lovable. She throws herself on the big twerp, destroyer of her car and her future, and scumbles against his expensive Irish-sweater, English Leather, deodorized chest, and she has never felt so fine or so furious in her life so far.

Doris helps Agnes stand. The little Puerto Rican girl looks lost. How much of all this is she taking in? With her arm around Agnes, Doris cups Elena's elbow. "This is the true spirit of the original Thanksgiving," she says loudly and slowly. "Sharing our wealth."

Elena draws back. Is that a crack? What, the family jewels? Or welfare? These old girls don't miss a trick. "Sharing *our* wealth is right," she snaps. We share, and you teach us to say thank you. Fucking imperialist lapdogs!

Mrs. Foster laughs. It won't be long now before they're sharing what little wealth she has left. She envisions the pagan ceremony, the sacrificial knife, she and Doris cast in the grave with the dog. If there is a dog. Now she wishes she were back in her nightie.

They march toward the kitchen. Doris cries gaily, "The three —"

"I have to stop in the little girls' room," Mrs. Foster says.

"Caballeros," Elena finishes. She wears the droopy countenance of the Disney parrot. She turns her head and sees her most recent client, pobrecito chico rico, stooped over Gidget Goes for the Jugular. Great. This town really ain't big enough.

Nick skitters through the kitchen as Angie is lifting out the turkey. "Watch out!" With the cross of Jesus going on before, he whisks through the back door and lets it crash into Joe, towing the front end of the cooler inside the slithery garbage bags. "Watch it, Nick!" The cat runs in and runs out. "Ah-oooh," howls Nick. Shane answers from his own backyard, and several neighborhood dogs begin yowling.

Brian's eyes are open because he's dizzy with lust. "Dr. Soto."

He closes and opens them again. She's still there — the fucking psychotherabitch his lawyer is making him see. His prick slumps. Has she been questioning Tess? Is she, like, haunting him?

Tess faces Elena. Brian's really weighing her down. She puts her hands on her hips and swells her chest, and the fringe on her dress twitters like leaves before a storm. Joe! That bastard! Did he set this up?

Elena ponders the pair of them: Tony and Maria at the dance. Joe's daughter doesn't look like anybody Elena wants to deal with or even see on a regular basis. "Hello, Brian." She's got to start behaving like an adult. How soon can she get out of here? When's the next flight to New York? Or Rio! Don't they have loose screws and unattached men in Rio?

"Aren't you going to introduce me?" Doris asks coyly.

"This is Brian," Tess perts, taking his hand. "Brian, Doris. And I believe you know Dr. Soto." She reams the name like a lemon.

"What a hunk!" says Doris. "Come and join us. We're just going outside."

"To bury Mutt," Tess explains. "And anybody who gets in the way." Her smile sparks like flint. Elena is now thinking the interstate and haul ass anywhere.

Mrs. Foster emerges. She's taken two pain pills and secreted the container in her pocket just in case. It's occurred to her that they probably won't kill Doris — she has family expecting her later — but rather use her to confirm that it's the *dog's* grave or whatever else they want the police to believe about Mrs. Foster's condition before her mysterious disappearance. Still, you can't count on hophead degenerates like this to be rational, and if Doris is going with her, Mrs. Foster can make sure she won't feel a thing. She just hopes they delay the actual butchery until she's had a taste of the turkey; it smells so good. There's nothing on this earth she loves so much as a juicy slice of white meat with all the trimmings.

Angie is the last to amble out to the pit. The sky is baby blue (strange expression — she remembers her baby, blue and then buried and now blurred) and feathered with high clouds. The sun is soft-boiled. A soft wind stirs the bare branches of the trees and leaves scattering over the ground. Palooka races back and forth among them, feinting at birds, insects, and squirrels, at nothing, sniffing the cooler and darting up the fence and down again. Otherwise, it's very quiet. Shane has run over from his house. He has permission to stay for the ceremony if it doesn't take too long and he doesn't get dirty. He's spruced up, clutching a bunch of yellow mums. He and Nick stand together, watching Joe and Mason punch holes in the garbage bags and knot slippery half hitches through the cooler's handles to lower it with the appropriate pomp and then release for retrieval. Nick holds the cross like a picket.

"Are we ready?" Joe straightens to see some big lug in a baseball cap draped over his daughter, who is dressed as a bar girl. He never thought he'd miss the guttersnipe look. "Who's this?" He sneers at the ox until he glimpses Elena's disapproval. She looks really out of place in his yard, like a social worker in Dogpatch.

Elena is wondering which will work most against the boyfriend — the criminal charges or the fact that Joe has to look up at him. Mason is thinking about his own daughter. Who's gonna stand up to the clowns who want to mess with her?

"This is my *friend*," Tess spits back. "You don't say anything about mine, I don't say anything —"

At the same time, Brian is saying "Brian Clark, sir," slanting forward to extend his hand a ridiculous length over the ditch so that if Joe reached for it, he'd fall in.

Brian? Wait a minute. Brian of Spanish class? Brian of the
trashed car? Brian of the drug possession with intent to sell and
deliver? Doesn't Tess hate this Brian? Isn't he the source of all her
woes, the bane of her existence? Unless she's been lying about
everything, and he's her partner in crime. Joe finds Angie, standing on the other side, somewhat behind Tess. She has her fist over
her mouth. She's thinking about Vince. It socks him. He almost
forgot. But it was raining that day, cold and foggy. They buried
what was left of Vince, after his spare parts had been recycled
through the hospital, on a bare slope near Joe's parents' place,
under a flapping green canopy. They stood side by side; they
never moved an inch apart, so they never looked at each other;
and neither of them knew what the hell they were doing there —
posing. Angie's smiling. Joe can tell even though her mouth is
hidden. Elena's studying him, trying to get her bearings, and she
looks like the most wholesome of forbidden fruits. How's he going
to break it to her that he can't go through with this? Especially as
he was the one who promoted it. "We'll talk about this tomorrow,"
he mutters.

Elena sees his eyes soften on her, and she thinks of being
packed in molasses.

Tess tracks Joe's gaze across the grave to Angie and realizes,
Vince. She remembers how, when Vince was buried, she had enjoyed, in some really sick way, the attention — her costume, her
performance, standing still in the cold rain, people whispering
how well she was handling it — and she shivers. Angie puts her
hand on Tess's neck so that her back is crisscrossed by arms —
Angie's and Brian's. They feel like wings.

"You know, you're ruining those shoes," Joe has to put in.

The spikes are rooting. Tess pulls them off. "If you'd do something with the yard, maybe —"

Angie and Elena laugh. Their glances tangle; they like each

other — how mature. They have so much in common: they both want to savage Joe. Mason feels hung out to dry. He craves some little body notched to his side, knowing him, nailing him, down the years. The ribbing — it's one of the things he likes about Angie, and he owes it to her marriage, her kids. He's falling for Thanksgiving — what a turkey!

Mrs. Foster leans heavily against Doris. Nobody remembers Richard's funeral, nobody remembers poor little Vincent. It's all a joke to them. So maybe it's for the best. She doesn't want to see any more loved ones buried, and she doesn't want to live in a world that won't mind seeing her go.

Doris is getting worried about Agnes. She tries thrusting her more upright. "Agnes, darling, you need a chair? You don't want to fall in!"

"Did she fall" — Mrs. Foster titters — "or was she pushed?"

While Joe runs to the porch for a chair, Angie girds her mother's waist. Mrs. Foster looks pretty rocky. What if she drops dead? And Angie half-wishing she would for several days. Not now, Mother, she thinks. Joe puts the chair under the old lady, and Angie helps her rump find it.

"Well, gang" — Angie takes charge with third-grade-teacher authority — "What's the drill? Nico?"

"You know. You sing a song. Then we talk about Mutt, and then we sing about him, and then we cover him up, and I plant the cross —"

"We all plant the tree," says Tess. "It's a great idea. Where'd it come from?"

"Mason," Angie says. He's moving the cooler to the head of the grave and stretching out the ropes.

"Oh," says Tess. That better be all of his they're planting. She intercepts the look he slashes Angie and snatches her eyes away.

"When do we lower the cooler?" Joe asks.

"Maybe first? First or last —" Nick consults Shane. Shane wants to see that dog go under before his mother calls him. He's not interested in the talking. In his opinion, Mutt was a lot like a bath mat.

"What about a prayer?" Tess doesn't want Brian to think they're atheists. "'Dearly beloved' or 'ashes to ashes' or whatever."

Angie and Joe, Mason and Elena simper. "It's up to you," Angie says. "If it feels good, do it."

"'Yea, though I walk through the valley of the shadow of death,'" Mason recites, "eh, bro?" Joe nods. Saw it everywhere in Nam: I will fear no evil. Because I am the evil. Mason draws a different conclusion. Anywhere you been, Jesus been there before you.

"Don't you have to say it backwards?" Mrs. Foster chuckles.

Doris shakes sympathy at Angie and pats Agnes's back.

"That sounds good," Nick tells Mason. "You do it. Last."

Joe and Mason gather the ropes close to the handles. Mason suggests the boys hold the very ends "for maximum security." They love the idea. Elena takes Shane's flowers. Nick passes the cross to Angie. "You do the singing. Something, you know — good."

"A dog song?"

"No, that's later. Something — you know!" he stamps.

"Hold on," Joe cuts in. "Somebody banging the door."

"Justis. You guys carry on." Angie hands the cross to Tess and runs through the house to the door. It's Chemo Sabe, wearing a floppy tennis hat, a suit and tie, thin and pale and looking around as though he expects a trapdoor to open under him. "Hope I'm not —"

"Hey, guy! Welcome! Glad you could make it. Look, I know this doesn't make much sense, but we're in the yard burying our dog. Dinner to follow. There's everything you need in the glove box of the car up the driveway. If you wouldn't mind going around the house, just help yourself, but please try to be quiet so my crew won't notice. I've got two pounds in the trunk we can move later. Okay?"

"Pounds?" Chemo Sabe's bulbous eyes tear left and right as if he has something to fear beyond his prognosis.

"Yeah, harvested. In a garbage bag. It'll be the last for some time. But there's an open ounce in the glove box. My neighbors aren't home. It's pretty secluded up there. You'll be all right."

"Thanks, Angie. You're a lifesaver."

Her lips buckle. "Yeah. And then join us. Maybe come through the house so I can say you had to use the john or something."

"Will do. Sorry about your dog —"

"He was old." Angie dashes back through the kitchen, checks the warming dishes, and out in time to miss the fight over who holds the cross and who speaks first and to hear the last of Tess's reflections on her loyal retainer.

"He was my true friend" — mascara puddling under her eyes and Brian's arm over her shoulders. "He was there for me." She doesn't say, Like nobody else was. She sobs into Brian's sweater as if he were Mutt.

"'His wants was few,'" says Joe.

"Remember the time he runned away?" Nick asks, the cross slung casually on his neck so he can be more expressive with his arms. "We looked everywhere for him and drove around and called, and when he finally came home he'd rolled in something gross, and boy, did he stink! P.U."

Shane's laugh jitters.

"He was all dog," says Joe.

"He was happy!" Nick imitates Mutt's tongue-lolling smile. "Joe had to use kerosene on the gunk. Remember how he loved to stick his head out the car window? He sure could drool. Remember his grody tail swishing in your face?"

"I always said, Why did they have to keep such an unappealing animal?" Mrs. Foster laughs. "And he was worthless as a watchdog." Unless — could that be why he had to be destroyed? She pictures Mutt as Lassie, leading the police to the yard, scratching at her freshly dug grave. Mutt certainly liked to roll in dead things.

Tess knuckles her tears, frowning. Grandma is such a bitch, and the boys are getting silly, and of course her parents are hopeless. "Remember how he waited for me to come home from school?" she defends Mutt staunchly. "Or at night, he'd wait up? How he'd run with me? How he could jump? That time in the park he stole the Frisbee from the Ultimate Frisbee jerks and took off? How he loved to fetch?"

"Yeah," jeers Nick, "you'd throw his ball, and he'd bring it to somebody else —"

"A real crowd pleaser," says Joe, tousling Nick's hair. "Good with children, especially babies."

"He hatched Vince." Angie smiles with wet eyes, and Joe's eyes brim, and it's as if they're clicking glasses.

"Who's Vince?" Elena asks. Mason is wondering the same thing. Angie and Joe look astonished love at each other.

"Who's making that racket in the alley?" Doris asks, blowing her nose.

A whoop-whoop of siren, honking, calling, the crotchet and maunder of a squad car radio. Angie moves to the fence. Two uniformed police, a man and a woman — she's poring over some papers — are coming up the drive. Chemo Sabe is hunched, struggling to shut down his operation and creep from the car. As soon as he opens the door, smoke bellows out. Angie thinks of Tess; she thinks of Mason. She smiles and shoves out through the gate. "Hey, there!" she calls, hoping she's shielding Chemo Sabe's escape. She features herself as Veronica Lake in *So Proudly We Hail*, strolling toward the Japanese with a hand grenade in her blouse. The only thing she's got in her blouse worth mentioning is her rusty ticker.

"We're looking for the owner of —"

"That'd be me," Angie says. She holds out crossed wrists.

"What's this all about?" Joe picks up his pace.

Tess and Brian file through the gate, closely followed by Elena and Mason, Nick, bearing the cross, and Shane. "What stinks?" Shane asks. He and Nick both think, Mutt! and their stomachs sink.

Mrs. Foster and Doris bring up the rear. "What's that smell?" asks Doris. "Like concentrated mildew."

Tess knows what it is. Brian! Would he have toked up in the car? She glazes over — see no evil, smell no evil, speak no evil — not anymore.

Brian wonders if Tess has been smoking. She had that ounce. Maybe the whole family smokes — bunch of Deadheads. Get in the car, pretend they're going somewhere, sing. Run over the dog. That's one he's got on the shrink.

Chemo Sabe inserts himself beside Mason. Mason can smell the smoke on his clothes and clasps him to his sweaty side.

So the kids have been smoking pot out in the car, Elena thinks — big fucking deal. Her fist balls on her hip. Let them come after her!

"Is that Angie Die —" The policewoman, reviewing the papers, "Pee-tro?"

"That's me. I'm the one you want. Joe, don't worry. I won't say a word. I won't talk at all. My lips are sealed." Angie smiles like Stan Laurel.

The male cop is sniffing, inspecting the big black guy. Wudn't he at the courthouse t'other night? Who's the little worm with him? And that girl — reminds him a them Manson girls — Squeaky Something. And what's with that there cross? Some kind of cult foolishness? Fucking-A weird. "Somebody want to tell me what's going on?"

"You tell me," says Joe.

"Doris, we're saved!" cries Mrs. Foster. "Look in the trunk!" she instructs the officers. "Look in the trunk!" She wilts against the fence, piously linking her hands in — thanksgiving.

"You got a warrant?" Joe asks.

"It's open." Angie smiles.

Joe slaps his forehead.

"Biff bam, thank you, ma'am." In seconds, the male cop locates and confiscates the pot in the glove compartment. "I'd call that probable cause." He dangles the Baggie. He notes some suspicious stains on the seat — could be blood. "I want to see in the trunk," he tells Joe. What if — what if these are part a that cult what slashed up the Green Beret doctor's family over in Fayetteville? Promotion, for sure!

The policewoman folds the paper into her belt and clicks the cuffs on Angie. "You have the right to remain silent." Angie smiles deliriously. Shane hears his mother hollering, but there's no way he's missing out on Mrs. D getting busted.

"And there's a cooler in the backyard." Mrs. Foster feels it's best to cooperate. "They say the dog died of natural causes — if it is a dog." She shakes her head sorrowfully. "My only daughter," she tells the policewoman, "she's been drugging me." Maybe Angela can get off on an insanity defense. The psychologist? Mrs. Foster will *loan* Joe the money to hire an American.

They must have all had a hit, the cops are thinking.

"Wait a minute!" Joe feels like he's screaming.

"He is so dead!" Nick yells. "I found him!"

"Joe, listen, it's really all right." Angie broadcasts what she hopes is reassurance. "I know what I'm doing. I won't tell them anything, I promise. Tess, get my purse, please. And would you throw in some Tampax? I'm seriously on the rag," she explains to the female cop.

"Maybe it's PMS," Mrs. Foster suggests. "Or, no, during — DMS. Anyway, she needs to have her uterus removed."

"You need to have your tongue removed," says Joe, and Mrs. Foster raises her eyebrows at the cops. "Angie, let me do the talking. Officers, I'm a lawyer. I'd like a private word with my —"

"Now hold on just a minute —" The male cop doesn't like those two kids disappearing into the house, but he'd need a warrant to go in after them, and he's not screwing up a righteous bust, especially if this guy really is a lawyer.

Tess pushes Brian ahead of her like a walker. She wants to tell him everything, so he can explain it back to her — he's begging her — but her tongue is coated in cement.

"Look, Officers, could you step aside for a minute while I confer with my —" Joe brakes just short of physically prying Angie free. Both cops have hands on their gun butts. "Angie, what in the name of —"

"Joe, I promise you, I know what I'm doing. Listen, everything's ready on the stove. Don't forget to serve the cranberry sauce."

"Angie —"

"Dessert's on the kitchen table. Mom, you show him. Don't forget her medication. Also, there's this homeless person I've been feeding — under some blankets over by the high school gym. Could you take over a plate in some foil? You just leave it there, under the magnolias, that's all. And call the Sore? I'm signed up to —" Angie's talking so fast nobody can make much out.

"Angie? Listen. Don't say —"

"Oh, and weren't we going to write up a ten commandments for Tess —?"

Tess is back. At a look from Angie, she hands the purse over to the policewoman, who extracts the car keys and tosses them to her partner. Angie kisses Tess's forehead. Tess thinks of Judas. Her intestines wring.

The male cop opens the trunk. Removes and looks in the trash bag. "Ooowee, that's rank!" He hefts it. "Must be pounds. Come on, lady. We're going to the station."

"I'm her lawyer; I'm coming with her."

"Joe, no! You'll ruin Thanksgiving! I'll be fine."

"You can do what you want to, Mister. She's coming with us."

Nick rushes at the policewoman, pummeling her viciously, so Angie can run. He's counting on Shane and Joe to help. The policeman grabs him around the waist and carries him, kicking, biting, red-faced, to — the black babe is the only one who seems competent. "Look after this boy, will you?"

Not on your life, Elena thinks, backing away from Nick's violent and muddy boots. We're talking dry cleaning, if not injuring a favorite body part. Mason takes him. Nick falters. "There, there, my man." Mason kisses his hair, his ear.

"Joe" — Angie smiles at her husband as the policewoman recovers and pilots her toward the street — "you still got to pull the dirt up over Mutt and sing 'Hound Dog.' Take care of Nick and Tess — and my mom. Please — it's Thanksgiving."

"By the way" — the policewoman pulls the papers out again and passes them back to her partner — "what you want us to do about this abandoned vehicle over in Lockwood Close?"

Chapter 8

In the Road

Joe stares down the driveway, trying to think. He's staving Nick off at arm's length. Squirmed away from Mason while Joe was signing for Tess's car to be towed to the body shop, Nick tore after the cops, a lashing live wire. Joe barely caught him, and now Nick is kicking and swinging, landing the occasional shin breaker, knee breaker, ball breaker, tears spurting like angry bees. At the fence, the line up waits to be dismissed with the ambivalence of witnesses to the fatal fall of a Flying Wallenda. Only Shane had the courage to run away, roused by the imperative in his mother's voice. Elena taps his dry yellow mums in the crook of her elbow like a billy club. Mrs. Foster laughs.

"Joe, you go on." Doris comes to first. "We'll see about the dog and dinner." Who's this we? Agnes — demented — give her the carving knife — and the colored couple — at least they'll know what to do in the kitchen — and the two teens and — "Where'd you come from?" Doris squeaks. Some skinny bald guy — not one of them Harry Krishners? Not AIDS! What next? Dopey? Grumpy? How much of what Agnes has been raving about is on the level? Doris knows one thing: anybody in her family asks how her day was gets an earful.

"Justis Greer, ma'am." Chemo Sabe prigs the brim of his hat.

How can he explain why he's here, feeling no pain, while their beloved wife-and-mother is headed for the slammer? Why didn't he come forward and testify? Because two in the hand is worse than one in the bush. And his sky is falling. And he's starving. He thinks of saying, If it's any comfort to you all, I'll be greasewood in hell soon. He thinks of asking, When do we eat?

Mason shifts to scope him out. This is the dude he's risking his ass for, the dude Angie just got taken down for — Mr. Pitiful. Those rabbity, lashless, browless eyes. Mason's whole body is sodden. He encircles Justis's scrawny white neck and slaps his hairless cheek. He really wants to pop him. Pop that child, Joe, squealing like a fucking pig! You want him to grow up squealing over every fucking thing? Go after your woman, man. Lock and load. Shit. What froze up Mason's own action when the law took down the woman he's telling himself he loves? Practical considerations, dig. His cool. And what's she gone give up? *Who?* Should he be pulling up stakes? Dissing this dream? Driving on? How many times can a man come back from scratch? At once and with a certainty that zaps him like a radio falling in the bathtub, he knows Angie will turn over nobody but herself. Those blown-out eyes. It's a fucking heartache: the better she gets, the more impossible it becomes. He and Justis exchange shit-eating grins.

Nick looks up, sees, like Mister Rogers standing next to Mason — "It's a beautiful day in the neighborhood" — loses his steam. He takes one last dejected swack at his father just as Joe completely snaps and slaps his face. Infrared handprint. Nick touches it, shocked. Joe clutches Nick to his groin. Nick's sobs resonate through him like hunger pangs.

Nick thinks about nailing his father's nuts. He can't! He doesn't *know* why! He wants to turn inside out like a sock.

"Let's deep-six the dog and get that turkey on the table," Elena orders. It's a chick thing, she thinks, seeing crazy Angie sleep-walking to the patrol car again: solidarity. Shit, situation comedy. She brandishes the dry mums. "Tess — help Doris with your abuela. Brian, Mason, let's go, ándale, get the lead out, get the shovel! Joe — see to your wife, hombre."

Their eyes meet. A click of consummation, perfect intimacy, perfect communication: goodbye. He feels a rush of love like rough surf. She feels a dove beating its wings in her chest. Next year — somewhere else. Somewhere the men know how to dance. Let the job come to her. Yes!

Nick retrieves the cross, and, chipping it into the dirt like a pick, then scything grass, flipping it into a sword, a crutch, he tramps back to the grave. Mrs. Foster watches in horror.

The others follow.

Where did the cops go, Mrs. Foster wonders. When are they coming back? They really are never around when you need them. Why did they take Angela and not this Mason? (Mason! Are there black Masons? Or is it *Manson*?) Maybe Doris will take Mrs. Foster with her to her son's — although a redneck Thanksgiving might be out of the frying pan and into the trailer park, where they're always getting liquored up and shooting each other when they're not committing incest. If Angela's just mixed up with some screwy Masons, maybe things aren't so bad. Mrs. Foster's mother's people were Masons. Secret handshakes, that kind of thing. Maybe this is all just a big misunderstanding.

"What in the fuck is going on?" Brian whispers to Tess. Tess sternly turns an invisible key in her lips.

"I really feel the need to pray," Justis confides to Mason.

"That's good. That's real good, man. That's exactly what we need here. You do that. Just add a few kind words for the dog."

Angie's sitting on a bench while the cops check to see if she's got a record. There's more activity than she would have imagined; apparently, give some people a day off with their loved ones, all hell breaks loose. She feels about eleven years old — excited and curious — but also lost. Maybe they'll buy her an ice-cream cone and tell her where she belongs.

Since now every drunk to her is Alaska, she thinks she's delusional when he actually bumbles in or that maybe her vision is going the way of her plumbing. His eyes are purple-green-black, his upper lip stitched and swollen, his hair flat and dark with grease. But that's the sweatsuit she put on him yesterday? Yesterday, after the fire extinguisher festival, the recognition eventually filters through his features. shows the broken tooth. "Angel," he exclaims, "well, would you look at here! Good friend a mine," he tells the cops escorting him, hoping his stock will rise. They turn their attention elsewhere. He edges in beside her. "You doggin' me, woman?"

Angie is so astonished to see him she almost kisses him, and he leans toward that stalled kiss. "I thought I left you in good hands," she says. He tries to gesture with the cuffs behind his back. She rubs her own wrists, freed almost immediately after she got to the station. "I don' know why I cuffed her," the policewoman had laughed. "The way she was holdin' 'em up there, it was like tyin' a bow on a birthday present."

"Don' think I don' 'preciate your kineness, Angel. I guess I han' finished out my drunk. An' it was so hot in there. An' we were locked up. An' there were all these crazies. You oughta be proud a me makin' my escape. Wudn' easy." Inside the rotten plums, the black pits are steady. "This here ain' about your daughter?"

Angie shakes her head. No. She's telling herself that. But how did the cops know about the pot in her car? How did they know about the acid that kid Brian got busted with the other day? Angie tries to imagine Tess fingering her. The Tess who helped her dress this afternoon, that Tess, placing the call. That Tess, wanting to get rid of her. Angie sees herself through the eyes of that Tess. "I come home from school and my mother's stoned!"

"Everything's fine," Angie says. She's touched that Alaska remembers she has a daughter.

"Yeah, right. You jus' ain' talkin'."

Her smile ratchets.

"Yeah, I know you." His puffy eye soaps up her thighs to her breasts. "You know how good you look? Mmm-mmm-mmm." He brings his lips close to her ear. He smells like a fusty diaper. Angie sits up straight. He slouches back. "You wanna hear a great story? You know, I shoulda been a writer, but a course I has to devote myself to my drinkin'. But, so, get this. I'm in a package store, gas station, somethin'. I'm gonna buy as much wine as I can tote an' hike on home. Well, don' this woman come in an' spot her son? He's been, like, on the lam I find out later. Anyways, she starts layin' into him an' screechin', 'Call the police!' which the clerk does. So here I come with my booze — no wallet, mind you — tha's back at the ranch, only I don' know it — I'm takin this one step at a time, you know what I mean" — he slaps a laugh — "ooh, son of a bitch, it hurts to laugh — and so here's this dude whippin' up on this po' defenseless woman, right? An' nex' thing, we's all goin' down to the station. I din' even get a drink. Fuckin' Thanksgivin', man — can' find a bar nor nothin' open." Alaska cracks his loud, leathery laugh, tears cutting the white creases in his blotched face like rain ruts a dry dirt road.

Heads turn to see who's having fun.

"Oh me!" He licks his sore lips. "I think maybe I done broke my wrist. I'm still feelin' the effects a the drugs they give me, but pretty soon I'm gonna start shakin', and the walls'll start crawlin', and when tha' happens, I'm tellin' you, Angel, I don' wanna be in the tank."

"You're so scared." She has to sit on her hands to keep from touching his cheek. He really seems to be vibrating, as though a giant is gaining on him.

He strains against the manacles. "I don' wanna be an alcoholic, Angie."

"Hold that thought, my friend. Do something with it."

"I'm goin' down this time." He looks over his shoulder and back at her. "First time in my life I got the feelin' I ain' gone make it."

"Sure you will."

"I mean, why try? A life like mine — you ever heard a more mis'able life than mine? Mos' people can' b'lieve it. If I had any guts — I mean, wha's the point?"

"Turn it around, guy. Do something sensational. You can always die."

Alaska laughs. "God, I love you. In for a penny, in for a pound. Listen, can you go my bail?"

Angie laughs.

"No, tha' was wrong. Scuse me. I shouldn' a asked that a you. Tha's way too much to ask."

"Wow," Angie admires; she's surprised he's not laughing too, "you sure know how I work."

"You sayin' I'm a son of a bitch?"

He's serious. She gets serious. "I only know you're a drunk. But here's the deal, pal: I can't help you. I am totally outta my league."

"Yeah" — his face crumples — "me, too."

From a room down the hall, a suit reads off Angie's name.

"You know what iss like to disappoint yourself every single day?" Alaska asks her.

Ah! "I got problems all my own," she says, rising.

"Maybe I can talk 'em into takin' me back to the hospital," Alaska muses, watching her recede. "I musta broke my damn wrist. Think they'll go for that? Hey, can I call you later?"

Angie doesn't turn around. She's emptying sandbags. She's gaining altitude. It's cold and clear up here.

Joe has to drive to three automatic teller machines — one is out of order — to collect the cash bond he thinks he'll need to get Angie released. He doesn't care if it takes time. He strikes up a pointless conversation with a security guard; he finds a gas station open and buys a large coffee and some Little Debbie snack cakes and nurses them, sitting on the hood in the parking lot, until he's ready to puke. What kind of lunatic behavior has she been indulging in? He couldn't get a straight answer from the menagerie chowing down right now on his Thanksgiving dinner, but it's not personal use. She's either baking psychedelic brownies for some wacko fund-raiser — Betty Crocked — and shades of the Rasta and the Ding Dong defense — or it's connected with the dying people at the Sore, with Baldy. Better Baldy than Tess. Joe would put money on Saint Angela, Hostess to the Hopeless.

But does she have any idea what she's playing with? He knows she did jail time twice back in her student riot days, once in Chicago and once in Kent; she gave the name Valvoline Vavoom on charges that might be summed up as "lip." What's some cracker judge going to make of a record like that? He wonders if she comprehends how lucky she is never to have been written up on even the most minor drug violation. He'll enjoy scaring the shit out of her. What really burns him is that she didn't automatically turn to him. Doesn't she at least respect his professional competence? Doesn't she trust him at all? Why would she? Has he trusted her? Respected her? Respected himself? What's he been up to at the office lately? Recalling the scene with Elena, his dumb cock looks up; his relationship with his sex organ reminds him of Abbott's with Costello. He's cleverly ended a really promising affair just when there's nothing left of his marriage. The way things are going, Elena may soon be seeing everyone in his family except him. She'll be able to assure them that their problems *are* his fault, and he'll get to pay the bills.

He finds Angie in an interview room with two white, male, thirtyish detectives, one buff, one burly. They're pissed. They're not gritting back on turkey either. Like him, they're hot and uncomfortable in coats and ties. Joe changed to enhance his credibility, and then, of course, he loafed on the hood of his filthy car eating gooey, crumbly cakes and guzzling acid coffee in a gasoline- and urine-soaked parking lot with the rest of the outcast population. Angie's pale and serene in his moss green suit, hands folded limply on the table, and the black T-shirt gives her a clerical aspect; she looks like she's counseling them.

Burl is saying they can make it easy on her if she cooperates. Why doesn't she get it off her chest? Get honest.

"Just a minute," Joe intervenes. "What are you offering?"

The detectives swivel as he comes up behind Angie and grips her neck.

"Hey, Joe," she murmurs, "where you goin' with that —?"

He yanks her braid before they decide to pat him down.

"So she *can* talk," Buff grumbles. "Be a lot simpler if you'd talk to us, lady."

"I have the right to remain silent." She smiles.

"Who are you?" Burl asks Joe.

"Her husband. More to the point, I'm her lawyer. Joe Di-Pietro." Joe extends his hand.

Burl tags it. "That so?" he asks Angie. She nods and lowers eyelids thick as enamel.

"I remember him from a child abuse must be three year ago," Buff tells Burl. "Got the sumbitch off."

Joe settles in a chair beside Angie and addresses the cops. "You were saying?"

"She be willing to submit to a drug test?" Buff asks.

"You first," Joe shoots back. "You know, those steroids'll ruin your sex life."

Buff grins. His teeth are also in shape. "Nothin' to hide."

"How about nicotine?" Joe badgers. "Caffeine?"

"Look, it's open and shut." Burl takes over. "She was caught with the goods, admitted in front of witnesses it belonged to her. Something like two pound — we're talking felony possession with intent to sell and deliver. Now, of course we can't make no promises, but since she's been clean the past few years —"

"Last quarter century" — Joe frowns — "and before that —"

"As far as what the record shows." Burl gives Angie's beatitude the fish eye and returns to Joe. "The D.A. might look a little more kindly on her if she'll give up the grower."

"Who? Juan Valdez?" Joe imagines the cheerfully colonized Colombian coffee icon materializing with an M16, hoisting Angie onto his burro's back, spraying the room with bullets.

Neither detective chinks any amusement. "This stuff is fresh. Local," Burl says. "We don't tolerate that kind of mess in this county.'

"Unless it's the tobacco company's," Joe drawls.

"You know well as I do that's a load a crap. The people who's growin' —"

"Might be kin to you." Joe stretches his legs.

Burl, in fact, has an uncle out in Wilkes County —

"Hey, your wife is in big trouble here, bright boy." Buff is a hard sell. "You got kids?"

Above the vinyl smile, Angie's brows knit.

"We don't want to take a mother away from her children" — Buff's eyes chew her face — "but we got to think about the children, Angie. The pot finds its way to them, their lives are down the toilet."

"She's not giving it to children," Joe retorts.

"She don't know that. She can't control where it goes."

Angie smiles into her hand. Story of her life.

"You remember back a few years, a young mother was shot where she stood through the picture window in her livin' room?" Buff prods. "Shot dead? That was pot. They was smokin' pot and drivin' around shootin' at the lights, remember? 'Shoot at the lights,' this bitch in the backseat kep' sayin'. Victim was watchin' TV, hemmin' a dress, got up to close the curtains, that's all she wrote. That woman had little children — three-year-old girl and another in diapers."

Burl chimes in, "Look, Angie, we want to help you, hon. We need the source, everybody involved, every name you can supply. You may think these people are your friends, but they'll sell you out in a heartbeat. Show us somethin', honey." Burl's eyes implore. "You cooperate, we cooperate."

Buff looks at Joe. "You know how it works."

"Fine. Thanks. I'd like to confer with my client alone now."

"If you're afraid, we can protect you," Burl tells Angie. She looks sorry for him. Shakes her head.

"Can we stay in here, or do we have to go elsewhere?" Joe puts his arm around her shoulders.

The detectives wigwag and rumble out.

"Quarter century?" she asks when the door closes.

Joe holds the side of her face. "Baby, let's go home." She looks about eleven years old to him. Her eyes are blue as chicory, the wrinkles beside them the faintest bird tracery in the finest crust of sand. He wants to hide her inside him — slip his arms inside the green jacket, have her stand on his feet, and walk her out, whistling. Whatever she's been losing, she's lost a little more of it. He's frightened. "I've got your bond. We go before the magistrate, he releases you on your own recognizance, we're outta here."

"I dunno, Joe. I think maybe I oughta go to jail. Everything I do or say hurts somebody." Her eyes twinge. "Including this."

Joe takes her hands. They feel waxy and cool against his gummy palms. He must be melting. "Angie. What's going on?"

"Oh, Joe." She brings her forehead to his so she doesn't have to look into the hot tar of his eyes. He's sweating. Even his hands feel sticky. "You think they're listening?"

His head shakes hers. "Let's hope so. Ruin their case."

"I'm guilty," she whispers.

"Explain it to me, kid."

"Okay." Angie draws back. For some reason, she's remembering the night they conceived Vince. She can pinpoint it because she'd been using the exhaustion, because of tending to baby Tess, as an excuse not to fuck him. Everything about Joe rewarded her as nothing else ever had or would except the way he took her to bed. She thought time would fix that; she thought she could teach him. She was sure. All you need is love, right? But she didn't get off on teaching, and when she went crazy on him, she embarrassed herself. He was trying to get in and out without encountering the other side — commando mission. It hurt.

That night he'd brought home two bottles of some good Italian sparkling wine and a dozen red roses. A big case won? Something. The roses put out like chloroform; Tess colluded by falling asleep fast and hard. They sat at the table telling stories, laughing, and as night crept on, she asked when did he want to eat, and he took her hands and said something like, "Explain it to me, kid."

She remembers her mouth went dry. Too dry to speak. Her eyes. She couldn't hurt him. She couldn't lose him.

Then she was pregnant. No, Joe, I'm too sick; no, Joe, I'm tired. Vince — her son darts through her mind like a shining needle — that's what Vince was made of. Tender abrasion. Road rash. Lies. Compromise. Love. She's never been able to explain it.

Joe kisses her. He webs his fingers around her head and drinks sweet milk from her mouth like a shipwreck draining a coconut. His lips cling when she pulls back. Her heart aches with wary hope. "So this bail money?" she inquires softly. "Earmarked for Tess's college education or taking care of my mom?"

Joe throws up his hands and starks his hair like a mad scientist's.

"Friend's been growing dope for me to give to people with cancer and AIDS and shit. Eases the pain, the nausea, helps them get some food down — like functional munchies. Can't say I haven't skimmed off the top — liberally." She takes Joe's disdain as though she's in the stocks. "I also drink too much. I drink too much, and sometimes I drive, but not with the kids." She blinks. "Yet. Anyway, my friend wanted out and turned the harvest over to me. I should say I've been screwing him for six months. The last in a series."

"Tell me something I don't know," Joe rasps. Then he hears *last*. He advises himself not to make too much of it.

Angie bumps over that one. He knew? She's not even a good cheat. How hard did she try? "Okay, so how's this gonna play to your clients? Right? Or the court. I mean, I haven't been too worried about your career either, our — livelihood. And what about the Sore? Thanks to me, from now on it may be associated in the popular imagination with the distribution of street drugs. Maybe get it shut down. You can just see the paper or one of the local channels picking up on this, some hotshot reporter — some alderman — crusading against downtown shelters, treatment programs, humane terminal care, race mixing, who knows what? The people at the Sore — they're so good, man, they're *corny*. I make them look corrupt — completely fuck them over. You know? The best people on earth. And who's gonna take up the slack? If the Sore closes? Because it's just getting slacker out there, as I am living proof." She bows. Show's over. Silence. Empty house.

"What are you gonna do?" Joe asks curtly.

"I dunno. I was thinking maybe — okay, I'm caught. I do my time. Where I can't hurt anybody else. You tell people I went away, died — something."

"And you raise little tweety-birds in your private cell overlooking the bay. Fantasyland."

Does he have to be such a fucking hard-ass? "Or — could I be like a test case? You know? If it all has to come out anyway. At least raise the issues around legalization, the contradictions. Suppose we won? On to the Supreme Court!"

"Yeah, right. Liberty Leading the Potheads. Think how that's gonna sound to the people around here — New Age. Bizarre. And how's your character gonna hold up under cross? You given any thought to your children?"

"Look at my children," Angie says sadly, and now she has to look down. She wants to tell him her suspicions about Tess turning her in, but she can't. Simply as Dad, Joe can snuff his daughter's self-esteem without saying a word. And Joe will say the words. Who knows what Joe will say or do? Is that Angie's fault, too? She bites her lip. "Tess already ran away from me. And Nico — he's so angry."

"Your ego, you know? Pretty fucking amazing. Fucking Godzillian. You think you're in this alone? Look at me, how's about? Damn it, look at me!" Joe doesn't trust himself to touch her. The half-halo shine on her hair in this penitent posture makes him want to smash her skull. She raises her stricken face, and it's worse. He sees his handprint on Nick's cheek. He cranks up out of the chair and down again. He slams the table with his fist, and she jumps without budging. "You wanna get honest? Let's get honest. Let's smear ourselves in it. I've been getting some on the side myself." He hears that and sees Elena's eager breasts, her candid eyes, her cushy resistance, and he's choked with self-loathing.

Angie's every expression — is that sympathy? fuck! — infuriates him. "What'd you expect? Jesus! I'm trying, I'm trying all the god-damned time, and what do I get? You spreading for any jock who knocks and locking up tighter than grim death when I lay a finger on you. I'm not gonna tell you I took up with this woman — Elena, damn it, it's Elena! — incredible, beautiful Elena, right? — for your sake — shit, you were the last thing on my mind, you fucking bitch — but I let her go for your sake, and I am damned if I understand why."

Burl raps the door and puts his head in. "You all right in here?"

"Five more minutes," Joe says.

Burl's eye quizzes Angie. She nods. The door clicks.

"I knew — about Elena," Angie gets out. He let her go?

When did she know? Who else knows? "I couldn't deal with it." He raps his fists together on the table, and his ring nips his knuckle. "To give her what I wanted, what she deserves, I would've had to leave you" — his eyes scorch her — "and I can't."

Angie's insides grip. She can feel blood leaking into Joe's cor-duroy trousers. What can she do about it? Excuse herself? Now?

"Vince was my son, too," Joe gets out.

Angie is crying. She wants to touch Joe, but it seems so cheap and condescending, and she's repulsive, bleeding, foul. She holds her elbows and cries with the high-pitched whine of ice splinter-ing, her teeth jammed in the pad behind her upper lip to contain the noise.

Burl puts his head in again. "You about ready?"

"Five more minutes!" Joe barks.

"We haven't got all day, Counselor. There's —"

"I want five more minutes with my client —"

"Yeah, well —" This time Burl lets the door slam.

Joe fingers away her tears. "Ange, I'm sorry, baby, listen —"

"Oh, Joe." She has to pry her hands off her elbows. Her arms jerk open, and she throws them around Joe's neck. They nose blindly into each other's humps, tightening and tightening, two monkeys clinched to a slippery tree. When the spasm passes, Joe has corduroy welts on his cheek. Angie's chafed from his wool blend and burnished with tears. "A quarter century down the road" — she gulps and snuffles — "I still want five more minutes with you. I'll always want five more minutes with you." She grabs him. "But, Joe, I'm bleeding all over what would otherwise be a beautiful pair of pants."

"That's it." Buff and Burl stride in, Burl doing the talking. "Fish or cut bait. We got cases backed up —"

"Angie" — his blood roars so loudly, Joe can't hear himself — "let's go home."

Elena has got to be gone before Joe gets back, you understand, got to *be* — and what if she just packed up for good? fuck the furniture! fuck the lease! fuck the recommendation! fuck the future! — but she can't see leaving these poor fish by themselves. They look like the driven little campesinos on the minor tarot cards — No! Shit! They're the Pilgrims! Can't even feed themselves, in Paradise. And then they bite the hand that feeds them. Mason feels the same way — it's the damnedest thing. They both know that everybody would be glad if they'd never come but are scared witless to see them go. They're the surrogate parents. Slaves — of God, of Love. Suckers.

Their sappy compassion may have something to do with Mutt's burial. As Brian and Mason lowered the cooler into the hole, Nick tried to make them sing — howl — "Hound Dog," but Tess stood there mute and unmoving as if she were bound head to foot in bandages, and none of the rest of them really knew the words, and it struck all of them as ludicrous.

"*Mom* knows it! She said everybody knows it! She —"

Justis touched Nick's nape. Doffing his hat to expose his shiny baldness, he looked like a spaceman to Nick, the supersmart, old-baby kind. Justis took Nick's left hand in his right and Mason's right with his left, and then they all linked up, Brian operating Tess, and Justis talked about how since Jesus suffered the little children to come unto Him, He'd smile on a dog like Mutt. Nick pictured Mutt panting up to a bunch of dirty, skinny, barefoot, nightgowned kids with Jesus. Justis said something about sheep and green pastures that still has waters, which sounded maybe okay, and everybody said, "Amen," almost together. Filling the grave, planting the tree and the cross were very satisfying. Nick did practically everything. His mom will think it looks beautiful.

Now Doris is at the table with Mrs. Foster, Brian, and Nick. Nobody told Nick to wash up, but he did it, with a funny-serious feeling that he was helping Mom and Joe. Tess tried to bolt for her bedroom, but Elena taloned her wrist and imposed the bowl of stuffing, so Tess is muling back and forth with the food and drinks, which is probably better than putting her head on the windowsill and slashing the sash cords, although who does this bitch think she is? Mason is just finishing carving the turkey. It's his first, it's dry as chalk, and the knife is dull.

When they're all seated, Nick appropriates a hunk of white meat off the platter and plugs it in; Justis asks Mason to say grace, and Nick feels stupid and gross with his mouth gorged up. Mason keeps it short for Angie's mother, who's staring fixedly at her plate as if they're going to make her bob for it, and for Justis, who looks close to swooning, or else he's really wrecked. Mason tacks on an apology for his carving before they say amen.

The dishes circulate. Doris heaps her own and Agnes's plates, harping on how good everything looks and smells, under the circumstances — i.e., the arrest of the cook. Doris feels witty, as though she's in something heartwarming on the Hallmark Hall of Fame.

Mrs. Foster never noticed before how much Doris resembles a witch — she must have been in league with them all along. Mrs. Foster is resigned to being poisoned, but, with her wrist, does she have to saw at these clumsy lumps of turkey? He's probably used to pulling the meat off the carcass, tossing the bones over his shoulder. At least the gravy is hot and, of course, thick, as are the yams and the dressing. Maybe the idea is to choke her. Or drown her in the tub later. You can drown in three inches of water; she'll sink like the *Titanic*. She actually would prefer death to explaining about her daughter in the clink and the colored cult to her bridge club.

Elena wonders if all white people like their food dry, pale, bland, and heavy. The pasteles in their pretty green wrappers almost bring tears to her eyes. She wishes she'd kept them for herself.

Brian has never felt so comfortable. There's nothing in the place he could be the first to mess up; some things he could fix. And the food — humble peasant fare, he thinks — especially the turkey nuggets, which, he's sorry, he likes, if only there were dipping sauce. And the people, whoever they are, whatever they're doing here (his shrink?) — like the flight crew of the starship *Enterprise* — way cool. Imagine Mrs. DiPietro as your *mom* — like Madonna, only — a little less — material. And Mr. D — okay, he lost it with the kid, but he had a right to be pissed; at least he cares and doesn't mind showing it. He's a *man*. The shrink: she hasn't tried to score any points, which, for an adult in her position, is pretty amazing, and it's nice to catch her with her man, looking sexy and playing hard to get — she's fucked up, too. And her guy — if he pulls out a musical instrument, any kind, a nose flute! — Brian will believe he has died and gone to heaven. The bald dude — you wanna talk spiritual! Even the bratty little brother. Brian wants to stuff him like a sausage with advice. Put it this way: nobody's told him to take off his cap *yet*, not even the two old ladies. Except what's with Tess? She looks like she's having an out-of-body experience. He's got to get alone with her, and he doesn't have much time; he's due home before dark. How soon can he talk to her about getting married? Realistically speaking?

Justis savors his yams. The sweet glaze like the sun on a perfect day. He sees it lining him like fleece in a shearling coat. He sees the cancer cells smothering in it. "If you ladies had anything to do with the preparation of this sumptuous repast," he congratulates Doris and Mrs. Foster, "I thank you from the bottom of my heart."

Mrs. Foster believes he means it. "I think I can tell you — what was your name again?"

"Justis —"

"Was your father a lawyer?"

"No, ma'am. He works for AT and T."

"I thought he'd be a lawyer — or a cowboy." She laughs. "I'll never understand the South as long as I live. Imagine looking down at a baby and calling him — Or — Is that your cult name?"

"Excuse me, ma'am?"

"Did they give you that name in the cult?" Mrs. Foster aims her fork at Mason. She doesn't care anymore. Get it over with. "Him?"

Mason is caught opening his yap for some green beans.

"I don't rightly know what you mean, ma'am." Justis takes some beans himself — ramparts, tough as logs. Chewing vigorously, the fiber weaving a green mesh that will surely repel the cancer as well as floss his teeth, "My folks are Baptists, ma'am, decent, God-fearing Christians, and I've never set eyes on this gentleman before in my life."

"Same here," Mason garbles, fumbling with a napkin in case he has to spit the stringy gobbet out.

"Just because I'm getting on doesn't mean I don't know what's going on." Mrs. Foster chuckles slyly, her eyes rolling from one end of the table to the other as though they're shipboard in high seas. "I'll bet your real name is Jim-Bob. And what do they call *you* around the sanctuary?" she challenges Elena, "Chastity?" Mrs. Foster silently shakes with laughter. "Purity? Oh me!"

"Are you taking some kind of medication for your wrist?" Elena asks quietly, laying down her silverware and consulting Doris with her eyes.

Nick's wondering what happens when these other people go home. Him and Tess and Grandma? Not even Mutt. And Grandma's off her nut. Suppose something bad happens. When's Mom and Joe coming back? Maybe he should sleep over at Shane's.

Doris is happy to help clear things up. "Agnes has got this fool notion you're all part of a Satanic cult. It's the television she watches."

"A cult!" Justis cries, spewing crumbs. "Why on earth would she think that?"

"Why wouldn't she think that?" Elena cocks her head. "Look at us."

"What else could she think?" Mason asks. "What else would explain blacks and whites in the same room, breaking bread together?"

Both he and Elena feel trapped. They both want to make their excuses, but neither will strand the other. Their eyes keep meeting over Nick. There's no point *not* liking each other, just because it's a stupid, racist setup. They smile at each other, and their eyes bloom like blown coals.

"And the sensational journalism," Doris adds. "Waco, that type

of thing. Come on, Agnes. A cult? Give me a break! Get real!"
Doris hoots. "Oh, mercy!"

"In answer to your question," Mrs. Foster addresses Justis in the
backwash of their risibility, "I believe I may say, without fear of
contradiction, that I'm the one to thank for this Thanksgiving
dinner."

Tess rushes from the table. Brian looks around and when no
one else makes a move or says anything, follows.

"When's dessert?" Nick forlornly asks the tablecloth.

"Tess? You all right?"

Tess can't believe Brian's talking to her through the bathroom
door. Like fucking Romeo! "But soft!" He actually wants to lift the
lid on these smells, these noises, and communicate with their
source. Not only are her bowels blasting, but she's started her period. Her eye makeup is smutching her face with the sweat and
tears. She's a sewer. She's a total disgusting skank mess, inside and
out. The real her. What an idiot he is. If he got a load of the real
her, he'd probably turn gay. She feels like telling him, I sold you
out! I sold out my own mother! She wishes she could pummel
him to a pulp! How would he like her honesty then? But she's
never opening her big fat mouth again. If she'd just kept her trap
shut, if she'd never said anything or, for that matter, eaten anything, she wouldn't be sitting here, erupting, now. She grasps her
burning gut. She wants to flush herself. She beats her heels on the
tiles with rage.

"Tess? Tess?"

She wants a cigarette. How do you turn him off?

"Listen, Tess, I gotta go soon. My mom said if I wasn't home by
dark she'd set the dogs on me."

The dog's dead and buried, boy.

"You're not doing anything dumb in there, are you?" He jiggles the knob.

And what would that be?

"Tess? You're scaring me. If you don't —"

He's threatening, but *she's* scaring *him?*

"— I'm going to —"

She flushes the toilet. The pain in her abdomen has subsided; she tracks it moving off to the northeast like a storm spiral on the local news Doppler radar. She cleans herself up, a long, complicated process she feels obliged to substantiate with exaggerated sound effects. Washing her hands, she studies her face; objectively, that's misery. She commands herself to wash it, too. She's just figured something out: she's stuck with herself. She strains a manic smile and watches her features slump through vacuity to a face she recognizes, accepts, even likes, wouldn't trade. She goes to the door and turns the knob, and it comes off in her hand. The other side is in Brian's hand. They stand on opposite sides of the door looking at their disconnected doorknobs.

"Tess?"

"Hey, Tess!" Nick peels around the corner and kicks the door. "Move it! We wanna have dessert." He sizes up the situation, plucks the doorknob from Brian's hand, and bangs it on the plate. Tess pushes the post through, and they turn together.

She appears, sheet white, her hair sleeked back as though she's been swimming, the makeup gone. She looks like a vampire mermaid to Brian. He lithifies with desire. Nick stuns her by fastening around her waist. Her heart feels like a rubber-band ball.

"Tess? When's Mom and Dad coming home?" he asks her.

She shakes her head, lips compressed.

"So it's you and me and *Grandma?* For how long?"

And not even Mutt. She pictures them moving about the darkening house. She crouches to her brother. Brian gets a shot down her dress at her pointy boobs. What a shit he is! Her white shoulder blades look like budding wings.

"You know when Joe hit me before?" Nick veils his eyes and lowers his voice. He wishes this big dumb jerk would get lost.

Tess tightens her hold.

"I'm not mad at him anymore. I just want him to come home."

Tess nods. Brian knows he should leave, but he doesn't see how. He feels like the donkey in the manger. And he's got a hard-on like a peg leg.

"I mean, why do we always have to understand?"

What's the little guy thinking? How's Tess gonna explain it's not about *him*?

"They're mad I'm not Vince," he whispers.

Tess sinks to her knees and grabs the sides of Nick's face as if it were a falling mirror. "No. Never," she tells him, emphatically — no screwing around; he's got to believe this. He feels so small, but so *real*, so sturdy. She surges with power. Brian is looking at her like he's totally in love with her. Which he should be.

"The sun sets over Toytown," Joe narrates as they crest the hill in the Chevy. It's a nice view: the high school auditorium, the park, a city-league ball field, a scattering of wits'-end shops, bungalows and mansions, tall old trees, a steeple, a pizza place. The only modern intrusion is the hospital. The sun is orange and gilds the blue around it. Joe pulls over to the curb and cuts the engine. He puts his hand in Angie's hair. She rubs his leg. They sit a few minutes.

"I'm glad to be out," Angie finally says. "I didn't really picture it — you'd *never* be alone, would you?" She shows him wide eyes. "I mean, thanks for bustin' me out, Slats." She presses his knee.

"Is that what you want, Slim? Alone?" Joe spots a hawk circling and wonders whether it's free or tethered to the unseen rabbit. He feels surprisingly calm. He has options to weigh. He could be a hot commodity — good-looking, *experienced* guy like him.

"You always let me alone." Angie smiles.

But nobody moves him like Angie.

She ticks her chin at the landscape. "You've given me a really nice life."

He shows her his skepticism. "Is that why you gave yourself up? Your nice life? I thought you wanted to be alone."

"I dunno, Joe, maybe I should be alone. I'm just so sorry I got us into all this. I really owe you for sticking with me." Angie knocks her mouth with her fist and looks out the window to her right. She sees the big white house of a woman who went through a terrible divorce. Two young children. Friends divided over who was at fault: not the children. "Joe, I didn't turn myself in. I think Tess did. But I was afraid to tell you because I didn't know what you'd do."

The handprint on Nico's cheek. "Yeah, but you're wrong —"

"No, look, we have to be able to talk about these things — that's what you've been saying, I know. But, man, you can't hit the kids. We've got to deal with them."

"Yeah, okay, you're right, but —"

"No, look — the long version is it's all my fault, trust me, but Tess planted that ounce in my glove box. I think she might also have planted the acid on that kid Brian to get back at him for the car or the trouble in Spanish. And then running away — Don't you see? She's saying one of us has to go. And any way you look at it, man, this is fucked."

"No, but listen, you're wrong about Tess."

"We have to face this, Joe. And Nick — these tantrums —"

"Listen, Ange, shut up a minute. You're right about my temper. I slapped Nick's face before. Something I never thought I'd do. I was out of control. It was horrible. It won't happen again." He stops. He has to slow himself. "I hear how that sounds. But I get so angry, I don't know what I'm doing. I'm so frustrated. You know?" Every muscle knots. "We could have everything, you dumb shit, but you just won't —" He's blaming again, and she's taking it again. Is there any hope? "And there's no cure I believe in, no therapy I believe in, there's nothing I believe in" — he realizes this sharply, like the punch line of a bad joke — "except you."

"Oh boy! Do we have a hope in hell?" Her lips curl. "Hope in hell is what you are to me."

They kiss to break the suction of their eyes, the pressure of the moment.

"But you really are wrong about Tess," Joe says mildly. "The cops were here about her car. I never got around to calling them or the insurance, and meanwhile, it was reported abandoned. They have to make contact before they can tow. It's in your name, right?"

"Joe!" She cracks her fist on her forehead. "The things I was thinking! Hooray!"

"This smiling, you know, Ange?" He brushes his knuckles over her laugh lines. "You're getting to be just like your mother."

"Whoa, Joe, my mother! Alone in the house with Tess?"

"We call it *el día del pavo,* the day of the turkey, which, if you think about it, is pretty funny." Mason asked, so Elena's talking about Puerto Rico. They're both resigned to baby-sitting until Angie and Joe get back. Elena brewed a vat of stiff coffee, and they're lingering at the table with Tess and Nick, Mrs. Foster and Doris.

Justis left a while ago for his own family's Thanksgiving; he didn't want to lose his chemically induced appetite and hurt his mother's feelings, although if his father or any of the rest of them perceive that he's under the influence, he could be thrown out for good. They have this insane suspicion that what he's really got is AIDS from a secret, depraved lifestyle, and sometimes they rail at him for not telling them the truth, although they also believe, as does Justis, that AIDS is God's judgment on faggots and would turn their backs on him if he had it. Justis only wishes he'd thought to pocket that ounce. Angie might be free and the two pounds in his possession, and he could fake recuperation until the day he kicks. But he's got to take his medicine, or lack thereof: man was born to suffer — must be so he won't mind dying. He didn't mind leaving, either.

Brian also had to leave. He wanted Tess to come out on the porch so he could rub up on her and ask her for some kind of commitment, but she was all wrapped up in her pesty little brother. She didn't seem to realize they might not have another chance again soon. He wondered if he'd done something wrong, or if she's just a selfish bitch after all.

Tess was glad to see him go; you'd think he'd understand her priorities. Men are so completely self-centered.

Doris has been making noises about leaving but can't seem to get her ass in gear. She's having a fabulous time. She hasn't tasted coffee like this since she quit the Greek's. And she loves talking to educated, well-traveled people like the colored couple. She also doesn't care if her family has to wait on her for a change.

Mrs. Foster wishes she'd never asked Doris; she's obviously enjoyed herself as much as if she were really an invited guest instead of merely a stooge to thwart what Mrs. Foster still believes could have been a Satanic cult, if you look at the evidence. In *Rosemary's Baby*, they all had normal jobs and went to church and so forth, and that was based on fact.

"But I don't remember turkey," Elena patters on. "We ate a million other things — pasteles, fried bananas, sausages, pumpkin, yes, but not sweet" — lifting her eyebrow at Angie's ravaged pie plate. "After the meal, candied fruits, coconut, flan. The one time I was actually on the island in November, mi mama had sent me to my abuelita. I was having" — she smiles at Tess, who stares straight through her, thinking no wonder she's so fat, all she talks about is food — "I guess you could say adolescence hit me hard. Suddenly, all my papi said was no."

What's she smiling at? They still don't have anything in common, and even if they did. What's she hanging around for? Why doesn't she go home? Back to Puerto Rico. Take Shaft with her.

"Anyway, I spent a month with my grandma — from Thanksgiving to Los Reyes, Three Kings Day, which is like Christmas — in her little bohío in the country. No school. I lay in a hammock on the porch in the shade of the mangoes and the flamboyan, and the roses were blooming, and she made me herbal tea for pimples and cramps." Here she goes again, probably confirming every stereotype they have — start singing that Anita song from *West Side Story*. And Mason — well, he's no doubt expecting the guided tour between her legs. Why does she always make the island sound like her pussy? (Nostalgia!) "You get the picture. Finally, I missed the Brooklyn Public Library. We ate fish. Rice and beans. No turkey."

"I always wanted to take in the islands" — Doris sighs — "but I could never talk any of the girls into a cruise." She nudges Mrs. Foster, who bares and deliberately clacks her false teeth.

"Filthy place! Diarrhea! You have to enjoy the trots! The turkey trots!" Agnes cackles.

El día que la mierda valga algo, los pobres nacerán sin culos. The day shit is worth anything, Elena thinks in Spanish, the poor will be born without assholes. It's a saying. Apropos of nothing. She looks at her watch. Maybe they're both in the cell.

"But you're not Puerto Rican?" Doris hurries to ask Mason — trust Agnes to say exactly the wrong thing — and before he can answer, "So where did you two meet?"

"Here," Mason says, "just now." He looks at his watch. Hot prospects all over town going stone cold, and he's talking turkey with the Addams Family.

Nick's ears prick — ratatat up the steps, and when the front door opens, he's there. His mom bends to embrace him. Joe is posted above them with his hands dabbling their hair.

On this rock I will build my church, Angie thinks. Then she imagines her church — a tattered scarecrow in a fallow field. She struggles to stand without weighing on her son, his frantic hands printing all her joists. They hobble for the dining room like skating partners coming off the ice. Joe follows. Palooka, who pranced in with them from his enforced exile, makes for that lovely bird smell. He'll dance in their dirty dishes! Track gravy everywhere! Piss *next to* the litter box!

The trio pauses in the doorframe, surveying the hospitable table. Angie gratefully attributes the lack of casualties to Mason and Elena. She hopes her face conveys this. She notices they're beautiful together: walnut by cherry. Mrs. Foster seems somehow stronger, firmer; she looks like the one doing time — a lifer; she's not smiling. Doris, however, is radiant — lit, most likely, and is there any of that left, and will Angie let herself have a snort? But what's the matter with Tess? Flimsy and pale as paper, she's pasted to her seat. Where's Brian? What went on between them? Angie wants to feel the back of her daughter's neck for fever.

Mason rises, stirred by Angie and Joe's handsome unity, their mutual solicitude. He's a little anxious about what her quick release means — what advice Joe might have given, what deal he might have cut, how much he knows, how much he cares. Mason feels like the two birds that one stone is aimed at.

Joe wishes both Mason and Elena would split, and now; also the old dame — he's still not clear who the fuck she is. He wants to down some turkey and half a bottle of wine, strip, watch a little tube, and crash. Then he remembers his mother-in-law is using his bed. He's sleeping on the floor. Everybody else probably has a more serious agenda — board meeting. He motions Mason to sit and throws off his jacket.

"What can I get you?" Elena asks, hopping up — vestigial impulse triggered by the sight of a man shedding a coat — Latina training, for sure: use me! Is this why she jabs her right heel into her left ankle?

Doris is also up. "You must be famished!" She and Elena pedal to the kitchen, putter back and forth with cups, glasses, bottles, plates, until anything anyone could possibly want is restored to the table; then they sit.

Angie moves to the empty chair next to Tess and feels her daughter's neck, her forehead, studies her listless eyes, her nose, like a bulb of garlic, takes her hand. Nick lugs his chair to his mom's other side as if she may ask him to pass her the smelling salts or a scalpel. Joe, loosening his tie as well as his belt buckle, parks near Mason. He gulps off some coffee — ooh! high test! Elena — he leers at her and pours more. Now if she'd just give him a massage —

In your dreams; Elena's mouth crabs.

"Hey, so thanks for hanging in here, everybody," Angie says, trying to project particular contrition at Mason, whom she has formerly berated for ditching women and children. She sees, in fact, that he's the one who's held, maybe longer than he should. "Above and beyond. How was the turkey?"

"Never mind the damn turkey," Mrs. Foster squalls. "What happened to you?"

Joe's teeth are sunk in his yams. He looks at Angie.

"How you doing, baby?" she asks Tess. Tess looks away. "Well, Joe bailed me out. As usual."

"It was all a big misunderstanding," Joe interrupts, lettuce fringing his teeth. "The police needed Angie's permission to have Tess's car towed —"

Tess starts.

"What?" demands Mrs. Foster. "Don't talk with your mouth full!"

"— and Angie thought —"

"No, listen, Joe, it's all gonna come out eventually." Angie squeezes Tess's hand.

Everybody tenses.

"Been scoring marijuana for some of my sick people —"

"Shit!" exclaims Doris. "All this fuss over a little pot. When they gonna make it legal again?" She taps Agnes. "Remember the speakeasies?" She remembers the children. "Excuse my French."

"You're a narc?" Nick asks his mother. Angie touches his hair.

"A curandera — a healer, like my abuela — my grandma," says Elena. "Good for you!"

"So we plead guilty," Joe munches away. "She'll get a fine —"

"How much?" Mrs. Foster asks.

"We can handle it." Joe chews.

"Not with Tess's college," Angie protests. "Nobody should have to pay for this but me. I'm gonna get a job. A real job. I want to. I was thinking" — she addresses Tess — "Carol's old job — teaching girls in prison? Maybe it's still available —"

Joe puts his fork down and looks at his wife with bemusement.

He feels as though he's married to some fairy-tale heroine — or who's the straw-into-gold wench?

"What are you going to teach them?" Mrs. Foster asks wryly. "How to inhale? Who's got a cigarette? Tess!"

"Mom!" Angie exclaims. "What are you thinking? Since when —?"

"What's it to you? Richard made me stop years ago, and look where it's got me. Tess! Fork one over!"

Tess looks brained. Doris opens her purse and produces a pack and a lighter. "I indulge occasionally," she explains. Mrs. Foster takes one and lights up. She sucks in with a vengeance. "Nick!" She flippers the smoke. "Keep away!"

She won't have to say that again. Nick's trying to make sense of what his mother is in trouble for. Giving drugs to sick people? He can't put it together with Officer Susie and the cop shows. He hates this feeling, like his head is full of cloth.

"Yeah, okay, a fine." Doris picks up the thread as Mrs. Foster exhales a lifetime of constraint. "Is that it?"

"Yeah, this job," Mason asks, "you gone do it on the inside or out?" His insides are just beginning to unkink.

"I think we can count on her being out." Joe upends some red wine. "My best guess is two, three years' probation, some kind of treatment program, counseling, and community service."

"Maybe they'll let me work at the Open Door," Angie says.

Mason huffs back against his chair and laughs.

"This is rich," Elena says. "I have a new respect for the U.S. justice system." Where white people are involved. She salutes Joe. "Actually, I'd have more respect if they just let her go on giving it away." Now she takes in los pocos locos — Nick's puzzled peepers, Tess's anomie. "To the sick, I mean."

Joe looks at Angie and Tess. "I thought we might all take advantage of that counseling."

"Dios mío! A miracle!" Elena crosses herself. She feels for the counselor taken advantage of. She imagines facing their siege mentality, lined up like the defenders of the Alamo. "I'll give you a recommendation," she says. Somebody she hates!

What's done is done

*E*rna buzzed me into the office earlier today. Alaska was there. He looked good, cleaned up, headed for a treatment program in the mountains. In the spring, hopefully, if he can stay straight, he's back to the shack near Purgatory. Weezie may go with him. (He said she *will*.) He doesn't remember much of what happened between us. He searched my eyes. "I just know I owe you."

"Forget it," I said, and then I realized he had.

He laughed. "I'll be in touch." He touches something in me that scares me. Going down with this guy would feel like hang gliding. I've sworn off the hot line.

Now I'm on a secret mission to pick out a puppy at the pound. I'm tooling past the high school gym when I see the island of blankets under the magnolias. They haven't been there since Thanksgiving, when I didn't show with the turkey. I've been thinking of them leaving in a huff. Oh, and much worse. But it's a lousy time for Blank to be setting up camp; temperature's dropping — looks like snow. I pull over and climb out, and full-tilting down the hill, I trip over a root and fall face-first into the filthy, mildewed fluff and hit something hard. "Blank?"

The blankets draw up and toss me. Muffled: "Get your own!"

I grab hold of the big wad, and I will not let go unless I'm blessed.